Suzanne Arruda, a zoo keeper turned science teacher and writer, is the author of several biographies for young adults. An avid hiker and gardener, Suzanne lives in Kansas with her husband, and her cat, Wooly Bear.

You can reach her at
www.suzannearruda.com
and follow her historical blog at
http://suzannearruda.blogspot.com
for more about 1920s Africa.

MARK OF THE LION

After driving an ambulance along the front
lines in the Great War, Jade del Cameron can
fire a rifle with deadly precision. She may
look like a pin-up, but she's smart and tough
and doesn't shy away from a challenge. So
when she agrees to fulfil a fighter pilot's
dying wish — that she investigate the death of
his father and track down his half-brother
— she sets off for the wilds of colonial Africa
. . . never expecting to become involved in
murder.

SUZANNE ARRUDA

◆

MARK OF THE LION

A JADE DEL CAMERON MYSTERY

Complete and Unabridged

CHARNWOOD
Leicester

First published in Great Britain in 2010 by
Piatkus, an imprint of
Little, Brown Book Group, London

First Charnwood Edition
published 2011
by arrangement with
Little, Brown Book Group
An Hachette UK Company, London

British Library CIP Data

Arruda, Suzanne Middendorf, *1954 –*
Mark of the lion.
1. Del Cameron, Jade (Fictitious character)- -
Fiction. 2. Women private investigators- -Kenya- -
Fiction. 3. Murder victims' families- -Fiction.
4. Americans- -Kenya- -Fiction.
5. Missing persons- -Fiction.
6. Kenya- -History- -*1895–1963*- -Fiction.
7. Detective and mystery stories.
8. Large type books.
I. Title
813.6–dc22

ISBN 978–1–4444–0828–5

Published by
F. A. Thorpe (Publishing)
Anstey, Leicestershire

Set by Words & Graphics Ltd.
Anstey, Leicestershire
Printed and bound in Great Britain by
T. J. International Ltd., Padstow, Cornwall
This book is printed on acid-free paper

This work is dedicated to Mom (Woofy), who always loved everything I wrote, and to my dad (the Dad) for everything he's done for us and still does for Mom.

Acknowledgments

My thanks to the members of the Joplin Writers Guild for support and critiquing; Max McCoy for all his assistance and encouragement; the Pittsburg State University Axe Library Interlibrary Loan staff for all the books; Neil Bryan, John Fields, and Ellen Benitz for the lessons in firearms, and the National Wild Turkey Federation's Women in the Outdoors program for the opportunity to handle a rifle, a shotgun, and a bow; Helen and Dr John Daley for valuable critiquing and information on historical weapons; my agent, Susan Gleason, and my editor, Ellen Edwards, for taking a chance on a new author and their advice and encouragement; and my sons, James and Michael, for their love and support. I especially wish to thank my wonderful husband, Joe, for setting up my Web site but mostly for all his love, support, and encouragement.

1

'Despite Britain's attempts, East Africa is still a dangerous land. Perhaps that is part of its charm for so many of its visitors.'
— The Traveler, Compiègne, France — May 1918

Jade del Cameron's third and last run from *poste de secours* to the evacuation hospital began as dawn broke. She yawned, tired after a long night of driving. As her friend Beverly used to say with her typical British understatement, 'War's deucedly inconvenient in the dark.' Of course, that was the only time it was relatively safe to drive so close to the front and evacuate the wounded. Safe enough, that is, if the moon wasn't up, and one drove with the lights out and managed to avoid the treacherous shell holes, unexploded grenades, and piles of rotting horses, or 'smells,' as they were called. The horizon before her glowed with a beautiful rosy pink gilded with tangerine. A delicate golden yellow brushed the edges of the wispy clouds that flicked their tails in the sky like wild mustangs.

Beautiful, thought Jade. Just like sunrise at her parents' ranch in Cimarron, New Mexico, only she was hell and away from Cimarron. She was attached to the French army and went where the army went. At present, that meant Compiègne, the front lines, and evacuation duty. The latter required the driver to go alone on cratered roads to God only knew where, at all hours, in all conditions, and in a car that was generally not in any shape to handle the trip. Both Jade and Beverly considered themselves incredibly lucky.

Jade studied the rough track ahead and replayed the night's events in her mind as she drove. It began, as did most runs, when their supervisor, Second Lieutenant Loupie Lowther, met the women as they lined up by their trucks.

'Same area as yesterday, ladies,' Lieutenant Lowther announced. *'Poste de triage*. Remember to turn left at the first 'smell.' '

Jade had started to drive off when Miss Lowther motioned her and Beverly to wait, then came alongside their cars. 'Are either of you ladies game for a new assignment? I need someone to go to *poste de secours* tonight.'

'Ma'am?' Jade asked.

'I just received a follow-up message over the wireless. Seems they need an additional ambulance after yesterday's shelling. African corps, but I can only spare one of you.'

Beverly grinned and urged Miss Lowther to send Jade. 'Did you know she has Moors among her ancestors?'

'I do trust you and your flivver more than the others, Jade,' said the commandant, addressing her Ford Model T by its slang name. 'Might be rough, and you're a better mechanic if there are problems, you know. I was asked to send my most trusted driver.'

Jade nodded but said nothing. Her arms tingled in excitement. The *poste de secours* sat right behind the batteries, as close to the front lines as any ambulance driver ever got.

'This is a bit of a sensitive situation as well, and I'm not certain all of the girls would understand,' Lieutenant Lowther said.

'I appreciate your trust, ma'am. I won't ruin it.'

'Very good. Don't turn at the first 'smell.' Drive another kilometer beyond. There should be a rather large tank that was shelled in the road. An orderly will be there watching for you.' Their commandant patted Jade's arm and smiled. 'Good girl, Jade. I trust you'll handle everything splendidly. You western Yanks have a way with situations like this.'

Jade's mind returned to the present and her load of wounded Africans. She'd heard of the African corps and knew the French treated their wounded at the same hospitals as the other French soldiers. She admired that blatant disregard of traditional color barriers. Having a darker complexion herself, she knew real or implied discrimination firsthand and detested it. Hell, she thought, Beverly was probably right about the Moorish ancestry. She glanced at the wounded black corporal of the Chasseurs d'Afrique sleeping next to her. Before Corporal Gideon had succumbed to exhaustion, he had explained his motives for fighting.

'We are the front, mademoiselle. The Bosch, they are very afraid of the Chasseurs d'Afrique. And now I have proven my manhood. I can take a wife when I go home.'

Strange idea, Jade thought, *having to kill someone before you can get married*. Jade

3

mentally sorted through all the wounded she'd driven. Many were the Les Joyeux, convicts given a second chance at redemption and marked with a fleur-de-lis. To earn a Croix de Guerre medal carried a further reduction of sentence, so those men tended towards incredible recklessness. Jade understood why *they* fought, but she wondered what prompted a man to leave the warm climate of Africa for the harsh winters of Europe to fight in someone else's war.

She peered again at the sleeping African corporal. Surely no one had to travel that far just to find someone to slay. Then again, since they lived in French colonies, maybe they had no choice. Whatever their motives, they deserved care and comfort, and Jade did her best to avoid jarring ruts. Speed was essential, but so was the well-being of her passengers. The rule was twenty-five kilometers per hour maximum with a load.

The first shell slammed into the ground about fifty yards from her, a 220, judging by the impact. The shock wave rocked her Model T ambulance and sprayed her face with gravel and mud. She heard a ping followed by a plop as something hard ricocheted off the top of her wobbly helmet and struck the dazed Somali corporal next to her. From her right, the French returned fire.

No point in driving slowly now. Jade pushed the lever of her trusty old vehicle forward, and gave it the gas. Someone in the back screamed, a high-pitched, gut-knifing wail. Whether he screamed from terror, a rude awakening to pain, or both didn't matter, as she couldn't stop and tend to him now. Corporal Gideon groaned next to her, his eyes masked by swaths of bandages.

Jade peered through the smoke and debris, searching for the bloated pile of horse carcasses. The 'smell' marked her final turn toward the evac hospital. Finally she spied the pile of rotting horses stacked to one side of a caisson a hundred yards ahead. Naturally white, they'd been dyed red while alive to make them less visible. Now their color ran and bleached them to a sickening pink.

Another high-explosive shell exploded on impact to her right. 'Damn!' she swore. 'They're firing whizbangs.' Jade felt a sudden longing for a good old, dependable howitzer shell. At least they had the decency to give you a little advance notice. She chanted her own personal fear-controlling mantra aloud.

'I only occupy one tiny space. The shells have all the rest of France to hit.'

Almost in answer to her words, a shell exploded directly in the road ahead. It landed far enough away to miss her, but close enough that she couldn't avoid the crater at her current speed. Quickly she forced the wheel to the right to avoid the deepest part and felt the truck drop down on its left side with an agonizing shudder. A fresh scream exploded from the back.

'Come on, flivver. Hold together now,' she coaxed from the cab. She tried to climb out of the hole. The right front tire spun uselessly, spraying dirt. 'Damn!'

Jade jumped out of the cab and ducked low

beside the truck, scuttling crablike around the ambulance as she searched for the problem. She found it. The right tire was hung up on some lump instead of making contact with what remained of the road. *Probably a rock.* Jade opened the wooden toolbox on the side.

'I'm going to kill Beverly when I get back,' she muttered to the tools. She imitated her friend's British drawl. 'Madame Commandant, send Jade to fetch the African soldiers. She's so swarthy herself that they'll feel more comfortable.' *My aunt Fanny,* Jade thought. As if her coloring made her a better candidate to move African wounded. It was just another one of Beverly's ideas of a joke. Almost funny, too, if it wasn't for this accident. Her helmet, oversized to fit a thick roll of hair that she no longer had, slipped from her head and slapped her on the ear.

Jade extracted the crowbar from the box. Then she slid on her belly around the side and began leveraging the ambulance off the rock.

Only it wasn't a rock. Rocks should be hard. This one wasn't. The shell had landed on the 'smell' and spewed horseflesh everywhere. Jade set the crowbar at the rear of the horse meat and pushed the carcass forward. It worked. The slab of meat slid out from under the axle, and the truck dropped back down onto four wheels.

Good! No broken axles. Then she saw the small black spot on the crowbar. 'Blast it.' *Probably a crack in the oil pan. That's it! Beverly owes me now.* Best friend or not, she would pay. Maybe the next time Jade went on leave to visit David at the aerodrome, she'd tell on Bev to

6

David's friend, Lord Dunbury, whom Bev flirted with so shamelessly.

With the crowbar, Jade dragged the horse remains out of her way and inspected the rest of the huge crater. It was steeper in front than behind and would be difficult to climb out of, at least going forward with her low gas tank. No way to go around the crater either without risking a puncture on shrapnel. While she pondered her options, she heard a sound that made her flesh crawl. Above her head in the ambulance, one of the shell-shocked wounded reacted to the shelling with insane laughter. It started out as a low, tentative giggle and soon swelled into high-pitched, rolling cackles.

'Dear Lord, no,' Jade murmured. A cold sweat erupted on her skin. Of all the horrible sounds along this hellish front, that hideous laughter was the one she could not deal with.

The booming reverberations around her were deafening. Unfortunately they could not drown out the screams of terror from one passenger and the insane giggles from another. The giggling increased in intensity and volume. Jade shouted a few words of encouragement in French to the back as she climbed shivering into the cab. The corporal next to her was in a dead faint. 'Lucky you,' she whispered as another shell slammed to her left. She turned the ambulance around in the crater to take the steep side in reverse.

Jade had started in the unit driving a Fiat, but after one week she'd decided she preferred the light maneuverability of the Model T. She also enjoyed being able to pilfer replacement parts from stranded Model Ts or rigging up make-do parts. The flivver was a rather accommodating vehicle for that sort of thing, and Jade took pride in the fact that it was as American as she was. Most drivers found the system of three foot pedals and a side lever maddening, which meant no one tried to pinch her car. But it had one problem. It could climb steep hills only in reverse.

A Model T worked with a gravity-fed gas tank under the driver's seat. If a climb was too steep when the vehicle was going forward, fuel didn't reach the engine. Jade refused to risk that even on this short climb. She heard the T groan in protest and shouted encouragement. 'Come on, sweetheart. If you fall apart now, Beverly won't let me hear the end of it.'

Slowly the durable machine heaved itself out of the crater. 'Thataboy,' she coaxed. 'Show them what a Yank can do.' Jade kept it in reverse until she found a level spot wide enough to turn in. Then she drove hell-bent for the second coming, as her father used to say. But no matter how fast she went, the maniacal laughter hung on behind her, like a dog with a can cruelly tied to its tail. It couldn't be escaped. The creeping sensation crawled down her legs, and she felt them quiver.

Jade tore down the rutted road, riding higher on the passenger side in the ruts. She sang 'The Star-Spangled Banner' at the top of her lungs to drown out the hideous whoops of laughter behind her. It didn't help. Her shaking hands slipped from the steering wheel. The T lurched to the left. Jade clamped down harder on the wheel and brought the T back onto the road. She veered around a battered caisson and raced on towards the evacuation hospital. Another shell burst somewhere overhead. Shrapnel rained down to her right. The fringes of that shower pelted the top of the ambulance and her already loose helmet. The helmet slid off to one side.

Jade took turns muttering curses towards herself for cutting off her hair, for the lice that had made her cut her hair, and for the clear night that had kept her from lowering the canvas canopy over the cab in the first place.

On the plus side, the reverberation from the last shell had silenced the patients. In that welcome quiet, she heard the drone of an aircraft. Jade glanced up and saw rings within rings painted on the underside and knew it for one of theirs. Who was on the dawn reconnaissance run? Could it be David? The plane was a Sopwith Camel, and most of the experienced pilots preferred the Camel, with its agility in tight turns. She blew a kiss to the unknown pilot and pulled into evac as a bomb dropped in the center of the hospital base.

Shouts of fear and disbelief emanated from the makeshift hospital. Jade ducked behind the ambulance, but not quickly enough. She felt a hot, stabbing pain bite into her left knee. A wetness trickled down her leg. Her hand brushed aside her skirt and automatically grabbed her knee. Warm, sticky blood coated her palm. She prodded the area with her fingers and felt a hard chunk of metal stab back.

Jade bit back the pain and tugged. Her wet

9

fingers slipped off the shrapnel. She wiped her hand on her skirt, placed her hand inside her shirtsleeve for a better grip, and pulled again. This time the chunk came out. Jade fumbled in her pocket for a handkerchief and tied it around her bleeding knee just above her boots. Then she limped around the back, opened the ambulance doors, and helped the orderlies move the wounded. Another bomb slammed and detonated in the road, just missing the hospital. Screams exploded around her as a rain of debris clogged the air. *These aren't whizbangs or howitzers. Who the blazes is firing on a hospital?*

Jade looked up through the dirty haze and spotted the second airplane and the black Iron Cross on its fuselage. The pilot banked and came about for another run on the hospital, and the Camel raced in immediately on the German's tail. Jade cheered an instant before she caught sight of a black horse painted behind the propeller. *David!*

Her grimy olive face lit up in a broad smile, and she shouted with the orderlies. 'Vive l'Angleterre,' they cried out. 'Long live England.' The planes sped away from the hospital towards the front lines, the Camel biting the backside of the German plane with its machine gun. From a distance they saw black smoke belch out of the enemy plane. Its engine sputtered, and the plane began a death spin towards the earth. The Camel pulled away and proceeded on to its original scouting mission along the front lines. Jade watched with pride as it flew off and wondered if she should think more seriously of David's

10

recent marriage proposal.

One of the orderlies hugged Jade and kissed her on both cheeks. When he would do more, she pushed him away with a laugh and limped back to her ambulance. She was just pulling out when an additional droning hum to her right arrested her attention. David had been spotted and challenged. The two planes flew by, chasing each other with the aerial agility of dragonflies and the ferocity of hawks.

Jade shaded her eyes against the rising sun's light and watched. The first plane was David's Camel. The second was obviously German by the black cross on its tail, but she'd never seen one quite like it before. The Fokker E.III only had one wing. This one had two. She recalled David telling her the Germans had another Fokker called the D. VII. It was deadly.

The Camel came around and fired on the Fokker's tail, but the German pilot looped up and over, neatly avoiding the machine-gun fire. Now he was behind David and returned fire. David banked left and then right, trying to avoid the barrage of gunfire.

Jade shouted encouragement. 'Come on, David, shake him. Show him how a Camel really flies.'

The two orderlies joined Jade by her ambulance and gaped openmouthed at the intense aerial joust. The new Fokker was fast and every bit as maneuverable as the Camel. It hung on to David's tail like it was tethered.

'Lose him in the sun,' someone yelled, and Jade recognized her own voice.

11

As if the pilot heard her, he plunged into a nosedive with the intent of leveling out nearly on the ground. Perhaps he hoped the rising sun would make him invisible to the pursuing Fokker. Perhaps he hoped the Fokker would follow and crash before pulling up out of the dive. Whatever his plan, his plane had other ideas.

The Sopwith Camel, named for its humped fairing over the guns, often bit its owner just like a real camel. Its rotary engine carried a powerful torque. This increased its amazing agility, but that same torque put many novice pilots in a fatal spin at low speeds unless they compensated with right full rudder. David was no novice, but his damaged rudder didn't respond adequately enough to counteract the gyroscopic effect of the engine. The plane rolled over in a ground loop and crashed on the starboard wing.

Jade watched for a split second as the plane skidded along upside down across the field, leaving chunks of wood, fabric, and tubing behind it. Then, as if acting on instinct, she gunned her vehicle across the field towards the wreck. The Ford shuddered and protested as she pushed the vehicle to fifty kilometers an hour. Her helmet slid from her black hair. It hung on the back of her head by its strap and tugged at her throat as though trying to hold back any outcry.

Jade skidded to a halt ten yards away and hit the ground in a dead run towards the wreckage. Panic and pure energy prevented her from feeling the pain in her damaged leg.

12

'David!' she screamed. With inhuman strength born of fear, she ripped away part of the plane and exposed the pilot. Jade fought back the rising taste of bile in her throat and worked to free him before the plane caught fire. Several orderlies raced down the field with a stretcher as she slid him out of the cockpit and onto the ground. There she probed gently for wounds.

'Jade,' he whispered. Blood dribbled from his mouth.

'I'm here, David. Don't talk.' She unfastened his leather flight helmet and slid it off his brown curls, sticky with blood. She bound his head with his aviator's scarf.

With tremendous effort, David brought his shaking left hand over to his right, tugged a ring from his bloody finger, and pushed it into Jade's hand. She heard him try to speak, a hoarse croaking sound, and bent forward to listen.

'Find . . . my . . . brother. Mmmm-mi . . . '

She stroked his head. 'Hush.'

The young pilot persisted. 'Father's death, suspic . . . '

'David, you're going to be all right. The orderlies are here. Just hold on. Please!'

But already she spoke to a spiritless shell.

★　★　★

Beverly tiptoed into the farmhouse basement as softly as her boots allowed. Jade hadn't moved from her bunk.

'I'm awake, Bev.' Jade's lusterless voice rang hollow in the dim room.

13

'I brought you a cup of coffee, love.' Beverly pushed the cup into Jade's hand and heard the tin cup clink against the ring she was holding. She took it from Jade, sat beside her on the cot, and gazed at the beautiful green stone, almost the same color as Jade's eyes. 'Do you know where his brother is stationed?' asked Beverly. 'If not, I can write home and get help looking in the rosters for him.'

Jade sighed once, a deep, soul-shuddering groan. 'He doesn't have a brother.'

2

'Many travelers to Africa make the mistake of choosing their destination based on a preconceived notion of romance or adventure. This can lead to disappointments. Let the itinerary be a blank slate, and let the adventure write itself.'
— The Traveler, London — *February 1919*

'Please tell Mrs Worthy I'm a friend of her late son.' Jade stood in the entrance hall of an old London town house and waited impatiently for the butler to show her to a drawing room, a library, a study, or whatever room polite society used nowadays. She'd have been just as happy to settle for the kitchen if it meant sitting next to a warm fire and getting out of her wet coat. Unfortunately, the butler seemed reluctant to show her anything but the way out. She shifted her weight to her good leg and grimaced. Her wounded knee troubled her more today with the rain. Jade wondered if there was still a fragment of shrapnel stuck in there somewhere.

'Do you have a card, miss?' insisted the butler.

'No. Please, tell her I was with David when he died.'

'Very good, miss.' The butler tipped his head, probably as much of a bow as he felt this lowly American female deserved, and left her in the entryway.

David had rarely discussed his family, so Jade

15

didn't know much beyond the fact that his father had died a few years ago in East Africa. She glanced around for clues to the Worthy family. None jumped out at her. The hall's sparse appointments included little beyond the requisite umbrella stand and a low table and crystal bowl for leaving calling cards.

Several cards waited in the bowl. *Madam must not have been receiving this morning.* She fingered through them. A Mrs Hartford and a Mrs Nattington had called. There was also a card from a Mr Jacobs of Smith, Wetherby, and Harrison.

Her ears caught the soft sound of a closing door. She quickly released the cards and returned to her original place. If Mrs Worthy wasn't receiving earlier this morning, chances were she wouldn't see her now. Jade wondered if she should have done a bit of name dropping and mentioned her friend Beverly Heathington, lately engaged to Lord Dunbury. The butler returned.

'Madam will see you in the library, miss.' The man inspected her brown wool coat and her pre-war broad-brimmed hat with its faded green ribbon band. 'Your wraps, miss.'

Jade removed the hat first and handed it to the elderly man. His eyes widened for a brief instant in shock at the sight of her bobbed hair before he regained mastery over his face. He left her alone again to hang up her coat before returning to conduct her to a sitting room.

'This way, if you please, miss.' He led the way down the corridor to a side room. 'In here, miss.

16

Madam will be down momentarily.'

He left her standing alone on a lovely paisley Persian carpet worked in autumnal colors. Floor-to-ceiling walnut shelves covered three of the walls. Books primarily filled the shelves, but a large quartz geode prevented *Birds of the British Isles* from getting too familiar with a section of British poets. On the opposite wall, an elephant carved from blood-red jasper held back Shakespeare's histories. No novels or anything remotely improper. Jade heard a door close somewhere down the hall.

She glanced expectantly towards the door and spied a portrait of David's father, Gil Worthy. Jade took in the family resemblance of oval face, hazel eyes, and brown curly hair. Mr Worthy had posed in a smoking jacket, his hands crossed in front to reveal gold cuff links. One bore a G and the other a W. Above the portrait hung the motto 'To Be Truly Worthy.'

Underneath the portrait stood a small glass-fronted barrister bookcase. Jade recognized many of the works: Burton's *Wanderings in West Africa from Liverpool to Fernando Po*; Andersson's *Lake Ngami* and *The Okavango River*; Cameron's *Across Africa*; and James' *The Wild Tribes of the Soudan*, to name a few. She looked in vain for Mills' *The English in Africa*, or Lord Cranworth's *A Colony in the Making*. It seemed that none of the titles were more recent than the late 1880s. The books sat alongside an exotic necklace of whitened bones and yellowed teeth. The teeth, long and pointed, came from a carnivore and a large one at that. Jade had bent

17

down for a closer look when the butler coughed softly and announced Mrs Worthy's arrival.

Jade straightened at once to meet the woman who might have become her mother-in-law, had events and her own feelings taken a different turn. Mrs Gil Worthy was a slender woman of medium height and delicate facial features with light brown hair pulled back in a French roll. She wore an ankle-length black silk dress with elbow-length kimono sleeves. A high-waisted satin belt threaded through the sides of the gown, leaving it to hang loosely at the back like a robe. A necklace of jet beads draped her white throat.

Fashionable mourning, observed Jade. It seemed Mrs Worthy had enough money to maintain appearances with the latest in haute couture.

Jade extended her hand, but Mrs Worthy kept hers clasped in front of her. Jade took the hint and dropped her own. 'Mrs Worthy. Please accept my condolences on the loss of David.'

'Thank you, Miss del Cameron.' With a graceful sweeping gesture, the widow indicated a golden brown wingback chair next to a low table. 'Please sit down.' Mrs Worthy perched herself on the edge of a matching walnut brown chair and conveyed the impression that she didn't intend to occupy it very long, so there was no point in getting comfortable. The butler returned with a silver tea service and set the tray on the low table without a word.

'You may go, Winston,' ordered Mrs Worthy. Winston bowed and left the room, shutting the door behind him. Mrs Worthy poured tea into a delicate Wedgwood cup. 'Milk or lemon?'

'Neither, thank you,' replied Jade. She loathed tea. The only thing that made it remotely palatable was a thick dose of honey, and she didn't see any on the tray. Not even any sugar. Mrs Worthy handed the cup and saucer across to Jade, who received it with as gracious and as insincere a smile as the one on Mrs Worthy's face. She waited until the hostess had poured another cup before tasting hers. *Dreadful*.

'How is your tea, Miss del Cameron?'

'Fine. Thank you.'

Mrs Worthy replaced her own cup on the tray and folded her lily white hands in her lap. 'You knew my son.' There was no warmth or encouragement in her statement.

Now it begins, thought Jade. She set her own cup on the tray and steeled herself. 'Yes. I drove an ambulance in France.'

'But you're an American?'

'Yes, ma'am. I am.' She watched David's mother take in her dark olive complexion and saw the hint of a question in her eyes. Jade waited.

'I do believe David mentioned knowing an . . . American person,' Mrs Worthy said, her tone cold. 'It was very good of you, I'm sure, to do your bit.'

Jade despised that phrase as much as tea, so she decided to get to the point. 'I was with David when he died. I pulled him out of the wreckage.' She watched the woman maintain tight control over her outward demeanor. It would be a lot easier, Jade thought, to feel some sympathy for this woman if she acted as if she had a heart.

'I'm certain you did all you could for him.'

'No, ma'am, but I intend to. David made a last request of me. I'm here to carry it out.' Jade debated getting the ring out of her cloth bag, but her every mental alarm cautioned against it. It was not meant for the mother anyway. 'He told me to find his brother.'

Mrs Worthy was well schooled in hiding her emotions, but in the lengthy silence that followed, Jade detected a few traces of feeling. The woman's eyes widened for an instant; then the tiny lines around her lips lengthened a fraction as they tightened. It wasn't astonishment or disbelief Jade read behind those fleeting facial twitches. It was fear. *What is she afraid of?* Jade wondered. *Exposure? Scandal?* Here was a widow who recently lost her only son. Or had she?

The moment passed. The woman froze into an emotional iceberg again. 'You are wasting your time. David was an only child.'

'He didn't seem to think so.'

'Miss del Cameron,' the woman said in a tone used to instruct an ignorant child of her proper place, 'I was told David suffered a dreadful head wound in his crash. It is obvious he was delusional at the time of his death. He has no brother.' She rose gracefully from her seat.

Jade stood as well. All the polite smiles were gone, packed back into cold storage. Jade struggled inwardly to retain any shred of sympathetic feeling for this ice queen. 'I apologize if I was indelicate.'

Mrs Worthy sniffed. 'An American trait. I'll forgive you for it.' She walked to the door and tugged on a tasseled cord. 'Thank you for your aid to my son. Perhaps I can offer you some remuneration?'

Jade squelched her rising anger at the blatant insult and reached for the doorknob before Winston arrived. 'That won't be necessary. I was only *doing my bit*. The French gave me a Croix de Guerre, and David gave me his trust. That's reward enough.' She yanked open the door just as the butler gripped the other side and almost pulled the old man into the room. 'My hat and coat if you please, Winston,' she said authoritatively.

Winston, not yet recovered from his less than graceful entrance, said, 'Yes, miss,' and hurried off to fetch the garments. Jade marched down the hall and took a last stand by the card table. She glanced down at the crystal bowl, and a devious smile grew as she pocketed a card.

Winston arrived with her coat and hat and held her coat for her as she slipped her arms into the sleeves. Stepping out into the damp February air, she hailed a taxi, climbed into the backseat, and massaged her sore knee.

'Where to, miss?' asked the driver.

She consulted the business card in her hand. 'Twenty-six Willowbrook Street.'

★ ★ ★

On Willowbrook Street, which had no willows to speak of, Jade located the firm of Smith, Wetherby, and Harrison. Mr Jacobs, a solicitor for the firm, received her with warm smiles, polite bows, and an offer of tea. She accepted the first two with gratitude and declined the latter.

'Thank you for taking the time to see me so quickly, Mr Jacobs.'

'My pleasure, Miss del Cameron. I am most intrigued as to how I may help you with regards to Mr David Worthy.'

Jade settled herself more comfortably in the soft leather chair. 'David was a friend of mine.' She paused to see if he understood. Judging by the twinkle in his brown eyes, she decided he felt he did. Jade wondered if *she* did. She and David had been close friends with a mutual interest in planes. When she had turned down David's marriage proposal, he vowed to win her with feats of daring. One of those feats had killed him. Now guilt, as much as affection, drove her. 'I was with him at the time of his death, and he entrusted me with an important request.'

'His last request,' breathed Mr Jacobs as though he were about to hear the most sacred secret.

'I saw your calling card on Mrs Worthy's hall table. I assume you are her solicitor.'

'Her late husband's actually.'

Jade considered this tidbit of information. 'She won't assist me. Quite adamant about it actually. I'm hoping you will.'

'If I can, miss. What was his request?'

'He asked me . . . no, he *told* me to find his brother. He had never spoken of a brother before then. But despite his mother's claims, David was not delusional before he died. What he did took clear presence of mind. The short of it is, I believe him and I intend to find his brother. I'm hoping you'll help me.'

Mr Jacobs chewed thoughtfully on his lower lip. 'You said that what he *did* took clear presence of mind. Just what, may I ask, did he do?'

Jade responded by opening her pocketbook. She pulled out a bundle wrapped in soft gray flannel and unwrapped it. 'He pulled this ring off his finger and put it in my hand. I believe he meant either for me to give it to his brother or for it to be a clue in finding him.' She handed the ring to Mr Jacobs, who took it reverently.

'Yes,' he said softly. 'David inherited this from his father when he came of age.' Mr Jacobs rose from his seat and crossed to a large safe in the corner of his office. There he bent his tall, spare frame and carefully worked the combination while he attempted to hide the dial, not an easy task considering he was built like a beanpole. Jade discreetly looked to the other wall lined with legal books until she heard the safe door clang shut.

'I think you will find this a most interesting problem,' he said. Mr Jacobs held a small teak box in his slender hands. He placed it on the edge of his desk next to Jade.

'Open it, Miss del Cameron.'

Jade obeyed. Nestled inside on a small silk

23

pillow sat an exact replica of David's ring. 'I don't understand.'

Mr Jacobs reached into his coat pocket and smiled as he held up Jade's identical ring. 'This,' he said, nodding to the one in his hand, 'is the ring you handed me. You now hold its counterpart.'

'The ring for the brother,' guessed Jade.

'Exactly! Mr Gil Worthy had two of them made, one for each of his sons.' He handed Jade's ring back to her.

'If I'm guessing correctly, this other son is not Mrs Worthy's.' Mr Jacobs nodded. 'But you know about him and you'll take care of the situation?'

This time Mr Jacobs shook his head. 'Would that I could, Miss del Cameron, but it's not something I can do from behind the desk, and I don't know the entire story myself.' He shifted in his chair. 'I am going to take you into my confidence, Miss del Cameron. I feel I may do that because you and I share a common duty. In fact, the more I think of it, the more I see that you are the solution to my own dilemma. Allow me to explain.' Mr Jacobs settled back in his chair, tented his fingers together, and took on the aura of a storyteller.

'Mr Gil Worthy decided long ago that his fortune lay in Africa. He wanted to start up a farm, sisal perhaps or coffee. He was very keen on it and tried to get his family to go with him. David was only a little tyke, four or perhaps five at the time, and Mrs Worthy wouldn't have it. She insisted on staying

24

behind until her husband managed to make a suitable home for them.'

He paused and cleared his throat. 'I sincerely doubt she ever intended to leave London at all. Well, to make a long story brief, Mr Worthy was away for over four years. I believe he tried several ventures, but unfortunately, he contracted malaria and came home without realizing his fortune. Then six years ago, he approached me with that ring and a larger strongbox to be opened after his death only by David or his other son. Said he'd give me the particulars later. I gather he didn't know himself exactly where to look. That is where the second problem begins.

'You see, Mr Gil Worthy took it into his head at the start of 1915 to go to Africa and find this son. He took with him a sealed packet for the lad explaining everything. But instead of finding his son, Mr Gil died in Africa under evil circumstances.'

'Evil circumstances?' asked Jade.

'Yes, Miss del Cameron. Gil Worthy mailed that sealed packet back to me unopened. He said in a brief letter that he feared he was in some danger and didn't want the information to fall into the wrong hands.'

'May I see that letter?' Jade asked. Mr Jacobs extracted it from a file and handed it to her.

January 28, 1915
Jacobs:
  This infernal war makes it difficult to get anywhere. Trying to get out of Nairobi and

make my way back to Tsavo to pick up old trails. Going to look for an old Boer I met there. I'm sending the packet back to you for safekeeping. I think someone is following me, and if something should happen to me, give the packet to David and tell him to continue the search. Don't give it to my wife, Olivia. Must go. I'm sending this to the post by way of a Kikuyu lad I trust.

Gil

Jade handed the letter back to Mr Jacobs, who continued his narrative.

'Of course David had already joined the Royal Flying Corps and left for the war by then. Then we received news that Mr Gil Worthy was found dead in his hotel in Nairobi.'

So that's what David meant when he said, 'My father's death, suspic . . . ' 'Isn't Mrs Worthy at least concerned about her husband's death?' she asked.

'She insists his health was bad and won't hear anything else.'

'And David never opened the strongbox?'

'He had no opportunity. It would appear that Mr Worthy told him something of this situation since he mentioned the existence of a brother to you. Did he have any letters in his possession?'

'Not that I was able to see,' Jade replied. 'All his personal effects were sent home to his mother. She's probably burned anything regarding another son. Can't you open the packet?'

Mr Jacobs shook his head slowly. 'The instructions were explicit — only David or this

26

other son. My hands are tied.'

Jade fidgeted with frustration. 'Is there at least a name for this other child?'

'Abel. At least that's what Mr Worthy wrote on the packet. But beyond assuming he still lives somewhere in Kenya with his mother, I have no knowledge of his exact whereabouts.' Mr Jacobs shifted his long legs under the desk. 'Miss del Cameron, to be perfectly frank, your visit is a godsend. I need to find this boy, or rather, this young man, and I truly want to bring Mr Worthy's tormentor to justice. If someone caused his death, then it's murder plain and simple.'

'And you want me to help?'

'Yes.' Mr Jacobs warmed to the subject. 'You're bright. You certainly are no stranger to travel or difficult conditions, judging by your wartime contributions. You knew David. You appear to have a passion for fulfilling his dying request . . . ' He leaned across the desk with a hopeful, pleading smile on his angular face. 'In short, you are perfect for the job.'

Jade stroked the ring that David had entrusted to her and carefully rewrapped it in the square of gray flannel. 'Just so I understand you, sir. You want to hire me to go to British East Africa to look for a young man of nineteen to twenty-some years, whom no one has seen or heard of before and who may not even live there anymore, to give him his lost father's legacy. *And* you want me to investigate Mr Worthy's possible murder?'

Mr Jacobs clapped his hands together. 'Yes, that about sums it up. Shouldn't be difficult.

How many Abels can there be in the colonies?'

How many indeed. For all Jade knew, every Tom, Dick, and Harry was named Abel. *David died trying to prove himself to me. I owe it to him.*

'I was about to begin a job as a writer and photographer for *The Traveler* magazine,' she added almost to herself. 'I could request the colonies for an assignment and use it as a cover.'

'That's the ticket, Miss del Cameron,' said Mr Jacobs enthusiastically. 'Then you'll do it for me?'

Jade tucked the ring in her bag and rose. 'I'll do it for David.'

3

'Nairobi is a thriving colonial town, planted by early colonists such as Lord Delamere and cultivated by goods from Mombasa via the Ugandan Railway, sometimes referred to as the 'lunatic line.' Among the many modern comforts are electric lighting and shops featuring such amenities as exotic foods and modern fashions. Any traveler to Nairobi will also be delighted to experience the luxury and comfort of the Norfolk Hotel, affectionately known as the House of Lords.'
— The Traveler, Nairobi — *June 1919*

Heat waves shifted in transparent rippling ribbons as Jade stepped off the stifling, noisy train onto the equally hot and far more raucous Nairobi station platform. It was late afternoon, and she had no idea whether the thrice-weekly train was on time. Probably not, considering that in addition to the numerous water stops, a herd of wildebeest had blocked the tracks for three-quarters of an hour. Another delay had occurred near Voi, when some young British bucks spotted a lion and insisted on wanting a bit of sport. The lion didn't and vacated the area as soon as the train halted.

Jade emerged into Babel, where not only a cacophony of sounds vied for her attention, but sights and smells as well. Sunburned whites in

29

European dress or bush clothing greeted one another in the king's English. An occasional Boer spoke in Afrikaans. Turbaned Sikh sentries shooed begging children away in thickly accented Swahili, while African women held up various goods and loudly expostulated their wares' merits in more exotic tongues.

The African women had beautiful coffee-colored faces with clean features glistening under shaven heads flattened by years of carrying heavy loads on their backs held by head straps. Some wore strapless dresses of colorful calico wrapped above their breasts in swirls of crimson, turquoise, and ochre. Others sported animal-skin garments. All jingled with multitudes of bangles and copper wire as they waved bananas, sweet potatoes, exotic fruits, and live, squawking chickens in the air.

A young African warrior strolled by clothed in a robe of red cloth tied toga-like over one shoulder. His plaited hair hung in strands dyed with ochre, and a large wooden, beaded block plugged an immense hole in one distended earlobe. A breeze fluttered his robe and exposed, along with his natural assets, a hunting knife hanging from a beaded belt around his bare waist. The man walked with liquid grace and a selfconscious air in front of the women, as though he knew he was beautiful to see and was bored by their admiration.

Most of the European men wore bush-style clothing with multipocketed khaki shirts. Broad-brimmed felt hats lined in red protected their heads from the equatorial sun's strong rays. Jade considered them the African equivalent of the cowboy — men who wrangled coffee, horses, and an occasional antelope instead of hay, steers, and elk.

The aroma of dust, foodstuffs, locomotive grease, and human bodies in various states of cleanliness mingled freely with the scent of grasses and wild animals that wafted in from the plains. Jade inhaled deeply. After the stench of war, the sooty air of London, and the close smell of hot machinery and moldy leather seats in the train, this smelled like perfume. She brushed a coating of red dust from her waltz-length brown linen traveling suit and stepped forward.

A loud explosive bang popped a few yards away. Jade immediately ducked and waited for the falling shrapnel. None fell. She rose, feeling a little foolish at her reaction to a backfiring car.

'Memsabu, memsabu.' An African boy waved to her from the far end of the platform and pushed his way through the crowd. 'You are Memsabu del Cameron,' he stated. 'I am here. I take you to the hotel.'

The boy stood about one foot shorter than Jade. She examined his smooth features together with his height and reckoned him to be around ten or eleven years old. He wore a uniform of the universal khaki complete with knee-length shorts and sandals. Black eyes sparkled intelligently back at her.

'Thank you,' she said. 'And you are?'

'I am here. I take you and your bags to the hotel,' he repeated as though reciting a memorized piece.

31

'Yes, and I thank you, but what is your name?'

The youth looked bewildered by the question, as though no one had ever found his name worth knowing before. Perhaps, thought Jade, they hadn't.

'I am Jelani,' he said shyly. 'Please, your bags, memsabu?'

Jade turned towards the train as a rail worker handed her luggage down from the car. 'Ah, here they are, Jelani. Just these two. I can carry the other and my rifle myself.' Jade picked up a leather satchel containing her precious Graflex camera, shouldered her rifle, and waited. 'Are you certain you don't need another boy to help, Jelani?' she asked.

He shook his head vigorously. Then he hefted a large leather case and nodded his head towards a small wooden rickshaw. 'This way, memsabu.' He began to drag the trunk behind him by one handle until Jade took hold of the other. Together, they wended through the noisy throng, past open coaches dripping with people, their friends, and their baggage; a few old private motorcars; and an official-looking coach with a uniformed guard.

'Just call me Jade,' she said. 'Careful with this trunk,' she added. 'It has bottles in it.' She hoped she'd packed her limited supply of photo developers carefully enough. 'How did you know I was here?'

Jelani shrugged under the burden. 'I am told, bring Memsabu Jade del Cameron to the hotel. Where else would you be?' Together, they placed the luggage in the back of the rickshaw. Jelani indicated that she should climb up into the seat. Then the boy positioned himself between the two long poles in front. Jade hesitated, one foot on the floorboard, the other in the street.

'Wait a minute,' she said. '*You're* going to pull me?'

'Yes, Memsabu Jade,' he said with a puzzled look on his face. 'I pull. You ride.'

Jade saw several other Europeans being pulled in rickshaws by African and Indian men of varying ages, mostly young lads. Customary or not, using fellow humans, especially children, as beasts of burden caused revulsion in her. She put her bag and Winchester on the floor next to her other luggage and stepped down.

'If you don't mind, Jelani, I have been sitting too long in that cramped railcar. I need to walk. You may pull my luggage. I would like to practice my Swahili with you.'

Jelani's face twitched in initial shock, which quickly dissolved into amusement. 'Memsabu speaks English funny,' he volunteered.

'Yes. I am an American, Jelani. I am trying to learn Swahili. Will you help me practice?' Jelani nodded vigorously, and Jade suspected he really wanted to hear how badly she would pronounce that language as well. Considering she only had the boat trip over to study out of an evangelical mission language guide, Jade thought with amusement that the topics would be as humorous as her pronunciation. After all, how often would sentences like 'Quick, there is a baboon in the bathroom' and 'The drunken Englishman is sick' come into use? She decided

33

to start simply with *Jambo, habari?* — Hello, how are you? — and build from there.

Jelani proved to be a patient tutor, responding to her questions and prompting her with polite questions of his own. Jade, for her part, spent a good deal of time asking in Swahili 'how do you say' followed by an English word. Jelani patiently answered and corrected her mispronunciations. She inquired about his name, and the boy proudly answered that it meant strong. Jade smiled to herself as she recalled Corporal Gideon puffing up as he explained that his name meant great warrior. Did all African mothers name their sons 'warrior' or 'strong'? Probably, she decided. After all, where names held meaning, why risk a male child's future prowess with a weak name?

Shops made of galvanized tin lined the straight, mile-long dirt street to the Norfolk Hotel. Colorful banners masked the shops' shabby appearances as the shopkeepers displayed pots, fabrics, and other wares under the iron awnings. A heady aroma of spices wafted from one unstable-looking structure, and Jade thought she detected the delicious scent of coffee among other smells.

She asked Jelani about several of the items and had increased her basic vocabulary considerably by the time they approached the fence delineating the hotel grounds. The magnificent two-story stone hotel and its wide, sweeping double veranda arrested her attention. After the unstable appearances of the street shops, this edifice announced itself with a solidity that spoke volumes for British determination to graft a permanent part of the empire here.

A half dozen whites lounged in the lower veranda's shade and sipped beverages from tall glasses. Jade observed their startled faces staring at her. Glass tumblers hung motionless in their hands. A middle-aged woman in a flowered hat turned to her mustached companion and whispered a few words. At first Jade thought it was because of her dusty attire, then realized it was because she was walking and conversing familiarly with the young African. *Pompous bastards*, she thought, and proceeded to ignore them.

'Jelani, thank you for the most interesting lesson.' Jade reached into a skirt pocket for a few rupees she kept for tips and handed him several. He took them with a gracious bow and proceeded to gather her satchels from the rickshaw, calling another boy to help with the trunk.

'Please, memsabu. You go in now,' he said softly. His speech had returned to its original formality. Jade hoped she hadn't caused him trouble. She hoisted the bag with her camera in one hand, her rifle in the other, and preceded him into the cool building. As she passed the lounging colonists, she overheard two men in a heated discussion.

'I tell you, we need to go on a hunt and clean out all the damn hyenas. I heard they've started hunting the natives.'

'You'll never clean out the hyenas,' replied a young man. 'There are too many of them. What if they do take a native or two? I'd rather they eat natives than my cattle.'

Jade was about to turn and show the last speaker a piece of her fist when a cheerful voice called from behind the lobby counter, 'Miss del Cameron. So glad you arrived safely.'

'Thank you,' replied Jade. She set her satchel on the floor and propped her rifle against the lobby desk. 'I'm surprised to be addressed by name before ever introducing myself.' She looked at the short balding man with an expectant smile.

'Your magazine, *The Traveler*, arranged for your room,' he began by way of an explanation. 'We knew when your boat arrived in Mombasa, and . . . ' He flourished a hand in the air like a magician about to make the invisible visible. 'Your solicitor, Mr Jacobs, also requested a motorcar. I'm doing my best to secure one for you, but at present . . . ' He shrugged.

'That's all right,' said Jade, wondering how she was going to get around without it. 'Then I must have been the only guest you were expecting?' she asked with a hint of incredulity.

The man's round face turned a shade pinker. 'Well, no, Miss del Cameron. But I must own that you look exactly like the description given in Lord Dunbury's letter, and he was *quite* insistent that we take the very best care of you.'

Jade smiled. *Beverly, you've been a busy girl.* Everything became crystal clear to her now: the lad with the rickshaw, the expectant and highly solicitous hotel keeper. Bev must have wheedled her fiancé into sending a personal endorsement to the hotel. In fact, if she knew Beverly, the dear girl probably wrote the letter herself and simply had Avery Dunbury sign it. Jade thought of the personal letter of introduction from Lord Dunbury in her bag. They were taking no chances of her receiving a cold shoulder among the Nairobi elite.

'I should think this red dust made everyone virtually unrecognizable,' Jade said. 'Every time someone opened a window on the train, it swooped in on us.'

'A nice hot bath in your room will take care of you. Not every room has a bath attached, but for you . . . ' He smiled broadly and waved his hands as though he conjured a private bath out of thin air. 'And we can have your traveling costume cleaned and pressed for you as well. Just leave it hanging outside your door. The boy will see to it.' The manager looked towards the far wall, where Jelani had melted into the shadows. 'N'ja, come here!' Both his voice and his fingers snapped. Jelani and the second boy sprang forward with her bags. 'Take Miss del Cameron's trunk to her room. And, miss,' he called after Jade, 'I'll have tea sent up shortly.'

Jade halted in her tracks. 'No! No tea please, if you don't mind.' She added more gently, 'You wouldn't by any chance have some coffee, would you?'

'Yes, Miss del Cameron. Coffee it is. Lots of coffee growers in the colony.' He smiled. 'I forgot you are a Yank, what with your London solicitor also sending letters of credit. So many people looking after you,' he added.

37

Jade pondered the various groups looking out for her. Mr Jacobs' influence might get her financial credit, but it wouldn't get her far with the tightly knit colonial set. It appeared Beverly and her fiancé knew that as well. Suddenly Jade remembered that Gil Worthy had supposedly been found dead in his rooms here.

'Tell me, sir. Do you recall a Mr Gil Worthy? I believe he visited in January 1915 and passed away suddenly in this hotel.'

The manager's eyes opened wide in horror. 'Merciful heavens! I recall no such thing. But,' he added, 'I shall make inquiries concerning him if you wish.'

'Perhaps I could check the register?' asked Jade.

'Later, Miss del Cameron. That year is in the safe with the others.'

Disappointed, Jade took her key and followed the boys up the stairs to her room. She wasn't sure what she had expected, but her preconceived notions certainly didn't include the beautifully crafted oak four-poster bed, the matching lion-footed chairs upholstered in warm golden velvet, and the large French doors that exited onto the upper terrace. Letters from lords had their advantage, since she couldn't imagine the magazine's request for a room would have warranted one this richly appointed. Jade saw with pleasure that the room also had electric lights.

Jelani waited for further instructions, which Jade gave in her best Swahili regarding filling the bath and then later bringing coffee and a light meal. He responded with minimal giggles and a few gentle corrections as, once again, Jelani became the relaxed, friendly boy of before. Jade felt they'd get on famously, as Bev was so fond of saying.

Jade washed the red dust of the Athi Plains from her slender body and short black hair, and put on her ambulance corps trousers and a white blouse. The only thing missing from her uniform was the overskirt. She signaled that she'd finished her bath by hanging her soiled traveling suit outside the door. Jelani appeared in a few minutes with a quarter of a cooked chicken, bread, an orange, and a pot of that blessed coffee.

'Oh, thank you, Jelani.' Jade poured a cup of precious black nectar, sipped it, and sighed. 'You don't know how much I've missed coffee.'

'Memsabu not like tea?' he asked innocently in English.

Jade made a sour face and stuck out her tongue. Jelani laughed. 'No,' she answered. 'Memsabu does *not* like tea.' She finished the first cup, picked up a chicken breast, and retired to a wingback easy chair and footstool. 'What is your tribe, Jelani?'

'Kikuyu,' he answered.

She offered him a seat and a chicken leg. He refused both. 'Do you live here?'

'I live with the others,' he said, leaving Jade to wonder where the staff stayed. 'But in a year I will return to my village and become a warrior.'

Jade nodded, her mouth full of chicken. 'I'm sure,' she said, swallowing, 'that you will be a

39

fine warrior. You must be very strong already, carrying everyone's bags and pulling people in rickshaws.' She leaned forward and poured another cup of coffee. 'And who will you fight when you are a warrior?'

Jelani's face turned stony. 'The *laibon*.'

Jade paused in midsip and peered over the cup rim. 'And what is a *laibon*?'

'He is a . . . ' The boy paused as he searched for an English word to explain. Jade took another swallow while she gave him time to think. When he spoke, he spat the word as though it were poisoned. 'Witch!'

Jade nearly choked on the coffee. Her sudden coughing worried Jelani. He shifted from one foot to the other in hesitation over what to do. Finally Jade managed to set her cup down and regained her voice. 'A *witch*?' The boy couldn't be serious. Then she saw his young face transformed by a mixture of fear and loathing. 'Who is this *laibon*? What does he do?'

Jelani hesitated before answering. 'He sends his beasts to kill us, but it is not good to talk of him.' He pointed to her chest. 'Already he stopped your air.'

'My cough? No, Jelani. I swallowed the coffee wrong, that's all.' She could see his skeptical frown. He probably believed some witch made her choke just because of his unwitting comment. Jelani fidgeted some more, impatient to leave. Jade handed him a few more coins, thanked him again, and allowed him to return to his other duties. She watched him take down her soiled traveling dress before he shut the door and

40

left her alone with her thoughts.

For several months, she'd avoided idle times like this. Immediately after leaving the Hackett-Lowther ambulance unit, she returned to London to tie up some loose ends in her language studies at Winsor College. Too restless to stay in one place, she took a Christmas trip home to her parents' New Mexico ranch and occupied it with hiking, hunting, and ranch chores. She went out of her way to pack every moment of every day with something useful to occupy her mind so she didn't have to think about the front and David's death. Especially David's death. It wasn't until New Year's Eve when the crisis came to the forefront.

Her father's foreman and ranch hands had sequestered some Roman candles to shoot off in celebration. Jade was in the living room of the big stone house with her parents when the explosions began. New Mexico suddenly dissolved into the French front lines. After first hitting the floor behind the chair, she raced out into the night, searching for her ambulance. Later that night, she woke screaming from a nightmare in which she carried David's bloody body across fields of broken airplanes.

That was when her father suggested it was time to put David to rest, and the only way to get rid of the burden was to carry out his last request. He convinced her she didn't know everything about David, including any illegitimate siblings tucked away somewhere. He also said she needed independence, so he contacted an old editor friend who decided that her language skills and adventuresome nature made her ideal to write travel articles for his magazine. Jade went back to London in February and began the search for David's brother.

Together, Jade and Mr Jacobs had surmised a few key points: the second son was four or more years younger than David and was sired in East Africa during Gil's first trip. The name on the packet hinted that the young man's name was Abel, and since Gil wanted to pick up a trail in Tsavo, the son might still live there. Now here she was in Nairobi with the second ring and the sealed packet tucked away with her clothes. As far as she knew, she was still a thousand miles away from a conclusion, but she'd made her resolve, and that was the first step towards the end and her own recovery. The chicken bone dropped from her hand onto the carpeted floor as Jade slipped into an uneasy sleep filled with diving planes and wild hyenas with eyes glowing like the stone in David's ring.

4

'The residents of Nairobi are as diverse a set of people as any group of pioneers. Some go to help build the empire, others to seek personal fame and fortune, and still others look for adventure and freedom from the rigid confines of society. They all carry treasured parts of civilization with them as well as a spirit of rebellion.'
— The Traveler

'Grab your rifle and head for the flume!'

A loud shout woke Jade with a start, and she jolted upright in her chair. When she realized the room was dark, she reached for her pocket watch to see the time. *Funny. I don't remember turning out the lights.* Perhaps Jelani had come back for the tray and, seeing her asleep, had switched them off. She glanced at the table beside her. No, the tray was still there. She felt her way to the far wall and flipped the switch. Still, no lights.

The power must be out. More shouts from the street drew her onto the upper veranda. A crowd milled below in the fading daylight. Several men called for help at the generator flumes, and suddenly Jade had the urge to tag along. She grabbed her leather notebook and ran out the door and down the stairs to the street.

Outside, people raced for cars and horses. She spied a slender middle-aged woman and a tall man walking towards a box-bodied car. Jade ran after them. 'Please,' she called, 'may I ride with you to the generator?' The pair turned and looked at her in openmouthed surprise. 'I'm an American reporter for *The Traveler*,' she explained. 'I'd really like to see what's happening. May I ride with you?'

The lady whispered in her husband's ear. He nodded, and the woman responded with a broad smile. 'Delighted, Miss . . . '

'Jade del Cameron.'

'Miss del Cameron,' the lady repeated as though tasting the words. 'Please do get in. A reporter. Gracious me. This should be a novel addition to your piece.'

The gentleman helped them both into the car, a put-together job made from at least three models, including a Dodge and a Wolseley. Jade got in the back. The man slid behind the wheel next to his wife, and they sped off down the dirt streets of Nairobi and into the wild plains beyond. Several people in cars and on horseback preceded them.

The lady turned in her seat and shouted to be heard above the noisy motorcar. 'I'm Madeline Thompson.' One hand clamped her flimsy ribboned hat on her head and the other indicated the driver. Jade noticed the woman's rough hands and lightly browned arms as the sleeves of her blue cotton dress fell back. She looked to be in her mid-thirties though the sun had done its best to advance her wrinkles. Obviously a working woman, not averse to tackling manual labor. Jade warmed to her immediately.

44

'This is my husband, Neville Thompson,' the lady continued. 'We're coffee farmers. Our place is north of here near Thika.'

'Delighted to meet you,' Jade shouted back. 'Just what is going on? What are we racing to in such a hurry?'

'Oh, well, it ought to be good sport, really,' called Mr Thompson. 'You see, Nairobi means sweet water in Maasai. Anyway, the town has a flume of sorts that carries some of that water to a generator to make the electricity. Sometimes something gets into the ditch and stops up the water.' He gestured back towards the town and the car veered right. Neville replaced both hands on the wheel. 'That is why the lights are out.'

'Do you mean something like a log?' asked Jade. She jotted a few notes in her book. The car bounced, and her pencil skidded across the paper.

'No,' answered Madeline gaily. 'Something as in a buffalo or other large animal. Maybe it can't get out or maybe it's just obstinate and doesn't want to. Anyway, here we go.'

'I knew this was a good time to come into the city for supplies, Maddy,' said Neville. 'And here you were afraid there wouldn't be anything of interest going on.' He laughed.

'You'll have to forgive us, Miss del Cameron,' said Madeline. 'The society life of a coffee farmer is different from that of some of the more genteel set in Happy Valley. We take whatever fun we can have.'

'I understand completely, Mrs Thompson,' said Jade. 'I was raised on a ranch. I know what

45

work and isolation do to pique a person's appetite for adventure.'

Madeline's brown eyes widened. 'Did you hear that, Neville?' she said. 'I told you this looked like an interesting young lady. An American, too,' she said while trying to discreetly take in Jade's dark olive complexion, green eyes, and wavy bobbed black hair. Her own long sun-bleached brown hair was escaping in strands from an elaborate bun. 'Are you by any chance an Indian?'

'Maddy!' snapped her husband. 'Don't be impertinent.'

Jade stifled a smile. 'It's all right, and no, I'm not. Sorry.' Jade saw the disappointed pout on Madeline's face and made a quick decision. Normally a private person, she realized if she wanted strangers to confide in her, she'd have to go first. 'My mother is full Spaniard, and my father is some Spanish-Irish-French mix. In short, I'm a mutt.'

'Well, you're lovely,' said Madeline. She nodded to Jade's hair. 'Very smart. Is short hair the fashion in America?'

'I really can't say,' answered Jade. 'I drove an ambulance in France during the war. For some of us, it became a matter of practicality.'

'Drove an ambulance,' Mrs Thompson repeated with awe. 'Neville, did you hear? Miss del Cameron drove an ambulance in France during the war.'

'I say,' Neville called back to Jade. 'That's bloody exciting. Red Cross?'

'No. Hackett-Lowther unit,' answered Jade.

She held on to the car seat as the vehicle jolted over the remains of a termite mound. 'Mostly British girls. I was at Winsor College for a year and joined up. We were attached to the French Third Army at the front lines.'

'Bloody marvelous,' he exclaimed. 'Madeline, she must stay with us for a while. You can be my wife's latest pet, Miss del Cameron,' he added over his shoulder.

Jade didn't care to be anyone's pet, but the opportunity seemed too good to pass up. Making personal inroads without having to use stuffy letters of introduction seemed nothing short of miraculous. Besides, these people were anything but pretentious, an affectation she hated. And if they'd been farming a long time, perhaps they knew about other pioneers, including Gil Worthy. Jade had decided not to openly announce her mission until she could glean more information. When she held at least a glimmer of knowledge of who the principal characters were in this melodrama, then she'd openly admit her underlying purpose.

Madeline joined her husband's cause with a wholehearted urgency. 'Neville is quite right. I would *love* to have you stay at our farm. Of course, it's nothing so nice as the Norfolk. The town people call the Norfolk the House of Lords. We're more the House of Commons, but we do have a good cook and a spare room. Do say you'll join us.' Mrs Thompson nearly jiggled in her seat from excitement.

'I'd be delighted,' Jade replied. 'As long as you're sure I won't be any bother.'

47

They both poohed the idea, exclaimed their own delight at her agreement, and pressed her for information about America.

'Ah, here we are,' exclaimed Neville just as Jade began to tire of repeated inquiries concerning wild Indians and desperadoes.

They'd driven about fifteen miles out of Nairobi to Ruiru, a small river crossing that boasted a hut or two. Papyrus waving plumed tufts in the air like a Persian cat's tail announced the welcome presence of water.

'There's a dam here,' Madeline explained as she straightened her hat, 'and a flume carries the water down to Nairobi's generator.'

Several Africans in rust brown robes and carrying spears stood next to the flume, staring down into it and shouting, *'Kiboko.'*

'Kiboko,' echoed Jade. 'Doesn't that mean hippopotamus?'

Neville hopped out and reached in the back for a double rifle, the ever popular Enfield. 'Correct, Miss del Cameron. Perhaps you and Maddy should stay here. Hippos are a nasty lot when they're angry, and they *always* seem to be angry.'

Mrs Thompson frowned at her husband's back and looked at Jade to see what she would do. Jade watched the growing number of people and decided, no matter how dangerous the hippo, the greater danger sat more with high-spirited and heavily armed hunters shooting each other in the cross fire. In that case, she'd be no safer from a stray bullet by sitting in the car than standing at the flume.

'I'm going to take a look,' Jade said. The two women joined the growing ranks of spectators at flumeside. Out of that crowd, three men argued over resolving the situation.

'Well, are we going to shoot it or not?' demanded an old man dressed in black-tie evening attire. He carried a Mauser rifle and looked as if he thought this was a formal safari. His drooping white walrus mustache jiggled as he spoke.

'It's not full grown,' answered a slender young man. He wore jodhpurs and riding boots, and his smooth baby-face features made him look more like a teenaged boy who should be under adult supervision than a hunter. Jade recognized him as the young man at the Norfolk who preferred the hyenas eat natives rather than his cattle, and felt her right fist tighten again.

'What bloody difference does that make?' retorted a third man, whose khaki trousers and bush jacket showed signs of heavy wear. Impatience marked his voice, and his broad shoulders strained his shirt. Not a man to make angry, thought Jade.

'Well, it hardly seems sporting to just shoot a young hippo stuck in the flume, Harry,' retorted the young man. 'Besides which, we'll have to haul out a deadweight.'

'Better a deadweight than being gored by the blighter,' argued Harry, the man in the bush jacket. He took a wider stance and flexed his powerful arms.

Mr Thompson joined in the debate. 'Now see here, chaps,' he said. 'Roger has a point. If this were a full-grown bull or even a cow, we'd have no choice but to shoot it in the ditch. But this bloke's too young to be territorial over some harem. I've got rope. I say we haul him out. Let the natives send him packing with a spear point in the rump.'

A loud crack ended the argument when the walrus-mustached man in evening attire shot the beast. 'Can't trust a hippo at any age,' he said as he lowered his weapon, 'especially a frightened one. Get your rope, Thompson. Let the natives pull it out. I daresay they'll appreciate the meat. If not, it will give the hyenas something to chew on besides my goats for a change.'

Harry pulled his wide-brimmed hat tighter on his head and scowled. He muttered a few curses that encompassed everything from hippos to meddlesome old coots, then stomped over to his horse, a beautiful black creature, and galloped back to town.

Jade looked questioningly at Madeline, who leaned towards her conspiratorially. 'Never mind Harry Hascombe. He's been here long enough that he fancies himself the best shot in Nairobi. Probably didn't like being robbed of his chance to show off in front of a new lady.'

Jade looked around and spotted no other women besides herself and Mrs Thompson. 'Me?' she asked. 'I doubt he even saw me.'

'Oh, Harry noticed *you* all right. Harry's a hunter in more ways than one, Miss del Cameron. He's just gone back to Nairobi to sulk a bit. He'll be all right in the morning.'

Jade noticed that the young man in jodhpurs,

Roger, also rode off in disgust. Jade took notes as the remaining men supervised the 'hauling of the behemoth,' as the event quickly became named. She imagined in the truest sense of hunters everywhere, that the animal would rapidly become bigger and fiercer with each telling. After much struggling and heaving, the men towed the carcass out of the flume and the water resumed its course to the power generator. Jade wondered if there'd be cheers and back-slapping all around in Nairobi as the lights came back on.

On the return trip, Madeline insisted on riding in back with Jade so she wouldn't have to turn around in the seat to talk. Neville received instructions to drive to town more slowly so they could have a longer visit and enjoy the cool night air and the rising moon. Madeline questioned Jade about her reporting job and hoped their farm might be mentioned in an article.

'Why not,' Jade answered. 'I'm also supposed to write a second feature about safaris. Perhaps you could give me some advice. I plan to go to Tsavo.'

'A safari!' squealed Madeline. 'We'd dearly love to go along. And, of course, we could help you arrange one.'

'That means me, of course,' said Neville with a chuckle. 'But it sounds splendid. Haven't been on safari for years.'

Jade spent most of the remaining ride fielding politely nosy questions about America in general and Westerners in particular. She answered them patiently if evasively and succeeded in turning a few questions back around on them. They

51

weren't the only ones wanting information.

She learned the Thompsons had been in the colony for eight years. That made them relative newcomers who probably wouldn't know anything about Gil Worthy's original visit. But perhaps she could meet some older residents through them. British East Africa covered a lot of land, and the chances that Gil had spent time in this area were slim. Still, she had to try. Deep inside, she believed her coolness had driven David to the recklessness that had killed him.

'Now, we must have breakfast tomorrow and arrange for you to come back with us to the farm,' Madeline said. 'Are you an early riser, Miss del Cameron?'

'Please, call me Jade, and yes, I am,' she answered, wondering what early meant here. On the ranch it meant predawn.

'What a lovely name,' said Madeline. 'And doesn't it suit her, Neville, with those delicious green eyes. I always thought — '

Bang! Whatever Madeline thought never came to light as a gunshot echoed from the hotel's interior.

Jade vaulted over the car's door and raced for the hotel. 'Someone's been shot,' she shouted. In an instant Nairobi vanished from her mind and, once again, in its place poured the sounds and smells of the front lines. Her gut wrenched into a tense knot, and her pulse quickened as she tore into the lobby. At any moment she expected a canister to explode near her, but she couldn't hesitate. Seconds meant a life.

Jade skidded and stopped dead in her tracks

mere inches before colliding with a beautiful black horse, the one Harry Hascombe had ridden to Ruiru. And there, astride the animal cutting circles in the lobby and firing his sidearm in the air, sat Hascombe himself. For a moment, she couldn't reconcile the animal with her reflexive reaction to the gunshots. When she did, her five-foot, seven-inch stature felt very short compared to this massive British centaur in front of her.

Harry spotted Jade, pulled his horse to a stop, and bowed low from the saddle. His face rested a few inches from hers. She saw the gray creeping into his day's growth of whiskers and the heavy lines creasing his broad brow.

'Welcome to Nairobi, miss,' he said with a trace of a slurred voice. Jade smelled the alcohol on his breath. 'A pretty lady needs a proper introduction to our town.'

As he bowed, he let his gun hand drift down within reach. Jade struck his wrist with catlike speed, using the side of her hand. The gun clattered to the floor, and the hotel clerk hastened forward from behind his desk.

'Mr Hascombe, I protest this intrusion in my hotel. Now you ride Whiskey out of here this instant. Save that nonsense for the Muthaiga, where it belongs.'

Harry Hascombe turned his horse's head towards the door. He reared once, waved his hat in salute, and raced outside and down the steps. Jade heard the cheers and general laughter that marked his progress down the street. Then she picked up the fallen gun and handed it handle first to the hotel manager.

'He'll probably want that later,' she said. He stared at her, mouth agape.

'Thank you, Miss del Cameron,' he murmured at last and mopped his sweating forehead.

The Thompsons stood in the door and gazed at her with something bordering on respectful awe. Jade smiled and nodded to them. 'Breakfast at seven?' she asked. They nodded dumbly and went up the stairs to their own room.

Jelani appeared beside her, beaming with pride. 'Would memsabu wish more coffee?' he asked.

'Yes,' Jade answered without hesitation. 'Bring a pot to my room please, Jelani.' She started to turn towards the stairs when the manager spoke to her in a whisper and stopped her in her tracks.

'Miss del Cameron, I did a bit of checking around for you about your Mr Worthy.'

Jade's attention snapped towards the pudgy little man. 'Yes?'

'Well, Miss del Cameron. I got to thinking that I was not here in 1915. Holiday, you know. So I inquired of a doctor in Nairobi. He said he did recall such a man dying here. Said it was most peculiar.'

Jade felt her impatience rising. She wanted to grab the little round man by his lapels and shake the story out of him. Instead, she merely nodded and urged him to continue with a simple 'Please go on.'

'The doctor said that this Mr Worthy was mauled to death by an animal, possibly a hyena.'

'I don't understand,' said Jade. 'What is so

54

peculiar about that?'

'The man was in his room on the second floor. How would a hyena get in there?'

'How indeed,' murmured Jade as the manager walked away.

'Memsabu,' Jelani said in a serious whisper. 'There is another Swahili word you should know. It is *hatari*. It means danger.'

5

'Africa's voice is neither the siren call luring men to promised fortune nor the primal scream of bloodlust and danger. It is the whisper to the sleeping soul, a call of awakening that seeps out of its ancient rocks like a hidden, life-giving spring. It can be drunk and accepted as is or it can be dammed and converted to power. The response depends entirely on the soul.'
— The Traveler

Sweat, urine, and something more nauseating filled the dank and windowless mud hut. The odors forced their way into every crack in the mud, through the rotting grass fibers in the roof and into the pores of the human form hunched over the glowing coals. From there they insinuated themselves into his muscles. He threw two gristly bones on the coals and watched them dance. The tendons tightened reluctantly in the heat and screeched in protest before snapping in two. Marrow sizzled inside and whined through gaps in the bone as though begging to be released from the torture.

The man sucked in the pungent smoke, letting it bully its way into his bloodstream. He mumbled incantations in what sounded like gibberish, focused his thoughts on his hate, and grabbed power from smoke, words, and emotion. How dared they push their goats onto his land!

How dared they compare their miserable little beasts to *his* cattle, *his* money, *his* manhood. He'd sent one of his messengers before to harvest their goats. He sent one again to take one of their own, a puny old man whose very bones were now blackening on his fire. Now they strengthened their thorn *bomas* and huddled in their huts, too frightened to go out, too foolish to leave.

This time he must go himself. A beast can be taught to kill, but it doesn't understand revenge. That took a human's touch. Even his former mentor, who could do this much more easily than he, would not suit his purposes tonight. He took a lion's form and killed too quickly. No, tonight he needed to choose the victim and make sure that the others heard the screams.

The man reached into the fire with a third bone and knocked one of the blackened ones out onto the dirt by his feet. He picked up the sizzling femur and bit into it. The brittle bone cracked under the pressure of his powerful jaws. Hot marrow scalded his mouth, and he swallowed quickly without tasting. Power coursed through his muscles, honing them, molding them. Red coals turned white and the yellow smoke appeared gray as his eyes lost their color sense. But what he lost in color, he gained in sharpness of contrast.

He grew aware of previously hidden sounds — a small lizard in the thatch, termites gnawing in the walls. His ears gradually shifted to hone in on the different locations, listening, discarding the unimportant noises. He lifted his face and tested the air. A new smell wafted in through the low door. It was the smell of humans: cowering, frightened humans. He opened his mouth and flared to capture the scent of their acrid sweat. He longed for the coppery smell of blood but it wasn't there. Not yet.

The hunching man tried to sit upright but couldn't. His spine locked in the hunch. Ropy muscles thickened and tugged at his legs. He drank in the pain and let it feed his hatred, sorry that there was less pain each time he did this. But then, he reasoned, what he lacked in hate, he supplemented with scorn. And it got easier every time. Already he was as good as his teacher. No, better. The figure stalked out from the hut and laughed a hideous, giggling laugh.

6

'*Nairobi enjoys the benefit of an extensive society including clubs, polo grounds, and golf courses. Horse racing is very popular in Happy Valley, and horse breeding is less an occupation and more an avocation. How could any horse not do his best when surrounded by the grandeur of the Athi Plains to the east, Mount Kenya to the north, and Mount Kilimanjaro to the southwest? The challenge to race is given by the native springbuck, impala, and zebra, and taken up eagerly by the Thoroughbred.*'
— The Traveler

'Your soft-boiled egg, miss, with ham and toast.' The waiter placed the porcelain egg cup on her plate next to one minuscule circle of thin, dry ham and set a rack of toasted white bread next to it. A jam pot joined the other items. Jade's shoulders slumped in disappointment. She'd envisioned a thick, juicy ham steak and at least two eggs fried in the drippings. There weren't even any hashed brown potatoes. *And Britain considers itself a civilized nation.* At this point she could kill for several slabs of bacon. She wondered what fried hippo tasted like. At least her cup held coffee and the waiter left the pot.

'Good morning, Miss del Cameron,' sang a cheery voice. 'So sorry we're late. Mmmm, looks delicious,' added Madeline as she eyed Jade's breakfast.

Jade looked up from her plate to see both Madeline and Neville. 'Good morning,' she echoed. 'I hope you don't mind my ordering already. I'm starved. And please, call me Jade. After last evening, I feel we're past the formalities.'

'Then you must do the same for us,' Neville added.

Jade waited as Neville held a chair opposite Jade for his wife and then seated himself next to Madeline. They ordered the same breakfast she had and insisted she continue before her egg chilled. She obliged by tapping the top off her egg with her spoon.

'Did you enjoy your introduction to Happy Valley society last evening, Jade?' inquired Madeline.

Jade loaded her egg with salt and pepper. 'Happy Valley? Is that what the generator flume is called?'

Madeline's laugh was a delicate musical ripple. 'No. Happy Valley is where the Nairobi elite live. The polo fields, the country clubs, the government house, all of it.'

Jade wondered if the nickname had originally been meant to be sarcastic and decided not to inquire. 'I enjoyed meeting you and Neville.'

Madeline beamed at the compliment. 'Then you are still planning to stay with us at our farm? You haven't changed your mind?' The waiter brought the Thompsons' breakfast. Jade noticed the same small circles of ham. Must have been cut with a cookie cutter.

'On the contrary, I'm looking forward to it. I'm grateful to have met you on my own without resorting to stuffy letters of introduction.' She uncapped the jam pot, scooped out a dollop of golden orange marmalade, and spread it on a triangle of toast while she waited for this little bit of news to penetrate. *Bait and wait.* Jade didn't have to wait long, but with traditional, well-bred British tact, the Thompsons inquired obliquely about these supposed letters.

'I agree, Miss Jade,' said Neville, who couldn't quite get as familiar as his wife. 'There is no good way to go about using a letter of introduction short of thrusting it on someone, er, no matter *who* wrote it.' In that last clause, he two-stepped around wanting to know the author.

Madeline picked up the marmalade spoon. 'Neville is quite right,' she added in an attempt to dance a little closer. 'And then, what if no one really knows the letter's author? How horrid!'

Jade stifled her smile. They really were too cute, and she felt a pang of guilt for toying with them. Still, she always enjoyed playing the game, so she dropped the juiciest bit of bait on them. 'Oh, absolutely. And, Madeline, you hit the nail on the head, as we say in America. That was my very concern. What if no one knew Lord Dunbury? What would I do then?'

Jade bit into the toast. From the corner of her eyes she saw Madeline's brown ones widen perceptibly. The marmalade spoon slipped from Mrs Thompson's fingers and landed with a clang. Neville threw himself into the breach

61

while his wife retrieved the spoon.

'Ah, Miss Jade, your fears are, er, in this instance, unfounded. Er, Lord Dunbury is a name known to all British, although, er, as an American, perhaps you were not as aware of that fact.'

Jade widened her eyes to look innocently naive. 'It's very good of you to tell me this, Neville. Still, I suppose I shouldn't risk hurting Dunbury's feelings by not using the letters. Not after he addressed them specifically to Lord Colridge and to the governor.' She drank her coffee while Neville nearly choked on his tea and Madeline dropped the spoon again before recovering from this final bit of news.

'Are you calling on them today?' asked Madeline hopefully as she wiped marmalade off the tablecloth.

Jade nodded. Bait taken and subject fully hooked. It only remained to reel them in. 'Actually, only on Lord Colridge, but isn't it too far to take a rickshaw?' she asked. 'I saw a motor garage in town. Is it possible to hire a car? I'm supposed to have one, but . . . ' She shrugged.

'Nonsense. We can drive you in our car,' exclaimed Neville. 'I insist.'

Madeline studied her own simple, pale yellow frock. 'Perhaps I should change?'

Jade glanced down at her brown huck split skirt, shirtwaist, and war boots, the female equivalent of bush dress. 'If you do, you'll make me look bad. I'm afraid my wardrobe for the past year or so has consisted of a uniform complete with trousers.' Jade winked

62

at Madeline. 'Besides, I secretly plan on blaming all my social faux pas on being an American.'

Madeline laughed. 'Lord Colridge will think you're charming.'

Neville finished and patted his mouth with his napkin. 'Do you have an appointment?'

Jade nodded. 'Our worthy host here sent my letter around for me yesterday evening, and I received a return message this morning. I'm to call on His Lordship after midmorning. I believe he is busy with his horses before that.' She poured another cup of coffee from the pot and held up the nearly empty toast rack as a signal for more. 'He's one of the original colonists along with Lord Delamere, isn't he?'

'Yes,' agreed Neville in a voice that hinted of hero worship. 'Pre-railroad. Actually, you saw him last evening. He's the old gent who shot the hippo. The one in evening kit. Er, Lord Colridge, not the hippo.'

Jade arched her brows in interest, encouraging Mr Thompson to continue while she ate her ham. He did.

'He's a colorful man and prone to escapades not unlike Mr Hascombe's last night. Once, he used one of the stuffed lions at the Muthaiga Club for target practice. By the way, you were most impressive removing the gun from Hascombe last evening.'

Jade scowled. 'Probably made a fool of myself. Somehow the screams and shots threw me back into France.'

Madeline put a work-roughened hand on

Jade's. 'There, there, you poor thing. You mustn't fret. You looked very charming.' Her brown eyes twinkled. 'You might even say you were *disarming*, isn't that right, Neville?' She cast a sideways glance at her husband as if to communicate some secret thought along with her pun. If Neville understood, he didn't let on.

'Speaking of shooting escapades,' said Jade, routing the subject away from the war, 'I suppose there are quite a few injuries or even deaths around here with all that wild shooting going on.'

Neville shook his head. 'Not that I've ever heard of. Most deaths here are due to disease or wounded wild animals.'

'Indeed? There are records, I suppose?' asked Jade. 'Hyena maulings, too?'

Madeline's mouth gaped open in horror. 'Certainly you don't want to write about that, do you?'

'Not exclusively, no. But a sense of danger will pique my readers' interests.' Jade gave up any hope of getting another slice of warm toast and took the last cold piece. 'I hope His Lordship will tolerate all my questions. I do need to know more about the colony's earliest days, including the struggles the settlers faced. I'd also like to learn about the ones who gave up. Maybe you've heard of some of them yourselves? I was told that a Gil Worthy was one. Did you know him?' Jade looked from one to the other, hoping either of them had something to offer.

Neville shook his head. 'Name sounds vaguely familiar, but then we've only been here eight

64

years and even that was broken up with the war. I daresay that Lord Colridge would know a great deal about the early years.'

'If His Lordship doesn't wish to discuss anything with you, I'm certain Mr Hascombe would be glad to,' said Madeline. 'He's been here a long time, too.'

'You must forgive my wife, Miss Jade. It appears she has matchmaking on her mind.'

Jade sipped her coffee and stared over the rim at Madeline. She used silence and her brilliant green eyes to her advantage. Very few people, with the possible exception of Beverly, could withstand that look. Madeline pouted.

'Harry is an interesting man, and there are so few single ladies coming into the colony,' she explained. 'I cannot help it if I'm a romantic.'

'My dear, you are embarrassing Miss del Cameron,' said Neville gently but firmly. 'As far as we know, she has a young man back in the States.' He glanced at Jade for confirmation.

'No,' whispered Jade softly. She poked her cold toast with a knife.

'Now see what you've done, Neville,' scolded Madeline. 'You've made her unhappy.'

'I have made her unhappy! Now see here, Madeline, you were the one who — '

'Oh, pish tosh, Neville,' interrupted his wife. 'We mustn't quarrel about it. We have to drive Jade to His Lordship's residence.'

Jade coughed into her napkin to hide her smile.

★　★　★

65

Lord Colridge's estate lay sprawled between the Tana and the Athi Rivers, where the latter arched its back like a lazy cat and stretched on to join the Tsavo farther southeast. The massive stone house and sweeping veranda testified to the farm's age and prosperity, as did the expansive stone stables behind it. Like many of the original settlers to the protectorate, Lord Colridge had survived by growing a variety of crops, and he finally succeeded with maize and a smaller field of sunflowers. He eventually gave in to his passion for horses once his farm could support them.

Lord Miles Colridge met them halfway between the stables and the house, wearing jodhpurs and a long-sleeved, collarless white shirt. The ever popular red-lined solar topee sat perched on his head, its worn brim showing its age. The old gentleman walked with a youthful spring in his step despite his snow white hair, lined face, and liver-spotted hands. He stood only one inch taller than Jade, but his stiff aristocratic bearing and commanding voice conveyed the impression of greater power, rather like a bulldog.

Jade extended her hand. His Lordship took it warmly and made a slight bow over it. 'Very pleased that you should come to see me, Miss del Cameron. Very good of Dunbury to write that letter. Of course, the young lord is nearly a stranger to me, but I knew his father. Old Hector Dunbury was a marvelous man. Did you know him?'

Jade opened her mouth to reply in the negative

when Colridge answered for her. 'No, of course you didn't. How is young Avery?'

Avery was the new Lord Dunbury, Beverly's betrothed and David's best friend. Jade had met him a few times at the aerodrome, but later he had been too occupied with Beverly to notice anyone else. Still, Jade had learned enough about him from Bev to feel she knew him well. 'Very well, thank you, Lord Colridge. He's engaged, now that the war is over, and back home.'

'So he fought in the Great War, did he? Of course he would. He's a Dunbury. Where?'

'A pilot in the Royal Flying Corps, Lord Colridge. I met him while stationed in France.'

'Yes, of course. He wrote that you drove an ambulance. Said you earned a Croix de Guerre. Very good of you, an American, too, to help out the empire in her time of need.' His soft blue eyes looked her over appraisingly as he might have studied a new horse to determine its merits. Whatever he saw must have met with his favor because he nodded to himself as if verifying some private thoughts. 'I should like to meet him someday.'

'I believe he's very anxious to see Africa, sir, and is planning a honeymoon trip here.'

'Very good.' Suddenly Lord Colridge noticed the Thompsons and snorted lightly, blowing his walrus mustache outward. 'Mrs Thompson, my apologies,' he said with a bow in her direction. 'Thompson, you must forgive me ignoring you and your lovely wife.'

Madeline and Neville each made polite bows and recited, 'Lord Colridge,' in unison.

67

'Mr and Mrs Thompson have been good enough to take me in,' Jade explained. 'I imposed on them last evening. They've not only acted as chauffeurs for me, but also offered to let me stay at their home.'

'Quite right. Now come inside and tell me how I may be of service to you as well.' He offered Jade his right arm and extended his left towards the front door. 'Thompson, escort your wife. I'll see to Miss del Cameron.'

Lord Colridge led the way into a spacious living room appointed in a blend of traditional comforts and exotic decorations. A simple English-style sofa and tea table bordered a leopard-skin throw rug. Portraits in oil hung on the wall between the massive head of a male lion and a Maasai shield, and gorgeously embroidered pillows with oriental designs adorned straight-legged teak armchairs. The scent of pipe tobacco hung heavily in the air.

'Please have a seat. My manservant, Pili, should be here shortly. I've ordered refreshments to be served. I've taken another liberty, Miss del Cameron. Once I was aware you were a particular friend of Dunbury's, I arranged for a dinner party at the Muthaiga Club for Saturday night. You'll meet a good many of the colonists there. Of course, Mr and Mrs Thompson, you are invited as well. Eight o'clock. Black tie.'

Jade and the Thompsons thanked him warmly as a young African man in a gleaming white robe entered with a loaded silver tray.

'Ah, there you are, Pili,' Colridge said. 'Wondering what happened to you.'

The delicious scent of warm cardamom wafted from the rectangular slices of cake, and Jade inhaled deeply to take in the aroma. With it came the unmistakable stench of tea. At least, she noted, there was sugar this time. She studied the young man as he poured. He possessed a graceful heart-shaped face with skin the color of antique bronze, and his short black hair formed soft curls around his temples. A gold cross dangling from a chain slipped out from his robe as he bowed over the tea service. He silently offered a cup to Jade, who proceeded to take the tongs and drop five sugar cubes into the cup.

'How do you like your tea, Miss del Cameron?' asked Colridge after she took a polite sip.

'Left in the pot, sir.'

Madeline's eyes opened wide in shock, Neville's jaw dropped, and Lord Colridge roared with laughter. 'By thunder,' he said, 'I'd forgotten how refreshingly frank you Americans are. Pili,' he said, addressing the young servant, 'fetch something else for the lady.'

'What would the lady like?' asked Pili. Jade detected a slight French accent to his English.

'Coffee?' suggested Jade. 'If it is no trouble.'

The young man said he would see to it immediately and left. Jade noticed his stately bearing and arched one brow in inquiry.

'My manservant is a French Somali, Miss del Cameron. Most are Muhammadans, but this one has somehow been put upon by one of the missions here. Went to school there. Poor chap isn't quite sure what to believe now. He's damned fine with horses, too. All Somali are.'

'I take it you don't approve of the Christian missions?' asked Jade.

'They ruin a perfectly fine native,' snorted Colridge. His brushy mustache fluttered about his thin, wrinkled face like a tattered banner. 'Fill their heads with all sorts of rubbish they'd do perfectly well without.'

Jade assumed Lord Colridge espoused what she called the 'Country Club School of Religion,' where one chose a house of worship based on its acceptable social status. In that light, he would hardly see any merit of evangelizing Africans. She turned the subject to his farm and his horses and planned to eventually broach the topic of early settlers in general and Mr Gil Worthy in particular. She didn't count on Colridge's ability to carry on a lecture rather than a conversation.

The older man warmed to the subject immediately and spoke at length about his land and especially his horses. 'Sent my finest filly as a gift to His Majesty last year,' he proclaimed proudly. 'Do you ride?' he asked Jade.

She swallowed some of the delicious cake. 'Yes, but more of a Western style, sir, and on a more rugged type of horse. Most of my father's horses are bred from the wild mustangs left by the Spanish Conquistadors, but he's thinking of breeding Andalusians if he can get a good stud.'

'Perhaps those mustangs came from ancient Arab stock,' suggested Neville, who wished to enter the conversation.

'Perhaps, perhaps,' muttered Colridge. 'Well,'

70

he exclaimed loudly and slapped his gnarled hands on his legs. 'You must come and see mine. Thompson, Mrs Thompson, come along, all of you. There's a good lad.' He shooed them out the door like one of her father's working dogs patiently running livestock, and as the dogs did, occasionally snapped at them to speed them along.

Jade, resigned to not seeing the coffeepot, stepped onto the veranda. Their host led them at a brisk pace to the stables and to his pride and joy, a magnificent bay stallion.

'This,' he said proudly, 'is Bakari.'

Jade reached out and stroked the soft, sensitive nose. 'He's beautiful.'

'His name means noble promise in Swahili, and he has kept that promise. Sired four champions already.' Colridge led them two by two down the rows of the stable and outside to a paddock that housed two young zebra. 'Raising these from foals,' he explained. 'Going to train them to pull a carriage. Can't break the grown ones. Too temperamental.'

Jade took another stab at changing the subject. 'Lord Colridge, you've done very well, but my editors are interested in the early beginnings of the colony as well as its present state. Can you tell me about any of the other people who began settling here along with you and some of the things they tried? Perhaps some who didn't make it or died trying?'

He fluttered his mustache. 'Don't like to dwell on failures, young lady. Not good for the colony, you know.'

'I agree,' she countered, 'but understanding the hardships at the start certainly does enhance the present success of yourself and others like you.'

'Hmm,' he mumbled and stroked his white mustache.

Jade sensed his rising impatience and thought of a strategy to occupy his mind. 'May I take some likenesses while we talk? Perhaps your photograph with Bakari?' Maybe posing him with his prize horse would relax him enough to speak freely.

Colridge nodded, and Jade hurried back to the Thompsons' car to retrieve her handheld 4 × 5 Graflex and a box of film sheets. His Lordship consented to a photograph of himself, then insisted on calling out Pili to handle the horses while he directed the remaining shots. Jade went along with him and only pretended to take most of the remaining pictures. She didn't have the film or developer to spare. She did take one of the Somali steward with a mare. Pili made a perfect model, quiet and serene, and she wished she had more plates to devote to his striking, youthful features with his bronzed skin and soft hazel eyes. The Somali were, indeed, a handsome people. She remembered Corporal Gideon and wondered if he had survived the war.

Colridge led the trio around his grounds and showed them his sawmill powered by an old steam locomotive, the various outbuildings, and the house garden fenced against hungry wildlife. An old hound with long floppy ears and sagging jowls joined them, and Jade stroked his head.

While they walked, the Thompsons exclaimed and admired, His Lordship puffed out with pride, and Jade tried to steer the conversation when it began to wander too far away from the struggles of early colonists and too much into the merits of various root crops. It wasn't easy. Once the man got going, angels announcing the second coming couldn't get a word in edgewise.

'I would say most failures fall into two categories,' Colridge concluded. 'Bad planning and lack of perseverance. Some of those chaps just wouldn't stick it.' He looked over at Neville for confirmation. 'Take you, for example, Thompson.'

Neville stood ramrod straight at attention. 'Sir?'

'It hasn't been all easy going for you and your wife, has it? No, I didn't think so,' he said without waiting for an answer. 'But you stuck it out. And you've been here seven years.'

'Eight, sir.'

'Eight years, that's what I said. Can't expect the crops to come in right away. Coffee trees take two years to produce at least.'

'Three at the earliest, sir.'

'Three years, just as I said. Then later you might expect five pounds per tree.'

'Three pounds per tree, sir.'

'Yes, of course. As I was saying, Miss del Cameron, a planter such as Thompson here has to stick it out, isn't that right, Thompson?'

Neville answered like any acolyte around his idol. 'I couldn't agree with you more, Lord Colridge.'

'What sort of endeavors made poor choices then?' asked Jade.

'Geraniums! Some fool decided geraniums would be an instant cash crop, put thousands of acres into geranium cuttings before some blasted disease wiped them out.' He waggled a finger at her. 'That, my dear young lady, is poor planning. Putting all your eggs in one basket, as they say. That young Forster is another example.'

'Roger?' asked Madeline. 'Didn't he have an ostrich farm?'

'Exactly. Put everything into raising those vicious brutes for their feather plumes for ladies' hats,' exclaimed Lord Colridge with a contemptuous snort. 'Failed to take into consideration the fickleness of women and their fool fashions. Motorcars are putting an end to his dreams of fortune.'

'Motorcars?' echoed Jade. She jotted snippets of the conversation into her notebook.

'The feathers are badly beaten up in the wind,' explained Madeline. 'Certainly not practical for a driving hat.'

'Rog is a resilient sort of chap, though,' stated Neville. 'Born in Africa. Doing more safari work nowadays, I believe. And he has a few cattle.'

His Lordship snorted again, and from behind him, Bakari gave an answering snort from his stall. 'Fool's gotten himself badly into debt. Overborrowed. Always scampering about, too. He needs to stay put and make that cattle ranch work, not go running off to Mombasa at every whim.' Colridge waved a walking stick in the air to emphasize his point. 'Then there's malaria.

Mosquito netting, quinine, good air,' rumbled Lord Colridge. 'Poor planning again.'

Jade knew that Gil Worthy left Africa the first time sick with malaria and once again tried to direct the topic to him. 'Your Lordship,' she began, 'did you know — ' She got no farther. A native runner raced towards them, panting from exertion.

'Bwana Pua Nywele,' the man said, addressing Lord Colridge rapidly in Swahili, and Jade struggled to catch some of the conversation. She did manage to make out the words *toto* or child, and *fisi* or hyena. She also thought she heard the word *laibon*. She wondered if this man spoke of the same *laibon* that Jelani had mentioned yesterday. She looked to Madeline and Neville for help, but they were too intent on the story to observe her quizzical expression. Finally, Colridge held up his hand for the native to stop and briefly answered him. The man seemed satisfied and ran back in the direction from which he'd come.

'What happened?' asked Jade. 'Is there trouble?'

'Bloody damned nuisance,' exclaimed Colridge. 'Oh, not you, Miss del Cameron. This business. Yes, seems a hyena has killed an elder's son, a small boy. The creatures have been a regular pestilence recently.'

'What was that bit about the witch?' asked Neville before Jade had a chance to ask.

'Superstitious bunk,' said Colridge. 'Can't have a normal hyena attack. Must involve witches somehow.'

75

'But why would a hyena attack a village? Aren't they primarily scavengers?' asked Jade.

'That's not entirely true,' replied Neville. 'Most any predator will take ready meat if it's there for them. Lions, too. It is true the hyenas do a nasty bit of undertaking for us, though.'

'It's the Kikuyu's fault,' exclaimed Colridge. 'They don't bury their dead.'

'Well, sir, in defense of the Kikuyu, it wouldn't make much difference if they did,' said Neville. 'Unless they bury someone very deeply, as we do, the hyena will dig it up. And we've certainly done our own bit to feed the brutes around Nairobi.'

'How is that?' asked Jade.

'The slaughterhouse did a brisk business feeding the troops during the Great War,' explained Neville, 'and simply discarded the refuse of the cattle outside the town. Then there were all those influenza victims, including thousands of natives, all of which fed a growing population of hyenas. The troops and influenza are gone now, and the hyenas were left starving. I've seen them chewing on cooking pots.'

'Quite right, Thompson. Quite right,' agreed Colridge. 'Dreadful situation. We've created a pestilence. That's why I'll go shoot this hyena for the Kikuyu. But we must convince them that there is no witchcraft involved.'

'I still don't understand about the witch though,' said Jade. Madeline looked equally perplexed, so Lord Colridge obliged them with the barest of explanations.

'Some of the natives believe that a witch

controls the hyena or some other creature for revenge killings. Still others believe the animal is the witch's shadow soul roaming abroad. If he's very strong, he can change himself into a hyena or other night creature. Either way, they're afraid to kill the animal themselves for fear of angering the witch further.'

'Like the man-eating lions at Tsavo,' added Madeline. 'I remember reading that a pair of lions attacked the railroad crews during the construction of the Tsavo bridge. All the natives thought they were spirits until the engineer, Colonel Patterson, killed them.'

'Yes,' agreed Colridge. 'Said they were ghosts of chieftains or some such nonsense.'

'Where is this hyena problem, Lord Colridge?' asked Neville.

'Near the southeastern edge of my land. Got so bad the natives left for a while.' The older man sized Neville up. 'Care to join me, Thompson? I'll have Pili organize the tents and equipment. We'll leave from here tomorrow at dawn.'

'I'd be honored, sir,' replied Neville. He looked like a little boy being asked to accompany his father on a first hunting trip.

'I'd like to see this myself,' said Jade. 'Be a good addition to the story I'm working on.'

Miles Colridge sputtered several times. Snippets of sentences such as 'no place,' 'young woman,' and 'frightening,' found their way out from under his bristly white mustache, and Jade waited patiently before she replied.

'You forget, sir, I was raised out west. I'm accustomed to hunting.'

'We're not going after rabbits, Miss del Cameron,' he exclaimed with a snort.

'When I was sixteen, a mountain lion took some of our stock. We lost several lambs.'

'And I suppose your father took you along on the hunt, did he?'

Jade looked directly at the aristocrat until he felt the weight of those emerald eyes boring into him. She kept the tone of her voice very factual, careful to omit any trace of bragging. 'No, sir. My father was gone at the time. I took out that cat myself.'

7

'Many Nairobi residents hire the neighboring
Kikuyu on their farms or in their establishments.
But every Kikuyu lad works with a thought of
the day when he will be a man and own his own
shamba, or garden, and his own herd of goats.'
— The Traveler

They came back. The fools came back to their
old village and brought their stinking beasts with
them. Did they think he would not know? That
he would not smell their stench? True, they kept
their goat herds away from his cattle and his
streams, but it was only a matter of time before
they would be back like an infestation of ants.

He was too busy himself to bother with them;
his teacher too proud to attend to them. 'They
are bugs,' his mentor said. 'Why should I risk
myself for bugs?' So he picked one of his own
beasts, a young male hyena, to remind these
fools that he would not tolerate them. He took a
stone knife and shaved his mark into its fur.
Then he chose a bone bead, carved from a
human finger, and tied it into the animal's short
neck ruff. The bone would guide the killer to its
chosen prey.

He turned the animal, and squatting in front
of it, stared into its face. They locked eyes for
several minutes as the man murmured and
chanted before it. At first, the beast shifted and

tried to scratch his neck. Its hind foot paused halfway there and hung in the air. Then it slowly dropped back down as the animal tensed and stood catatonic. The man's will passed from gaze to gaze and into the animal's brain. The beast quivered and whimpered. Then, with one rapid movement, the man stood and released the animal. The hyena trotted away towards the village, and the man knew his messenger would not return hungry.

★   ★   ★

Jade's stomach rumbled as she squatted on Colridge's veranda. An answering rumble rolled from deep in the house's interior as the brusque voice of Lord Miles Colridge issued orders. Jade held her suede wide-brimmed hat in her hands and fiddled with the frayed brim. Just enough moonlight shone in the yard to see without tripping, but very little penetrated under the veranda's roof. Neville's and Madeline's forms next to her were barely discernible in the dark.

'That Kikuyu man,' Jade began in a hushed voice. 'He addressed our host as Bwana Pua Nywele, didn't he? What does that mean?'

Madeline snickered, and Neville answered in a whisper. 'That is the Kikuyu's name for him. It literally translates as Nose Hair in Swahili. His mustache is rather famous.'

'Does everyone out here get a name?'

'Most generally, yes,' Madeline said. 'At least the men do.'

'What is yours, Neville?' Jade asked. 'If I may inquire.'

Madeline answered before Neville had a chance. 'He is called Bwana Mbuni. Mbuni means ostrich. You have to picture the setting. We'd just arrived in Nairobi and had never seen our land before. The oxcart ride was hot and dusty, but Neville found an ostrich plume along the track and stuck it in his hat like a musketeer. When we finally arrived at our land, he leaped off the cart, whipped off his hat, and made a rather dashing bow to me. Trying to act the part of a courtier,' she added with a giggle. 'Naturally, I was very impressed. Of course, some of the locals saw him and the name stuck.'

Jade smiled. 'I can think of several worse scenarios in which to be caught and named,' she said. She wondered if Gil Worthy had managed to acquire a name in his four years here.

Her hand went to the small lump under her shirt where David's ring hung from a leather cord. She had donned it early that morning in her hotel room along with her corps trousers, boots, and a new bush shirt purchased in town. The ring became a tangible reminder of what her mind still struggled to accept: the proof that David once existed and the hard, cold actuality of his death. Now, as she sat in the dark quiet of the African night and waited for dawn, both the war and David seemed unreal. Someone once told her that denial was an initial reaction after a loss. She couldn't deny the ring around her neck or the second ring securely stored in one of her bags.

Lord Colridge's voice boomed again from within. 'Perhaps we should lend a hand?' suggested Madeline.

'Absolutely not!' exclaimed Neville. 'Lord Colridge expressly ordered us to wait here.' His finger jabbed at the veranda steps. Neville got up and paced back and forth several steps before he leaned against the railing, arms folded across his chest. 'The last thing we want to do is antagonize him. His favor in the colony could be very helpful to us. He knows people, Madeline. Important people.' He sliced the air for emphasis. 'People who might pay more for coffee, or loan us money in a bad year.'

'You're right, of course, Neville,' replied Madeline. 'Only I do feel like so much excess baggage waiting to be loaded up.' She sighed. 'I do wish he would have at least let us bring our own horses.'

Jade thought of young Jelani at the Norfolk. The boy hadn't been the least bit happy about being told to stay behind. She wondered if it was his village that was being harassed. Perhaps he knew the child who had been killed.

'I suspect Lord Colridge has horses in excess,' Jade mused aloud. 'Possibly a matter of pride to be able to outfit us all.' She caressed the walnut stock of her Winchester.

A great deal of noise from the stables interrupted their conversation, and Pili approached leading two chestnut-colored mares saddled for riding. 'Horses for the memsahibs,' he said softly as though not to disturb the sun during its rest. A boy walked beside him carrying a lantern. In its

82

glow, they glimpsed two sturdy, dependable animals bred for strength and hardiness from northern Abyssinian stock.

'Mount up!' bellowed Lord Colridge. He led his own mount, a white Abyssinian stallion. Behind him walked another lad leading a third mare, black with a left white stocking. 'There's your horse, Thompson. Step lively. Dawn's breaking. Time to move out.' As if it waited for his direct order, the sun pierced the dark gray horizon. Light spilled across the ground as though thrown from a bucket and bathed the landscape in golden rays.

'When Lord Colridge commands, everything obeys,' whispered Jade behind her hand to Madeline. She slid her Winchester into a saddle holster and her camera and film sheets into the saddlebags. Six native Africans came around the side of the house carrying large bundles on their heads. Colridge barked a few curt orders, and the men departed in a brisk trot.

'They'll head towards the village and set up a camp for us,' Colridge explained. 'Only a morning's walk for them. We'll take a more roundabout way. I want to show you my land.'

Pili reappeared with a small basket containing four cloth bags, and Jade detected the spicy scent of cinnamon. Her stomach growled again in response to the fragrant aroma.

'Almost forgot breakfast,' groused Colridge. 'Scones, if I'm not mistaken. Take a bag then. No time to dawdle with fancies.' He took a sack for himself and issued a few orders to Pili concerning the horses. Pili inclined his head slightly and disappeared into the house.

'He's not coming with us?' asked Jade as she mounted her horse.

'Whatever for?' answered Colridge in genuine surprise at the idea.

'I suppose I thought he was your manservant and perhaps acted as your gun bearer or oversaw the camp.' Jade found the silent young man interesting and had hoped to talk with him.

Lord Colridge made a deprecating noise, and his white mustache fluttered in the outburst. 'Pish tosh!' he exclaimed. 'For a *safari*, yes. But for this little excursion?' He snorted. 'Should take care of this business tonight and be home tomorrow early.' He urged his horse forward and ended the discussion.

Neville fell in immediately beside Lord Colridge, and Madeline aligned herself with Jade. For some time, they rode past the fields and native workers and munched on the delicious scones while Colridge pointed out various features of his farm. Later, after leaving the cultivated areas behind, Jade dropped back a few more paces from the men. She wanted to ask Colridge about Gil Worthy, but Neville monopolized the conversation with questions. Madeline fell back with her.

'Is this what you expected?' asked Madeline.

Jade looked at Madeline and arched one brow in confusion. 'I'm not sure what you mean. The expedition?'

Madeline made a quarter sweep of the landscape with her right hand. 'This,' she said.

'Nairobi, the protectorate, Africa. Is it what you expected?'

Jade rode along silently and breathed in the clean, heady scent of wild grasses and the horse under her. Her perceptive eyes drank in the expansive horizon as they left the farm's buildings and fields behind them. The Athi Plains spread out in the distant foreground as a sea of tall brown grass punctuated by an occasional umbrella-shaped acacia tree. Dark spots shifted position, and Jade knew they would eventually resolve themselves into entire herds of wildebeest, zebra, or perhaps giraffe. To her left, the shadowy summit of Mount Kenya loomed blue-gray like a colossal whale breaching the sea of blue around it, the ever present clouds like foaming waves. Like the sea, Africa and the sky continued to roll and swell on beyond her vision. Perhaps if she listened carefully, she would hear the earth's heartbeat, which she knew would match her own.

She nodded. 'Yes. I expected grandeur and beauty, and there's certainly an abundance of both.'

'I'm coming to love it, too,' admitted Madeline. 'It took some getting used to, though.'

Jade nodded and waited for more of Madeline's story.

'I grew up very close to London. There were always carriages on the roads going to and from the towns. If you traveled longer than a day, you ran out of country and fell into another village. Here, you never run out of country, and there aren't all that many roads, much less towns.' She sighed. 'It's a lonely place.'

'The Easterners back in the States have that same problem when they travel west of the Mississippi,' said Jade. 'The land just keeps unrolling itself, and the sky goes with it. You aim for a mountain range' — she nodded her head towards Mount Kenya — 'and it never gets any closer no matter how long you ride. One day, you actually reach the mountain and stand on its summit, thinking you finally made it to the end. Then you look down on the other side, and the land's still rolling on.' She smiled at Madeline. 'What you have to understand is that we outlanders feel boxed in if we aren't surrounded by land and sky. This doesn't feel any different from home.'

Madeline nodded. 'Neville sent me home for nearly three years towards the middle of the war. I stayed in London with my sister. Do you know, I actually missed this openness then? All my neighbors seemed too close. Have you any idea what I missed the most?'

Jade shook her head.

'I missed the sounds,' she said softly. 'All of them. You can hear them out here, you know. You can't hear sounds in London, only noise. Why do people like all that noise?'

Jade thought about it for a moment. 'Have you ever noticed that little children are afraid of a strange or loud noise? But you rarely hear of a child being afraid of the quiet. That's a grown-up fear. Noise keeps us from feeling alone with our thoughts. Maybe we're actually just afraid of ourselves, so we surround ourselves with noise to

86

drown out our thoughts.'

'We whistle in the dark, so to speak?' suggested Madeline. 'That's an interesting idea.' She glanced sideways at Jade. 'Somehow, I don't imagine you're afraid of very much.' When Jade arched her brows in surprise, Madeline quickly apologized. 'I don't mean to sound impertinent. You have to forgive me. Living out here has apparently made me tactless. What I mean is, I saw how you reacted to Harry's shooting the other evening. Everyone else held back, but you . . . well, you rushed in there and took the gun right out of his hand. Wherever did you learn to do that?'

Jade shrugged. 'A person learns a lot of things growing up near Cimarron, New Mexico.'

'I don't believe anyone can teach you to respond the way you did. That's instinctive. You must not be afraid of anything.'

Only terrified of failing David.

Jade noticed the graceful arch of the Athi River in the valley before them and the play of long black shadows stretching out beneath the spindly thorn trees across the undulating brown and tawny-colored hills. Tributary channels cut deeply into the red soil and converged like bloody claw marks into the Athi. Beyond the river, the land rose into a gracefully rounded hill topped with a thick hardwood forest. The shadows shrank from view even as she watched. 'You're wrong. I'm *afraid* I'll miss photographing this gorgeous play of light and shadow,' she said.

She urged her horse into a canter and caught up with Lord Colridge, who was busily lecturing

87

Neville on the merits of the chestnut-vented sandgrouse for sport. Neville, for his part, acted as though he'd never before heard of the bird and hung on every word.

'Lord Colridge,' Jade called as she rode up to him. 'Pardon me, but I'd like to stop and photograph that view.' Seeing the old aristocrat's irritation, she added, 'I promise you, sir, it will only be the matter of a moment. My camera has a fast lens. I don't need a long exposure.'

'Very well, Miss del Cameron. I suppose you must.' He shifted in his saddle. 'Er, I'll just wander over to those trees to the left and, er, scout around a bit.' He turned abruptly to Mr Thompson before leaving. 'I depend on you, Thompson, to keep an eye out. Never know what comes out of those ravines there: buffalo, lion.'

Neville gripped his rifle firmly and nodded. Jade, in the meantime, dismounted and took her Graflex out of the saddlebag. She inserted a film sheet, pulled up the collapsible viewing hood, took a wider stance for stability, and shot. She inserted another sheet and took a second shot a little to the west of the first, making certain to overlap a portion of the two pictures. With careful cropping, she'd have a splendid panoramic view. Next she pulled a small leather-bound notebook and a pencil from the camera bag and jotted down a few notes as Colridge returned.

'You're finished?' he stated in a tone that expected an affirmative answer.

'Yes, sir. May I ask, what is that hill across the river?'

'That's what the Kikuyu call Kea-Njahe. It means the Mountain of the Big Rain. They believe it's one of the homes of their supreme being, Ngai.'

Jade jotted the name into her notebook. 'It's beautiful,' she said. 'Do Kikuyu live there?'

'Only on this near side of it, though they graze goats farther up the slope. Harry Hascombe's ranch abuts their land, and Roger Forster has his ranch on the southernmost base.'

'So these Kikuyu that you're helping, they live on your land?'

'No. Mostly on Forster's and Hascombe's, but so many of those villagers have worked for me that they come to me to settle problems. I've often wondered why they don't bother Forster or Hascombe instead, but Hascombe employs more Maasai than Kikuyu. Forster's probably off on safari again.'

Jade remounted and fell in line behind Lord Colridge and Madeline. Neville had been directed to bring up the rear and keep a watch out for any danger from the brush. Jade checked her own rifle to be certain of its ready availability. Experience had taught her never to count on someone else, but only a bushbuck, startled by their approach, leaped from one of the brushier ravines. His coat flashed rusty brown in the sunlight, but whether that was his natural coloring or if the reddish dust from a wallow aided in the tint, Jade couldn't tell. It was a male, and Jade admired his long, nearly straight horns with their one tight spiraling twist. The animal reminded her of the pronghorn in size and markings.

They descended to the Athi River and let their horses pick their footing through the slope's tall grass. The long rains had ended two weeks ago with the close of May, but even when the tributaries turned to dry gulches, the Athi itself maintained a steady if somewhat lower flow. Jade's sensitive hearing detected a persistent churning rumble characteristic of rapids or falls.

'We'll cross below the falls,' Colridge shouted back, verifying her guess. 'Safer there. Crocs don't care for a fast current, and it's too shallow for hippos. Miss del Cameron will probably insist on taking a photograph, so, Thompson, you be at the ready for trouble behind her.'

The low grumble grew more distinct but the high wall of a volcanic dike on the right hid the source from view. Jade scanned the top of the rocky wall for overhead wildlife and, seeing none, followed Colridge and Madeline along the trail at its base. Small mica sheets and quartz crystals flashed out of rich black feldspar.

A full and spectacular view of the waterfall cascading over the volcanic rocks greeted her when she rounded the corner of the outcrop. The falls initially dropped from a height of at least ten feet before tumbling the last three over two shorter stair steps. Fine white spray ricocheted off the dark boulders and splattered the surroundings with refreshing dampness. Lush, flowering shrubs and vines clung to seemingly impossible places on the rock, their roots grasping for a purchase in the precious, wet environment, while feathery papyrus heads undulated gracefully along the shoreline. A kingfisher, resplendent with a large turquoise-colored crest, dived from its perch into the basin at the foot of the falls. He emerged a moment later with a fish every bit as long as himself in his massive red beak. *It's Eden*, thought Jade.

She stopped her horse in midstream and unbuckled the saddlebag. Her horse twitched a hind leg and swatted a fly with its tail, and Jade decided not to chance the exposure to her mount's steadiness. She slid off the saddle and landed with both boots in a foot of churning, frothing water. Two boulders stabilized her as she took a photograph. She wanted to linger, but knowing that Lord Colridge's patience wouldn't last, she jotted a few notes in her book and packed up her gear. Jade led the horse out of the river shallows and remounted on the bank.

'Thank you, Lord Colridge,' she said. 'I appreciate your giving me this time when I know you must be anxious to press on.'

Colridge waved a hand in a gesture of benevolent dismissal while Neville Thompson crossed the river and joined them. 'We are nearly at the village. I'll talk to their headman and scout around for spoor, but to be frank with you, we cannot do much of anything until nightfall.'

'Why not?' she asked.

'I don't intend to trudge around all afternoon and evening looking for a blasted hyena. Don't want to miss tea. If this one is as bold as the runner told me, he'll show up again tonight. Especially,' he added, 'if I leave him some bait.' He turned his horse away from the river. 'Come along. No time to dawdle.'

Jade smiled. One moment, the old man allowed a break for photographs because there was no need to rush. The next instant the flutter of his bushy white mustache punctuated an imperial edict to quit wasting time. The Kikuyu had named him well.

The quartet rode on to the northern base of Kea-Njahe and found a narrow path that wended tortuously through the brush, as meandering as an old stream doubling back.

'The Kikuyu put a good value on their safety,' explained Madeline. 'I suspect this sort of path is easier to defend physically as well as with magic charms.'

The path eventually broke into the village, a collection of round thatched huts that sat like pointed beehives around a clearing. Small *shambas*, or farm plots, of banana trees and sweet potatoes clustered around the periphery, and thorny *bomas* made safe enclosures for goats. An elderly man dressed in monkey skins and a multitude of copper ornaments came forward to receive them. He, like the other elders, lacked the braided pigtails of the young warriors, and a snuff horn hung around his neck as a badge of service.

'*Jambo*,' said the old man, using the Swahili word for hello.

'*Jambo. Na furie sana ku wanana na wewe* — I am happy to see you again,' replied Lord

Colridge. The elderly man returned the compliment with a small, stately bow and invited them to sit outside his hut to speak. Jade caught snatches of the conversation, enough to make her frustrated, Madeline sat next to her and whispered a condensed translation along with a brief history of tribal politics, which Jade recorded in her leather notebook.

'The Kikuyu have elders, but the government finds it easier to deal with one headman, so they appoint a chief,' Madeline explained. 'Colridge asked him how many people the hyena has killed. The chief says only one since their return, his youngest son, but many goats have been taken since the long rains stopped. He says this hyena is strong. It breaks into the *boma*.'

'Why did Colridge say *simba*? Doesn't that mean lion?' asked Jade.

'He wants to be certain it's not a lion doing this. The chief says the tracks are not lion. They are hyena. He says it's a witch's hyena with his spirit soul guiding it. He claims someone is trying to make them move their village again.'

'Does he say who?'

Madeline listened for a while longer and shook her head. 'No, and Lord Colridge isn't pressing for that information, either. He's asking for practical facts: time of night, location, that sort of thing.'

Jade photographed the conference between Lord Colridge, the chief, and the other elders. Neville sat next to Colridge like a young disciple. Jade mentioned as much to Madeline.

'Yes,' Mrs Thompson agreed, 'Neville is

93

fascinated by any of the pre-railroaders, especially Lord Colridge. Just being a part of this adventure may be Neville's finest hour.'

The men rose and walked to one of the *bomas*. Jade and Madeline followed. The chief pointed out the most recently repaired section of the thorny fence and a clear paw print. Jade was trying to decide if the print would show up distinctly enough on film when she recognized a young voice calling from behind her. She turned to see Jelani run into the village.

'Memsabu Jade,' he called.

'Jelani, what are you doing here?' she demanded.

'This is my village, memsabu,' he said, panting. 'I have come to help.' He then pointed to Jade and proceeded to relate with great feeling something in the Kikuyu tongue to the chief and other village elders. At one point he struck his left wrist with his right hand in an elaborate pantomime. The chief nodded and said a few words in Swahili to Lord Colridge. Jade saw Colridge's eyes widen and heard Madeline stifle an outburst. Jade demanded a translation.

'I didn't catch everything, mind you,' said Madeline, 'although that swiping hand gesture spoke volumes. Something about a mongoose striking a snake. I think he told the chief about your rather dramatic encounter with Harry the other night. Congratulations, my dear. You might be on your way to earning a name for yourself.'

The Kikuyu chief looked at Jade for the first time and spoke to her in Swahili. 'Will you help kill the witch's hyena?'

Jade understood more this time, thanks to Madeline's previous translations and to her own ability to pick up languages quickly. She asked Jelani to help her answer. 'I am happy to help, but I am certain that Bwana Pua Nywele can handle this without me or my rifle.'

The elder nodded and said something that made Colridge puff his bushy mustache in a derisive snort. Jade looked to Jelani.

'The chief says it is well you do not help because you might not be powerful enough or fast enough to escape the witch's anger when you kill his hyena. Then he will send revenge against you. Bwana Pua Nywele is strong with the English king, so the magic will not hurt him.'

'Please ask your chief who is this *laibon* that bothers his people,' Jade said.

Jelani posed the question, but the old man shook his head adamantly. 'He will not tell me, memsabu. Already the *laibon* has taken his youngest son.'

Colridge clasped her arm and pulled her aside. 'Rightly he doesn't know because there's no witch, Miss del Cameron,' he exclaimed. 'Don't support their superstitions with foolish bunk!'

'I beg your pardon,' she replied flatly. 'Only doing a journalist's job.'

'I daresay Lord Colridge is correct,' echoed Neville. 'Best leave the business to him.'

'Why, Mr Thompson,' whispered Jade, 'I do believe your nose is getting a bit brown.'

Neville stared down at his nose cross-eyed before he took out a linen handkerchief and swiped at it. 'Probably just the sun,' he said. Jade covered her smile with her hand.

Colridge conferred with the chief again. Eventually he put several coins in the Kikuyu's hand, and the old chief turned and gave some orders to one of his warriors. The young man trotted to the *boma* and returned dragging a goat behind him.

'Our bait,' explained Lord Colridge. 'We'll tie it up near the *boma* where the other goats were taken. I've ordered the construction of an elevated blind for tonight and paid the chief for the goat as compensation in case the hyena kills it before I bag the blighter.'

Jade saw that the old nanny was long past her prime and near to drying up for good. Hardly a loss if she was killed, and not worth near the amount that Colridge paid for her. Like most leaders, the old Kikuyu man knew how to turn a bad situation into a potential gain.

'Come along then,' ordered Colridge. 'No use waiting around here for the next couple of hours. I want my tea.' He started to walk past Jade and paused to look her in the eyes. 'I daresay you would like coffee.' Jade grinned.

The four of them had begun riding out of the village when Jade noticed Jelani following. She stopped and waited for him to catch up. 'Jelani, what are you doing here? You'll be in trouble.'

'I told them I must take care of you, memsabu. I tell them you asked for me. I came here after you left for Bwana Pua Nywele's house.'

'Jelani, you could have been hurt. I told you to stay, and you know it.'

'Please, memsabu. A warrior cannot hold back because of fear. This is my village. I have to help you fight the *laibon*. Do not send me back.'

Jade didn't know if he meant to the village or the hotel, but not being the best at following orders herself, she understood the boy's sentiment. She certainly couldn't fault his courage. 'Well, you're not a warrior yet, and you've run far enough. Give me your hand and jump up.'

Jade scooted up in the saddle, and Jelani settled himself behind her. The others had stopped to see what kept her, and Jade detected an expression of surprise mingled with impatience on Lord Colridge's face. Madeline looked amused, and Neville appeared about to panic lest they offend his newly adopted patron. Jade ignored them all.

'Tell me a story, Jelani,' she said. 'Tell me about the hyena we will hunt tonight.'

'That is a good story, memsabu,' said Jelani, and he proceeded to relate it in the pattern of all good storytellers, with a lilting, musical quality in his voice. 'The first hyena saw some ravens with something white and shining in their beaks. She thought it was fat to eat and wanted some. She asked the ravens, 'Where did you get that fat to eat? I want some for myself.' The ravens looked at each other and answered, 'On the other side of the sun. Come, take hold of us. We will take you there.' So the greedy hyena, she took hold of the ravens and they flew up and up and up. Soon the earth disappeared below. The ravens asked the hyena, 'Can you see the land?'

'No,' said the hyena, so the ravens shook themselves and shook loose the hyena. The hyena fell a long way to the earth and landed on the hard ground, for it was the dry season. She broke both her hind legs. That is why all the hyenas walk like they have broken legs.'

'That is a *very* good story, Jelani. Greed often brings ruin. Now tell me this. Do witches always use hyenas for their evil work?'

'Not always, memsabu. The witch can send his soul spirit into many animals. Night animals are best. You can tell the witch animal because it carries the mark of the witch on it. If the *laibon* is strong enough, he can enter the body himself. I have even heard where a powerful witch changed his own body into an animal.'

The universal werewolf stories, thought Jade. 'So do *you* know who this witch is?' She felt Jelani shrug behind her. 'Well then, do you know why this witch is angry with your village?'

'No, memsabu. Only that someone wants to hurt us. Perhaps they have hired the witch to make us leave in fear. He made us leave once, but we came back. We had nowhere to go.'

'Hired the witch,' echoed Jade in surprise. 'I thought the witch himself was the one angry with your people.'

'Not always, memsabu. All I know is, someone is angry with the chief. They fight over the village. We have a saying: When two elephants fight, it is the grass that suffers.'

Jade pondered the truth of that African

aphorism as they rode into the camp. She also considered the idea of a man cruel enough to send a trained hyena to kill for him. Only a coward would send an animal to kill a child, and if she could find a way to thwart him, she would.

8

'The colors of the African uplands are cool. Round, smoky blue hills dot the landscape like the bloom on ripe grapes and cast deep violet shadows over the blue-green grass. They blend with a marbling of white clouds by day and fall under a sparkling blanket at night. Yet beneath this soothing veneer is an underlayer of hot red blood.'
— The Traveler

Three canvas tents complete with cots, mats, and canopies ringed a small campfire in military precision. To one side of the fire, the Thompsons, Lord Colridge, and Jade sat and sipped drinks. Behind them stood a small camp table decked out with linen napkins and a tablecloth. The three colonists drank wine, Lord Colridge because he preferred it, the Thompsons because Colridge drank it. Jade chose coffee to top off a splendid dinner of chicken cooked in burgundy with assorted vegetables and freshly baked bread.

Jade had grown up with campfire cooking and considered herself very capable of making delicious meals in Dutch ovens over hot coals, but Colridge's cook used a collection of empty five-gallon paraffin tins, or *debes*. If the cook's skill impressed Jade, the lavishness of the table setting astounded her. They ate dinner from

100

Wedgwood china, and her three companions drank from crystal goblets. Even her coffee, brewed in an iron pot, was poured from a silver carafe.

'Can't let civilized behavior slide, Miss del Cameron,' Colridge said. 'It's inexcusable out here.'

'Yes, then we risk becoming savages ourselves, don't we,' exclaimed a man's baritone voice from behind Lord Colridge.

Everyone turned towards the speaker, Jade suddenly, the others in a more relaxed manner, as though they had expected the intrusion.

'Harry,' said Colridge, rising out of his camp chair. 'I wasn't certain if you were around or not. Good of you to drop by.' He signaled one of his servants. 'Another chair.'

Harry Hascombe approached the table with the smooth walk and proud bearing of a well-fed lion who was king of his realm and knew it. He wore the same worn bush clothing from the other day and carried his Mauser rifle slung across his back. Brown sideburns tinged with gray and a wrinkled brow peeked out from under his felt hat. Jade guessed his age to be past forty.

She studied him with interest and observed a tremendous amount of power in his broad chest and well-muscled arms. His rectangular face bore a strong jawline highlighted by a day's growth of whiskers. Harry returned the look and scrutinized Jade almost to the point of rudeness. Jade, who, much to her mother's annoyance, could stare down a bear, never shrank from anyone's gaze and locked her grass green eyes to his dark brown ones. Harry flinched first.

'Miss,' he said with a slight bow and a touch to his hat brim. 'I didn't expect to see you, or you either, for that matter, Thompson. Good evening to you, Mrs Thompson,' he added with another bow. 'If I'd known the ladies were here, I'd have come sooner.'

'Miss del Cameron, may I present Harry Hascombe,' said Lord Colridge. 'Harry, this is Miss Jade del Cameron. A friend of Lord Dunbury. Out here to do a story for a magazine.'

'We've met,' said Harry with a grin. He took a seat next to Jade and leaned back after placing his rifle beside him. 'I should apologize for my outrageous behavior the other night.'

'I heard about it, Harry,' said Colridge. 'From a Kikuyu lad, of all sources. Really, you should be ashamed of yourself.'

Harry slapped his thigh, tossed back his head, and laughed. 'Now, Miles, it's not like you haven't pulled a few stunts yourself. I recall in particular one night at the Muthaiga — '

'Never mind the Muthaiga,' interrupted Lord Colridge. 'I daresay Miss del Cameron doesn't want to hear a bunch of wild nonsense.'

Actually, Jade thought, *I'd love to hear some of these stories*. She decided to wait and press Madeline for details later rather than risk antagonizing her current host. Instead, she offered a comment on a subject guaranteed to touch the vanity of any outdoorsman: his shooting ability.

'I was told that you are one of the best shots in the colony, Mr Hascombe. I'd like to hear about

102

some of your less controversial adventures sometime.'

Harry grinned, showing a multitude of white teeth, and leaned forward. 'I would be delighted, Miss del Cameron, at any time.'

'But not now, Hascombe,' groused Colridge. 'We have business to attend to soon enough. Your stories will have to wait.'

Harry folded his arms across his chest. 'What are you after in this territory, Miles? Off your own turf, aren't you?'

'One of those damnable hyenas is plaguing the Kikuyu,' replied Colridge. 'Takes their goats and some of them as well. Most recently, a child.' Colridge produced a pipe and tamped in a bit of tobacco from a pouch in his shirt pocket. 'Of course, they claim witchcraft.'

'When don't they?' Harry replied. 'But then, Miles, you and I have both been around the bush long enough to have seen and heard some pretty strange things.'

'Pig's wallow, Harry!' Colridge lit his pipe and puffed on it ferociously before replying further. 'Since when did you start paying any attention to native mumbo jumbo?'

Harry Hascombe shrugged his broad shoulders. 'More things in heaven and earth, Miles. I've lived around Maasai long enough to know that. Anyway, I and my gun are at your disposal.'

Colridge waved his pipe magnanimously. 'Your expertise is always welcome, Harry.'

'How did you know we were here, Mr Hascombe?' asked Madeline.

'Natives talk, Mrs Thompson. Some of my

103

cattle herders saw you.' He turned back to Jade. 'So you're a reporter, Miss del Cameron? Enjoying your visit to East Africa?'

'Yes, I am. It's beautiful land.'

'That it is,' he said and leaned forward for a better look at her face. 'And I know beauty when I see it,' he added with more of an attempt at gallantry and less brashness than at their previous meeting. To her surprise, Jade discovered she found him intriguing and wanted to know more about him, but Madeline intervened before she could ask him any questions.

'Jade drove an ambulance in France and earned a medal. She's quite an adventuress.'

'Really?' Harry said with interest. 'I'd like to hear about it.'

Jade's smile vanished. 'There's very little to tell. Fill an ambulance with wounded, drive to a hospital, return for more, scrub out the vomit and gore when you're done. I'm sure you had your share of it here as well.'

'There were certainly a good many hospitals set up in and around Nairobi,' agreed Madeline. 'I worked in one at the beginning before Neville sent me back to London.' Jade didn't reply, and Madeline, apparently eager to see Harry and Jade get together, tried another tack. 'But it must have been very romantic,' she urged.

Jade glared at her new friend for a brief instant before she looked down at her boots. 'If you find gas patients puking their guts out in your ambulance romantic.'

Harry noticed her reluctance to discuss war horrors. 'You're probably wanting to write about

104

a safari, if I'm any judge of the current fancy for them.'

Jade smiled gratefully for his gallantry at turning the conversation. 'Yes, I am. But I also want a flavor of the colony. That means knowing something about its start.' Here was an opportunity to finally ask about Gil Worthy's first trip without revealing her underlying purpose. The more she knew of those earlier years, the more likely she was to discover clues to his missing son and possibly to Gil's own killer.

'I'm told, Mr Hascombe,' Jade continued, 'that you've been here since before the railroad extended up to Nairobi. Perhaps you can tell me about some of the others who tried their hand at colonizing but didn't make it.'

'Well,' he said and rubbed a hand over his square-cut jaw. 'I might be able to give some assistance there.' His brown eyes took in her soft black waves of hair and oval face before they traveled down her lithe, well-toned body. 'Perhaps we could have dinner together and discuss it?'

Madeline, in her matchmaking joy, grabbed for her husband's arm and startled Neville out of a private reverie. The touch roused him with a start, and he jerked his arm in surprise. The cook, walking past his chair with a fresh pot of coffee, jumped aside. Harry saw the pot fly out of the man's hands and pulled Jade out of her chair before the scalding liquid doused her.

Jade tumbled into Harry Hascombe's chest, muttering in surprise and fury as she struggled to regain her balance and her freedom.

Reminders of the war had left her tense to begin with, and she responded to this assault with more violence than grace.

'What the devil are you doing?' she snapped as she pushed herself free.

Harry and the others stared in admiration as she stood rigid before them. Black curls fluttered in a tousled mane, and green eyes shot angry sparks beneath the black brows. With her feet apart and fists clenched, her entire attitude spoke of a readiness to fight with very little doubt of her success. Harry's eyes lingered on her glowing face, then dropped to the ring that had slipped on its thong out of her shirt.

He rose to his feet and touched his hat respectfully. 'Sorry, Miss del Cameron. You were about to get hit by a pot of hot coffee.'

Jade looked around at the dripping brown stain on her chair back. Steam still issued from it in testimony to Harry's tale. 'Oh,' she said softly. 'Thank you, Mr Hascombe. I'm sorry I nearly punched you in the face.' Harry simply smiled back at her.

Neville offered his chair to Jade, pulled up a wooden chop box marked flour, and sat on the other side of Harry. Jade took the vacated chair and sat down sheepishly next to Madeline, apologizing again for her rude outburst.

'Oh, never mind that, my dear,' Madeline said. 'Tell us about that ring. I've never seen anything like it. Is it an emerald?'

Jade noticed the exposed ring for the first time and gripped it in her fist. 'No.'

106

'It's stunning. May I please see it?' begged Madeline.

With a sigh of resignation, Jade pulled the cord over her head and handed it to Madeline. She hadn't intended to reveal the ring to anyone, but now she had little choice. The others clustered nearer to take a closer look.

'This must be a family treasure,' said Madeline. 'I'll wager there's a fascinating story behind it, too. Please tell us,' she urged.

'Only if it's brief,' countered Lord Colridge. 'We must be on the move shortly.'

Harry took the ring from Madeline and, after a detailed examination, handed it back solemnly to Jade. She slipped the cord over her neck and tucked the ring inside her shirt before replying. 'With everyone staring at me, I suppose I must.' She sat back in Neville's chair.

'As Madeline said, I drove an ambulance during the war. My unit was one of the few women's corps that worked the front lines. Towards the end, a . . . ' She paused, searching for the right words. ' . . . a good friend of mine, a pilot, was killed when his plane crashed near the evacuation hospital. I pulled him from the wreckage. He died in my arms.'

'How awful for you, Jade,' whispered Madeline. She reached over and gently stroked Jade's arm.

Jade politely waved her away. 'Yes, well, to make a long story short,' she said and nodded at Colridge, 'he gave me this ring just before he died and charged me with finding his brother. As near as I or anyone can tell, no one's ever met this half brother of his, but he's purported to live somewhere here in the colony, possibly in Tsavo. My job here is twofold. I *am* working for *The Traveler*, but I've also been retained by the family's solicitor to find the half brother.' Jade decided to keep the search for Gil's killer a secret at present. For all she knew, she might be talking to him.

Neville roused himself from his lethargic silence and broached the question on everyone's lips. 'Does this missing chap have a name?'

Jade thought for a moment before replying. By nature, she had a cardplayer's philosophy of dealing with people. She found silence and a good poker face useful, and it helped to keep information in reserve. In that instant, she tried to assess these people's characters enough to determine how much she should reveal. Caution won out over trust. 'I know the father's name. Gil Worthy.'

Jade checked everyone's face for their immediate reaction. Madeline kept the same piteous expression, but both Neville's and Colridge's eyes opened wider in surprise. Harry, on the other hand, frowned and rubbed a large hand over his chin stubble.

'I *know* I've heard that name before,' said Neville to no one in particular.

'I say, Hascombe, didn't *you* know Gil?' asked Lord Colridge.

'Yes, I did. We came over about the same time, actually, when I was still a green lad. Followed the railroad.' He looked up from examining his boots and met Jade's eyes. 'I never heard anything of Gil having a child here. He had a wife and son back home. David, I believe.'

Jade nodded. 'David was the pilot, my friend, who died and gave me the ring.'

Harry shrugged. 'Another son ... that's a stunner.'

'Man probably had an affair in Mombasa before he left,' proclaimed Colridge. 'Or when he arrived. Happens often enough.'

Madeline's eyes opened wide in shock. 'Honestly!' she exclaimed.

Jade wondered if the old aristocrat spoke from experience or not.

'I know! Didn't he prospect?' asked Neville. 'I believe I heard his name while talking to some of the chaps out looking for gold before the war.'

'We both did for a while, down in west Tsavo,' said Harry. 'Hellish work and worse country except for hunting. I gave it up as a bad deal, but Gil held on longer. Last I heard, he caught a nasty case of malaria and went home.'

'He came back,' said Jade, 'near the start of the war in 1915.' Once again, she opted to keep the details to herself and wait for information to come to her.

'By thunder, she's right,' exclaimed Colridge. 'I remember hearing about it at the Muthaiga. Damnedest thing, too. Stories went round that he died of a mauling.'

Neville sat up abruptly and slapped his right hand on his knee. 'That's where I heard his name! Throat torn out at the Norfolk Hotel!'

'The devil!' Harry snorted. 'I don't remember hearing about that.'

'Probably while you were running supplies, Hascombe,' said Colridge.

'So if I want to find this son,' summarized Jade, 'I'd better look to west Tsavo, where he prospected?'

Harry shifted in his chair. 'Lord Colridge is right. Look to Mombasa if you have to look anywhere.' He paused and rubbed his chin. 'Inheritance, right? If it's worth a lot, it might help you find him.'

'It's a lost bet, Miss del Cameron,' said Colridge. 'Don't waste your time looking for a bastard in a haystack.' His expression softened as he spied Jade's shocked expression and he placed a fatherly hand on her arm. 'You've done your best. Can't do more.'

Madeline patted her shoulder. 'Poor dear,' she cooed.

This level of sympathy felt dangerously close to Jade's wallowing point, so she roused herself and addressed Lord Colridge. 'Should we be getting back to the village soon, sir?'

Colridge puffed out his mustache. 'Most definitely. Need to be there before dark.' He fixed his eyes on Jade. 'I don't suppose you and Mrs Thompson would consider staying here? No, didn't think so.'

'Would your own wife have stayed behind, Miles?' asked Harry.

The old man chuckled. 'Lady Colridge not go on a hunt? Not even if she had to be bait. But,' he added quickly, 'I knew *her* value as a marksman. I don't know Miss del Cameron's.' He looked sideways to Jade. 'You'll have to stay

110

out of the way. By the by, we walk back. Horses would be in the way at the village. Besides, the boys have already groomed the ticks off of them.'

Harry picked up Jade's Winchester and examined it with interest. 'I believe your President Roosevelt used a Winchester, didn't he?' He shouldered it and sighted down the barrel. 'For myself, I prefer my bolt-action Mauser.'

'A fine weapon, Hascombe,' agreed Lord Colridge. 'Thompson, what did you bring?'

'An Enfield, sir.'

'Very good,' proclaimed Colridge as the rest of the party, including Jelani, fell in behind him. 'Proven weapons.'

'Just what is the recommended placement for taking out a hyena?' asked Jade.

'Hard to kill one cleanly,' admitted Colridge over his shoulder. 'But I'm not terribly interested in the pelt, unless you are, Harry.'

Hascombe shook his head. 'Perhaps Miss del Cameron would find it amusing, though. Or,' he added, 'Neville and Mrs Thompson might have a use for it.'

Neville Thompson declined any such need, and Madeline shook her head vehemently.

'Thank you,' Jade said. 'I'm sure my father would enjoy adding it to the wall with his black bear.' She recognized Colridge's answer as an attempt to evade her question. *Probably thinks if I don't know how to kill a hyena, I won't try.* 'But to return to my question, where would one shoot to make a clean kill?'

Harry Hascombe walked alongside Jade. 'A

111

head shot is out of the question,' he said. 'The head's too small, and the skull's rather thick. A better choice would be to go through the front shoulders or angle through the chest into the off shoulder.'

Similar conversation filled the brief walk back to the village, and Jade relaxed after the initial anxiety of exposing the secret of David's ring to these relative strangers. The worst result so far was Madeline's obvious desire to mother her. At best, she'd actually confirmed Gil's attachment to Tsavo. Her thoughts had trailed off to a safari there when Harry's deep baritone at her side recalled her attention.

'I beg your pardon,' she said. 'My mind must have wandered.'

'Not a difficult task once old Miles begins drawling on about his exploits,' said Mr Hascombe. 'I asked how long you intend to stay in the colony.'

'Several weeks, I should think. The Thompsons volunteered to keep me at their farm while I photograph Nairobi and Thika. After that, I'm to write a second feature on a safari.' She paused as though the idea had just come to her. 'You know, I read Colonel Patterson's account about those Tsavo man-eaters. I think I'd really like to see Tsavo. Perhaps I might learn something about Gil's son while I'm in the area.'

Harry frowned. 'Tsavo is a mean district, Miss del Cameron. Scratchy thorns everywhere, killer lions. You would do better to go to the Serengeti or Kapiti Plains.'

'Gil didn't prospect in those places. I'm not a

112

delicate flower, Mr Hascombe,' she added.

'I can see that.' His brown eyes ran slowly over her. 'You're all woman, but — '

Jade interrupted before he got more personal. If this man knew something about Gil and his treks in Tsavo, she meant to have his assistance. 'Besides my own interest in the matter, my editor also suggested Tsavo as a possibility. The romance of the name might sell more copy. I could use a man of your expertise.'

Harry shrugged his broad shoulders and leaned closer. 'Suit yourself. If you insist on Tsavo, I just might tag along to be of assistance.'

'Fine. My magazine is arranging the safari through the outfitters in Nairobi: Newland, Tarlton, and Company, I believe. Perhaps they could hire you as one of the safari guides?'

'I know the outfit, Miss del Cameron. I worked for them once before with a neighbor of mine, Roger Forster. I'm sure it would be no problem.'

'Excellent,' Jade concluded. 'You might as well be paid for your expertise as not.'

Harry frowned a little at this last remark, and Jade knew he took her intention to be businesslike rather than social. Good. All the signs pointed to his being interested in her, but she wasn't in the market for courtship. Better not to send any false messages. A man of Mr Hascombe's ego might intentionally misread her interest beyond an academic one. Still, he definitely had an aura about him.

The walk to the Kikuyu village took them down from an airy, elevated plain and its shorter grasses into the knee-high vegetation and woodier brush of the lowlands. The hike itself was not difficult, but Jade wondered what it would be like going back in the dark and uphill when they were tired. She looked down, pulled a tick from her trousers, and tossed it aside.

Once inside the village, Lord Colridge directed everyone to their places. By previous order, the Kikuyu had retired to their huts, though the droning whispers from within spoke of their intention to keep vigil. Jade sent Jelani off to the huts as soon as they entered the village.

'Thompson, you, Hascombe, and myself will wait over there.' Colridge pointed to a slightly upraised blind of poles and thatch that the Kikuyu had constructed for him. 'The ladies will wait it out in the *boma* with the goats, where it's safer.'

Jade and Madeline immediately protested, but Colridge shushed them with a dictatorial hand motion. 'Miss del Cameron, you will be able to see perfectly well through the breaks in the *boma*, especially with this moonlight. Mrs Thompson, I trust you'll want to keep her company.'

'I was under the impression, sir,' argued Jade, 'that the hyena broke into the *boma* in the past. I'd hardly call it a safe place.'

'But there wasn't any bait out for it on those nights,' Colridge said, his voice patronizing. 'The hyena is a lazy brute at heart, like most predators. It won't work any harder than it needs to for a meal.'

114

'I'm going to scout around the perimeter,' said Harry.

Neville turned to his wife. 'Off you go, Madeline. Be a good sport about it.'

'I don't care to be treated like a child, Neville,' she whispered lest Lord Colridge overhear her.

'I know, darling,' said Neville. 'But this is no time to argue.' He nodded sideways at Colridge and contorted his face into a grimace to convey to his spouse the importance of the man's patronage and approval.

Madeline took the hint. 'Yes, of course, darling,' she said in a louder voice. 'You are absolutely correct. We'll just be going into the *boma*.'

Jade reluctantly followed Madeline through a small gateway and pulled the brush back into place behind them. The goats paid no attention to their arrival and settled down on their knobby knees in the dirt. A few kids butted their mothers' udders to be fed. Outside the *boma*, the sun sat low on the horizon and filled the sky with gorgeous splashes of scarlet and gold. Long shadows bathed the village and surrounding hills in cool, grape blue shadows. Nearly a quarter hour later, they heard Mr Hascombe return and enter the blind. Then, as the sunset plunged the world into darkness, they heard a scratching at the *boma* gate. Jade lowered her rifle when a voice from without called softly.

'Memsabu, it is me.'

'Jelani? What are you doing out there? I thought you went into a hut.' She trotted over to the entrance and pulled back the brush from the

115

opening. 'Come inside at once,' she ordered.

Jelani slipped in through the opening, and Jade pushed the brush back into place. She took the boy by the shoulders and brought her face down to within an inch of his. 'We must be silent,' she whispered. 'When the hyena comes, it should only hear the goat outside.'

Jelani nodded and tiptoed in front of Jade along the wall and away from the opening. A few goats trotted before them. A patch of white appeared dimly ahead — Madeline's shirt. 'Over here,' she whispered.

They squatted down near her and peered through various gaps in the brush towards the stake that tethered the goat near the blind. Jade reckoned the distance to be about twenty yards, an easy shot. But bad luck and the gently rolling topography put the raised blind barely above the line of her fire. If she missed the hyena, she risked hitting one of the men. For that matter, from their current position the women risked being hit in the cross fire. Under her breath Jade cursed Lord Colridge and his antiquated chivalrous attitude.

They moved farther aside and sat in the dark for nearly half an hour more before the moon rose overhead and washed the landscape with its iridescent glow. The bait had long since knelt down in the dirt with its head resting to one side, and Madeline had given up on kneeling in favor of sitting with her legs curled to the left. Jade shifted from one knee to the other until her wounded knee began to ache. She shifted again when she realized Jelani was not by her side. She

116

looked for him and saw him standing at the gate, trying to peer out. Before she could call him back, a mad cackling laugh erupted from outside the rear of the *boma*.

The skin along Jade's forearms prickled and tingled. She shivered involuntarily. The laugh repeated itself. Erratic, high-pitched notes touched with insanity rolled through the night, the type of laugh she had heard from the shell-shocked victims. The darkness, the ghostly light, and the inhuman sounds triggered the memory of a particularly harrowing night ambulance run when the insanity behind her seat went on for endless miles.

Her breath came in rapid gasps. The nearly instinctive panic, the urge to flee the war with its smells, sickness, and death, oppressed her and pushed her to the limits of reason. She closed her eyes and fought the fear, mentally reciting her old shelling mantra. Then the laughter ceased, and Madeline gently shook her.

'Jade,' she whispered. 'Are you all right? You look ill.'

Jade pulled a kerchief from her hip pocket and wiped the sweat from her brow. Now she knew how a grouse felt as the dogs edged closer and closer until it finally gave in to its panic and flew out into the open. She also knew she must find a way to conquer those panic attacks or she would forever be in danger. Any sound, any smell might trigger them. Why they needed to be conquered was not the issue, but how.

'I'm fine,' Jade answered. 'That laugh, bad memories.'

'Hyena,' explained Madeline.

The old nanny outside had heard the eerie, quavering calls as well. It stood up and stomped its hooves nervously as its ears twitched from side to side, listening for danger. If another animal had entered the village, it kept itself out of sight. Jade took a deep breath, held it, and listened. Then she heard it, a soft scrabbling at the *boma* gate, right where Jelani stood.

'Jelani,' she whispered, 'get back now!'

Madeline crept closer to her. 'What is it?' she whispered.

Jade didn't reply. She shouldered her rifle and steadied herself. Jelani started to back slowly away from the gate. His right hand clutched a slender object. It glinted in the moonlight, and Jade saw it was a knife. 'Damn,' she muttered. Jelani seemed intent on becoming a warrior sooner than necessary.

Suddenly the *boma*'s gate bowed inward with a groan and a crackling snap. The low head and high shoulders of the spotted hyena pushed through. Jade chambered a round and waited. The animal hesitated and sniffed the air. A shot now was impossible. Jelani stood in the way, and if Jade moved, the hyena might charge. Jade concentrated on keeping her breathing slow and regular and tried to ignore the intense throbbing pain in her knee.

The powerful animal eyed Jelani and stalked into the *boma* towards him. Its massive jaws quivered slightly, glistening wet with saliva. The shorter hindquarters tensed themselves for the rush. Jade set her sights on the animal's chest and shouted.

'Jelani, run! Now!' She trusted in the immediate obedience of the boy, who had learned to take orders, but she underestimated the predator's speed and power. Jelani jumped out of the line of fire just as the hyena charged. The beast knocked the boy to the ground with a glancing blow from its massive shoulder. Jade saw her shot and squeezed the trigger as she exhaled. The animal yelped and leaped into the air.

'Madeline, get Jelani,' ordered Jade. Madeline darted around the nervous, bleating goats and pulled the Kikuyu youth aside as the hyena bit its own shoulder to attack the source of its pain. Jade worked the lever smoothly, chambered another round, and waited for her opportunity.

'Over here, you *toto*-eating monster,' she shouted. The hyena glared at her and presented its open chest to her sights. She fired again, and the hyena jerked, fell, and lay still. The sound of running feet came from the direction of the blind. Colridge, Hascombe, and Thompson rushed into the *boma*, rifles ready.

'Hold your fire. It's dead,' Jade said and rose from her position. The pain in her knee disappeared. 'Madeline, how's the boy?'

'He's fine,' Madeline answered. 'Just some scrapes.' She nodded to the hyena. 'Are you sure it's dead?' Jelani broke free of Madeline's protective embrace and plunged his knife up to the hilt in the hyena's throat.

'It is now,' Jade said.

119

'Bloody hell,' muttered Colridge. 'The damned brute went for the *boma* goats after all.'

'He went for Jelani,' said Jade.

Neville squatted down beside the hyena and examined the body. 'Marvelous shot, Miss Jade,' he said. 'You went straight into the heart and . . . My word.'

'What?' Jade knelt beside him.

Hascombe leaned over her shoulder for a better look. 'I don't see . . . '

Lord Colridge stood by Madeline and helped her to her feet. 'Well, are you going to tell us what it is or are you all going to stammer like imbeciles?' he scolded.

'You'll want to see this for yourself, Miles,' said Hascombe.

'See what?' demanded Madeline.

'The fur's been shaved into geometric patterns,' said Jade. 'And there's a bone knotted into the neck ruff.'

'It is the sign of the *laibon*, memsabu,' Jelani explained. 'We killed his hyena.'

★   ★   ★

Later that night, the man crouched by the now smoldering fire and thought about what had happened. His beast was dead. He had felt his own will driven from it in its death throes. He also knew who had killed his creature. Had he not seen her through the beast's very eyes? In his rage he slammed his fist into the ground. How dare the Kikuyu attempt to defy him! Calling for

120

that stupid old man to help. Thinking his magic was stronger because he was under a king's protection. What could an English king do here? He let his hatred ferment inside him. It would be useful later, a power to be tapped.

While the man had watched earlier through his animal's eyes, the fool Colridge tried to set a trap for his familiar. But the man was too clever for them all. He, like his teacher, could control the animal, but unlike his teacher, he had learned more, much more. And why not? Wasn't he smarter? Wasn't his teacher a tool to be used just like the hyena? The human bone knotted in the ruff had turned the animal away from the old nanny towards human prey. When his familiar had hesitated, he directed the hyena with barely whispered incantations away from the trap and into the *boma*, towards the scent of the boy and the women.

His eyes mirrored the fire's sparks as they flashed in anger. That woman! She would bear watching, and eventually, she would have to pay. But all in good time.

All predators learned patience.

9

*'Most races or groups of people believe they
are superior in some way to others.
The Maasai know they are.'*
— The Traveler

The Sopwith Camel plummeted into a nosedive,
wind screaming over its wings. Jade squinted
against the wing's reflective glare and ran across
the field. I must warn him before he goes into a
death roll. Too late. The plane hit the earth with
a sickening thud. A shout came to her throat,
drowned out by the maniacal laughter of the
shell-shocked wounded all around her. Bloody
hands snatched at her hair and clothes. She
plowed her way through the endless mob, but as
she reached the downed plane and the pilot, a
hideously large hyena sprang in between her and
David, snarling in defense of its carrion prey.
Jade launched a right hook at the brute's
slavering jaws. Her fist swung in the empty air,
and she woke in a cold sweat. Outside, a sweet,
high-pitched chirp announced another beautiful,
cool morning.

Jade lay panting on her cot and sorted
nightmare from fact. Last night's hyena was real,
no doubt about that, but it hadn't attacked
David. Just as she felt something akin to relief,
the weight of the ring on her chest reminded her
of that other reality, David's death.

122

'I'm sorry, David,' she whispered and clutched the ring through her bush shirt. 'I told you I'd find your brother, and I will. You have to give me more time, please.'

Her boots stood upright beside her cot, and Jade shook each one upside down before slipping them on. The action itself, perfectly normal and advisable on safari, triggered another place-time distortion. She caught herself looking for Beverly and listening for the commandant's call.

'I need some coffee,' she muttered and stepped out into the cool air of a highland morning.

Miles Colridge, sitting at the table, ignored her disheveled appearance and greeted her. 'Good morning, Miss del Cameron. Splendid morning. I trust you slept well. Good, good,' he said without waiting for her answer. 'There's coffee in the pot. Help yourself.'

'Good morning. And thank you, I believe I shall.' She picked up the pot with a towel and poured a mug full of the black brew. The fragrant aroma wafted up to her nostrils, and she inhaled deeply with a contented sigh.

'By thunder, Miss del Cameron, that was fine shooting last night. I underestimated you, and Mrs Thompson, too, it seems. If I understand the story rightly, she pulled the Kikuyu boy out of the way.' He chuckled and puffed out his bushy mustache. 'Lady Penelope would've been proud.'

'Your wife, sir?' inquired Jade. She blew on her coffee and took a tentative sip. Nectar!

'My late wife, yes. She loved Africa. Loved

everything about it.' The old man stared into his own cup, and Jade detected a twinge of sorrow cross his grizzled features. She waited patiently for him to continue or not, as he chose, and offered a word of support.

'A fine lady,' she said as a statement rather than a question and took a seat. The sun hadn't risen yet, but it would soon enough. Most of the stars were invisible, and there was an expectancy in the air, a stirring of hidden life in preparation. The waning moon hung low over the western horizon as though it waited for permission to set.

'A remarkably fine lady,' said Colridge eventually.

Jade wanted to ask how and when she had died and whether or not they had children, but British reserve wasn't something one pried into, especially when speaking with an aristocrat. But something in his fidgety mannerism told her he needed to speak, wanted to speak, wanted to be asked. She did. 'May I be so bold, sir, as to inquire?'

'A year ago. One of the first influenza victims.'

'I'm sorry, sir. It's a loss to you and to the colony.'

The old man looked up gratefully. 'Good of you to say so, Miss del Cameron. Our son survived the war. He's in London now, but I daresay he'll come home soon.' A noise outside the other tent roused him to his old self. 'Ah, Thompson, Mrs Thompson, you are awake. About time, the sun is already rising.'

True to his decree, the sun sent its first golden spears over the hills and spilled light into the

124

campsite. Jade marveled at the man's sense of timing. It spoke of a long partnership with Africa.

'Good morning, Lord Colridge, Miss Jade,' said Neville. 'Hascombe rode back to his ranch last night after all?'

'Just a few miles away,' answered Colridge. 'No spare tent. Sensible thing to do. Did say he'd come back for breakfast. Should be here now, in fact.'

Harry Hascombe, unlike the sun, did not obey Lord Colridge's imperial commands. It was a full half an hour later before he rode up on Whiskey, about the time they were digging into warm, sweet scones and slices of salted bacon, fried crisp. Jade was in heaven; well, nearly so. A large side of golden hashed brown potatoes seasoned with bits of onion would have done the trick. Jade looked up from her plate and noticed that the powerful rancher had shaved.

Harry seated himself in the coffee-stained chair and helped himself to a heaping plate of food. Finally, she could ask about the incredible hyena hide. Harry brought up the subject himself.

'Well, Miles,' he said, 'still doubt the witchcraft stories?' Colridge only snorted loudly. 'Should be quite an interesting trophy for you, Miss del Cameron.'

'I've never seen or heard of anything like that before,' Jade said. 'That is, except for incomplete references made around here and Jelani's statement. Would someone explain it?'

Harry grinned broadly. 'Most happy to oblige

125

a pretty huntress,' he said with a slight bow. 'The Kikuyu told our host here that a witch sent a familiar, if you please, after their flocks and themselves. Like any good, God-fearing Englishman, he sorts out the witchcraft angle but goes after the hyena. This time, the Kikuyu were right. Someone owned that hyena. That geometric pattern shaved into the fur had some meaning, perhaps the witch's secret name.'

'Like a cattle brand?' suggested Jade.

'Exactly,' agreed Harry. 'The bead in the fur may be a talisman or mark of power. Or maybe it all worked together to call up some magic power on the animal, an incantation.' He drained his cup. 'Of course, I'm speculating. Witches don't readily reveal their secrets.'

'And where would this witch live?' asked Jade. Harry extended his arms to indicate anywhere in Africa. Jade persisted. 'Surely he must have a tribe?'

'A *laibon* is a shaman,' explained Harry. 'He could be Maasai or one of the tribes related to the Maasai. Perhaps the Samburu. These *laibon* generally deal with day-to-day problems such as illnesses, fidelity, or bringing rainfall. One class helps the warriors defeat enemies. The English tend to see these men as seats of power. In reality, elders make the decisions for the *kralls*, or villages.' He paused and thought a moment. 'Well, maybe not the warrior-class villages.'

'So if we went to the closest Maasai village,' Jade said in summary, 'we might find this *laibon* and confront him?'

Harry leaned forward in his chair, his brow

126

furrowed, and his square-cut jaw set. 'Well, if you do, you'll do it without me. Those men may or may not have power, but I'm not making any enemies of the Maasai.'

'Quite right,' Colridge declared. 'No need to borrow trouble. We killed the brute animal. Problem solved.'

'Where is the hide now?' asked Madeline.

'I took the brute, as Miles called him, back last night and skinned it out, Mrs Thompson,' said Harry. 'It's already curing on the side of a hut for Miss del Cameron.' He touched the brim of his hat in salutation. 'And may I congratulate you in advance of your victory celebration?'

'What victory celebration?' asked Jade in confusion.

'Er, the Kikuyu wish to hold a *ngoma* for you tonight at the village,' said Colridge. 'That is their name for a big celebration dance.'

'What a smashing addition to your article, Jade,' said Madeline. 'That is, if we stay for it,' she added, looking at Lord Colridge like a pleading child.

'*I've* no time for it,' said Colridge, 'but I don't deny Miss del Cameron should be there. Thompson, I depend on you and your wife to accompany her. Hascombe, too. Myself, I prefer the Muthaiga for celebrating. Miss del Cameron, remember I have a dinner party set for you at the club on Saturday. Of course, Harry, you are invited, as well as Mr and Mrs Thompson.'

Jade again thanked the old lord. Neville looked as though he would burst with pride, Madeline appeared delighted, and Harry simply sat looking supremely amused by it all.

'Might I make another suggestion, Miles,' Harry said and continued since the question was rhetorical at best. 'As you are leaving this jolly group, allow me to take them to my ranch for the day. I'll escort them to the *ngoma* tonight, bring them back to my ranch, and see them and your horses safely back at your farm tomorrow.'

Jade felt something strike her booted foot. She looked sideways to see Madeline smiling impishly, mouth incompletely hidden behind her hand. Jade kicked her back.

'Very good, Hascombe,' replied Colridge. 'I depend on you and Thompson, too.'

'We should return to the farm,' said Neville. 'I have plans for a water-powered sawmill, and I must get started with the flumes. If Harry takes care of Miss Jade, I'd be free to carry on.'

'Good lad! That's the kind of dedication that makes success, but steam is what you want,' stated Colridge in a tone that allowed no debate. 'I can arrange for you to purchase an old locomotive just as I have for minimal cost. Make you a loan if need be. We'll discuss it when you return the horses. Wouldn't think of you leaving your wife out of this or behind with a scoundrel like Hascombe.' He chuckled and winked at Madeline.

'I don't want to be a bother,' said Jade. 'Surely we can stay here at camp.'

Madeline's eyes opened wide. 'Nonsense, Jade! You *must* see Harry's ranch, for the Maasai if for no other reason. They're really a marvelous race.'

Jade's interest grew. 'You have Maasai working on your ranch, Mr Hascombe? Could there be a *laibon* there as well?'

'I only hire a few warrior-class men who work in return for one of the calves. They are by far the best cattlemen you can ever hope to meet,' he answered.

'They do know cattle,' agreed Colridge, 'but it's a damned waste of animal flesh and good pasturage, considering they never eat them. Always wanting more land for the beasts, too.'

A dark brow arched in question. '*Never* eat them?' Jade asked. 'Are they like Hindus?'

'No, they drink the milk and curdle it in calabashes, gourds, to eat,' explained Neville. 'That and they bleed the bulls and drink the blood. Never take enough to hurt the animal.'

'Most curious,' murmured Jade.

'The Maasai breed cattle, hunt lion, and occasionally raid villages for more cattle,' added Hascombe. 'Cattle are their money and a mark of their manhood.'

'Money which they never spend,' sputtered Lord Colridge. 'Ridiculous economics.'

'Well, not really,' countered Jade. Everyone looked at her with open mouths. Very few people contradicted Lord Colridge. 'It seems to me a system of economics exactly like that practiced by many rich capitalists who never touch the principal but live entirely on the interest. And isn't that what they're doing when they only take the milk and a small amount of blood? They're living on the interest.'

Harry Hascombe laughed heartily and slapped

his palm on the table, which sent the coffee mugs and plates recoiling from the impact. 'Most delightful, Miss del Cameron.'

Lord Colridge puffed and snorted like an old bull, but to Jade's discerning eye, it seemed to be more for show. Once she even caught him stifling a smile with a cough. Ah well, he did have a reputation to maintain.

Breakfast completed, they bade His Lordship farewell. Then the two groups broke apart and traveled their separate ways, which left the porters to take down the camp and carry everything back to Colridge's farm. Jade wanted to clean her gun before leaving, but Harry suggested she wait until they reached his ranch. He'd brought a double-barreled Holland with him that morning and assured them that he, 'and Thompson of course,' could protect them very well for the short ride.

Mr Hascombe pointed out his herds of cattle in the distance and explained how they had grown so much that there was barely enough grazing land left for them. 'I recently made an offer to Roger Forster, my neighbor, to join up our ranches, but he's not interested,' said Harry.

'Why should he be?' Jade inquired.

'Roger's had a run of bad luck. First, the failed ostrich farm; then his cattle had to be destroyed due to anthrax. As a rancher's daughter, you know what that means.'

Jade reflected on the fear that the soil bacteria would land as spores on plants and be eaten by the cattle. Then an entire herd might have to be destroyed to prevent the risk of it spreading. But

130

the disease was considered rare. 'Is anthrax a common problem here?' she asked.

'It wasn't until the war,' replied Harry. 'The bloody Germans actually tried to spread it in some areas.'

'I say, I didn't know Forster's cattle had anthrax,' Neville interjected.

'Not sure they actually did,' stated Harry. 'But someone in the colony made the claim to the authorities and that was enough. He's trying again, but he's got two overdrafts at the banks already. Thought my offer might help him out, but Rog is a proud man.' Harry shrugged. 'Well, negotiations were friendly enough. Who knows, we may make some sort of partnership yet.'

Hascombe's single-storied house stood up on a rise and oversaw various vegetable gardens and metal outbuildings. Like Colridge's house, it sported a large veranda that ran the length of the home. Unlike Colridge's, no flower beds graced the borders, and the roof was an untidy-looking assemblage of tin cut from empty paraffin *debes*, the universal building material in the colony. Jade considered the overall effect to be that of a bachelor who didn't care to be inconvenienced either by a poorly made home or by the maintenance of any beautifying factors.

As if she read Jade's mind, Madeline pulled alongside of her and whispered, 'It needs a woman's touch.'

Jade furrowed her brows and glared at Madeline, who glanced away almost immediately and spied a spotted pelt tacked onto a mud hut. 'Oh, look, Jade,' she exclaimed and pointed. 'I

131

believe that is your hyena over there.'

'Correct, Mrs Thompson,' said Harry. 'Care to take a look at it?' They dismounted and handed the reins over to a stable boy in white robes, then proceeded on foot to the outbuilding.

'Should be a very fine addition to your personal trophies, Miss del Cameron,' said Harry. 'And after last evening, I've no doubt that they are many.'

Jade shrugged. 'Not so many. At home we hunt for meat; elk and deer mostly. Sometimes we shoot black bear or mountain cats that harass the livestock.' She touched the stiff hide and traced the symmetrical zigzags shaved into the fur. 'Of course, we keep the hides for coats, leather, or rugs, but I rarely mount the heads unless I need a new hat rack.'

'I'll send this to the Norfolk Hotel when it's ready,' Harry said. 'They'll hold it for you.'

Jade stood entranced by the pattern in the hide. 'This is incredible,' she finally said. 'To think someone would train an animal like this.'

'Then you believe it was a trained animal?' Harry asked.

'Consider the facts,' Jade replied. 'Someone certainly had his hands on this animal. Otherwise, those patterns and that bead wouldn't be there.'

'So perhaps a native captured a hyena, did that, then released the animal back into the wild,' Neville suggested.

'Why? To what purpose?' argued Jade.

'Well, to strike fear,' Neville said.

'But what are the chances anyone would ever

132

see it unless it attacked someone?' Jade countered. 'And despite your hyena problem, it seems unlikely that this one would just happen to show up at the village.'

'Then you do think it's witchcraft?' asked Neville.

Jade shook her head. 'Not necessarily. Why should the explanation be supernatural? If the animal is intelligent, it's trainable. Perhaps someone taught it to hunt goats or even humans.'

'I've never thought of the hyena as intelligent,' volunteered Madeline, 'but since it is usually a pack predator, I suppose it must be. Otherwise how could they cooperate?'

'Exactly,' said Jade. 'Wolves are another social predator, and they're very smart. I'd imagine the lion is as well.'

'Well, some might be,' said Harry, 'but old Percy is rather dim-witted.' He led them to a set of bamboo pens behind the outbuildings. 'Come, let me introduce you to *my* little menagerie.'

Grunts, screeches, chirps, and an assortment of other sounds grew louder as they approached the pens. The musky aroma of a large cat mingled with the sweeter scent of big herbivores and the mildly putrid smell of pig. A magnificent male lion greeted them first. He shook a thick black mane, yawned, and exposed a cavernous mouth of wicked-looking teeth.

'Percy here was a cub four years ago. We killed his mother much as you had to kill your mountain cat, Miss del Cameron. I hadn't the heart to shoot this little bloke, so I raised him for a pet.'

'Surely you don't actually let him out, Mr Hascombe,' exclaimed Madeline.

Harry laughed. 'No, ma'am. Oh, I used to take him out for a walk when he was a tyke, but I quit a year ago. He is a lion, after all, and even in play he's a bit rambunctious.' The huge beast approached the bars at Harry's voice and rubbed his massive head against the cage like any house cat. Harry obliged by reaching through and scratching him behind the ears. 'Like I said before, Percy is a bit dim upstairs. I never could teach him not to eat my hats and boots. But come meet some of my other companions.' He led the way down a row of similar compartments that housed zebra colts, a Grant's gazelle doe, and a grunting warthog.

Jade stared in wide-eyed wonder at the assortment. 'Lord Colridge keeps some zebra in hopes of breaking them to the harness, but this . . . this is a genuine zoo.'

Harry grinned broadly. 'We colonists like to consider ourselves eccentric and this is one of the best ways of proving it.' He looked at Madeline for confirmation. 'I daresay you have a pet or two, Mrs Thompson.'

'I do have a little duiker,' she admitted. 'That's one of the smallest antelope, Jade. He only comes up to my knee. I would like a mongoose someday, too.'

'I'll see what I can do for you. Roger may have some. He keeps some animals himself.'

The comical pig ambled around its pen, tail

134

spiked straight up like a flagpole. Jade was about to photograph it when a pretty birdlike chirp behind her arrested her attention. She turned to encounter a tall, fierce-looking Maasai warrior holding a leash. Attached to the other end and sniffing her boots was a beautiful, full-grown cheetah.

The cheetah chirped again, folding its upper lip as if to whistle, and entwined itself around the Maasai's bare legs. With his long spear, red blanket robe, and regal carriage, the keeper was every bit as handsome as the animal. His ochre-dyed plaited hair hung fore and aft, and a lion claw hung from each slit earlobe. The man didn't smile but spoke to Harry in some African language other than Swahili. Harry answered and, judging by nods in Jade's direction and at the hyena hide, explained his visitors to the warrior. The tall, slender Maasai only nodded curtly, but Jade thought she detected a note of curiosity when he looked at her. At least his glance lingered longer on her face.

'My man, Ruta, here has special charge of Biscuit, a position of great honor.'

'Biscuit?' exclaimed Madeline. 'You named this beautiful cheetah Biscuit?'

'He had a propensity for eating every one off the plate at teatime when he was a cub. Still does.'

Jade held out her hand, palm down as she would to a new dog. The slender cat first sniffed it, then licked it. Jade scratched it behind its rounded ears, and Biscuit sidled up to her for more.

'You've made a friend, Miss del Cameron. Biscuit is perfectly tame, but he gives his affections reluctantly. Ruta has always held them.'

Jade glanced up to see Harry looking at her intently. 'Animals are a great judge of character, Mr Hascombe,' she explained. 'They know a true animal lover when they meet one.'

'Indeed,' he replied and turned back to Ruta to speak with him.

'Ruta will allow you to walk Biscuit anytime you wish, Miss del Cameron.' He handed the leash to Jade, who accepted it readily. 'Simply return the cheetah to him when you're done.'

'How will I find him?'

'Only look behind you. He won't leave your side as long as you have Biscuit.'

She admired the beautiful cat. 'Well, perhaps just as long as we are touring the grounds, I might keep him with me.'

'Splendid. Now allow me to show you the house gardens.' He indicated the path with his hand. Jade hesitated.

'What's in those other pens farther down?' she asked.

'Only some baboons, but Biscuit dislikes them immensely. I'm afraid they aren't making very good pets. They've taken to throwing rocks and charging at the natives. However, if you wish to return Biscuit to Ruta, we could see them.'

Jade felt the cheetah rub its head against her thigh and sighed. 'Take us to the gardens,' she said and followed the others. Biscuit walked stiff-legged beside her. His non-retractable claws

136

made ticky sounds on the flagstone walkway as his shoulders rose and fell in rhythmic stride.

Ruta walked behind her as Harry said he would. She decided to speak with him about the cat and turned to greet the warrior and then asked him if Biscuit hunted. Ruta only shook his head slowly. Jade tried again, keeping her Swahili simple in case she was inadvertently confusing him with improper sentence structure. 'Biscuit hunts?' she asked.

'Ruta doesn't speak Swahili,' said Harry. 'The Maasai language is based on what is called the Nilo-Saharan languages. Swahili, on the other hand, is a Bantu language with a strong Arabic influence.' He lowered his voice as if speaking a confidence. 'Frankly, he understands it perfectly well, but he considers it beneath his dignity to admit it. They're a warrior tribe, you understand, and come to manhood by killing a lion with a spear.'

'I'm surprised they demean themselves to work for hire, then,' said Jade.

Harry shrugged. 'Their warrior village is nearby, they take pride in raising cattle well, and to be honest, when they no longer care to work for me or anyone else, they leave at a moment's notice. One really has to admire that sort of independence.'

Jade wanted to ask the Masai about his tribe. What were these warrior villages like and did they all have *laibons* were questions that came to mind. Mr Hascombe, though, seemed more inclined to show off a vegetable garden tended by some Kikuyu natives. The Thompsons

137

discussed plant stocks with their host, so Jade turned her attention to Biscuit and his soft, woolly-textured spotted fur. Eventually the tour moved indoors, and Biscuit made himself as much at home inside as out. The cat sprawled across a leather sofa, and Jade perched on the arm next to him.

'As you can see, my house is small, me not being a family man.' Harry again stared at Jade, who met his eyes. 'But,' he added, 'I have very comfortable grass and thatch guest huts, assuring you of complete safety and privacy. Perhaps you'd care to rest or bathe before we dine?'

Madeline wanted to rest, and Neville was content to sit outside with a government publication on grafting fruit trees, which he had found lying about. Jade wanted to talk to Harry in private about Gil Worthy, but he announced that he had some important business to attend to. She decided to use the time to clean her rifle. Only Biscuit and Ruta stayed behind with her.

She pulled a wooden chair from out of her bamboo and thatch hut and sat down outside with her Winchester and a rag. Biscuit lay at her feet like a large dog, panting open-mouthed in the afternoon heat. Ruta stood on one leg like a stork and leaned on his long spear. Jade pointed first at him then at a second chair inside, but Ruta shook his head. Jade shrugged and turned her attention to her rifle.

The big Winchester .38–55 was a gift from her affectionate parents many years ago and had quickly become her favorite rifle. With it, she felt safe from any danger posed by an irritated and hungry male black bear or an overprotective mother bear. She'd bagged her first elk with that rifle and now her first, and hopefully last, hyena. Jade's father had taught her the value of a well-maintained firearm, and the black powder used in these cartridges left a residue that needed to be cleaned thoroughly after shooting.

Biscuit rolled over on his back and flashed his pale underbelly just like her old tomcat, Rupert, back home. She rubbed the cheetah's tummy and murmured a few of the usual nonsensical things that most people said to their pets when engaged in such undignified activities. The cheetah responded by closing its eyes and promptly fell asleep, purring contentedly.

'*Duma nzuri*,' Jade said to Ruta while she pointed to the cheetah. 'Cheetah pretty.' The tall, slender Maasai looked at her but didn't respond. Next she smiled her friendliest smile, pointed at Ruta, and asked, '*Laibon?*' Ruta's mouth tightened a fraction, but he made no reply. Frustrated, Jade tried one more phrase, one that she trusted would gain a response simply because it sounded more urgent, which in fact it was. '*Choo kiko wapi?*' Where are the toilets? At this request, the warrior grinned and pointed to an outhouse behind the main house. Jade thanked him and handed him Biscuit's leash. Harry was right. Ruta understood Swahili and possibly English. She wondered what else he knew but kept hidden.

10

'Every culture honors brave deeds. Some do this with tediously long and boring banquets that often serve to teach the recipient to avoid future honors. The Kikuyu hold ngomas.'
— The Traveler

Jotting notes on the previous evening's events in her leather notebook helped Jade pass most of the lazy afternoon. Finally everyone, including Hascombe's neighbor, Roger, gathered for an early dinner of wildebeest steaks and garden vegetables. Mr Hascombe had sent a runner to him with the invitation not only to dinner but to the *ngoma* as well.

Roger Forster looked as young as Jade remembered him from the generator flume. His limpid blue eyes and upturned brows carried a confused puppy look. He stood in the doorway with his hands in his jodphur pockets and waited for an invitation to enter. All in all, he struck Jade as one pitiful young man. In fact, she mused, he hardly seemed capable of making his earlier cold comment on native deaths. Jade wondered if perhaps she had misheard him.

'Roger. About time you got here,' said Harry. 'Don't just stand there, man. Get in here and greet my guests.'

Roger removed his broad-brimmed felt hat and stepped softly into the living room. His

140

sandy-brown hair flopped over his forehead from a crooked side part. 'Hello,' he said and nodded to everyone. He noticed Jade and, for an instant, stared at her before he recollected himself and dropped his gaze to his dusty boots.

'Roger, you know Mr and Mrs Thompson. This young lady is Miss Jade del Cameron. She's an American doing a story on the protectorate for some magazine.'

Jade extended her right hand and, after a brief hesitation, he shook it gently. 'Very nice to meet you, Miss del Cameron,' Roger said. 'You'll pardon my earlier rude stare, but I believe I recognized you from the generator flume.' Jade nodded.

'Miss del Cameron is a crack shot, Rog,' said Harry. 'She killed a hyena yesterday with a Winchester .38. Same weapon Roosevelt used when he came through here.'

'No,' corrected Roger before Jade could reply. 'Mr Roosevelt's Winchester took a .406 caliber cartridge.'

'Exactly,' said Jade, impressed by his knowledge. 'And I have a model 94, not a 95. But how did you know about President Roosevelt's rifle?'

'As an aspiring safari leader, I've made a point to learn what others have successfully used. I read his account in *African Game Trails*. Most interesting.'

The dinner conversation tended towards safari talk. Harry suggested that Roger also lead her safari to Tsavo. Jade agreed and asked Madeline and Neville to come along. They discussed options and supplies until the time came to ride

141

to the Kikuyu village. Roger rode up front with Mr Hascombe. The Thompsons flanked Jade until the trail narrowed and they rode single file.

Jelani stood watch for their arrival and ran back into the village to announce them. He looked ghostly, and Jade initially thought he'd taken ill with an infection from the hyena scrape. Then she discovered he had covered himself in a pale, reddish chalk, as had the rest of the villagers. The chief greeted them and paid particular attention to Jade. Harry explained Lord Colridge's absence, and everyone in their party was invited to sit on logs around an open flat area. A pile of wood had been laid in the center and several small fires were lit nearby.

One young maiden dressed in a traditional leather apron and a large quantity of copper and bead ornaments brought a banana leaf with roasted meat first to Jade and then to the others. Harry explained that the Kikuyu rarely ate meat except on ceremonial or celebratory occasions. Then a ram would be killed. Judging by the toughness of the meat, Jade decided they had killed the old nanny goat destined originally for the hyena.

A grizzled old man with piercing black eyes pointed a bony finger at Jade, and Jelani ran forward to fetch her. Jade went willingly and followed the old man into a dimly lit hut with the usual dirt floor and thatched roof that rustled from the resident lizards. He squatted down on the floor and with a hand motion bade her do the same. Jelani stood beside her.

'This man is the *mundu-mugo*,' Jelani

142

explained. 'He is a good sorcerer, not like the *laibon*, who is evil.'

Jade greeted him respectfully in Swahili, and the man grunted his acknowledgment. He set several long gourds in front of him, each plugged with a stopper made of an animal tail. Two small gourds hung from a leather cord around his scrawny neck. He removed them and set them beside him. Next he scooped out a small depression in the dirt and placed a banana leaf in it. Into the leaf went several finely ground powders out of the large gourds, a few drops of liquid from the small ones, and the coarse hair of some unnamed animal.

Jade longed to ask Jelani what the man was doing but didn't dare break the reverent mood. Instead, she squatted patiently and watched as the sorcerer built a small *boma* of twigs around the banana leaf and muttered several incantations. Then he stirred the mixture into a thick paste and smeared a small amount on Jade's hat, belt, and boots.

The paste smelled rancid with an acrid tinge, but Jade didn't protest or flinch. Finally, the old man bundled the remainder of the paste in the banana leaf, secured it with a creeper vine, and handed it to her. He spoke at length in the Kikuyu language, nodding to her and to the bundle, as if explaining its power. Then he sat back and waited. Jade looked to Jelani for a translation.

'The *mundu-mugo* has protected you from the witch who will seek revenge for killing his animal. You must keep the paste with you at all times. He smeared it on your clothes instead of on you because he knows that white women would wash it off and forget to put it on again.'

'Jelani, please thank the *mundu-mugo* for me. Tell him that I will do as he says. I would like to ask him some questions, if I may.' She bowed respectfully to the old man, who nodded after Jelani finished. 'Please ask the *mundu-mugo* how the witch can hurt me if his hyena is dead.'

Jelani winced. 'Memsabu, the witch can do anything.'

'Then ask him who this witch is so I can stop him.'

Jelani posed the question to the old man, who shook his head and answered at length. Finally the ancient healer stopped and waved his bony hand for the boy to translate.

'Memsabu, he says an evil witch has many animals. The witch can become an animal if his heart is black enough. He does not know this witch, but he has seen something when his soul walks in his sleep.'

Jade looked inquiringly at the old man's withered face and read pity in his eyes. He spoke again briefly, and Jelani gasped.

'Memsabu, he says he saw two witches. One was an old black lion who taught a man. He says he fears for you because the new witch is younger and very powerful.'

'Jelani, tell the *mundu-mugo* that I want to find out what happened to a white man at the start of the big war. He died in the hotel you work at. A hyena killed him there. I have heard that a young Kikuyu had been his friend there.

144

He would be a young warrior now.'

The old healer spoke a few words to Jelani, who left the hut and returned shortly with a youth of about fifteen years of age. The *mundu-mugo* spoke to the youth briefly and nodded to Jade. The young man related his tale to her in a mix of English and Swahili, while Jelani knelt near the old man and whispered a translation in his ear.

'I am called Wachiru. I knew this Bwana Gil that you ask of. He gave me a paper box to take to the Englishman's post. He said to send it away across the ocean so it would be safe. Bwana Gil was worried about it.'

'Do you know why he was worried?' asked Jade.

The youth shrugged and then thought a moment. 'Evil things?' he suggested. 'I sent this box away and I came back to his room to give the rest of his money to Bwana Gil, but I heard strange noises in his room. It sounded like a man struggling to breathe. Then I heard a growl. The door was shut, so I peeked through the keyhole and saw a demon on top of Bwana Gil.'

'A demon? Can you describe what this demon looked like?'

The youth glanced at the old man, who nodded again. 'It looked like a hyena, memsabu. But I saw something around its neck. Something Englishmen wear. I was afraid, so I hid in an empty room.' The young man hung his head with shame to admit his fear.

'Did you have a knife or a spear with you?' asked Jade. The youth shook his head. 'Then you

145

were wise to hide. What happened next?'

Reassured, Wachiru went on with his story. 'Later, I went back to Bwana Gil's room. He was dead, but in his hand was the chain that the demon wore around its neck. I took it and Bwana's important paper from his desk so no one would steal it.'

'Do you still have them?'

The *mundu-mugo* interrupted and gave some orders for the young man. Wachiru left the hut and returned with an animal-skin pouch, which he handed to Jade. Inside she found a gold chain with a small carved bone strung on it. The carvings were geometric zigzags like the ones found on this latest hyena's fur. Could it have been the same beast? Next to the chain lay a folded paper that opened into a map showing Kilimanjaro, the Tsavo River, and the Chyulu Hills. At the bottom were the words: *Kruger, Dolie,* and *Abel, my second son.*

Jade felt a shiver race down her arms as she read the names, but before she could ask anything else, the old man dismissed the youth. Then the *mundu-mugo* took a small thorn and dipped it into a pot of dark liquid. He gripped Jade's left arm in his bony hand and traced what looked like a sickle blade on her inner wrist. The *mundu-mugo* spoke once more, this time in halting Swahili. He pointed to Jade and said, 'Msabu Simba Jike.' Jade recognized *msabu* as yet another variation on the original Hindu phrase *memsahib*, which had been incorporated into Swahili as a term meaning mistress. *Simba* meant lion, but *jike*? Again she looked to Jelani,

146

who grinned widely.

'Memsabu has a new name. You are the lioness. You fight the hyena to protect us.' He pointed to her wrist. 'That is a lion's tooth.'

The aging sorcerer took Jade by the arm and led her outside, where he loudly announced her name to the village. Jade returned to her seat feeling very conspicuous. Madeline's and Neville's mouths hung wide open in astonishment, Roger watched her with something akin to silent respect, but Harry's well-chiseled face bore a trace of a mocking sneer at the proceedings. Both Roger and Harry wrinkled their noses at the new smell, though, and Roger went so far as to sit on the other side of Madeline.

'Well,' said Madeline. 'Lioness. Very appropriate with those green eyes of yours, although I suppose most lions have golden-colored ones. I'm very jealous,' she teased. 'I'm only known as Mrs Ostrich, and I've lived here for eight years.'

'Ugh,' said Harry after Jade sat down. 'You smell like old piss.' He shifted farther away.

'Harry!' scolded Neville. 'There are ladies present.'

'I daresay they're all familiar with the subject, Thompson,' said Harry. 'But no offense meant.'

'It's this paste on my hat and belt,' explained Jade. 'It's to protect me from the witch.' She decided not to show them the mark on her wrist. She had no idea what their reaction to it would be, and it would probably wear off in a day or two, anyway.

'Well, if you keep that on, I doubt *anyone* will

147

approach you,' he said with a laugh.

The *ngoma* officially began as the Kikuyu warriors and maidens formed one large ring around the small fires. Several venerable old ladies sat inside the ring. Chaperones perhaps, thought Jade. They occasionally took wood from the large pile and fed their smaller fires. One man in the ring began chanting. The dancers stamped one foot forward, then stepped back forcefully on the other. Their bodies rocked fore and aft gracefully to the rhythm of the song. After a while, they began to move slowly sideways, still facing the ring's interior. An older man beat a goatskin drum in time. Once in a while, an exuberant young man leaped and twirled about.

Jade listened closely to the chant and tried to make out the words. She was naturally gifted with languages, and her understanding of Swahili had improved rapidly since her arrival in Kenya. Unfortunately, they sang in their own Kikuyu language. Madeline explained that the song probably recounted killing the hyena as well as the evil done by the hyena.

Gradually, the dancers broke into smaller rings around each fire and chose a preferred group or style of dancing. Other men took up the chant and recounted other tales. Little children ran from one group to the other with glee and imitated the steps of the young men and women. Harry explained that this was, in fact, a small *ngoma* and that the harvest ones were very large and involved many neighboring villages. He added that the dance would continue until dawn

148

and suggested they ride back before it became too late.

Jade made her farewells and thanks to the chief and the other elders in her broken Swahili and reluctantly left the village. There was something very dignified in the sedate dance style around small fires, and she keenly felt the honor given to her. She raised her head a little higher, and the night sky, set pavé-style with the gems of Africa, drew her attention.

The Southern Cross sparkled overhead in splendor and ruled the southern hemisphere with the Milky Way draped as its train. Scorpio sprawled out closer to the horizon, its whiplike tail ready to sting, but Sagittarius held his bow in front, ready to destroy the scorpion. Jade wondered what names and stories the Kikuyu or the Maasai gave to these constellations. Would Scorpio be a cobra or mamba snake? Would Sagittarius be a famous chief?

She looked around for any other familiar constellations and found them behind her. The Great Bear still pointed the way north, and Draco still wrapped itself around the Little Bear. She pivoted in her saddle to ease her neck, looked northeast, and picked out Leo racing above the eastern horizon. Jade touched the mark on her wrist. It seemed Leo was her personal constellation now, but she found she missed Orion, the first constellation her father taught her after the two bears. She missed David, too, and wondered if he watched from the back of Cygnus, the swan, as it flew across the

149

heavens. What other constellation could a pilot choose?

★ ★ ★

So the woman had protection, did she? Well, it was only Kikuyu magic, weak like their warriors, he thought scornfully. Had it protected any of them so far? No. Even his teacher's magic was weak compared to his own. He was stronger because his hate was greater. Suddenly, a new thought entered the man's brain. Perhaps this woman had strength, too, strength born of courage. That would make the Kikuyu shaman's ointment more potent.

The man found it difficult to believe that any woman had strength. They all tended to be weakened by their emotions. Why would this one be any exception? Still, he had underestimated this one's bravery. Through his beast's eyes, he had witnessed her coolness and heard her sharp, commanding voice through his animal's ears. Perhaps, he mused, she should be tested . . . tonight.

11

'East Africa is overwhelmingly vibrant. Nothing is done by halves. The daytime heat, the nighttime cold, the smells, and the sounds all do their utmost to make themselves keenly felt, but most especially the nocturnal sounds. Anyone who has huddled in a tent and heard the robust and husky roar of Simba announcing his lordship in the night will know that they have just heard the voice of indomitable Africa itself.'
— The Traveler

The excitement of the *NGOMA* subsided much like the spent energy of a flash flood, and like a flood, it scoured out hidden nooks and recesses in Jade's mind. It swept away the thin cavalier veneer, uncovered memories and raw emotions, and left her feeling exposed, drained, and utterly fatigued. She retired to her hut and pulled the bamboo door shut behind her. Since she had brought no change of clothes along, she limited her night preparations to slipping off her boots and standing them on the chair with her hat on top. Then she lay down on the cot in her trousers, shirt, and stocking feet with her Winchester beside her and listened to the night sounds.

Somewhere in the distance, a male lion announced himself with a deep, throaty roar. Percy took up the challenge from his pen and roared back lustily. The bellowing challenges continued for several minutes and finally ended in a series of deep, husky *harrumphs* that chugged like steam engines. Jade smiled. Percy still held his territory even if he had no harem of lionesses to defend. A night bird called in high, piercing trills, and Jade succumbed to sleep.

In her dreams, two sorcerers battled, transforming objects into an array of animals amid puffs of chalky powders. One grizzled and evil-looking witch with a raw red scar across his pale chest raised his hands high above his head and called up a hyena from the dust. The ugly brute shook itself and cackled its hideous laugh before it devoured three entire goats.

The second sorcerer, a shriveled old man, smeared Jade with a sticky paste, and she watched her body cover itself in a tawny fur. The new lioness slew the hyena as it lay on the ground, bloated and heavy with its victims. She roared her triumph, feeling the power well up from her chest and out her throat.

The scarred witch shook with fury and locked his hate-reddened eyes on Jade. Without breaking his hypnotic stare, he conjured up a massive, black-maned lion to attack. It grew out of the constellation Leo as first one star and then another took on muscle and sinew. The beast roared down at the earth, shattering the night sky with its thunderous bellow. A rain of falling stars cascaded to the ground and caught fire in the dry grass.

The lion leaped to the burning ground and padded around. Intense roars from his cavernous mouth announced his prowess. The footfalls of his huge paws sent tremors along the earth, and Jade felt the shock ride up her spine. She couldn't move. His deep, huffing grunts rasped out of his massive chest as he dared anyone to attack him. Then he, too, locked his amber eyes on Jade and tensed his hind limbs.

On her cot, Jade shivered and tossed as the dream grew more threatening. She tried to shout, but the cries strangled into a whimper in her throat. Then the soft sound of fur brushing against wood woke her. For a moment she lay still on her back and tried again to separate reality from the nightmare. The sound repeated itself. Jade froze.

Something scrabbled and scratched with large claws at the bamboo door. She strained her ears to listen. To her horror, the sound wasn't outside her door. It was inside. Something had pulled the door open and slid past it into her hut. Its footfalls, though muffled on the dirt floor, sent shock waves up the cot's legs and jarred her aching knee. Jade had prior experience with prowling, nocturnal black bears. This animal was a quadruped and a large one at that. *A lion?*

The distinct musky aroma of a male animal mingled with the sickening scent of carrion. Jade forced back the nausea rising in her throat. She'd never felt so helpless. Air raids, artillery fire, and exploding shells never shook her as did this silent, stealthy padding in the dark. A cold sweat trickled down from her forehead and dribbled into her eyes. She tensed to keep herself from the

153

convulsive shivers that threatened to give her away to the beast.

The animal stopped moving. She felt its warmth inches from her face. *Get a hold of yourself. Think!* A sudden move for the rifle would only alarm it. Jade wasn't sure what the reaction of *this* animal would be but doubted it would hesitate or run like a black bear. *Cats like moving prey.* She lay perfectly still and prayed it was only Biscuit wandering loose in the night.

She listened in vain for the cheetah's purr. The beast brushed against the cot beside her and moved the bed with its bulk. Her rifle clattered to the floor. A snarl was followed by a throaty growl that rumbled like thunder. Both sounds spoke of menace. *It's not Biscuit. Did Percy get loose?*

Visions of Colonel Patterson's man-eaters ran through her head, which swam in dizziness. Perhaps if she startled it with a sudden shout she'd have time to grab her rifle.

Hot, wet breath blew across her face, down her chest, before the beast sniffed at her belt. The creature snorted loudly in disgust and backed abruptly away. She heard the sound of the chair shifting, another violent snort, and the animal bolted out the open door.

Jade forced herself to sit up. She pivoted around on the cot and grabbed her rifle from the floor. Moonlight filtered in through the cracks and the open door. Her eyes adjusted to the darkened room and picked out discernible shapes from indistinguishable shadows. *Empty!* And the door was ajar. She raced over and stared out into the night. *Why is it so dark?* She looked up at the black, empty sky. *Where are the stars? Was the dream true? Did they really fall?*

Jade gagged from the fear knotting her stomach. One hand clasped her rifle and the other grabbed the door and quickly pulled it shut. *Why is there no way to bar the door from inside?* She removed her belt, slid it between the bamboo poles of the door and the hut, and tied the door shut. Then she collapsed back onto the cot and let her muscles give in to fear's quaking aftershocks.

Somewhere in the night sleep overtook her again, but it was fitful, and she woke often. At dawn, Jade got up and reached for her boots. Her hand stopped in midair. Before her loomed the muddy print of a huge cat's paw stamped on the chair. Jade remembered Biscuit's feet. Not only were they smaller, but a cheetah's claws didn't retract. They would have left scratches or muddy traces. These claws were retracted; a lion's print, and a monstrous one at that. *Percy?*

Jade pulled on her boots and hat, untied the door, grabbed the belt, and ran out of the hut towards the animal pens. Percy sat in the middle of his locked cage, serenely washing himself. He looked at her calmly, then returned to licking his tawny sides. Jade looked at the dirt in the pen, hoping to find the red mud that her nocturnal visitor had left behind. *Dry!*

A wild lion had found its way into her hut last night. *It stalked me, just like in my dream!*

Jade suddenly recalled the animal had sniffed her belt and snorted in disgust. She brought the

155

belt, still gripped in her hands, to her face and inhaled. The pungent odor of the sorcerer's paste emanated from the leather. She found herself considering the genuine protective properties of that concoction with gratitude.

12

'If society whirls, as people say, then the Muthaiga Club is the Nairobi pivot. Jackal hunts, polo matches, horse races, and safaris are planned here. They're also resurrected here with the prey becoming more elusive, the winning point more difficult, the horse faster, and the shot more impossible with each retelling. The flamingo pink building and its two dining wings (so divorced couples don't have to eat in the same room with their ex-spouses) has hosted innumerable parties for nobles and notables. Dine, dance, drink, and flirt with elegant abandon. Use the outdoor electric lights for target practice. Come in a dinner jacket and tie for evening dinner or in bush gear for a drink. The Muthaiga promises all its visitors good fortune.'
— The Traveler

Neither Madeline nor Neville said anything about hearing a lion in the night. Jade kept the event to herself lest they think her prone to delusions. Only Harry commented that she 'looked like hell' and asked if she'd had a bad night. After breakfast, Harry, the Thompsons, and Jade left Hascombe's ranch and rode to Colridge's farm. Roger tagged along, and he and Harry spent the entire ride together. Jade couldn't hear their conversation, but it seemed animated. She presumed Harry was renewing his bid for a merger. At the edge of Colridge's farm, Harry took off with Roger, and with them went another opportunity for Jade to prod Harry for more information about Gil. The Thompsons and Jade rode to Colridge's house, returned the horses, discussed the *ngoma*, and retrieved the Thompsons' old box-bodied motorcar.

Madeline nodded off during the drive back to town, to Jade's great relief. She still felt too frayed and exposed after last night to handle personal conversation. She needed time to rebuild her defenses. Neville pulled up in front of the Norfolk and Jade went in while Neville woke his wife. Jade ran upstairs to her room and washed; then she tossed Gil's map and the chain with the bone into her open suitcase. Since Jelani had remained in the village, Jade went back down and explained his absence to the hotel proprietor, who seemed to have not even noticed he was gone.

'The native lads come and go,' he said. But he was delighted to report that he'd secured a motorcar for her. 'The garage just purchased it from a Boer down south.'

'A Boer?' repeated Jade. 'Do you know his name? Was it Kruger?'

The man shook his head. 'I don't know his name. One of our local lads brought the car up. Not exactly new,' he explained, 'but it is American like you, miss. Are you interested?'

Jade admitted that she was and received directions to the garage. 'Please settle my bill. I'll pick up my luggage as soon as I come back with the car.' She turned for the front door to tell the

Thompsons and collided head-on with a man coming in. 'Excuse me,' she began.

'Not at all. I was hoping to bump into you.'

Jade recognized the baritone voice and looked up quickly. 'Mr Hascombe,' she exclaimed in surprise. 'You're the last person I expected to see today in Nairobi.' She stepped back a pace to allow him room to enter.

He touched his hat brim in salute. 'Roger and I rode straight here after we left you. Decided we'd better put our names down for that safari before you changed your mind. Told them I'd see to the details. Just left their office,' he explained, 'when I saw you come in here. Thompson said you were packing up, so I thought perhaps I could be of help with your luggage.'

'Thank you. I'm going to pick up a motorcar, but I'll be back shortly.' She slipped past him and escaped into the open air. *Amazing how one man can make a lobby feel so crowded.*

Neville and Madeline had headed down the street to pick up a dress she'd left for alterations and an ax he'd left for a new handle. Jade walked in the opposite direction, to the garage. To her delight, she found herself behind the wheel of a Ford. Its chassis had been replaced by wooden sides to make the standard box-body vehicle preferred in this rugged terrain, but the blood and guts of the machine was all Model T. When Jade puttered back to the hotel, she found not only the Thompsons but also Mr Hascombe waiting on the veranda with her luggage.

'I didn't expect you to already have my bags. I wasn't packed yet.' Jade rarely blushed, but the

159

thought of him fumbling with her undergarments nearly pushed her to it.

Harry Hascombe flashed a wide, toothy grin. 'Have no fear. The desk clerk went up with me. Everything was neatly stowed away except for your traveling costume. It had just been cleaned, so I bundled it carefully on top and brought everything down.' He nodded to the bags. 'You're not only tidy; you pack lightly. I like that. No need for all sorts of frivolities.'

Jade didn't think two men handling her clothes made the situation any better than one. But frontier gallantry aside, she decided to check the room herself for stray articles. It was true, she had repacked most of her belongings before the hyena shoot, but she wanted to be sure.

'Thank you, but I think I'll go up and make certain I have everything.'

'I'll go with you, Jade,' said Madeline. 'Neville will put your bags in our car.'

Jade picked up the room key and dashed upstairs. Madeline followed on her heels. 'I do apologize for Harry, Jade. He meant well. He's just used to his rough bachelor ways.'

Jade unlocked the room door. 'Please don't fret yourself, Madeline,' she said. 'I'm not all *that* offended.' She opened the various bureau drawers and found them all empty.

Madeline looked under the bed, while Jade checked the adjoining bathroom. 'I think he's taken an interest in you,' Madeline said with a note of hope in her voice.

Jade returned with a tortoiseshell comb in her hand. She stopped in front of Madeline and waggled the implement in her face. 'Madeline, I think what you are trying to do is sweet, but stop it. I like Mr Hascombe. He's very colorful, but I am *not* interested in matchmaking.'

Madeline pouted. 'But you two are perfect for each other. You're both adventuresome and intelligent — '

'And he must be at least twenty years my senior,' added Jade. 'Thank you again, but no. I'll gladly hunt with him, talk to him, and eat with him, but I draw the line at marrying him.'

'You poor thing,' cooed Madeline. 'Your heart must be absolutely broken. Perhaps if we give it time,' she suggested.

Jade knew enough to not continue the argument. Instead, she simply turned and fixed her eyes on her new friend. Madeline flinched and looked away. It worked every time. 'This is everything,' Jade said, holding up the comb. 'Shall we go?'

She returned the key, thanked the proprietor, and went out to the cars. Jade wanted to stop at the local doctor's office to ask about Gil's death, but Madeline wanted to get home, so she followed Neville to their farm eighteen miles to the northeast. There would be time, she reasoned, before the safari to come back to town. She'd see the commissioner then, too.

Madeline rode with Jade and described their coffee plantation, her gardens, their two dogs, and their assorted projects with a good deal of vivacity and color. 'Neville thought perhaps a good moneymaking project to help with our overdraft would be to herd crocodiles from the

161

rivers into traps and kill them safely there. I gather there's quite a good market for ladies' pocket-books and shoes in crocodile leather. Have you ever owned any?'

'No, but I did have a pair of boots that bit my toes every time I wore them.'

Madeline laughed at the joke, her voice rippling in merry peals. 'Oh, I do wish you'd marry Harry.' She sighed. 'I should so much like to have you as a neighbor.'

Jade smiled at the frontier concept of neighbor — anyone within fifty miles. They passed the Ruiru flumes and saw no trace of the hapless hippo. She wasn't surprised. Scavengers rarely left much behind.

'Forget herding crocodiles. You should write stories about life in the colony, Madeline,' suggested Jade. 'You'd be very good at it, and it sounds safer.'

'Do you think?'

Jade shrugged. 'Certainly. You must have dozens of stories about the farm, the Africans, and Nairobi. Your real characters are better than most fictional ones.'

Madeline beamed. 'Well, perhaps I could try one. I rather like romances.' She winked at Jade. 'I have just the right hero and heroine, too.'

The remainder of the drive's conversation revolved around the coffee farm and how the war had hurt so many farms due to neglect while owners were away at war. Between that and anthrax, many colonists found themselves forced to take out large loans.

'Not that our overdraft is so large,' Madeline

explained. 'Neville has flat feet, so he served nearby overseeing transport operations. He was able to keep an eye on the farm off and on.'

The Thompsons' home fell in a class between Lord Colridge's fancy estate and Harry's rectangular shedlike structure and assorted huts. The main house's stone foundation and walls rose to at least three feet in height, an indication that there once was enough money to hire a Sikh mason but not enough to complete the entire house. The upper portion was a put-together job of galvanized tin and wood from local hardwood trees. A separate building housed the kitchen.

Like Hascombe's house, gardens surrounded the building, and a veranda ran the length of one long side. Any similarity ended there. Blooming bougainvillea vines shaded both the veranda and the privy with aromatic flowers and cool leaves. Colorful blossoms ranging from flaming red-hot pokers to delicate pink roses alternated with assorted edibles in the gardens. Jade took this to be the 'woman's touch,' as Madeline had previously expressed it.

The day was far advanced by the time they arrived, so Madeline busied herself with urging the cook into dinner preparations while Jade unpacked in the guest room. Happily, the bottles of photographic developers were intact, as were the boxes of film and ammunition. Her clothing was another matter. The traveling dress sat in a rolled-up wad atop her other clothes and, since nothing had been strapped in, everything sat collapsed into a jumbled heap.

Men! Doesn't it occur to them to secure the

163

clothes inside before shutting the case? She shook out her best dress and draped it across a chair back. Perhaps the wrinkles would come out if she hung it over the tin bathtub full of hot water. She dumped the remaining contents on the bed, sorted them systematically, and put them in the dresser.

The dresser was a makeshift affair arranged from six of the ubiquitous, empty *debes*, wedged with the open ends facing out of a wooden frame with a wooden top. Jade refolded her undergarments and placed them in two of the cubbyholes. Two spare shirts went in a third, another set of trousers and her corps overskirt in the fourth, and a nightdress in a fifth. As she lifted the nightgown, Gil's map, the solicitor's sealed packet, and the ring box tumbled out onto the bed. She fished the hyena's chain from the pile and slipped it into her pocket.

Madeline rapped on the door and came in. 'Is there anything you need? I hope you don't mind our simple furniture,' she said. 'The bed is actually quite nice.'

'It's fine, Madeline. You can see for yourself,' she said as she pointed to her meager clothes in the *debe* drawers, 'I don't surround myself with luxuries. I hope I don't shock everyone with my trousers,' she added. 'I grew quite used to them during the war. Most of these items are my uniform pieces. Everything else was too out of style even for me. Didn't have the time or the inclination to get new things.'

'Lots of the farm wives wear their husband's old trousers at home.' Madeline sat down on the

164

edge of the bed and watched Jade sort her toiletries on top of the dresser. 'Can I hand you anything?' she asked and turned to the nearly empty suitcase. 'Oh? What's this? Is Abel your father's name?'

Jade turned suddenly and saw Madeline holding the packet in one hand. 'Please, if you would, just put that back.' Jade's stern voice startled Madeline, and she dropped the packet on the bed. Jade grabbed both the packet and the ring box and shoved them in a cubbyhole.

'I'm sorry,' Madeline said to Jade's back. She studied Jade in silence for a moment. 'You know, it isn't good to keep things inside. If you want to talk, I know how to keep secrets.'

'Thank you,' said Jade softly. She gripped the sides of the dresser and steadied herself. 'I appreciate your concern, and I'll keep it in mind. But not now,' she added, turning around. 'All I need now is a place to hang these two dresses.' She pulled two wooden hangers from her suitcase and slipped the good dress on one and the traveling costume on the other.

Madeline showed her the hooks on the far wall for hanging clothes and pointed out the nicer features of the room, such as the sanded wooden walls, a pull-down board that served as a writing desk, and the distant view of the south garden from the window. 'You can leave the shutters ajar at night. We have mosquito netting to cover the bed.'

After last evening, it seemed that mosquitoes weren't the only danger in a seemingly safe

165

bedroom. Jade shook it off. 'Is there time for a tour?'

'As long as you like.' The two women spent the remainder of the daylight hours strolling the grounds until dinnertime. Half of the coffee trees had been cut down to mere stumps after some fungus infected the leaves, and another five years would pass before they produced. The other trees, however, remained full and lush with young berries. These would provide ammunition against the overdraft. Neville joined them from his inspection of the coffee trees, and the three talked of coffee farming, both during and after dinner until they retired.

Jade slept fitfully. Her mind replayed the old Kikuyu's notion that two men were behind the native deaths. Could there be something to his dreams? And how would a hyena, controlled or not, get into Gil's room to maul him? It seemed Mr Jacobs' theory of murder was true, but for the life of her, she couldn't figure out how anyone had managed to kill Gil Worthy. With all this troubling her, Jade woke often and finally lit a lamp. She added her questions to her notebook, wrote an article on the hyena hunt, and penned a brief letter to Beverly before reattempting sleep.

Madeline again played hostess the next day and took Jade to see some of the local sights, including a small concrete reservoir that Neville had constructed and their citrus groves. Finally, as it drew on to midafternoon, Madeline decided it was time to prepare for Lord Colridge's evening dinner party. Baths were ordered and taken in turn using a tin tub in a small bathing room, and the three of them worked to make themselves look smart. Jade worked with less: less vanity, less at stake, and fewer resources at her disposal. She combed out her short, naturally wavy black hair and slipped on her dress, stockings, and shoes.

Her one new dress was a birthday gift from Beverly. The gown of apricot-colored silk crêpe had a short-sleeved bolero jacket trimmed in green satin ribbon over a straight shift that hung to her lower calves. Jade had refused to buy matching dress shoes and settled for wearing her slightly outdated black leather slip-ons. Jade wasn't against looking her best. She just wanted to be comfortable while doing it.

She sat on the edge of her bed and looked at her wrist. Despite all the scrubbing, the sorcerer's mark remained. *What will Nairobi society make of it?* She decided if she kept her left hand to her side or in her lap, no one would notice it.

Madeline came out in her made-over, royal blue satin dress with a high waist, and sighed. 'It isn't fair. You could be covered in soot and still look ravishing with that hair and complexion of yours. I need a bit of powder to hide the wrinkles, and it takes so long to sweep up my hair.' She patted her coiffure. 'I do hope short hair becomes the fashion. It would be so much simpler.'

'Why wait for Paris to decide? Set the trend yourself.'

'But what would people like Lord Colridge say

if I cut my hair?' worried Madeline. 'They might think I was improper rather than just trying to be practical.'

Neville caught the end of the conversation and tugged at his dinner tie and tight collar.

'Men's fashions could stand a bit of rational change as well,' he said. 'You may cut your hair as you please, Maddy, if I may chuck this blasted noose around my neck.'

'Perhaps we may do both *after* we have secured the steam engine from His Lordship,' suggested his wife.

Conversation lagged during the drive so that all eyes could concentrate on spotting potential road hazards in the dark. Finally the Muthaiga's pink exterior appeared from beyond its extensive grounds and beckoned them to escape from the cares and trials of colonial life. The Muthaiga greeted each of its guests with *Na Kupa Hati M'zuri* carved into the great fireplace's stones. 'I Bring You Good Fortune' might be an idle promise, but Jade hoped not. She needed some good luck to find David's half brother, if he still existed, and Gil Worthy's murderer.

Lord Colridge greeted them at the entrance to the lounge with less promise of prosperity than the fireplace but much more personally. 'Miss del Cameron, delighted to see you again. You look stunning. Hardly recognize you. Mrs Thompson, beautiful as always. Thompson, good of you to come. Think I have a line on that engine for you. Should do just the thing.' He shook their hands, the ladies' gently, Neville's with great strength. 'Come on, come on,' he said with a trace of impatience. 'Can't dawdle over pleasantries; there are people I wish you to meet. Been telling them about you and that hyena.'

He ushered them farther into the spacious lounge towards a short, burly blond man; a tall, effeminate-looking man with long black hair to his collar; and a buxom, heavily made-up middle-aged woman decked out in diamonds. A pretty red-haired lady stood meekly nearby.

The buxom woman's brunette hair was swept back in an elaborate roll held in place with a comb sporting two ostrich feathers. They reminded Jade of the papyrus heads by the Athi River. The redhead's hair was also rolled back but more simply, with only a tortoiseshell comb holding it in place. Both of their dresses were cut in the latest mode with form-fitting, sleeveless bodices. The older woman's gown sported a blue-and-silver brocade overskirt over a darker blue taffeta. Blue and silver tassels hung down the front of the skirt and sashayed saucily when she moved, which she did frequently just to set them in motion. The younger lady's pink taffeta dress looked equally expensive but more tasteful. Its embellishments were restricted to a wide, high-waisted satin ribbon tied and draped down the back.

Jade whispered to Madeline, 'I see a preening peacock, a fat pigeon, a turkey, and a mouse. And me without my rifle.'

Madeline whispered back, 'Now we'll see how brave you *really* are, Simba Jike. Some of these women will try to eat you alive.'

Jade's lips twisted in a wry smile. 'But I'm

prickly and hard to swallow.'

Lord Colridge did the honors. 'Mr Stanley Woodard and his lovely wife, Isadore. May I present Miss del Cameron,' he said as he introduced the short blond man and the buxom brunette. A series of 'how do you do's' and 'charmeds' went the rounds, followed by the second introduction. 'And this,' he said, indicating the tall, thin, pasty-looking man and the young redhead, 'is Godfrey Kenton, the second son of the Earl of Kenton, and his new bride, Leticia.'

Mrs Kenton stood passively beside her husband and only glanced up from the floor long enough to murmur a weak, 'Pleased to meet you.' Her wan spouse simply flopped a gloved hand in the air from an equally limp arm. The man dressed like the proverbial fop with an ascot around his neck held by a diamond stickpin.

Jade found herself repulsed by him. His lady certainly looked cowed, but he appeared to be too much of a milksop to be a physical wife beater. Jade concluded that he mentally abused her. He looked underdone in a way, like a newly molted crayfish, all pale and naked without its protective exoskeleton.

'Madeline, how good to see you again,' said Isadore Woodard. 'And how sweet your old dress looks all made over. Almost stylish. I do wish I had your touch for economy. It really is tedious to have to order new gowns from Paris every time the fashion changes.'

'How very true, Dorrie,' replied Madeline. 'And you have the added burden of knowing that you aren't supporting England or her colonies, which must be frightful. You have my complete sympathies.'

Jade maintained her diplomatic poker face with difficulty. This was a new side to Madeline. 'Lord Colridge must have told you that I'm a writer doing a feature on the colony,' she interposed before the claws came completely out. 'May I ask how long you have lived here?'

'Isadore and I have been here ten years,' said Mr Woodard. 'Sisal farm, you know. But my wife prefers to live in town, so I built a house close by the club for her.'

'And you, Mrs Kenton?' Jade asked the pretty redhead.

'Ahem,' replied her husband in a nasally drawl. 'My wife has lived in the colony longer than I have, though she's been away. We are both newly arrived here immediately since the war.'

Once again Jade tried to get the timid wife to speak for herself. 'So you lived here before the war, Mrs Kenton?'

The young woman looked up at her husband and, on receiving a nod of permission, answered, 'Yes, Miss del Cameron. My parents came to the colonies when I was a little girl of eight and began a farm. Father sent Mother and me back when the war began. Father was wounded during the war . . . unable to keep up with the more strenuous labor. My . . . husband was good enough to pay off his overdraft and enable him to return to England.'

And you, thought Jade, *came as part of the transaction*. She wondered what had happened

171

to the farm as she could hardly imagine this soft-bodied grub doing any manual work. A little salt on him and he'd positively shrivel up like any other slug. In any event, none of them could have known Gil Worthy. She lost what little interest she had in them.

'I have a few other people for you to meet, Miss del Cameron,' said Lord Colridge. He took her arm and led her away. The Thompsons followed, glad to escape further conversation with either of the couples. 'Some important people could not be here, I'm afraid. Short notice, you know. I should have liked to introduce you to Baron Bror Blixen and his wife, Karen. The baron is probably off hunting, and the baroness runs their coffee farm at Ngong.'

'No doubt Blix is hunting a pretty face,' said a deep voice. Everyone turned to see Harry Hascombe approaching from a back room. Roger Forster walked beside him, his face sullen.

'Hascombe,' said Colridge. 'I wondered where you'd run off to.'

'In the bar,' said Harry, 'hashing out safari plans with Roger.'

'Good evening, Mr Hascombe, Mr Forster,' said Jade. 'Good to see you again.' Roger made a slight bow but didn't speak. His hangdog face looked longer than before.

'Call me Harry, please.'

'Very well,' snorted Colridge. 'Miss del Cameron already knows you two. I have other people for her to meet. Now where the devil did Donaldson go?' He peered around the room in vain. 'Oh, blast,' he exclaimed and fluttered his mustache. 'Thompson, look after Miss del Cameron for me while I find that idiot Donaldson.'

'If he's an idiot, why do we need to find him?' Jade asked after he left.

Harry laughed. 'Because he's a *rich* idiot, and His Lordship puts a lot of stock in that.'

'And why not?' blurted Roger. 'Money means land and power out here.'

Harry scowled at his younger companion. 'Go back to the bar and have another drink, Rog, if you're going to be so confounded moody.' Roger took his advice and left the room.

Harry ran his dark eyes over Jade and flashed his teeth. 'My, you are beautiful.' He bowed. 'I meant that in a gentlemanly fashion, of course.'

Jade acknowledged the compliment and returned it. 'You clean up rather well yourself, Harry.' In his black dinner jacket, boiled shirt, starched collar, and white tie he did make a striking appearance. He had shaved again, too. Jade decided that the gray temple hairs looked distinguished on him.

Colridge returned with several richly dressed people in tow and introduced them to Jade, explaining their importance in the British protectorate. Donaldson, it seemed, raised very fine racehorses. The other man, a Mr Seton, and his slightly tipsy wife had something to do with the government, and Jade frankly didn't listen to what the others did. They were too pretentious and silly acting to be of interest, and too young to be of use in her search. Of more interest was

173

the hateful stare that Donaldson directed at Godfrey Kenton.

The tipsy wife spied Mr Woodard and trotted across the room to grab hold of his arm. Mrs Woodard, in the meantime, had sidled up to some other gentleman, a commissioner, if Jade heard Madeline correctly. No wonder she wanted a house in town, thought Jade. And no wonder Mr Woodard was so agreeable, Harry had stepped back to the bar for a moment.

'Mr Seton,' Jade said, 'I'm trying to look up some news of an old friend of the family, a Mr Gil Worthy. Perhaps you've heard of him?'

Mr Seton clasped his hands behind his back and rocked to and fro on the balls of his feet. 'Worthy, ah yes, I believe he died a few years ago. Mauling or something of that nature.'

Jade nodded. 'Yes. That much I've heard, but have you any idea what he was doing in Nairobi before his death?'

Seton shook his head. 'Sorry, Miss del Cameron. I was not privy to his business. Never knew the man.'

'Perhaps you could help me find someone else. I'm going on safari soon and I heard good things about a Mr Kruger. Do you know him?'

'Sorry, but the Boers keep to themselves, you know. Most just come and go. Good luck finding any particular one, especially one with a common name such as Kruger.'

Harry, who had returned with a fresh drink in hand, overheard the last part of the conversation. 'What are you up to now?'

Without revealing Gil's map, Jade explained

that Gil had the name Kruger written on a slip of paper. She thought locating him could be helpful.

'He could be someone Gil met in Tsavo after I left,' said Harry. 'Seton's right, though. It's a common name.'

Just then Jade spied another woman stumble over to Roger. Jade watched her gesticulate first impatiently and then imploringly, but Roger waved her off. He seemed preoccupied and disinclined to indulge the woman in whatever she wanted. Madeline came up beside Jade and said something about Cissy being drunk again, but Jade was now busy watching Roger's moon-eyed look towards the lovely Mrs Kenton. At that point, the young lady glanced up, and her eyes opened wide in surprise.

'Roger?' Leticia said in a tone of disbelief.

'Leticia,' he answered with tenderness.

The almost-an-earl looked around sharply at his wife's call, scowled at Roger, and hauled his bride away.

Madeline caught Jade's stare and whispered, 'Later,' before she said more audibly, 'Jade, would you care for champagne?'

'What? Oh, no, thank you,' she answered.

'I heard you had a dreadfully exciting encounter with a hyena,' said Mr Donaldson. 'Bravo shooting the beast. Important in their own way, I suppose, but a disgusting nuisance. They've been harassing my dogs. Have you anything like them in America?'

'Coyotes.' The man shook his head, signaling that he didn't understand. Jade explained, 'They

175

resemble a small wolf. Sheep ranchers hate them. It's rather curious, actually,' she remarked. 'Now that I think on it, the coyote is the familiar of Indian skin walkers. That's remarkably like the African *laibon* using the hyena.'

'How interesting,' said Neville. 'Don't you agree, Harry?'

'What it suggests is that witches everywhere recognize potential power in animals that others slight as cowardly pests,' said Harry. 'At least they exploit the fear of it, in any event.'

'Pish tosh,' exclaimed Lord Colridge. 'They are calling us to dinner. Come along. No more nonsensical drivel. I'm hungry. Someone fetch Forster from the bar,' His Lordship commanded, and everyone obeyed.

Wedgwood china worked in a rose pattern, delicate crystal goblets, and fresh red roses graced the linen-clad dining table. Jade found herself wedged between Donaldson on her right and the insipid Godfrey Kenton on her left. Harry managed to position himself opposite her. Roger sat like a faithful hound at his side and gazed longingly at Leticia Kenton through the entire soup course and then as often as he dared after. Jade reasoned that Roger had lost her to a more powerful — that is, richer — rival and would have sympathized if the young man showed a little more spine himself. She once caught both Roger and Harry glaring at Kenton with undisguised loathing.

Madeline had managed to get Neville between herself and Isadore Woodard. Poor Neville didn't appear comfortable being assigned the part of a protective chair by his wife to keep the catty woman on the other side at bay. Soup was followed by a fruit salad, then squab in a light cream sauce and asparagus tips. Wine flowed freely around the table, though Jade never allowed the level to drop in her own glass. Somehow, letting her guard down here seemed hazardous. Instead, she sipped water, made brief remarks when necessary, and listened.

'So the bullet went into the beast's spine, but you know the buffalo can't stop himself even to die. Worse than a rhino. Naturally, there was nothing left for me to do but . . . '

'Honestly, I caught him stealing from the storeroom, but how can you trust . . . '

'Your Lordship, how is your new Willys-Knight Overlander? Do you think . . . '

'You *must* go to Cissy's next party.' The voice dropped to a hushed tone. 'Of course, I don't know who her supplier is, but I hear the quality is top-notch . . . '

'I have it on good authority that he won't divorce her because she has all . . . '

Eventually, by the time custard was served, Jade knew one thing for certain — very few people spoke to Godfrey Kenton, and both Harry and Roger hated him. Since none of this helped her learn anything about David's father or brother, she thought about talking Madeline and Neville into leaving for the farm with her. That was when Isadore suggested everyone adjourn to the lobby, wind up the gramophone, and dance.

Jade rose with the others, not as quickly as

Harry, but certainly faster than the tediously dull slug, Kenton, next to her. At first she assumed that Harry had hurried around the table to escort her into the lobby, but instead he stepped up to Kenton, grabbed him by his lapels, and hoisted him out of his chair.

'I just heard from Seton that *someone* is claiming my cattle have anthrax. Now, just who do you suppose started that lie?' his voice growled low and menacingly.

Kenton whimpered something unintelligible, and Jade put a restraining hand on Harry's right arm.

'Harry,' she said firmly, 'please leave off pummeling Mr Kenton and escort me to the dance floor.'

Hascombe flung Kenton away from him like he would a bit of offal and gave Jade his arm. 'My apologies, Miss del Cameron. I should have waited till later to thrash him as he deserves.'

'No doubt, but I think he got your point. And,' she added, 'if I'm supposed to call you Harry, then you had better call me Jade.'

Hascombe grinned. 'Jade it is, then.' He escorted her into the spacious lobby.

The chairs and end tables had already been dragged to the sides to make room for dancing, and one young man wound up the gramophone while his partner flipped through several records, looking for something suitable. A fast foxtrot played, and Harry guided Jade through the rapid footwork.

Harry's physical strength blended with an easy grace, resulting in an excellent dancing form. He

178

led with a masterful assurance without overpowering his partner. Jade found herself enjoying it very much. The foxtrot ended and a tango followed. Harry muttered something about not knowing how, and before Jade could respond, Mr Holly, one of the silly set, grabbed Jade's arm and pushed it straight out to the side while he pressed her tightly against his body.

The man was obviously drunk and barely in control of his legs. His leering grin made it crystal clear what was on his mind as he staggered out the slow-slow-quick-quick-slow tempo. Jade pulled back and inserted her free left hand against his chest to maintain some space between them. The man had little sense or else he overrated his personal charm because he threw Jade back into a deep dip and lunged for her neck. Jade saw Harry trot towards them, but she was faster. Her right hand pulled back in a fist and let fly a strong shot to the drunk's eye.

Her partner's head jerked back, and Jade broke free of his embrace. Mr Holly held a hand to his eye and weaved around the room, mouth agape, as he tried to figure out what had happened. Some of his friends laughed loudly at his plight and congratulated Jade.

'He should have known better than to mess with Memsahib Simba Jike,' said Harry. 'What's a jackal to her after killing a hyena?'

The group applauded his speech, and Donaldson shouted, 'Throw out the jackal.'

The crowd took up the chant, grabbed the drunk by his jacket and trousers, and tossed him outside the Muthaiga. He landed sprawling in the dust, where he promptly passed out. The Thompsons, Colridge, Harry, and Jade watched as his friends hauled the drunken Mr Holly into the backseat of a car. Then Jade noticed that Roger wasn't part of the crowd and wondered what had happened to him. She looked around and saw him standing in a far corner with Leticia, engaged in what appeared to be a passionate declaration. He held her hands clasped in his while he made his case. Leticia looked more woeful than before. Her husband staggered out of the men-only bar, where he'd gone to reinforce his own manhood, and spied them together.

This time Harry grabbed his friend before Godfrey Kenton could start trouble. 'You'd better go, Rog,' he urged. Roger left with a backwards look at Leticia and her reeling spouse.

'It was kind of you to look out for Mr Forster, but I can't imagine what Mr Kenton could have done, aside from throwing up or passing out on him,' said Jade. 'He doesn't strike me as being a particularly formidable opponent.'

'Never underestimate a wounded animal, Jade,' Harry replied, 'and a jealous husband who thinks he's being cuckolded falls square into that category. Kenton's an underhanded bloke who'll try to swindle anyone. I should know, as you may have gathered. He's probably the reason Roger lost his first herd with that anthrax scare. He even cheated Maasai once.'

The rest of the dinner guests hadn't noticed the near encounter. They were busily engaged in sticking butter pats on the table roses and tossing

180

them to the ceiling to see if they'd stay. Mrs Woodard put on a waltz and cornered Mr Donaldson for a dance. Mr Woodard was nowhere to be seen, but then neither was Seton's tipsy wife. Lord Colridge snoozed on a chair along the wall, an empty wineglass in his hand. The sound of a subdued argument caught Jade's ear. She turned to witness Godfrey Kenton expostulating harshly to his browbeaten wife.

'The Woodards will drive you home, Leticia,' Kenton said.

Leticia made little fists and waved them uselessly in front of her. 'Are you seeing that woman again, Godfrey?'

'That is not your concern, now, is it? But if you must know, I have a business meeting.' He waggled a slip of paper in front of her face.

Jade's attempt to hear more was stifled by a respectful hand at her elbow. She turned to see Harry standing beside her.

'May I have this dance, Jade?' he asked. She nodded.

Neville and Madeline were already dancing together, and Harry took Jade's hand and caught her up in the slow, dreamy rhythms of the waltz. She found herself remembering her first dance with David in Paris. She closed her eyes and could almost smell his scent. When she opened her eyes, it was to Harry's intent gaze and, for the first time in her life, Jade felt in danger of losing the staring contest. Just before she looked away, she attempted to divert him with small talk.

'Where did you learn to dance, Mr Has-combe?'

He didn't answer at first and, when he did, Jade felt the words hit like a rifle's recoil. 'You need to forget him, Jade,' he said softly. 'I could make you forget him, if you'd let me.'

Harry stopped dancing and simply held her in his arms. His eyes traveled from her hair, down her face to her lips, and lingered there. She pulled away.

'Madeline, I'm very tired. Shouldn't we be going?' She woke Colridge from his nap, made her grateful farewell to him, and stepped outside into the cool night air.

Jade knew Harry had wanted to kiss her, but what had startled her was that she'd felt dangerously close to letting him.

13

'In Africa, one feels the book of Genesis has come to life and is being played out for the world to see, if the world would only stop and look. Gardens of Eden as vibrant as the flowing springs and as dazzling as the shimmering sunbird's wings grow wild here. Alas, it's after the Fall, and the lion would just as soon devour as lie down with the lamb. Into this backdrop of life, the missionaries have come afire with zeal, attempting to set the garden ablaze.'
— The Traveler

Despite the late evening, Jade woke up very early the next morning and put on the same conservative serge suit she'd worn on the train. It was Sunday, and she intended to drive herself to the French mission. The Thompsons had protested against such an idea. They flatly stated that she'd get lost or worse, but Jade held her ground and countered all their arguments. She spoke French fluently, was capable of navigating on her own, knew how to drive and repair her motorcar, and was experienced ad nauseam with maneuvering along cratered roads and tracks. In the end, Neville drew a map for her and instructed their headman, Juma, to accompany her.

They left before dawn in the leased Ford and reached Nairobi by sunrise. From Nairobi, they turned east toward the Ngong hills. There, in the flatlands below the hills, stood a sturdy gray stone church planted by French missionaries. Their cultivation of souls was so successful that the church structure had grown to the point of sprouting a bell tower. The mission buildings sat square in the middle of a well-maintained coffee plantation like a quaint and tidy European village. The bell chimed as she drove down into the main grounds, past the rectory, and across an arched stone bridge to the church. A few Africans emerged from their nearby huts and headed in the church's direction. Others sat outside in the morning sun.

Jade parked the Ford a respectful distance away from the church so as not to cause too much of a distraction. Juma opted to remain in the village, so Jade walked into the church alone for Mass, presented in a curious blend of French-accented Latin and Swahili.

After Mass, Jade introduced herself to one of the missionary priests. Father Jacquinet stood two inches shorter than Jade. The wiry little man wore a brown robe, and his flowing beard, which reached his waist, completed the illusion of a gnome. He expressed delight at being addressed in his native tongue and quickly bustled her off to the cool refectory for a breakfast of crêpes stuffed with ripe pawpaws and topped with thick whipped cream. Juma, Jade noticed, had found his own way to one of the native huts and dined happily with other Kikuyu.

Father Jacquinet introduced Jade to his two colleagues, the elderly Father Robidoux and the younger Father Duflot. Each of the three priests listened intently to her tales of the Great War in their beloved homeland. They mourned the destruction of so many lives and beautiful farms and praised her great bravery. She asked them many questions about their mission and the coffee farm, which they gladly answered, trading news of themselves for news of others in and around Nairobi. They seemed to know a great deal about the colony, and Jade hoped one of them might have known or at least heard of Gil Worthy. Eventually she explained her own mission. They listened sympathetically and with keen interest.

'You assume then, mademoiselle, that Monsieur Worthy fathered a child in Africa and that someone killed him when he came back to find his son?' said Father Jacquinet. 'Have you thought perhaps he found his son and the son killed him?'

Jade shuddered. 'What a horrid idea, Father. No, I had not thought that, but I have good reason to think otherwise.' She told them what she knew about Gil's death and about the hyena that killed a boy in the Kikuyu village. 'Fathers, have you ever heard of a *laibon* using trained hyenas to kill?'

The three priests looked from one to the other and all but Father Jacquinet shook their heads. 'Evil knows no country, my child, so I am not surprised at the tales the Kikuyu tell of an evil *laibon*. But I ask myself, why would such a man want to kill your Englishman? Is it not more likely that a hungry wild animal, attracted

185

perhaps by a cut or a scent of food on Monsieur Worthy, was drawn inside? During the war, Nairobi was in much turmoil, and that agitated the animals, too.'

'But,' protested Jade, 'the Kikuyu boy said — '

Father Jacquinet finished for her. 'The boy was of course scared to hear a wild animal in the hotel. But he was also ashamed to have run away. Perhaps he feared a beating for not helping Monsieur Worthy. So he embellishes his tale with the supernatural to give his actions greater justification.'

'And the neck chain on the hyena?' asked Jade.

Father Jacquinet shrugged. 'Something of Monsieur Worthy's, a trinket of Africa.'

Jade sighed and put her head down. Father Robidoux patted her hand gently. 'You have an awesome quest, mademoiselle,' explained Father Robidoux, 'but not an impossible one. First, because nothing is impossible with God's aid, and second, because you look for an Englishman. They are becoming more numerous, it is true, but there are yet not so many of them as to make it impossible. Add to it that you look for an orphan Englishman, young like yourself, and that narrows the search.'

'It is true,' agreed Father Jacquinet. 'And the empire likes to keep records of its subjects, does it not? Surely there will be a record somewhere of his birth.'

Jade shook her head to indicate none so far. 'But you have not met someone such as that yourselves?' Jade asked without expecting an affirmative answer.

The three priests shook their heads again, and Father Duflot rose to get more coffee. 'The English do not associate with us,' said Father Jacquinet with a smile. 'We are French, for one,' he added with a wink. 'But that is the way of the world. What is different is shunned. Even here, families reject those who do not fit, even if it is their own child. A young woman who marries into a different tribe, or has a child outside of their own wedlock, is just as likely to be cast out as in our own countries. Luckily, the missions are havens for those who find them.'

They mused on such tragedies in mutual silence while the younger priest poured more of the rich, dark coffee and placed a fresh pot of cream on the table. They visited for a while longer, and Jade asked permission to photograph the mission.

Father Jacquinet took her to the coffee plantation with its tidy rows of coffee trees. He showed her the best views of the church and waited patiently while she took a picture. They passed a small cemetery, and Jade remarked on the scarcity of markers. 'Does no one die here?' she asked.

The little priest chuckled. 'Of course, mademoiselle, but very few wish burial. It is not the Kikuyu manner. Those interred are either very devout in their new faith or not Kikuyu. For instance,' he said, pointing into the cemetery, 'a Sudanese trader left his ailing son behind one time, and *many* years ago, a French Somali woman and her little child came. She had been cast away from her family and traveled all this way back to Nairobi. She came to us very ill, succumbed within a few weeks, and is buried here as well. An old Boer who drove oxen fell ill with the influenza and died recently.'

'A Boer? What was his name?'

Father Jacquinet pointed to a newer stone. 'Von Tonden.'

Jade didn't know whether to feel sorry that Kruger had again eluded her or relief that he might still be alive somewhere.

Father Jacquinet sensed her anxiety, turned to her, and gently took her hands in his. 'There are many like that,' he said. 'Wounded souls that are wandering, searching, much as you are now.'

Jade flinched. Involuntarily, she grabbled hold of the ring under her shirtwaist. An idea flashed in her mind.

'Father, have you ever seen a stone like this?' She took the cord holding the ring from around her neck and handed it to the priest. He held the ring and examined it, carefully taking in every detail. The lush green of the stone came to life under the bright sun and sparkled from within with a cool, flashing glow.

'Never,' he remarked softly. 'It is most interesting and beautiful.' He peered deeply into the gem. 'It is not an emerald,' he remarked finally. 'At least, I have never seen one that clear and with that command of light.' His work-hardened fingers traced the etched patterns on the ring's side. 'This is of all most curious. Only lines and curves. Do you know what it means?'

Jade shook her head. 'No, Father, I don't. If it's a family crest, it is one that no one connected

188

to the family knew about. I thought perhaps it might be some form of writing, but it doesn't look like any hieroglyphs I've ever seen before.'

'No,' he agreed. 'It does not. Perhaps the written variety, though? What is it called? The hieratic form?' He handed the ring back to Jade, and she slipped the cord over her head. 'I am not perhaps the most educated man to ask,' he said. 'To me it looks more like a child's scribbles, such as the children here make with a stick in the dirt.'

'I'm beginning to be afraid that is all it is,' said Jade with a sigh. 'A favorite scribbling of a lost child.'

The little man put a friendly hand on Jade's shoulder. 'Do not fear, mademoiselle. We will pray for your success.' He blessed her, and Jade thanked him.

She found Juma pleasantly engaged with an elderly man who just happened to have a pretty young daughter. The girl waited on them while they ate, and Jade found it difficult to tear him away from such attractions. She succeeded, finally, and they walked to the Ford.

Jade eyed the gently sloping hillside and decided the car would do just as well in forward as in reverse. She drove off with mixed feelings. It hardly surprised her that Gil Worthy and the French mission had never crossed paths. After all, he wasn't Catholic. But a part of her had still hoped for a bit of enlightenment. Perhaps tomorrow she would have better luck when she spoke to the doctor who had examined Gil's body. She decided to quit focusing on her problem and asked Juma how he had enjoyed his morning.

'Very fine,' he said. He added that the food, a traditional millet porridge, was plentiful and tasty. Jade asked about the pretty girl. Juma said she would cost too high a bride-price in order to keep her in that area. Her father had moved there to escape threats from the Wakamba tribe and felt protected by the white God. Juma scoffed at that notion. 'The white God lives in a fine house, but he did not protect his people from the big war. Why would he protect the Kikuyu at the mission?'

Jade tried to explain that God loved all people. He was their father. But children fought among themselves and disobeyed. Their disobedience started the war.

'When a child in his village disobeys his father or the elders, they take him in hand,' Juma said, 'to correct him. Why did not your God do that to the white men?'

'Perhaps,' she said sadly, 'that is just what he did.'

★   ★   ★

The witch huddled beneath the hyena skin and felt it mold to his body, or perhaps it would be more accurate to say that his body fitted itself to the hide. An hour had come and gone since he had performed the ritual and by now there wasn't much manlike about him except for his human mind. Even that, he knew, became more sharply honed, like a well-crafted weapon. More remarkably, some of that mental crafting lingered even when his man-form returned.

He flexed his powerful jaw muscles and felt their strength. They could crush a man's skull or rip out his throat. Years ago his teacher told him to use a lion skin, like he did, but he chose the hyena instead, a true night predator. What little he lost in size, he gained in sharper night vision. To his delight, he found that the hyena had tremendous strength for its size.

Power! That was what drove him, the search for power. At first he wanted power only to control his destiny. Then he made his first kill for money and discovered a new kind of pleasure. He enjoyed toying with other lives such as the one he watched now. While the first kill was for money, now he killed for revenge and the sheer joy of killing.

The man called Godfrey Kenton paced back and forth not ten yards away from him, hugging himself against the cool early morning air in what Kenton would probably call 'an ungodly hour.' How suitable. The witch chuckled, but the sound came out as a low, gurgling laugh.

Kenton jerked around, fear showing in the beads of sweat that popped out on his forehead. The witch man smelled the sweat before he ever saw the beads. As he watched, Kenton fidgeted with the stickpin at his throat. His throat, thought the witch, and felt saliva form on his tongue and hate rise in his chest.

Kenton spoke aloud to himself. 'That blasted note said sunrise. Now where the hell is he? To think I came all the way out here to listen to that idiot's deal on a Sunday morning when I could still be warm in Cissy's bed.'

The witch saw the man handle something in his pocket and knew he had brought some puny little pistol along for protection. Time to finish him. He called Kenton's name, his voice a husky shadow of a human's but clear enough for Kenton to recognize it. He watched as Kenton turned towards his place of concealment and heard him say, 'Well, come on. I haven't got all day.'

He certainly doesn't, thought the witch as he gathered his muscular hind limbs and sprang for Kenton's throat.

14

'Coffee farming is a jealous spouse, always demanding attention of some sort. It's either time to start seedlings in a nursery, plant new seedlings during the rains, weed between the trees, or harvest beans. The growing trees demand to be shaded by banana tree fronds and to be debugged or manured until they come of age and finally pay their own way. Then the coffee cherries insist on daily picking, pulping, drying, and shipping. Following all this, it should be a sin to drink tea, but old British habits die hard, even in the colony.'
— The Traveler

The coffee cherries on the Thompsons' remaining trees started their yearly transformation from camouflaged green to flamboyant red. Neville's hands were literally full now, and two consequences clung to this bounty. First, Neville needed to stay behind from the upcoming safari to supervise the coffee bean pulping and fermenting. The second grew out of the first. Neville didn't like the idea of his wife going on safari without him, especially as he considered Hascombe to be a bit of a rounder.

'Neville, you're being childish,' Madeline protested on Monday morning. 'There is no reason for me to stay behind. You are so busy with the coffee, you won't even know I'm gone.'

193

Mr Thompson's eyes opened wide in shock. 'Madeline!' he gasped. 'How can you say such a thing. Of course, if you find running off with other men so much more attractive than being with me, well . . . ' He hung his head and shoved his hands in his trouser pockets like a pitiful schoolboy. The effect was not wasted on his wife.

'Oh, darling, you mustn't think that. I'm not one of those flighty women who engage in wife-swapping games in Happy Valley.' She tugged playfully at his sleeve, pulled his hand out of his pocket, and held it.

'Perhaps I should just wander off,' suggested Jade. 'I do need to drive into town today.'

'No,' they said in unison, and Madeline added, 'This concerns you, too, Jade. Neville, you can hardly expect Jade to go alone on safari with Harry and Roger. How would that look?'

'Lord Colridge will be there,' he protested. 'He'll look after her.'

'Another man,' scoffed Madeline. 'You didn't approve of that for me.'

'Please don't argue on my account,' said Jade. 'Madeline, you know I can hold my own against rowdy males. As for propriety, I don't really care if the good folk of Nairobi look askance at me. I'm just passing through.' Seeing Madeline's hurt look, Jade added, 'I'd love to have you with me, but I'm not going to be held responsible for ruining your marriage. Now, if you'll excuse me, I really do have to drive into town to post some letters.' She didn't add that she planned to call on Dr Montgomery, whose name she had gotten from the Norfolk clerk.

She hopped into the Model T with her rifle, camera, and a canvas bag with several packets. Besides her hyena hunt article for the magazine, she had an incomplete letter to Mr Jacobs, which she planned to finish after interviewing the doctor, and two personal letters to send. One went to her parents and the other to Beverly, who, if plans had gone through, should be Lady Dunbury by now. Madeline gave her an envelope to mail as well, an order to a seed catalog.

Jade had had another dream last night about glowing eyes stalking her in the tall grass, which left her feeling edgy, so she turned her mind from it and focused instead on the safari as she drove along the pitted dirt track to Nairobi. Harry had arranged for departure the middle of next week, but coffee harvesting would continue for weeks. Jade didn't mind losing Neville from the party, but she found herself hoping Madeline would still come. In many ways she was like Beverly: frank, brave, and certainly not flighty. Jade missed Beverly, her former 'comrade in axles,' as they'd termed themselves.

Until recently, oxcarts had been the main vehicles that traveled the track to and from Nairobi. The heavy wagons had plowed deep ruts in the pasty mud during the rainy season, which later baked into treacherous pits. The car jolted over one. Jade bounced a few inches off the seat. The car slid left, and Jade gripped the wheel and steadied it. The jolt reminded her about other rutted roads, and she half expected to see a caisson along the track. Instead, she saw red murram soil, clumps of grass with long, thin

195

leaves like wire, and warped thorn trees. An *Erythrina* tree practicing to be a contortionist held blazing red flowers at the end of its twisted branches. To her left, in the distance rose the rounded back of Kea-Njahe, the mountain near the Kikuyu village where she had killed the witch's hyena and earned her new name. So far, no new reports of terror had come in from the village, so maybe that problem was solved after all. She slipped off her hat and sniffed the brim. Yep, she thought, memories may fade but that odor lingered. So had the tattoo on her wrist.

The sun felt good on her head after the morning chill, so she tossed the hat atop the letter packets and enjoyed the warmth as it soaked into her black curls. On her right was a small *shamba*, where hardworking Kikuyu women decked out in shaven heads and copper bracelets hoed the rows with hand-fashioned bone and wood tools. Two younger women, each with a circle of hair on her head that marked her as unmarried, carried water in the ubiquitous four-gallon *debes* to some sorry-looking sweet potatoes. Jade wondered what everyone had used before empty fuel tins became available. Probably gourds.

'*Jambo*,' she called out and waved. The women looked up, and one waved back.

Jade looked back to Kea-Njahe and Harry's farm. An intriguing man, she thought. Possibly too intriguing for her own good. 'It's plain he's interested in you,' she said aloud. 'Now how do you feel about him?' To her surprise, she returned his interest, at least physically. 'What

196

would Beverly say?' she muttered. More to the point, what would David think? Jade felt trapped in a warped paradox. Only David could comfort her after so close a loss, but then, he was the one who was gone. Maybe, considering the temptations Harry posed, she'd better insist that Madeline go with her on safari after all.

Thinking about Harry and Kea-Njahe made her think about last night's dream, in which she stood alone in tall golden grasses in absolute silence. The grasses moved without any breeze to ruffle them. Overall, Jade recalled a sense of menace and the disquieting conviction that the grasses themselves were stalking her. *It was just a dream!*

She finally entered Nairobi, headed for the post office, and deposited her outgoing mail in the box reserved for such envelopes. Since the train wasn't in yet, neither was the most recent mail. Jade left the car at the garage with her camera and her rifle tucked out of sight and headed for Dr Montgomery's office.

Nairobi boasted several government doctors with a reputation of being unavailable to civilians, which left the commoner with a Dr Burkitt. Jade wondered if she should have sent her letter of introduction from Lord Dunbury ahead to make an impression on Dr Montgomery. After only a minute with him, she could tell it would not have made much difference.

'Miss del Cameron, you're not a member of the family, so I don't feel it is proper to show you Mr Worthy's death certificate.'

'I'm here on behalf of Mr Worthy's solicitor.'

She handed him a letter of introduction from Mr Jacobs, which explained her position on behalf of the late Gil Worthy and his son, David, and waited while he read it.

Dr Montgomery finished the letter with a tremendous sigh, folded it, and handed it back to her. 'I suppose that I must comply then.' He walked over to a wooden cabinet and pulled out one of the drawers. 'But I am really very busy.'

'I understand, Doctor,' Jade said soothingly. 'I'm grateful for your sparing me this time.'

Her words and tone of voice mollified the man. Finally, after much rummaging, he found the file he wanted. 'Here,' he said as he opened it. 'Death certificate for Mr Gil Worthy.'

Jade read the document. In brief terms, it ascribed the death of Mr Worthy on January 29, 1915, to trauma to the throat, possibly from a lion or hyena. She stared at the paper a few seconds more as if something else might magically appear there. Finally, she handed it back to the doctor. 'I heard that no one ever found the animal. How did you know the bite came from either of those two animals?'

'From the size of the bite marks, Miss del Cameron.' He set the folder on his desk and folded his arms. 'Perhaps you should go to the commissioner's office. He should know more of the matter. *If*,' he added, 'there is anything more to be known.'

'Unless Mr Worthy packed a hyena in his luggage, there's more. Thank you for your time.'

Jade next made her way to the commissioner's headquarters and inquired of an African soldier if she might see the commissioner. He showed her to a chair and asked her to please wait. A few minutes later, a white man in khaki military clothes came in and bowed.

'I understand you came to see me. How may I help you?'

Jade rose and shook his hand. 'Commissioner. Thank you for seeing me.' She handed him Mr Jacobs' letter. 'I'm here to inquire into Mr Worthy's death. Dr Montgomery could only tell me that he died of an animal attack in his hotel room, a fact I find most curious.'

The commissioner pursed his lips and rocked up and down on the balls of his feet for a few moments. Then he slapped his right leg and exclaimed, 'Quite right, quite right. Most odd, as I recall. Come into my office and sit down, please.' He escorted her inside and showed her a chair before taking a seat behind his desk.

'So you agree that the death was odd. Can you tell me more?' she asked.

'As I recall the facts, Mr Worthy was last seen taking breakfast on the twenty-ninth. When he never appeared the following day, the clerk thought he'd skipped out without settling his bill and went up to his room. Found him dead on the floor, throat torn out. Didn't find any identification — no wallet on him or in his room. It appeared he had been in the act of either making himself comfortable or getting dressed at the time.'

Jade arched her brows in an unspoken question.

'Cuffs open, collar undone, shoes off, that sort

199

of thing,' elaborated the commissioner.

'And no one reported seeing a wild animal enter or leave the hotel? Don't you find that to be a bit beyond belief?' asked Jade.

The commissioner shook his head. 'I do admit it was odd. The clerk, of course, sent for a doctor and someone came to fetch one of the *askaris*, er, native constables,' he explained. 'My men, of course, went straightaway up to the man's room and searched. In fact they looked in every room on that floor. No one ever found the beast. One of the native boys probably stole the wallet.'

Jade considered his words for a moment. 'Could someone have brought an animal in, say, disguised as a dog, and then removed it before your men searched?'

The commissioner snorted. 'Highly unlikely. Do you realize that you are proposing this was not an accident, Miss del Cameron? You're suggesting it was murder?' He shifted in his chair as though he were becoming impatient with her.

Jade nodded and then explained Mr Worthy's reason for returning to Africa and how he had sent the very parcel he came with back when he feared his life was in danger. She next described what the Kikuyu lad had witnessed through the keyhole.

The commissioner rose from his chair and leaned both hands on his desk. 'I can't help you at all about his illegitimate son, Miss del Cameron. I've only been in the colony six years. I'm afraid by now I can't help you much more with Mr Worthy's death. The case is old, Miss del Cameron. Mr Worthy died of an animal

200

mauling. Tragic? Yes. Odd? Decidedly. But during the war things did get a bit hectic around here and the animals responded. As to the idea that this was a demon animal, why, that is preposterous. I'm frankly surprised that an educated young lady such as yourself would even entertain such a notion. Case is closed.'

Jade rose, too, and faced the commissioner square in the eyes. 'I have one more question, sir. Do you know a Mr Kruger? Gil Worthy had his name written down.'

The commissioner shook his head. 'That's a Boer name. The Boers come and go through here with their oxen. If, as you tell me, Mr Worthy was about to go into Tsavo, then I expect that this Kruger was his man for buying an oxcart. Now, if you'll excuse me, miss?'

Jade thanked him again for his time and departed his office. Once outside, she made a few notes in her notebook and considered them. If someone brought in a hyena to kill Gil, they had to slip it in unseen. She wondered if a hyena could be disguised as a dog. Somehow she doubted it. This person would need great skill in handling dangerous animals, and the so-called *laibon* seemed to have similar control over his animal. But native Africans were not allowed as guests at the Norfolk. Maybe she'd find clues in Tsavo. She certainly wasn't having much luck here. She finished her letter to Mr Jacobs and decided to get her camera from the car and wait for the train.

Many of the Europeans stared at her

knee-length brown boots, trousers, and short-cropped hair as she walked back from the garage. Jade grew tired of their rudeness and countered by openly saying hello to them until they felt their own bad manners and looked away. *Honestly, I polished the manure off my boots before I left.*

A turbaned Sikh offered beautiful fabrics and scarves for sale in an open-fronted shop. Jade was framing a photograph when she noticed a familiar-looking woman staring at her with open-mouthed shock. Jade placed her as Cissy someone or other from the Muthaiga. The woman had been inebriated, so Lord Colridge had avoided introducing her. Now, with her elegant ankle-length suit of creamy white linen and matching broad-brimmed, red-lined hat trimmed in silk roses, she made an interesting contrast to the shopkeeper.

Jade held up her camera. 'Would you like to have your picture in a magazine?'

'Oh? Well, perhaps, of course, but really,' blathered the woman. 'Do you realize you have no hat on? The equatorial sun is very powerful. The actinic rays will destroy your brain and send you positively mad.'

'Ah yes.' Jade comprehended all the previous stares. Her trousers might be bad enough in town, but being hatless seemed unforgivable. 'I have a thick skull.' The woman looked more horrified than ever. 'I left my hat in my motorcar at the garage,' added Jade.

'Indeed,' replied the woman. 'Well, you had better fetch it before you addle yourself further.'

She blinked at Jade. 'Do I know you? You look familiar.'

'Possibly you saw me at the Muthaiga Club on Saturday evening.'

'Oh yes! Were *you* there?' Cissy blinked again. 'I'm Cissy Estes, but of course you must know that already.' She came in closer to Jade as though to whisper a confidence. 'Have you seen Godfrey Kenton? I cannot find him. I'm sure I saw him Saturday night, but . . . '

'No, I haven't. Sorry.' Jade started closing her camera's viewing hood when the lady stopped her.

'Of course, if you *insist* on taking my photograph, I understand,' the woman simpered. 'I'm sure Godfrey will turn up, and I don't suppose a few more moments without your hat will make *that* much difference. Er, what magazine did you say this is for?'

'*The Traveler*, ma'am,' said Jade.

The woman cooed her delight. 'How is this?' She struck a dramatic pose in which she critically examined a fringed shawl.

'Turn more towards me, if you would, please,' instructed Jade. 'Your face is in the shadow. There, that's better. Please hold that pose.' She took the picture. 'Of course, I cannot promise the magazine will use it.'

The lady reached into her handbag and pulled a small white rectangular slip of paper from under a small brown package. Bits of white powder, like flour, snuck out of a frayed edge. 'Here is my card,' she said. 'Please do send a print to me. Just address it care of the Nairobi

203

post. Jeffrey will like to have it so much.'

Jade glanced at the card and read 'Mrs Cissy Estes.' She wondered if Jeffrey was her husband or if she was divorced. Whoever he was, he had already supplanted her concern for Godfrey Kenton. Jade decided to make a print for the woman. The Thompsons had graciously given over one of the less leaky huts to her as a darkroom so she could develop her film sheets.

'I'll have a print for you in a few days if you like,' Jade said.

'How delightful, miss . . . do I know you?' she asked again.

'Jade del Cameron.'

The woman's eyes opened wider. 'I know that name. You're the *American* staying at the Norfolk, aren't you?' She placed her pale hand on Jade's arm. 'I heard at a party all about how you disarmed Mr Hascombe in the lobby and killed that dreadful hyena.' She blinked a few more times. 'Were you at that party?'

'Yes, that was me, ma'am,' she said with a sigh. Apparently something more than solar rays had addled this woman. 'But I'm staying with Mr and Mrs Thompson at their farm now.'

'Oh, at Neville's farm?' The lady ran the tip of her tongue along her upper teeth, and Jade doubted the extent of her attachment to Jeffrey. 'Perhaps I should call on you out there?'

Good heavens, thought Jade. Madeline would toss her out bodily if this predaceous hussy came out on a pretext of seeing her. 'No! I won't be there very long. Going on safari, you know. But it was nice meeting you, Mrs Estes.'

'Please, call me Cissy, and yes, it was fun. Now don't forget to wear your hat, Miss del Cameron. It's very dangerous not to, although with your rather, um, dark complexion you might be more immune. You know, like the natives.'

Jade left before the woman could make any more insinuations about her hybrid pedigree. Long, droning whistle blasts announced the train's arrival at the station. She bought an orange from one of the peddlers and sat in the shade of a young eucalyptus tree to eat it and wait. There she watched the general bustling activity of the rickshaw boys, sentries, and Europeans until the mail was delivered to the post office and duly sorted.

To her delight, she received a letter from her mother and one from Beverly. She sat down at the post office to read them, her back against the cool stone wall. Her mother's letter, dated just after Jade left London, announced the birth of a new foal and expressed how much they missed her. Jade felt a momentary pang of guilt that she hadn't written home sooner. What would they think of her new African name or tattoo? She opened Bev's letter.

Dearest Jade:

It is done, we are married, and I have only one regret. That you were not here to be my maid of honor instead of my sister, Emily. Avery felt the same way, but he said (and I quote him), 'I am not about to wait for that damned gypsy to quit gallivanting about the globe before we can get married.' Wasn't that

205

romantic of him? I won't bore you with all the details of the wedding in this letter. Suffice it to say that I was ravishing, of course, and Avery very dashing and handsome. Instead, I'll tell you in person. That's right, darling. As you read this, we are already on our way to Africa and should arrive in Nairobi by June 29 or 30. You had better be there, too, or I shall be frightfully put out with you. We know all about your safari plans. (Avery knows everything.) He contacted your magazine and discovered all the particulars. Of course, we intend to come along so make all the proper arrangements for more tents or whatever. I cannot wait to see you again. Till then, all my love.

Your dear friend,
(Lady) Beverly Dunbury

P.S. You must promise to let me shoot the first lion. I must have one before Avery, and I know you will be only too busy photographing to shoot.

Beverly in Africa! Jade grinned with pleasure. Just what she needed and longed for, and Neville wouldn't have to worry about Madeline going on the safari, either. Jade folded the letter and stuck it in her shirt pocket with her mother's. Madeline would worry if she didn't get back soon. She picked up the mail, mostly government publications and gadget catalogs for the Thompsons and a box of fresh photo chemicals

206

for her sent up from Mombasa, and headed for the garage.

The dusty street north out of Nairobi quickly returned to the heavily pitted wagon track. Three miles on, Jade slowed to maneuver one of the deeper ruts when the car jolted sharply. This time she heard a loud bang and felt the machine slide and pull to one side.

'Spit fire and save the matches,' she swore. 'Of all the times and places to get a blowout.' She stopped the car but left it running rather than trust it to start up again. 'Bev will be mighty put out if I manage to get myself eaten out here and spoil her safari,' she muttered.

Jade lugged over two large rocks and blocked the front tires. Next she retrieved her loaded rifle, worked a cartridge into the chamber, and set the hammer halfway as a safety. Finally she pulled out the jack and began the tedious process of changing the rear tire.

Experience had trained her ears to detect any sounds that might signify danger. Habit taught her to pick out the distant rumble of artillery, the high-pitched whistle of shells, and the droning whir of an airplane. The ruined tire already sat beside her on the dusty red ground when it occurred to her that those sounds no longer posed any threat. Suddenly, she felt confused, as if she had awakened in a strange place and didn't know how she had gotten there. Her head swam as she struggled to orient herself. This wasn't France. Africa spread around her.

Listen to Africa, she told herself. All she heard was silence. She had refocused her attention on the flat tire when a chill spread down her back and arms and prickled her skin. Silence itself was a dangerous sound. Active predators traded in silence.

The afternoon sun beat down. Sweat dripped off a limp black curl and rolled into her eyes. *Cissy Estes would pitch a fit.* Jade rose to get her hat from the seat before hefting the spare tire onto the axle. Halfway to the hat she froze. Something shifted in the tall grass. *My dream!* Slowly, very slowly, she crouched down and retrieved her Winchester. Her eyes stayed riveted on that one patch of grass. Nothing. Perhaps she had heard a ground bird, or maybe just the breeze? Jade waited long enough to see the shadows lengthen. *Nothing dangerous lurking out there. Panicking over a silly dream.* Rifle in hand, she retrieved her hat and moved around to the spare tire.

Putting the tire on took a matter of moments, but it required two free hands. That meant setting the rifle down again. She scanned the area carefully, let go of her Winchester, and turned her back to the open plains. Jade needed to hunker in close under the heavy tire to lift it into place. It didn't help that her wounded knee had started aching, too. As she readjusted her squatting position, hoping to relieve the strain on her left knee, her hat brim hit the car's frame and slid to one side of her head. A breeze blew from the side and caught the old, battered felt hat. It flipped off her head and onto the grass. Jade let it lie. The tire slid into place, and she started to secure it when she froze again.

208

Only a little sound arrested her. A soft cough, the type someone used to discreetly announce themselves, came from the car's opposite rear and whispered by her. Jade slowly leaned back and peered around the car. She stared straight into the face of a massive male lion. The beast shook his black-maned head, the mark of virile prime, and Jade couldn't help but sense a rising admiration mixed in with her fear.

On an impulse, she greeted it softly. '*Jambo, Simba.*' The lion threw back his head and bellowed a deafening challenge. The hellish sound, terrifying in its natural power, vibrated Jade's bones to the marrow. Long white daggers flashed in his open maw. Jade reached back slowly for her rifle, wincing from the pain in her knee.

The lion sniffed the air. *If animals can smell fear, this one's certainly getting a snootful.* He lowered his huge head and sniffed the ground. His black nostrils swept the road dust. As if the beast wanted to be certain, he opened his mouth and flared, his long, pink tongue curling upwards to taste her scent as well as smell it.

Jade oozed into a kneeling crouch and shouldered her rifle. She squinted down the metal sights, but the sun fell full in her face and made it impossible to see. One shot was all she'd get, if she was lucky. She needed to see clearly for that shot. The cat continued flaring as if searching for some particular smell. Jade reached back, snagged her hat, and set it on her head to put her face in the brim's shadow.

Suddenly the immense tawny-colored cat

stiffened. He sniffed deeply once, snorted in disgust, and turned. Jade stared down the rifle's barrel and watched the animal trot away. Her finger still held the trigger, but the lion and the tall grass blended as one in the distant haze.

She plopped into a sitting position. The danger gone, every muscle in her body trembled violently. Eventually, she leaned against the car for support, then removed her hat and fanned herself with it. The dank, rancid aroma on the brim made her wince.

'Phew!' *Was that what drove the cat away? But why didn't it leave before? After all, the sorcerer annointed my belt and boots with it as well and . . .* Jade paused in midthought. She'd polished her boots the other day after stepping in manure. There was no scent left on them. But the belt? Her left hand reached for it at her waistline. *Gone!* Then she remembered. She had taken it off to wash the trousers in the tub and never put it back on. Thank heavens for the hat. Mrs Estes was right: It was dangerous to go out in the midday sun without a hat.

★   ★   ★

His beast came back without the scent of blood on his breath, but he already knew the plan had failed. He had felt his control over his animal weaken despite his best efforts. *This one is strong. She is hard and swallows her fear, not like the other.* He smiled at the memory. The other one was weak, and he had enjoyed killing him. That simpering man had cringed and trembled as his powerful jaws shook him like a rag. The witch man reconsidered his strategy. The first time he had sent his former mentor, but the old man had weakened. This time he had sent a real lion, a very virile one. Each time he had underestimated the woman's strength. Not to worry; there were other animals under his control. Eventually, he would take care of the woman himself, when he had her alone, after he had toyed with her nerves. Even lionesses ran from a hyena.

15

'A successful safari requires stout tents, nourishing food, water, fuel, maps, and porters to carry all these essentials. But if only one person can accompany you, a good gun bearer is more vital than any tracker or other companion. This is the person to whom you will entrust the care and safekeeping of your rifles. Should it be necessary, his will be the shoulder on which you rest the gun. In other words, he is entrusted with your life.'
— The Traveler

Lord and Lady Dunbury's imminent arrival convinced Neville to let Madeline go along on safari without him. However, after hearing of Mrs Estes' designs on her husband, Madeline had second thoughts herself.

'If that painted trollop thinks she can just waltz in here and seduce my husband, she is going to find herself in the coffee pulper.'

'Maddy, I am in no danger of being seduced away from you. Besides,' Neville added with a wink, 'Cissy's body would ruin a perfectly good pulper. You may go on safari without me.'

The two women rode on the Thompsons' ponies to Colridge's farm that afternoon to inform His Lordship of the changes. They were met at the door by one of Colridge's many hounds and by Pili, As before, the young man wore an immaculate white robe that set off his handsome golden bronze skin, black hair, and hazel eyes.

The hound extensively sniffed Jade's boots and belt, which had undergone a thorough reapplication of the Kikuyu's paste, before insinuating his head under her hand for an ear scratching. *Well, dogs don't seem to be repelled by it.* If Pili found the smell offensive, he was too well bred to show it.

'It is good that you have come,' Pili said. 'Bwana Colridge is hurt.'

Lord Colridge sat in a wingback chair with his left leg raised onto an ottoman. White plaster bandages encased it and his head. He resembled an incomplete mummy.

'Please sit down, ladies,' he said. 'I apologize for not standing in your presence. You'll excuse the rudeness as you see the cause there before you. Blasted horse threw me yesterday morning, broke my leg. Damned near cracked my skull. Dr Burkitt came out from Nairobi. Good doctor. Preaches too much, though. Fractured tibia, he called it. Made some crack about having to shoot me if I were a horse.'

Jade stifled a smile, but Colridge caught it all the same. 'Is there anything I can do?' she asked.

'Yes,' added Madeline, 'that includes Neville and myself, Lord Colridge.'

'Nothing to be done unless you can work a miracle. The doctor may not shoot me, but he has put me out to pasture, so to speak. I'm out for your safari, Miss del Cameron. Thompson will have to see to you without me.'

'Neville is busy with the coffee, sir,' said Madeline.

'Eh? Well, perhaps, Miss del Cameron, you should cancel. Hascombe's a good shot, but I don't approve of the two of you going off alone with him off into the wilderness. Not proper. And you must stop gallivanting around on your own.'

'What do you mean, sir?' asked Jade.

'That blasted fool, Godfrey Kenton, is missing. Burkitt told me he disappeared sometime between Saturday night and early Sunday morning. Told his wife after the party that he had business to tend to. Hasn't come back.'

Madeline sniffed. 'Probably ran off to one of Cissy's wild parties. He seems the type.'

'I heard him tell his wife about a business meeting,' said Jade. 'But I saw Cissy, and she asked me about Kenton as well. Said she saw him Saturday night. I got the impression she meant after the party. You might be right, Madeline,' she added. 'If I read his character correctly, he's probably off cheating on his wife *and* Cissy.'

Jade turned back to Colridge. 'In any event, Your Lordship, we won't be alone with Mr Forster and Mr Hascombe. Lord and Lady Dunbury are arriving soon and intend to come along.'

'Oh? Young Dunbury coming, is he? A crack shot? Of course, he would be. Well, that changes matters. Sorry not to be along. Knew his father.' Lord Colridge continued to ask questions that he answered himself and make pronouncements until Jade interrupted him.

'I'll inform Lord Dunbury that you want to meet him, sir. In the meantime,' she added and pointed to his leg, 'leave breaking colts to your trainers.'

'I wasn't breaking any blasted colts, Miss del Cameron. Bakari threw me. A jackal, of all things, ran right under his legs. Damnedest thing. Ran right out of the hedge. Actually aimed for me. Never seen anything like it before. A jackal so close to the house, and in *broad daylight*.' Madeline shook her head in sympathy and fussed with the comforter on his lap. Lord Colridge snorted in surprise and fluttered his mustache. 'Here now! No need to fuss like a mother hen . . . I, er . . . well, yes, that is rather better.'

Jade hung back and watched the fun. It almost looked as if the old man were blushing. She decided to tease him a bit. 'I suppose this is the *laibon's* revenge for your interference.'

'Rubbish! Something frightened a jackal. It ran, scared Bakari, and I fell. Nothing more!'

'I'm sorry. Just having some fun. I suppose I'd better contact Mr Hascombe and let him know that you won't be joining us?'

'No need. I sent a runner over. I'll send another to tell him about young Dunbury and his bride. You'll start from Nairobi in any event. Train will take you south towards Tsavo. You'll join the bearers there. Did you know that? Of course, you did. Smart woman. Good shot.' He paused, and Jade waited for the next edict. 'The outfitters supply gun bearers, of course, but I had intended to take Pili along as my own man. Trustworthy person. Smart, too. You take him, Miss del Cameron. A good shot deserves a good bearer.'

Jade felt the praise deeply. 'Thank you very much. But perhaps we should ask him first? He may not appreciate carrying a gun for a woman or even leaving you behind.'

'Pish tosh,' snorted Colridge. 'A servant does what he's told to do. But if you insist, we shall speak with him. Pili,' he called. 'Pili, come here.' The young man appeared at the door, bowed slightly, and waited for the upcoming order.

'Pili, Miss del Cameron is going on safari. She shot the hyena at the Kikuyu village. I want you to be her gun bearer. She's a worthy shot and, er, deserves the best.'

Pili bowed again in acknowledgment of this implied compliment to himself. 'It is no problem for me, Bwana Colridge, but who will watch over you while I am gone?'

Colridge 'pish toshed' any need for extensive care as the doctor allowed he could walk with a cane for short distances. As to dressing himself or serving his meals, there were other house servants. In the end, there was little the young man could do but acquiesce. Madeline promised that Neville would come round and lend a hand later next week, and they took their leave. Outside, Jade spoke further with Pili.

'I don't need a personal servant, Pili. I'm more interested in your expertise with African game.

216

As far as I'm concerned, you're an equal partner in the expedition.'

Jade watched his face closely for any signs of disgust, respect, fear, uncertainty, or plain and simple tolerance but found few clues. His wide-set hazel eyes never betrayed any symptom of emotion. At least, not until Madeline asked one last question, where to find the privy.

Pili began to point the way, hesitated, and blushed. 'Memsahib must wait outside first. I must correct something before you may enter. It would not be proper.'

Jade and Madeline followed him. 'Now what do you suppose the old coot keeps in there that wouldn't be appropriate?' Jade asked. 'French postcards?'

'Well, he is a widower,' answered Madeline, 'and maybe, if half those tales are true . . . ' Just then Pili emerged from the privy with a huge coiled gray snake in his arms.

Madeline screamed, and Jade stifled a shout. *Something's queer about all this*, she thought. No one would keep a poisonous mamba in the privy, and even if they did, no one would be able to tote it around like that. She looked more closely. 'The blasted thing is stuffed!' she shouted.

Pili put the mounted specimen in a shed and closed the door. Then he turned back to Jade with a grin on his well-chiseled face. 'Yes, memsahib, it is stuffed. Bwana Colridge likes to play jokes on people. He enjoys watching them run screaming from the privy, but it would not be proper for Mrs Memsahib to do so.

217

Especially,' he added with a bow to Madeline, 'for the friend of the lady who killed the witch's hyena.' Madeline excused herself.

'Pili, do you believe the hyena was controlled by a witch?' asked Jade.

'Memsahib, I believe it was controlled by a very bad person. I do not know how. But I have seen men with dogs trained to fight. So I ask myself, why not a hyena?'

Jade nodded. 'Why not, indeed. Have you heard any of the men speak about this *laibon*? Do any of them know who it is? Because I think he needs to be punished.'

Pili shook his head. 'The Kikuyu men do not speak freely in front of me either for fear that the witch will overhear or for fear that I am the witch.'

'You? The witch?' Jade found that hard to believe. 'I thought the *laibon* was a Maasai or from one of those related tribes.'

'Do you believe in him, memsahib?' asked Pili.

'Please, call me Jade, and I'm not sure. Like you, I'm inclined to think someone wicked has trained a hyena to frighten others. I admit I have a very hard time believing in actual sorcery.'

Just then, Colridge bellowed from within and Pili grinned. 'The old bull stirs, and I must attend.' He hastened inside.

Jade waited for Madeline by the ponies. She took out her pocketknife, picked some gravel from their hooves, and thought about Pili's idea of a trained hyena. It was interesting to compare it to an attack dog; she had even said as much herself before. But from the recesses of her mind she recalled stories of Navajo skin walkers who reportedly turned into wolves. Her father had told her those tales and other ghost stories around the campfire when she was an impressionable child. Now she no longer believed someone could shape-shift, but it was curious that such a wide variety of cultures held on to stories of witches and animal familiars. If someone could train a hyena, could he control other beasts? She wondered if those lion encounters were not just accidental meetings, but animals trained to her scent intent on killing her!

As she pocketed her knife, a Kikuyu man ran to her. 'Memsabu Simba Jike,' he called, 'the jackal who harmed Bwana Pua Nywele, it was a *laibon's* jackal.'

'Did you see markings on it?' asked Jade.

The man shook his head. 'No, memsabu, but why else would a night animal attack during the day? The *laibon* is angry with the bwana. You must stop him.' Before Jade could respond, the man ran back to the fields.

Madeline returned. That was when the breeze picked up, and Jade noticed a rank smell. She looked around and spied a vulture landing a few hundred yards away in the citrus orchard.

'Maddy, let's go see what's causing that smell.' They remounted their ponies.

Madeline grimaced but followed Jade towards the trees. The smell of rotting meat became stronger, and Jade wondered if one of Colridge's goats had gotten loose and died here. Suddenly she reined in her pony and held up a hand, warning Madeline to stop.

'Stay there, Maddy.' Jade took her rifle from its saddle bag, slid off her mount, and listened for the sound of a predator hiding in the other grove. Nothing but the sound of a vulture scrambling about. She sidestepped lightly around another tree and stopped abruptly. Madeline, who had followed her anyway, gasped. The vulture hopped away into the open and took off.

Buzzing flies covered an elongated form in a seething mass before them. Jade kicked the swarm, and the flies lifted momentarily, bringing a fresh stench up with them. 'Sweet heaven,' she murmured and picked up a torn, bloody shoe. A rotting foot fell out at her feet and hit the rock with a sodden thud. 'I think we just found the remains of Godfrey Kenton.'

Madeline promptly disposed of her lunch behind the nearest tree.

★   ★   ★

Jade stood next to her car and watched the native *askari* put another body part into a wooden box. So far they'd found his head, both arms, and most of the torso in addition to the booted foot. Scavengers had disposed of the rest. After discovering the corpse, Jade had informed Colridge, then ridden with Maddy back to her farm. There, Jade had left the horse behind and taken her car into town to fetch the commissioner.

'We've combed the area, Miss del Cameron,'

said the commissioner 'and there's no sign of a weapon, no spent cartridge, no knife. Of course, the doctor will have a look at the, er, remains, but all the marks appear to be made by teeth. No question in my mind, he's a victim of an animal attack.'

Jade was less than impressed. She scowled. 'How did he get out here? Where's his car?'

'What do you mean?' asked the commissioner. His voice indicated he didn't care to be questioned by this American female.

'I heard Kenton tell his wife that the Woodards would drive her home, so presumably he wanted his car for himself. Where is it?' The commissioner frowned and rubbed his chin. When he didn't speak, Jade continued. 'His wife said he had a business meeting. I heard him tell her that, too. Who was he meeting? Where are they?'

'Miss del Cameron,' said the commissioner with a patronizing smile. 'You're a young lady, inexperienced perhaps in the ways of the world. Mr Kenton was well known to be a ladies' man. It is highly likely that he had *business* of a different sort, an assignation, if you will.'

'He was a rounder and cheating on his wife,' said Jade bluntly.

'Exactly. And if this was a married woman he was meeting, she wouldn't want her husband to know.'

'This doesn't look like the place to have an affair,' Jade said, pointing to the orchard.

'It's rather obvious he was attacked on his way home,' retorted the commissioner.

'Which brings me back to the fact that we

221

haven't found his car abandoned nearby.' Jade's voice rose with increasing impatience. 'His Lordship said he heard no car.'

'His Lordship,' countered the commissioner, 'was probably sound asleep. Besides, wild predators frequently drag their kill back to a lair. His car could be a mile away.'

One of the *askaris* brought a bundle of bloodied and torn clothing to them. 'These are the victim's clothes not associated with his body, Commissioner.' Jade recognized the silken scarf among the scraps.

'Put it in a sack and then add it to the body box,' ordered the commissioner.

Jade held up her hand. 'Kenton wore a diamond stickpin on that scarf,' she said. 'You might look for it. His wife would surely want it back.'

The commissioner sighed with evident impatience. 'Miss del Cameron, I have your statement and His Lordship's. There is no further need for you to be here.'

Jade recognized the suggestion as a curt dismissal. She plopped onto the running board and sat there a moment, thinking. Pili came from the house and joined her.

'Do you need help, miss, with cranking the car?'

Jade shook her head. 'No, thank you, Pili. I've done it many times. I suppose the commissioner talked to you, too?'

Pili nodded. 'I was in attendance on Bwana Colridge all evening.'

'And you heard nothing, either?' she asked.

Pili shook his head.

Jade thought aloud. 'The body parts were scattered, but small scavengers would do that. There were a lot of remains, too. More than I'd expect if a big predator killed Kenton for food.'

'So you do not think it was a predator, miss?'

Jade shrugged. 'The rip on the throat certainly looked like a killing bite. I don't know. Maybe I just don't know enough about African predators to make a fair conclusion.' She sighed and rose. 'We're scheduled for a safari in a few days. Maybe I'll learn something about them there that will help me make more sense of this.' And, she thought, more sense of what happened to Gil.

16

'The hyena is generally thought to be a cowardly brute, incapable of anything but scavenging. A few keen observers will tell you otherwise. It is curious that humans treat wild scavengers with such disdain. It's actually an activity that the colonists raise to an art form with every piece of construction made from old debes or other cast-off items.'
— The Traveler

Beverly arrives today with Avery. Jade hopped into the Ford and drove into Nairobi. Her mellow contralto voice broke into song as she neared the station.

'It's a long way to Tipperary, it's a long way to go . . . ' *To hell with witches and hyenas.* For the first time since the war began, she felt truly excited and happy. She was a child on Christmas Eve, and Beverly's friendship, complete with all its brusque, open mannerisms, was her gift. 'Goodbye, Piccadilly, farewell, Leicester Square, it's a long, long way to Tipperary and my heart lies there.' She pulled in at the railway station and waited for the train to arrive.

While she waited, Jade studied the people on the platform with a writer and photographer's eye. The same cluster of African women she'd seen when she first arrived still hugged the same section of the platform and hawked their chickens and fruits. Jade took her Graflex out of a canvas shoulder bag, inserted a film sheet, and waited. She caught the dangling, squawking chicken just as it targeted a succulent papaya and lunged for it.

Rickshaw boys arrived with their carts and jockeyed for position. A small troop of King's African Rifles dressed in khaki shorts, shirts, and fez hats lined up smartly to receive some expected dignitary. Various Happy Valleyites strolled about arm in arm and discussed the prospects of a good cricket match later. Jade had just finished photographing them with a handsome Maasai in the foreground when she heard the whistle blast from down the track.

The small locomotive with its unique front bench seat hissed into the station. Lord and Lady Dunbury sat like royalty in the open air on the bench dressed in unpretentious bush clothing, including a split skirt for Beverly. Both were nearly free of the ubiquitous red dust that assailed everyone in the cars behind them. Beverly spotted Jade and waved furiously.

'Darling, here we are.' Her husband, afraid she would leap from the bench in front of the still-moving locomotive, took a firm grip on her arm when she tried to rise. 'Avery, please let go of me,' scolded Beverly. 'I want to see Jade.'

'Yes, and I daresay she would like to see you, too, but in one piece and not mangled under the engine.' Beverly sat down again until the train stopped, then leaped off, ran to Jade, and hugged her.

'Jade, darling, you look wonderful.' She pulled

back and held her nose. 'But you smell a trifle ripe. I hope that isn't a new cologne you're wearing.'

Jade removed her hat and held it out for Beverly to see and sniff. 'No. It's a magic potion. It keeps witches away.'

'Oh?' said Avery as he strolled up. He kissed Jade on the cheek. 'Perhaps we should get some, Beverly. Maybe it will keep your sister, Emily, away.'

'Avery, dear,' said Beverly with a rippling laugh. 'She said it keeps *witches* away. You are confusing *witch* with another, very similar word. Emily is a b — '

Jade interrupted her before a respectable-looking woman next to them could be shocked by such language from a lady. 'You both look wonderful. Avery, you've grown a mustache since I last saw you. Beverly, you cut your hair.'

Beverly shook her short blond curls and laughed. 'How could I not after you paved the way? Besides, I do think it will become the latest rage, and you know how I love to set a style.'

Jade laughed, her smooth contralto contrasting with Beverly's airy soprano. 'Yes, your combination of cocoa powder and coffee was quite the trend in the unit.' She looked at them both and decided they made a very handsome couple. Avery's blond hair tended more towards a sandy shade while Bev's shimmered like liquid sunshine. He stood six feet to her five feet, six inches. Both had watercolor blue eyes that reminded Jade of the Mediterranean.

On an impulse she decided to take their

photograph and hustled them back onto the engine's front bench to pose. They sat seriously for the first photo, then relaxed for the second. Beverly leaned against her husband, who gazed down at her with a look of intense devotion. A sudden feeling of loss welled up inside Jade and blurred her vision. She choked it back down, took the picture, then turned her back to wipe her eyes before Beverly detected anything amiss.

Beverly noticed anyway but determined not to subject her friend to questions here on the platform. 'Avery, darling, what do you suppose we do about our luggage?'

'There are plenty of young native boys here only too willing to hire on to carry it,' said Jade. 'My car's over there.' She pointed to a cluster of carriages and a few other motorcars.

'Well,' said Lord Dunbury, 'let's find ourselves some likely lads and let them have at it.' He picked out two and, with Jade's help translating, sent them racing for a stack of luggage farther down the platform. 'Just what do they do with this money?' he asked. 'I can imagine them spending it all on some sweets like any other boys.'

Jade shook her head. 'Many of them are saving for a future wife. In the old days, before the colony outlawed tribal warfare, they could raid a village and steal some goats to pay a bride-price. Now they have to have rupees to buy goats.'

'Shocking,' said Avery. 'Why we should interfere with a perfectly good system is beyond my comprehension.'

'It's even worse for the Maasai and some of

the other more warlike tribes,' replied Jade. 'A young Somali wouldn't think of courting a bride without first killing another warrior.' She remembered Corporal Gideon. 'Now they join the army to do that.'

Beverly looked at her husband and shook her golden hair. 'How hypocritical. To think we send our own young men off to slay the enemy and then marry the returning heroes, but won't allow others to do the same. What is civilization coming to?'

The two youths returned hauling first one batch of suitcases, then another, and took them to Jade's made-over Model T. The boot had been removed in the makeover and an open bed surrounded by wooden sides put in its place. A narrow wooden bench served as a backseat. Lord Dunbury stowed the goods in the back. 'Will they come with us,' he asked, nodding to the boys, 'to help unload at the hotel?'

'I'm sure they will,' she said, 'as long as they aren't attached to a rickshaw. We'll create quite a scene, though, driving with them in the car. These colonists are very class conscious.'

Avery's eyes twinkled. 'A scene, you say? Sounds like ripping good fun. We're game, aren't we, love?' He looked across at his wife. Beverly smiled and nodded.

Jade's Swahili had improved markedly since her arrival due to constant practice at the Thompsons' farm. She asked the youths if they would like to come and help unload. After receiving an affirmative answer, Lord Dunbury grinned and pointed from them to the top of the luggage. The two young boys scrambled up to perch on top of the suitcases with delight spread in wide smiles across their faces. Avery assisted Beverly into the car and then got in himself after cranking the machine for Jade.

'Good heavens, Jade,' called Beverly from the backseat. 'Even out here you still manage to find a flivver to drive. Which reminds me, I heard the most marvelous joke the other day. Do you know the difference between a Model T and a wheelbarrow?' She waited for Jade to reply, savoring the moment. Jade merely arched one thick black brow and waited. 'A wheelbarrow only has one wheel,' said Bev. 'Isn't that a scream?'

Jade removed her hat, reached back, and slapped her friend on the head with it as she drove down the wide dirt road to the hotel. 'You'd be surprised at how many American cars there are in Nairobi. I've seen several made-over Fords and one Dodge. But,' she added, 'you'll be pleased to hear that Lord Colridge now owns a new Willys-Knight Overlander.'

'Old Colridge still alive, is he?' asked Avery. 'I suppose I'll have to visit the old man. He and my father were rather thick at one time.'

'He's expecting you,' said Jade. 'Actually, he was supposed to go on safari with us but just broke his leg. Seems a jackal ran straight towards his horse, and he was thrown.'

'My word. I hope it's not too serious,' exclaimed Avery.

'Just a fracture. If I know His Lordship, he'll order his leg to heal quickly.' She called back

229

over her shoulder to Beverly, 'Tell me all about the wedding.'

'Oh, never mind the wedding, darling,' scolded Beverly. 'I want to know what you've been up to. Here you are dressed in trousers and those old corps boots stinking like a pen at the London zoo. I do believe you need a keeper.'

'I told you back at the train, the smell protects me from witches.'

'You're not serious, are you?' Beverly tapped her husband on the shoulder. 'Avery, darling, I can't see her face. Tell me if she's serious.'

'She looks serious to me, my love, but I don't know her half as well as you do.'

'It's simple. If she's pulling my leg, she'll eventually turn up one side of her mouth in a pert little smirk. If she's serious, her lips don't move.'

Jade started singing an old war ditty.

'I believe her lips are moving, Beverly,' said Avery, 'but I can't say that they're smirking.'

'Oh, cripes. She's stringing us along,' Beverly groused. 'Very well. Two can play at that game.' She folded her arms across her chest for emphasis. 'I won't give you the gift we brought.'

'I'm sorry,' said Jade. 'I promise I'll explain everything, but not here.'

'If not here, then where?'

'Are you hungry?' asked Jade. 'The train came in early today. Must not have been anything worth shooting at on the way. You could ask the Norfolk to pack a basket for you while you get settled. I'll take you around, show you the sights, and give you all the *gory* details.'

230

The couple agreed. Jade saw to the lunch basket while Beverly and Avery went to their room followed by the two boys, still giggling from their ride atop the luggage. The desk clerk, used to many eccentricities, tolerated the outside youths better than he did Jade's aroma.

'Miss del Cameron,' he said and wrinkled his nose. 'How . . . good to . . . see you again. You aren't staying with us again, are you?'

'No,' she assured him. 'I'm a friend of Lord and Lady Dunbury. They would like a picnic basket packed, please. Some cold chicken perhaps, hard-boiled eggs, and fruit. Probably a nice white wine as well. Something simple will do.'

'Oh! For His Lordship? Of course.' He leaned forward to emphasize his assurances, but drew back as soon as he caught another whiff of Jade's hat.

Jade enjoyed the entire scene. She'd grown used to the scent and, being a rancher's daughter, didn't find it half as offensive as some of these dandified Nairobi-ites did. She wondered where Mrs Estes might be. *I'd like to show her my hat*, thought Jade with an evil grin.

'Er, would you care to have a glass of sherry on the veranda while you wait?' suggested the desk clerk.

'Actually, I still want to see that 1915 guest register. Do you have it?'

The clerk wrinkled his nose again, ran to the safe, and extracted the volume. Jade flipped the book open to January and ran her fingers down the list. She found Gil's name first listed on the

231

twenty-fifth. Next to that was a brief notation: *Jan. 30, found dead in room*. Few other names appeared, attesting to more people leaving rather than staying during the war. Jade took out her notebook and wrote down the names. One, she noticed, was a John Smith. He had taken the room next to Gil's on the twenty-eighth, and left late on the thirtieth.

'Did you find what you need, Miss del Cameron? Couldn't I get you that sherry on the veranda?'

'Coffee will do instead, please.' She went out before he fumigated the lobby.

As if thinking about trouble earlier now produced it, Cissy Estes appeared just as the Dunburys did. Her roving eye immediately landed on Avery's handsome face and athletic figure.

'Jade, whoo-hoo,' she called as though they were bosom friends.

'Who the blazes is this floozy?' whispered Beverly in Jade's ear.

The woman oozed up the stairs at a snail's pace. 'I was entertaining another acquaintance of yours last week.' Her words dripped slowly and dreamily. 'You'll never guess, so I'll tell you. Roger Forster. Such a charmer, that one.' She closed her mascara-lengthened lashes with a deliberate languor to emphasize her pleasure. 'Always adore seeing him. I believe he said he's running your safari along with Harry.' She moaned with pleasure. 'Mmmmm. You should have a wonderful time with those two. And thank you for the photograph. I adored it.'

No mention of Jeffrey this time or even the recently deceased Godfrey. Not with fresh prey in sight. 'Mrs Estes,' said Jade, 'how nice to see you again. As you can see, I have my hat today.' She took it off and waved it in the woman's general direction, hoping to keep her at bay. Mrs Estes' red-tinted lips puckered as though she had bit into a lemon. She stopped and swayed to some mental rhythm. 'I'm very sorry, too, for the loss of your friend Mr Kenton,' added Jade. 'I know you were very worried about him.'

Cissy swayed to and fro and blinked slowly. By the puzzled expression on her face, Jade assumed the woman was trying to remember who Mr Kenton was. Suddenly she drew in her breath with dawning recollection. 'Oh, poor Godfrey,' she said as she dabbed her dry eyes. 'I miss him so. Such a terrible accident. The funeral is tomorrow, I believe.'

'Yes,' murmured Jade, 'the commissioner did rule it an accidental death by wild animal, didn't he. I'm just curious as to what Mr Kenton was doing on Lord Colridge's land at the time.'

Cissy ignored Jade's statement and slid up the final step towards them. 'And who are your friends? You *must* introduce me to this very handsome man.' The woman nearly salivated as she extended her gloved hand. 'I'm Cissy Estes.'

'*I* am Lady Dunbury,' said Beverly. 'This is my *husband*.' She emphasized the word. Mrs Estes didn't seem to hear it. Beverly approached on the pretext of shaking the woman's hand and accidentally stomped on her foot. The woman didn't even wince.

'Oh, *Lord* Dunbury,' she cooed and crept closer. 'You must come to my flat and visit. I entertain many people there. We have the most divine parties. As I was saying, Roger — '

'I'm sorry, but we won't be joining you, Mrs Estes,' Beverly said. 'Perhaps we'll meet again. I presume you walk the streets quite frequently?' Beverly said this with the sweetest of smiles, but the heavily made-up woman couldn't help but catch her meaning.

'I must be going,' Mrs Estes said and threw one last predatory look at Avery before she turned and slithered back down the stairs.

'My word, Beverly,' declared Avery. 'You were an absolute tigress defending her own territory. I feel quite like a bit of prized meat.' He kissed his wife on the forehead.

'I don't think it would take a tigress to beat that one off, although I daresay she's handy with her needle,' retorted Beverly. Jade raised one brow in question. 'She's a heroin addict, my dear,' said Beverly in answer. 'You must have seen the signs: general slowness and euphoria, the fact that she didn't feel my foot stomp. And her pupils were positively pinpoints.'

'It is bright in the sun,' Jade countered, but in the back of her mind she recalled the powdery package in Cissy's purse.

'The sun isn't bright under that huge hat of hers. No, she's an addict. I'm sure her thighs are quite a mess from injections.'

'Who is this Godfrey person she pretended to cry over?' Avery asked.

'Godfrey Kenton. No one you would like,

Avery. Rich, self-centered, cheated on his wife, and, if the general gossip I heard was true, he may have tried to cheat a couple of the colonists out of property or livestock.' Jade watched Cissy's retreating back and tried to make her voice sound as casual as possible. 'Anyway, he went missing late Saturday or early Sunday. I found his remains on Colridge's property just the other day.'

'What?' exclaimed both Dunburys simultaneously. 'How horrid for you,' Beverly added. 'Did you have to identify him?'

'There wasn't much to identify really. His boot . . . with a leg stump in it and his head.' Jade looked around. 'Where is that lunch? I'm famished.'

The lunch basket appeared shortly, and Jade drove them straight to the Ruiru flumes, where her adventure had first begun. They sat on some rocks and ate while Jade recounted her experiences, ending with the lion by the car and finding Kenton's body. She even undid her cuff and showed them the small indigo-colored lion's tooth on her wrist.

'So you can see why I believe very strongly in this ointment. I'm not entirely sure what it does against witches, but it's very efficacious against wild lions.'

Neither Beverly nor her husband spoke. Beverly was too stunned, and Avery had a mouthful of chicken. He poured a glass of wine for his wife and held a second out to Jade. She declined it, taking water from a crockery jug instead. Avery drained his glass in two gulps.

'Beverly, do you have the feeling that we don't know our Jade as well as we thought?'

Beverly recovered her presence of mind enough to close her mouth and accept the wineglass. She drained it. 'You're quite right, my love,' she said in a soft voice. Then she added in a livelier tone, 'Only imagine that. Our own Jade is now a lioness. Simba Jike, indeed. I can only imagine what names we shall receive, Avery.' The newlyweds bantered several possibilities back and forth, ranging from the complimentary to the silly.

'Golden goddess,' suggested Avery.

'Oh no, Avery darling. That would never suit you,' Beverly replied with a laugh.

Jade sat motionless on her rock, rifle at her feet, and let them have their fun. To her ear and with her intimacy born of friendship, she detected certain nervous qualities in Beverly's voice. She concluded the two of them were larking to hide their worry for her. Beverly pulled *The Colonist's Swahili Language Lesson* from Jade's bag and looked up words.

'Oh, Avery,' she called out, 'you can be Bwana Mtemba for that pipe you insist on smoking. I'll be Manjano Swala. That means yellow gazelle . . . I think.' She patted her hair.

'Well, don't look now, my gazelle,' said Avery, 'but there is a lioness on that rock watching the both of us rather intently.' He took his pipe from his pocket and filled it.

Beverly wheeled around, eyes wide with fear. Instead of the expected big cat, she saw her friend seated on the rock with her arms wrapped around her knees, eyeing her. 'Jade, stop that. You gave me a fright. That habit of yours where you stare with those green eyes is positively unnerving and rude.'

'Sorry,' Jade apologized. She didn't move or look away. 'My mother would agree with you. She says it shows bad breeding, but then, I am a mutt, aren't I?'

Beverly pouted. 'Honestly, darling, you've always been brave and bold and perfectly oblivious to social conventions, but we are worried about you. I mean, well, you've smeared your clothes with who knows what unsanitary ointment, for heaven's sake. This is far beyond simply melting your Bovril chocolate bars with coffee and making up those awful limericks. Er, what did you call them?'

'Piss-sonnets,' answered Jade. 'And the chocolate and coffee was your idea, remember?'

'Exactly!' Beverly stabbed a finger into the air to emphasize her point before she lost it.

'What my adorable little wife is trying to say, Jade,' chimed in Avery, 'is that we fear you've taken this entire search to uncover what happened to David's father and his missing brother way too far.' Jade stiffened, and he raised his right hand in a placating gesture. 'David's loss was a blow to all of us. He was my best friend. But you must move on.'

'He made a request,' Jade said in a low, firm voice. Her green eyes locked onto Avery's blue ones. 'His final one. I understood that to be slightly sacred.'

Avery looked down at his empty glass. Beverly

237

verbally leaped into the breach.

'What Avery means, Jade, is that you are too close to this. You must let us help you.'

'Exactly,' stated Avery. 'Thank you, darling, for posing it so neatly. Jade, after my discharge, Bev told me a bit about your trip to see David's mother and their solicitor. I made some inquiries of my own, sent a few cables to some acquaintances in Mombasa actually, and saw to their replies when we docked.'

'And?' Jade asked. She arched one brow but didn't move otherwise.

'There's no birth or baptismal record for an Abel Worthy in Mombasa or Nairobi. For that matter, they couldn't find a birth certificate for an Abel *anybody*.' He leaned forward and clasped his hands together. 'Jade, it's a wild-goose chase. The two biggest cities, for want of a better term, don't have any record of such a person. You indicated that Gil's map said 'Abel, my second son.''

'That's right, Jade,' added Beverly. 'In the Bible, Abel was Adam's second son. Maybe he just wrote Abel as a metaphor, something to remind him that he had another child without knowing his real name.'

'The protectorate is large,' continued Avery. '*If* there was such a child, and that's a big if, finding him would be the proverbial search for a needle in the haystack, as you Americans say.' He looked at Beverly for support and added, 'What you told us about Gil's death certainly sounds unusual, but you said yourself that those hyenas have been bold since the war's start. Maybe Gil's

238

death was just an accident. Maybe a hyena slipped in during the night.'

Jade closed her eyes and inhaled deeply to steel herself against her inner turmoil. Her lips tensed and whitened for a moment before she reopened her eyes and clutched at the token inside her shirt. 'The ring is the key. I . . . I promised David.' Her voice grew thick and husky.

Beverly stood and scrambled up the rock to her friend's side. She put her arm around Jade to console her, but Jade didn't relax into the embrace.

'I knew David wore that ring,' said Avery, 'but to be honest, I never got a close look at it. May I?' He stood up and held out his hand.

Jade hesitated a moment, then slipped the cord from around her neck and handed the ring to Avery. 'He never explained it to you before? Never mentioned a brother or the circumstances around his father's death?' Her tone was skeptical.

'Oh, come now,' cooed Beverly. She hugged Jade. 'Can you imagine two British males sitting around discussing how one's father was a rounder? It's simply not done.'

'Remember, he never told you either, Jade,' said Avery. Jade winced at the gentle rejoinder. 'He probably didn't know himself until his father sent him that ring. I recall him receiving a letter and a box from his father one day, a few months before the old man died, in fact. David became rather reclusive after that. I asked him what it was about, but he said just some family matter. I don't know when he began to question his father's death.'

'I never got to see his personal effects to look for a letter,' commented Jade.

'No,' agreed Avery. 'All of that was sent off to his mother. She probably destroyed it rather than admit her husband had a child with another woman.' He stared into the stone, the green of a wet, lush, tropical forest, the green of fresh moss in a mountain stream. 'Is this an emerald?'

'No,' replied Jade. 'Even the best emeralds have little black specks, inclusions. And emeralds are sleepier. This one also plays with light as though it had its own internal fire.'

'Like your eyes, Jade,' suggested Beverly with a smile.

Avery studied the etchings in the side. 'How very odd.'

'Yes, aren't they,' agreed Jade.

Beverly scurried down the rock to her husband. 'Let me see.' She peered over Avery's shoulder. 'It looks like a little ghost peeking over at another one,' said Beverly. 'At least, you can see the back of the second one's head and the little topknot. He has a tear running from one eye.' She took the ring and turned it over. 'The other side looks like a snake with a tiny Orthodox-style cross on one side.' She handed the ring back to her husband.

'I don't understand it,' he said finally with a shake of his head. 'Bev's little pop-up ghost aside, it's all chicken scratches to me.' He paused and played with his mustache in thought. 'And

240

you said there is another ring? Is it the same?' he asked.

Jade nodded, then stopped. 'Well, almost,' she said. 'Beverly's pop-up ghost is alone without, in keeping with her metaphor, the tear. And the snake is more of a broad, shallow U. The cross is longer, too.'

'How interesting,' remarked Avery. 'Perhaps you hold them to a mirror and get a word or something. I daresay the meaning was in a letter to David, but it's lost now. What about in that packet?' he asked.

'That's sealed for the second son. Even the solicitor didn't have the authority to open it. If I find reasonable proof of the son's identity, I'm allowed to hand it over.'

Avery gave the ring back to her, and she slipped the leather thong over her head. 'Sorry, ol' girl. What you have is a very special reminder of David.'

Jade picked up her rifle and rose to her feet. A small bushbuck that had approached the flume to drink bolted out of the grass and raced away. 'We should leave before something larger decides to drink here,' she suggested. 'You'll want to rest awhile after all your traveling. And the Thompsons are joining us for dinner. They're wonderful people. Of course, Neville won't be coming on safari with us, but you can meet him. You'll like the Thompsons,' she added. 'Madeline is a lot like you, Beverly.'

'Stunningly beautiful, you mean?' suggested Avery. Beverly grinned but didn't blush. She was not a blusher.

'Well, I'm not tired and I don't want to go back to the hotel to rest,' protested Beverly. 'Let's visit old Colridge, shall we? But before we go,' she added, making it clear that the decision was already made, 'we must give Jade her gift. Did you bring it, love?'

Avery assured her he had and strolled to the Ford to fetch it from the back. Jade's jaw nearly dropped when he handed her a beautiful new Mannlicher bolt-action rifle. 'About time you had a decent weapon. Not that your Winchester isn't perfectly splendid for mountain cats and hyenas, but you can trust this to tackle a lion or rhino with a bit more efficiency. Perhaps,' he added with a smile, 'it will help you to leave off with that dreadful concoction you're wearing.'

Jade cradled the rifle in her arms and expressed her feelings with a simple but sincere 'Thank you.' However, she added inwardly, she had no intention of forgoing her protective ointment, not even for Beverly's or Avery's British sensibilities. She sighted down the barrel at another ravine and noticed a bright pinpoint of light wink back at her.

'Do you see something?' asked Bev. 'Perhaps a warthog attracted by your perfume?'

'Probably nothing,' Jade answered, ignoring the barb. 'There's something shining in that ravine.' She slid off her boulder and headed for the spot.

'Wait for us,' said Avery. He trotted up to her with his own rifle ready.

Jade neared the location and cautiously moved around, wary of unseen predators. The light caught the object and reflected off the glass windshield of an automobile. She stopped.

'What is it, Jade?' asked Beverly.

'Evidence that Mr Kenton wasn't killed in Colridge's orchard.'

★ ★ ★

She must stay alive awhile longer. Against all his inner thirst for revenge and desire to dominate, the witch knew the American woman must be allowed to live. Only recently had he learned that she carried information that could lead to potential wealth, and wealth meant power. It would not be forever, he reminded himself. Then he could deal with her as she deserved. He would make her suffer mentally as well as physically. He knew the terror that washed over her when she heard the hyena's laugh, a terror that would make him laugh long and hard. Then he would kill again.

17

'A visitor in Nairobi is immediately touched by the close-knit society there. Such tight bonds are important in a colony, as everyone depends one way or another on everyone else.'
— The Traveler

The day after Jade found Godfrey Kenton's car, a handful of Nairobi residents gathered to bid farewell to his meager remains. Leticia Kenton looked small and insignificant in a black dress several sizes too large for her petite frame. Dr Burkitt, who often led a local congregation in Sunday worship, conducted the service and read Psalm 23 while the young widow stood by. Her attention, however, was not on any 'restful waters' that her husband might be led to. Instead, Jade thought, she appeared to be looking for someone. Judging by the young woman's disappointed frown, that someone wasn't present. Perhaps she was looking for Roger.

Jade glanced around at the cluster of people. The number of people *not* present was more noticeable than those attending. Besides herself and Madeline, she saw the commissioner, Mr Donaldson, Mr and Mrs Woodard, and a reporter for a London paper. Mr Donaldson appeared to enjoy himself immensely. Harry, she knew, was involved with safari details, and

Colridge's leg kept him away. Roger was already on his way to Tsavo with the body of equipment.

Dr Burkitt finished the psalm, and Leticia threw a handful of dirt onto the coffin. No sooner had the clump left her gloved hand than a car pulled up, and Cissy Estes staggered out, wailing and moaning. The Woodards hurriedly pulled her away before she tripped and fell into the open grave.

'I say, good show all round.'

Jade turned and spied Mr Donaldson walking up to her. A wide grin stretched across his face. Jade arched one brow and waited for the explanation to his rude comment.

'I suppose that was in poor taste,' he said without a shred of remorse. Then, after seeing Madeline's chastising frown, he added, 'I was referring to Mrs Estes. One is never without entertainment when she's around.'

'I'm surprised to see you here, Mr Donaldson,' Jade said. 'I got the impression that you didn't care for Mr Kenton.'

'I didn't. He cheated me out of a broodmare last month.'

'Was that Mr Kenton's regular business?' asked Jade. 'Cheating people?'

'Yes, but the bast — er, the scoundrel always managed to do it legally, or at least in such a way that a man could not charge him with anything.'

Jade nodded her understanding. 'Then that explains why so few people came to mourn him. But back to my original question. Why did you come?'

'Satisfaction, I suppose. And to make certain

245

the man was really dead.'

Madeline made a slight snort of disbelief, and Jade put her hand on Maddy's arm. 'Oh, we can vouch for that, Mr Donaldson,' said Jade. 'They found most of him, but in bits and pieces. Most men don't recover from injuries like that.'

She paused a moment before asking him her next question. 'Do you think this was an accident, Mr Donaldson? I mean, what in the world could he have been doing out there?' Jade intentionally did not state just where 'out there' was. When she had told the commissioner about the car, she had suggested he keep the location of its discovery at the flumes quiet since only the killer would know it. It might lead the person into revealing something since everyone else assumed Kenton had died on Colridge's farm. The commissioner had not been overly impressed by the idea at the time.

Mr Donaldson put his hands in his coat pocket. 'I heard the old boy was in two spots, and I don't mean after his death.' He snickered. 'Probably met a lady friend at the flumes, then headed off to Colridge's estate for some dalliance,' he added as he waggled his eyebrows.

Jade gritted her teeth. Her suggestion to the commissioner had fallen on deaf ears.

'Then why hasn't the woman come forward?' asked Madeline. 'Why wasn't she killed?'

Donaldson chuckled. 'Several reasons, Mrs Thompson, perhaps not obvious to a polite lady such as yourself.' He ticked them off on his fingers. 'One, *she* killed him. Two, she's married and doesn't need trouble from hubby. Three, and my personal favorite, it's an accident, and she wasn't killed because she could outrun him.' He slapped his thighs in obvious glee. 'Anyway, he's gone and good riddance. If it was murder, and I doubt it, we'd all just as soon buy the guilty party a drink as turn her or him in. And,' he added, 'that includes the widow *and* the commissioner. Kenton caused enough trouble that the commissioner's workload will lighten visibly.' He touched his hat brim in farewell and headed for his car.

Madeline put her hands on her hips and shook her head. 'Well, that was by far the most outrageous . . . ' She ended with another exasperated sniff.

'Yes, it was,' agreed Jade. She caught sight of the commissioner and tugged Maddy's arm. 'I want to speak with him.'

Jade succeeded in capturing the commissioner's attention before he left the cemetery. 'Sir, why did you reveal where the car was found?'

The commissioner leaned back as though he sensed he was under attack. 'Miss del Cameron, I wasn't aware you headed our criminal bureau.'

Jade pressed her point. 'All sarcasm aside, sir, that was potentially valuable information.'

'Only if a crime was committed, miss. There is no evidence of that.'

Jade sucked in her breath in a frustrated hiss. 'The car's location *was* the evidence. It proves his body was moved.'

The commissioner puffed out his chest like a posing gamecock and looked down his nose at her, a task rendered more difficult as they were the same height. 'As we discussed earlier, a large carnivore dragged the body away.'

Jade shook her head. 'Carnivores don't drag full-grown men over six miles cross-country. He had enemies, sir. Lots of them. He cheated Donaldson out of a broodmare. He tried to get Harry Hascombe's cattle killed by starting another false anthrax scare.'

'He cheated on his wife,' added Madeline.

The commissioner raised his right hand for the two women to stop. 'Calm yourselves, Miss del Cameron, Mrs Thompson. Mrs Kenton does not care to have this matter pursued. She only wants to bury her husband and the past. And,' he added quickly when he saw Jade inhale in preparation for another attack, 'without other evidence of foul play, there is nothing I can do.'

Jade saw the futility of pressing her point. She took a different tack. 'Have you learned anything else about Gil Worthy that can help shed light on finding his son or his killer?'

The commissioner assumed a look of patronizing patience. 'Still on that as well, Miss del Cameron? You read too much into ordinary deaths.' He waved his hand at the headstones. 'Only look around you. You will find many deaths attributed to animal attacks here.' He saw Jade's dark brows furrow and stepped back a pace.

'I'm leaving the day after tomorrow on safari to Tsavo,' she said. 'When I return, I plan to continue my inquiries.' Jade pulled a slip of notepaper from her pocket. 'Here are the names

248

of guests in the Norfolk at the time of Gil Worthy's death. I presume you'll want to interview them.'

The commissioner glanced at the list. 'John Smith! You must be joking.'

Jade shook her head. 'I don't suppose there's much use in my asking about what's been done about this *laibon* that terrorized the Kikuyu village, is there? Kenton supposedly cheated Maasai out of cattle. Perhaps a *laibon* killed him.'

'Really, miss. Killed by native witchcraft?' He snorted. 'As I understand it, you took care of the *laibon* already when you killed his hyena.' He doffed his hat to them. 'Good day, ladies.' He turned on his heel and strode briskly away.

Jade folded her arms across her chest. 'Well, that was a waste of breath.'

Madeline patted her on the shoulder. 'You did very well, my dear. Really, one cannot move stubborn male mountains. But do you really suspect a *laibon* for all these deaths?'

Jade shoved her hands into her skirt pockets. 'I suppose it does sound silly, but I can't shake the suspicion that all these deaths are related.' What, she wondered, was the connection between Kikuyu natives, Godfrey Kenton, and Gil Worthy? Someone may have wanted to stop Gil before he found his son in Tsavo. That would also explain the attacks on her.

'When I find the son, I'll find the connection.'

18

'Safari. The very word conjures up more romantic notions than all the Arabian Nights tales. It is an incantation as powerful as open sesame. It unlocks the rhythmic chanting of porters, the excited whisper of the gun bearer, and the hypnotic eyes of the lion that studies you in the golden grass that seems to spring from its very mane. Enough danger, excitement, and adventure to generate a lifetime of personal sagas travel with you by day and camp with you at night as you relax around a fire, dine on eland steaks served on fine bone china, and swap tales of impossible shots. Of course, all this romance will cost your pocketbook and make it many 'pounds' lighter, but how can you put a price on legends?'
— The Traveler

The two days before the safari blew by in a whirlwind of last-minute shopping for 'woolies,' more socks, another pair of heavy trousers suitable for the thorny bush, and any other items deemed indispensable.

All nonpersonal items such as tents, cots, mess gear, blankets, and food had already been sent ahead in boxes with the hired porters and Roger on the return train after the Dunburys' arrival. They would travel by train as far as the Tsavo station, where an oxcart waited. From there, the porters would hike west towards Kilimanjaro and set up camp. Roger would wait for the hunting party at the Tsavo depot.

On the day of departure, the party convened on the Nairobi station platform in midafternoon to wait for the returning train south. The usual laughing children, scolding sentries, native women and their produce, and assorted colonists crowded the platform. Above all the ruckus rumbled the voice of Harry Hascombe, first hunter for the safari.

'Good day, Jade,' his deep baritone voice purred. 'Pity about poor Miles and his leg. I presume everyone else is ready.'

'Yes, and allow me to introduce you to Lord Avery and Lady Beverly Dunbury.'

Harry shook hands with Avery, and the two men sized each other up. They matched in height, but Harry's build was far more powerful than Avery's slighter, almost willowy frame. Jade didn't doubt, however, that in a test of courage, it would be a very close match. Avery had taken nearly as many risks as David during the war, and Harry had already shown at Ruiru that he didn't care to be bested by anyone. *This could be interesting*, she thought. *Two bulls sparring for dominance*. Jade wondered where Roger fit into this herding scenario.

'I brought the hyena skin to town with me, Jade,' Harry said. He released Avery's grip but kept his eyes riveted on the younger man's face. 'Took it to the hotel. They'll keep it for you.' Beverly, disgusted by the dominant-male staring contest, held out her hand.

'How do you do, Mr Hascombe?'

Harry tipped his battered, wide-brimmed felt hat to her and to Madeline, who stayed in the background. Pili sat quietly behind them near their luggage. 'Good day, ladies. Pleased to make your acquaintance, Lady Dunbury.' Harry kissed Beverly's hand. Avery scowled.

Beverly grinned. 'Mercy, I do love hearing people say my new name. I am pleased to meet you, Mr Hascombe. Jade has told us so much about you.'

'Don't believe everything you hear, Lady Dunbury.' He flashed a wide, roguish smile that exposed all his white teeth. 'I'm much worse than all that.' He turned back to Avery. 'What are you carrying for weapons, Your Lordship?' The title sounded mocking, coming from Harry.

'First of all,' said Avery, 'drop the title. There's little room for that nonsense in the field. I'd hate to see myself mauled because someone was busy spitting out 'Your Lordship' instead of just shouting 'lion.' '

Jade agreed. 'Reminds me of the American author James Fenimore Cooper. No one could have survived the wilderness if they talked as much as his Hawkeye did. He once spent an entire paragraph warning everyone to be silent lest the Iroquois hear them. With his gums flapping, they should have been dead, scalps neatly hanging on a belt.'

Everyone laughed and, with the previous tension relieved, Harry and Avery began conversing more genially about their hunting rifles. They were still talking when they heard the train approaching. Pili rose from his seat like a white phantom and picked up Jade's new rifle and ammo box. Harry noticed him for the first time and looked at him in surprise. Jade wasn't sure what surprised him more, her new rifle or having Lord Colridge's personal man for a gun bearer. She didn't ask. Memories of their last dance flooded her mind, and she decided the less private conversation she had with Harry the better.

They boarded the train with their personal gear and sped off towards Tsavo and Colonel Patterson's famous bridge. It was there that two man-eaters had claimed more than a hundred railroad workers as victims before Patterson managed to kill them. Harry sat alone in the back of the car. Avery seated himself next to Pili, and Beverly and Madeline sat together and compared Jade stories. Jade first sat in front of the other women, but after announcing, 'I don't need to hear all those blasted lies and tall tales,' she moved over closer to Avery and Pili.

The small-gauge engine stopped frequently for water, and the station names of Machakos Road, Kiu, Sultan Hamud, and Simba rolled out of the passengers' view and into their memories. Most of the stops were merely at water towers. Some had high-walled stone buildings maintained by the railroad for workers or for travelers on foot either hoping to catch the train or just there to pass the night in something more defensible than a ring of thorny brush.

Later on the train, a porter brought tea (to Jade's disgust), and they dined on scones (courtesy of the Norfolk) and tinned beef. The

253

party was in high spirits. At first, everyone amused themselves with looking through the smoked-glass windows at distant herds of wildebeest or giraffes and debated whether or not that golden tan lump in the grass was a rock or a lion. When the train whistled to chase away an animal, they placed bets on what it would be and laughed as the frightened kongoni or any other antelope raced away.

Avery declared his desire to try for one of the sable antelope if only the train would stop long enough for him to get off a shot and retrieve the carcass. He opened the window for a better look and was met with the universal red dust of the plains. His wife coughed loudly, the window was closed, and the sable antelope survived another day.

Eventually, the air inside their car became more stifling in the late-afternoon heat, the tinned beef lay heavily in their stomachs, and the passengers grew lethargic. Antelope herds ceased to interest anyone. No one cared about the pseudolions anymore, and Avery protested that the engineer should 'stop the bloody whistle and just run down any infernal animal foolish enough to stand betwixt the metals.'

Only Jade maintained her inner excitement. At its base lay a sense of coming closer to the truth about David's father and brother. Her large camera bag rested on the floor between her feet, and she nudged it gently. In the bottom, hidden from view, were the second ring, the map of names, and the packet marked Abel. Somewhere out there, she reasoned, was David's half

254

brother, and she wanted to be ready for him. Since Gil had listed the Chyulu Hills on his map, there was a good chance she could pick up his trail there. Perhaps she'd find this Kruger fellow nearby. Eventually the sun set, and stars crystallized out of the cooling night air. She drifted off to sleep, which, for once, was not disturbed by nightmares.

The train stopped at the Tsavo station just before one o'clock in the morning. Jade and Pili were the first to disembark and Harry the last as he made certain everyone in their party was off with their personal belongings. Nothing rustled in the distant grass or called out in the night except a few nocturnal insects that played the rhythm by which the stars arced across the sky. The first sound to send a ripple through the darkness was Beverly's sleepy voice.

'There had better not be any man-eaters about. It's positively uncivilized to be mauled at this hour of the night,' she said, and Avery growled behind her.

Tsavo boasted a better station than most of the previous water stops. Besides its famous bridge, there were several round huts, and a small, wood-frame station house. The usual veranda ran around the building, but the floor was packed earth without a platform. A little house for the Indian stationmaster sat farther back surrounded by thick, thorny scrub. The train started off for Voi and left them alone with the stars and whatever lurked in the brush beyond.

A small fire crackled a few feet in front of the

station door, and Roger materialized from behind it. He touched his hat brim in greeting. 'I took the liberty of setting cots up inside the station for tonight. Borrowed them from the old stationmaster. That way, we won't have tents to take down and we can snag another hour's sleep before starting out in the morning.' As he took in the party members, his eyes opened a little wider in puzzlement. 'I don't understand,' he said. 'I thought there were only two ladies in the party. Who are these other two people?'

'We replaced one lord with another,' said Harry. 'It seems Thompson and Colridge are out, but Lord and Lady Dunbury are in instead. Same number. Supplies shouldn't matter.' As an afterthought, he introduced Roger to the Dunburys.

'I see,' said Roger in a confused tone that indicated he didn't. He roused two natives from one of the huts and directed them to move the baggage into the station. Jade didn't wait for anyone to assist her. She left her untried Mannlicher with Pili, took her Winchester and the camera bag inside, selected a cot, and set them beside it. Beverly staggered in after her and threw herself on the very cot Jade had marked for her own.

Jade looked down at her and kicked the cot. 'Nice of you to think of us, Bev, and help out,' she said. Beverly only groaned.

'Let her be,' whispered Madeline. 'She's exhausted.' Jade made a scoffing sound.

Madeline and Jade moved one of the men's cots to their area without waiting for the porters

256

to do it, and Jade made certain to again 'accidentally' kick Beverly's cot in the process. This time Bev didn't stir, and Jade knew she'd fallen asleep already. Roger brought in blankets. Jade tossed one on top of Beverly, rolled herself up in another, and fell asleep.

She woke before the others and went out to stand on the tracks, facing west. She heard Roger wake the rest just after the first golden rays shot across the horizon from behind her. She heard Avery groan and Beverly comment on nocturnal ambulance runs. The comment turned into a mild swear, and Jade presumed Bev had discovered Jade's cot was empty.

'There you are, Jade.' Bev stood beside her friend, their long shadows cast like advance scouts into the scrub. Jade held her camera idly at her waist and gazed out to the distant hills while Beverly hugged herself against the morning dampness.

The Tsavo station stood on a sidehill and looked out over the Tsavo River valley with its steep gorges, buttes, rounded hills like native huts or sugar loaves, and expansive thornriddled grasslands. The scene spread before them like a golden brocaded cloak trimmed in plush velvet greens around the waterways.

'He's out there somewhere,' said Jade in a hushed voice. 'I'll find him, and once I do, I'll find out who killed his father.'

Beverly took Jade's hand in hers and gave it a gentle squeeze. 'Of course you will, love.'

Madeline called from behind them in a cheery voice, 'Good morn — Oh, sorry, I didn't mean

257

to disturb a private conversation.'

Beverly graciously eased the moment by releasing Jade's hand and extending her own towards Madeline in invitation. 'Good morning to you, Madeline. May I call you Madeline? And you must call me Beverly. I feel I know you very well after our little talk yesterday.'

'Lies, all lies,' muttered Jade.

Madeline joined them and yawned. 'Please do. I know I should feel dreadful this morning knowing poor Neville is home harvesting the crop, but I don't. I feel like a schoolgirl on holiday. Isn't that wicked?'

Beverly grinned. 'Terribly, and good girl, I say. But you and I also have an important job. Who knows what would befall our American friend here if we weren't around to take care of her? Only consider the mischief she's gotten into so far, killing bewitched hyenas and slapping pistols out of strange men's hands. And look at the consequences. Now she has to go about smelling like an incontinent ferret in heat.'

Jade glowered at her former ambulance corps comrade. Beverly looked away from that formidable stare but didn't apologize.

'I must be getting used to it,' suggested Madeline. 'I don't smell anything now.'

'It's worn off the belt and boots,' Jade explained.

'But not the hat,' added Beverly. 'Ah, well, I suppose in this environment, Simba Jike will blend right in with the elephants, rhinos, and other wild beasties at that.'

'If you're going to continue in this vein,' said

258

Jade, 'I'll just go see about our gear.' She pivoted and strode back to the station. Her friends followed hot on her heels.

Jade ignored them and found Roger talking with Harry and an old wiry African native dressed in khaki shorts and a red blanket. They spoke in some clipped dialect that sounded to Jade like the language Ruta spoke. Most likely Maasai. Harry saw her first, touched his hat brim in greeting, and walked off behind the station house.

Jade thanked him inwardly for having enough gentlemanly notions to avoid embarrassing scenes in front of her friends. She knew from their dance at the Muthaiga that he wanted her, and she half feared that he'd continue his pursuit out here. Jade smiled. *Half feared.* That meant that she half hoped, too. *Chalk that one up to feminine vanity.*

Roger spotted her, nodded, and dismissed the African. Jade stepped forward. 'Good morning, Mr Forster.' She pointed to the retreating figure. 'Who's that man?'

Roger's nose wrinkled and he stepped back a couple of paces. 'That is our tracker, Memba Sasa. I've worked with him before.'

'Very good. Where are all the porters? I haven't seen very many here.'

Roger's lips straightened into a rigid line like those of a schoolboy who resents being questioned. 'I sent the regular porters ahead with an oxcart the morning after we arrived. As soon as everyone eats, we'll load up the cars and drive west, Miss del Cameron. We'll catch up to them in no time with the motorcars.'

'Cars?' asked Jade. 'I thought you only used oxcarts on safaris.'

Roger pursed his lips with a look of mounting impatience and shuffled his boots in the dust. 'I sent one with the porters to carry the supplies, water barrels, and extra petrol, but I thought we would try something more modern this time. Ox can be a bloo — excuse me, a nuisance in this type of country. Too many lions about. The next thing you know, your transportation is being digested somewhere in the scrub. I had the cars brought up from a man in Mombasa. Box bodies made like lorries actually. And,' he added with the slightest hint of a relaxed smile, 'they're American like yourself, Miss del Cameron.'

Jade arched one brow as a question and waited for the answer.

'A Dodge and a Ford,' said Roger.

Beverly overheard the last part and groaned. 'Am I never going to see you drive something more suitable than an old Ford flivver, Jade?'

Roger looked from one lady to the other in confusion. 'Well, I hardly think she will be driving, Lady Dunbury — '

'Oh, just try to keep her from behind the wheel, Mr Forster.' She shook her blond head in disgust. 'Come along, Madeline. Let's find some breakfast. Maybe an impala fell into the pot. I am absolutely famished.'

Roger watched them leave and shifted his boots again as he tried to determine the best course of action now. Jade read something akin to annoyance in his body movements. She

260

decided he probably felt his authority was challenged and tried to put him at ease.

'Mr Forster, please excuse my friend. It's true, I am a very experienced driver. I drove a Ford along the front lines during the war. So, if you'll accept my offer, I'll be more than happy to help. But, of course, that is your decision. You and Harry are in charge.'

A faint smile resembling a sneer showed on Roger's face. *Honestly*, thought Jade, *no wonder he lost Leticia*. The man was surly bordering on irascible.

'I'll pass your offer along to Harry,' he said. 'Remember, he's actually first in charge on this hunt. This opportunity is his way of helping me stay a half step ahead of the bank and the overdrafts. But you really must get some breakfast now before the porridge gets cold. I'm afraid it's all we know how to make ourselves. I sent the cook ahead, too.'

Jade joined the others for a bowl of hot oatmeal, something she enjoyed about as much as moldy bread and tea. Thank heavens someone had made coffee. She poured a little on the oatmeal and stirred it around. Better, she thought. At least it added some flavor. Madeline, Avery, and Harry looked amused, Roger shocked. Beverly pretended she didn't see.

Breakfast over, one native man scoured the pot with sand, and the other stowed the gear into the motorcars. The cars looked like mutt dogs put together out of various parts. Like mutts, they were hardier for the mixture. Both the Dodge and the Ford owned only a little of their

261

original chassis after the transition to box-bodied cars. Wooden slats had been hammered together and held in place with bolts and wire to make the sides. Wire netting, roofing felt, and rolls of canvas made the vehicle relatively rain resistant and created places along the exterior from which to hang assorted baggage and cans of water. Makeshift benches had replaced the seats, so the vehicles held more passengers than would otherwise be possible, although far less comfortably. As Roger said, they resembled lorries or ambulances more than pleasure cars.

Harry delegated bodies to the vehicles. 'Roger, you travel in the Ford with our eager and hardy guests. I'll take Memba Sasa, Colridge's man, and the other two men in the Dodge.'

'I should warn you, Mr Hascombe,' said Beverly. 'Our American friend here will fight you or Mr Forster for the wheel. She's like a fire horse that way. Can't be kept out of the run. Especially if there's a flivver involved.'

Harry regarded Beverly with a look of confusion on his handsome face. She simply gathered up her new felt hat and climbed into the Ford with her husband's assistance. Avery next helped Madeline into the bench seat, then waited for Jade.

'Where's that blasted gypsy?' he muttered.

'She's photographing us, my love. Smile pleasantly, please, or all the world will see you scowl in some magazine. Mr Forster,' Beverly added, 'pose for future publicity.'

Roger was busy tying a satchel onto the wire-and-wood frame. He looked up, saw Jade with her Graflex, and jauntily posed by leaning against the Ford's hood. Jade finished her shot, packed up her camera, and trotted to the car. She waved away Avery's chivalrous offer of aid and neatly sprang up and into the passenger's side of the front seat next to Roger. One of the remaining native Africans cranked the machine and it sputtered to life just as Roger sneezed loudly.

Jade pretended not to notice while Roger nervously adjusted the magneto and fidgeted with the side lever. Whether he was in charge or not, she was about to push him aside and show him how it was done when Beverly rescued Roger by calling Jade's attention to the station-master's house.

'Look, Jade. Who's that little man with that horrid-looking implement in his hand?'

Jade saw a small turbaned man wielding what looked like a medieval battle-ax painted bright green. In that moment, Roger managed to find low gear, and the car lurched forward.

'Did I just see what I thought I saw?' Jade asked.

'That's the stationmaster,' said Roger. 'Curious man. Carries that grotesque ax around all the time. Claims there are very bad men around here. When they see his ax, they decide that he, too, is a very bad man and leave him alone.' Roger shrugged. 'Daresay it works. He's alive at any rate.' He rubbed his nose with his sleeve and tried unsuccessfully to hold back another sneeze. 'Miss del Cameron, I must ask you to remove that hat. I'm afraid whatever is on it is making me sneeze.'

Jade took off her hat and pushed it into a crevice under the seat. 'I'm sorry.'

Roger rubbed his nose. 'Horrid-smelling stuff. I'm surprised that you tolerate it.' He pointed to the canvas covering. 'The canopy will protect you from the sun.'

Jade sighed. 'I love this country. It reminds me so much of home.'

'You have men carrying battle-axes around at home?' asked Madeline from behind.

'Well, metaphorically speaking, yes. My father has one horse wrangler who never goes anywhere without this old, rusty bayonet from the Civil War. Claims it's the best guarantee against rattlesnakes. But we have counterparts to many of the people I've seen in Africa. Lord Colridge, from what I hear, used to ride down the streets of Nairobi and shoot out the streetlights.'

Jade looked across to Roger for confirmation. He nodded and she continued. 'There's a town called Cimarron near our ranch. The hotel has more bullet holes in the ceiling than I'd care to patch, and we have some wealthy landowners who are notorious for their wild escapades, too.'

'What about Neville and me?' asked Madeline. 'Who are our counterparts?'

Jade rested her left leg from the knee up on the seat and turned around. 'The farmers and ranchers who moved west searching for space and opportunities.'

'*I* came to Africa because Neville made me. He's never told me why he left England.'

'And what about yourself?' asked Roger. 'I

264

should think you're rather unusual.'

Beverly spoke up before Jade could answer. 'You won't find Jade's counterpart anywhere. She's an enigma, part adventuress, part wildlife. And,' Bev added, 'the bravest woman I've ever met.'

'Shut up, Bev,' growled Jade. 'Everyone in the outfit was brave.'

'True,' agreed Beverly, 'excepting Jane the Pain. She was a 'seeing Francer.' That means,' she explained to Madeline, 'that she only joined up to see Paris and marry an officer.'

'Unlike you, my love, who had to settle for an ordinary pilot,' said Avery.

Everyone but Roger chuckled, and Avery pressed Madeline for information about growing coffee. The noisy engine made conversation between the front and back difficult. Mr Forster made no more attempt at communication so Jade turned her attention to Tsavo's expansive grasslands. To her left was a green belt of trees marking the river's course. Rounded hills and rocky buttes dotted the landscape of golden grass and prickly thornbushes. Patches of reddish-pink dirt showed where animals had wallowed and exposed the laterite soil. *So this is the country of the famed man-eaters.* Colonel Patterson himself might have walked through here tracking the killers. Roger's voice roused her from her daydream.

'I said, are there people like myself in America?' asked Roger.

'Well, there's me, if you mean people actually born on the frontier, Mr Forster. At least, I was told you were born in Africa.'

'Yes, I was. Even with a brief run in the war, I've never been away.'

Jade was surprised that the usually sullen young man was making an effort to be friendly. She took advantage of it. 'May I ask where?'

'Where I was born or where I served?'

She shrugged. 'Both actually.'

'Not sure where I was born. Father was a prospector who died before I was born, but Mother married a likely chap willing to take on the role of parent to another man's child. My stepfather had a farm outside Mombasa. I even went to school there. Boarded until I was sixteen.' He paused and circumvented a particularly large ditch.

'Do your parents still live there?' asked Jade.

'No. They died of blackwater. I sold the farm and tried to make a go elsewhere with ostriches. Bought a farm already in the making when some chap wanted to move on.' He shook his head. 'Course, hell had just broken out in Europe anyway.'

Roger snorted in disgust. 'The man probably saw the handwriting on the wall and saw a green, young fool ripe for picking.' He stabbed his chest with his thumb and created a small cloud of red dust. 'Me! I daresay you've heard how *that* went. Next I tried raising cattle, but they were all put down due to an unwarranted anthrax scare. Right now I owe so much money to the bank, here I am, making a go at safaris to stay one step ahead of the creditors.'

He slowed as the car's left side dipped into a

shallow wallow that had been hidden by the grasses. 'Funny thing, really,' he continued after maneuvering the ditch. 'The motorcar was a death knell to feather hats. But here I am using one — the car, that is. You might say it's been a curse and a boon for me.'

'You're resilient,' said Jade in summation. 'But if you served during the war, you hardly had a chance to make your ranch work.'

Roger shrugged. 'I didn't see the sort of action other blokes did. Since I knew the country so well and spoke several native languages, the war office put me to work running transport and things such as that. Not very exotic or exciting. Spent a lot of time in Nairobi.'

'Not everyone can be a general,' offered Jade.

'No,' he said. He concentrated on maneuvering around a patch of wait-a-bit thorns and bit his lower lip in concentration. Behind her, Jade heard Madeline and Beverly laugh uproariously over something that Avery had said.

Jade waited for Roger to work through his thoughts and was rewarded with further revelations. 'I often thought I should have been a pilot, though. Not that I can fly or anything,' he added as he cast a sideways glance at her. 'It's just that my initials fit the job so well.'

'Oh? How's that?'

'R.A.F. Just like Royal Air Force. My full name is Roger Abel Forster.'

Excitement, nervousness, and disbelief rolled down Jade's back in miniature tremors. For a minute she sat mute and motionless. Finally her hand moved in slow motion with a will of its own to the ring at her chest. She clutched it through the heavy shirt. Her brain retreated back to France, to David's marriage proposal and her laughing rejection. She could almost smell the engine grease on his coveralls as he leaned towards her. That image faded into his broken body in her arms, and his rasping voice asking her to find his brother and what had happened to his father. Beverly's soprano shout broke through the trance.

'Look, pink elephants. I must be tipsy.'

Roger explained that the elephants took dust baths and coated themselves with the faded red soil of Tsavo. His words sounded distant, as though Jade heard only an echo. The foreground of her thoughts was entirely occupied with one word: Abel.

19

'The Big Four! Lion, elephant, Cape buffalo, and rhinoceros. No one argues that these are the four most deadly big-game sporting animals in Africa. Hunters only disagree as to their individual ranking.'
— The Traveler

Jade desperately wanted to question Roger further, but the landscape prevented it. The two vehicles jolted over the rough terrain and heaved their occupants about like rag dolls. If the cars ever possessed springs, they had long since died of exhaustion. Jade landed with a thud on the hard seat. The shock slammed up her spine, and she vowed to personally kick the man who'd let this car's underbelly fall into such disrepair. Thank heavens the canvas top was at least soft on the head.

Jade could think of two advantages to traveling in these instruments of torture. Comfort was not one of them. They did save time, and the fifteen- to twenty-mile-per-hour speed generated a minuscule but most welcome breeze. To say that Tsavo was hot was like saying hell was a trifle warm. Unfortunately, the cars also stirred up red dust, which stuck to every exposed part of their sweaty hides and congealed into a gummy, pink paste, covering them as it did the elephants.

'Let's hurry up and shoot something so we can all go home,' whined Beverly. 'As wretched as I feel right now, it might just as well be me.'

'As lovely as you are, dearest,' said Avery, 'I really don't care to have your head staring down at me in my study. I would rather have a lion or a rhinoceros brooding over me instead.'

'Your husband sounds exactly like Neville,' said Madeline. 'Doesn't he, Jade?'

Jade was too preoccupied with keeping her tailbone from slamming up into her skull, and with Roger's last remark, to attend to the banter behind her.

'Jade,' said Beverly, 'wake up and answer Madeline.'

'I'm sorry. What did she say?'

'They were speaking of how charming and handsome both Neville Thompson and myself are,' said Avery. 'You were asked to agree.'

'Jade,' said Beverly, 'fetch that little book of yours and look up the Swahili for 'bilgewater.''

'Anything for you, Beverly,' said Jade. She reached into the canvas bag and pulled the Swahili language lessons out from under the Graflex. 'Bilge, bilge, b, b, b. Sorry, I don't find 'bilgewater' but I did find 'bloody fool.' That's *pumbafu*.'

Avery grumbled a low warning behind her. 'If either you or my dear wife calls me Bwana Pumbafu, I shall be forced to do something drastic. Perhaps not in our present circumstances, but later. I promise you on my honor as a member of Parliament.'

270

Beverly giggled, something Jade didn't remember her ever doing before her marriage, and suggested that Jade search out something noble to call Avery. Jade turned several pages and was struck by what looked like the word 'pili.' She started to look more closely when the Ford thwacked either a rock or a sleeping warthog and jolted the book out of her hands. She gripped the side for stability and decided this wasn't the most opportune condition for reading. *Later!*

'Leave it to the Africans,' yelled Jade. 'They'll give him a name soon enough.'

'How far are we, ouch, driving, Mr Forster?' Madeline called from the back.

'We should cover about fifty to sixty miles, depending on how far the porters got. They have over a three-day head start, you know. That will serve as a base camp from which to work.' Roger patted the steering wheel. 'The motorcar is going to revolutionize safaris.'

'I say, I should think an aeroplane would be handy as well,' commented Avery. 'What do you think, Beverly? Should we bring one to the colony and go into the safari business?'

'You couldn't transport many people, could you?' asked Roger. 'I mean, doesn't it only fit the pilot?'

'A pilot and a gunner in some. But I'm not thinking of transporting people. Imagine someone flying overland to spot out the game. They fly back and drop word, perhaps literally, to the base camp. Tell them how far to go and in which direction.'

'Like a busy worker bee reporting to the hive,' added Madeline. 'That sounds positively fascinating. I must tell Neville. He'll want to be in on this venture.'

'Sounds as if you three are planning a corporation already,' said Jade. A low, angry buzzing from under the hood caught her attention. 'Stop!' she ordered.

'Whatever for?' demanded Roger. 'Are you sick?'

'No. Don't you hear it? The radiator is nearly dry. Stop the car.'

Roger stopped, and they all listened. Without their chatter to mask it, the noise like that of swarming bees rasped clearly.

'Oh, that's definitely an unhappy radiator,' agreed Beverly. 'Good ear, Jade.'

'Well, cripes,' swore Roger. 'The bloomin' thing shouldn't overheat that fast.'

'The seal is probably cracked,' Jade explained. 'Too much steam evaporating.'

Harry noticed the Ford had stopped and doubled back to see what was the matter. He found Roger gingerly trying to open the radiator cap without getting scalded in the process. Roger yanked his hand back without succeeding in removing the cap.

'Of all the . . . ' sputtered Harry. 'Didn't you fill the radiators before we left?'

'Of course I did,' Roger snapped back.

Jade wasn't sure whether her comments would help back Roger or not. *What the hell?* She'd put her two cents in anyway. 'Probably a crack in the cap's seal. The car's seen some wear, and whoever sold it to you skimped on the maintenance. Just look at the dirt around the engine. I doubt anything's been cleaned in a year.'

'Of course there's dirt, Jade,' snapped Roger. 'We're driving in the damned dusty scrub.'

'No. It's not *new* dirt, Mr Forster.' She pointed at the engine for him to look. Neither Harry nor Roger came any closer to inspect it, however, so she added, 'That's old, grungy dirt.'

'You'd better listen to her,' said Avery. He sat on the ground in the shade of the car's chassis with his arms folded around his knees. 'The lady was one of the best mechanics in her unit.' He looked up at his wife. 'Excepting you, of course, my dear.'

'Oh, I defer to Jade,' said Beverly. She sat beside her husband.

'Well, refill the damned radiator, cover the cap with something, and let's be on our way,' ordered Harry. Roger paced back and forth by the Dodge like a caged animal.

'It would be better to let it cool first before you open it,' suggested Jade. 'Might we eat a bit of lunch while we wait, Mr Forster? It's early, but I'm hungry.'

Roger looked up, an angry scowl on his face. 'Fine. We have some tins of potted meat. I'll break them out.'

Jade and Madeline joined Lord and Lady Dunbury on the ground to picnic. They kept their backs to the car and a rifle handy while they devoured the contents of several tins. Madeline asked about airplanes, and Avery obliged her with an entertaining history of his experiences.

Jade, always interested in planes, half listened, but a low, rapid conversation on the other side of the car caught her ear and drew her attention away from her friends. Eavesdropping seemed sneaky, but if the cars were in a bad way, she wanted to know. The words came in snatches, drowned in part by Beverly's melodious laugh and the hissing radiator.

'Did you tell — ?' Jade recognized Harry's baritone voice.

'I tried to — . . . ' replied Roger in his tenor.

'Are you cert — about this?'

'Yes, man! Do you . . . live in the shadows . . . life?'

' — risky.'

'Riskier than — . . . ? Trust me.' Harry again.

Jade listened for more, but the conversation broke off when the tracker, Memba Sasa, interrupted them in Maasai. Since the earlier conversation seemed more to do with Roger's personal life, she felt ashamed of listening to it. Roger came around to the front with several *debes* of water, and Jade jumped up to help.

'Where is that blasted gypsy going to now?' asked Avery to no one in particular except perhaps Jade. She ignored him.

'I think I can seal the cap,' she offered once Roger had it off.

'Oh?' asked Roger. He sounded skeptical, almost mockingly so. He emptied one *debe* of water into the radiator and opened a second.

'We can oil up a scrap of canvas and put it

274

over the hole before replacing the cap. There's certainly enough grease around the engine to do the trick, assuming that there's no other leak.'

'Might as well try as not,' replied Roger. He dumped a third of the canful in and waited for it to trickle down. 'There's canvas to spare on the side panels. Cut a piece off the bottom.' His tone was brusque. Jade wondered what it would take to be friends with this man. Even Harry seemed to have a dominating, older-brother relationship with him rather than a friendship.

Jade pulled the pocketknife from her trousers and carved out a corner of the canopy. She smeared it with the oily residue coating the motor and worked the grease well into the fibers. When she was through, she held a tolerable facsimile of oilcloth in her hand.

'This should do the trick,' she said and placed the square over the hole. Roger handed her the cap, and she screwed it on over the cloth.

'I didn't know I'd signed on a mechanic for the safari,' said Roger.

Something in his tone smacked of disapproval. Jade had heard it all before from frontline officers and decided not to let Roger's personal insecurities bother her. She changed the subject. 'Did your mother ever mention your father's name, your *real* father?'

Roger hesitated and shuffled his feet. Jade squatted down, ostensibly to wipe her hands on the dry grass but mostly to give him time. 'I'm not sure,' he said finally. 'She never talked about him much. Mother wanted me to think of my stepfather as my real father. I do remember she said he named me, or at least he told Mother what to name me if she had a boy.'

A fresh set of tremors rippled like aftershocks down her spine. Could he actually be Gil's son? It was too much of a coincidence that his father suggested the name Abel otherwise. She pressed the point. 'You mean he suggested naming you Roger? Was that his name?'

'No, Roger is my stepfather's name. I think my father's name might have been Abel, or perhaps his father's.' He glanced at her from the corner of his eye. 'Why do you ask?'

Does he suspect he's a bastard child? wondered Jade. *Is that why he lost Leticia?* She sidestepped the question. 'Female curiosity, I suppose. I promise you I won't use it in my article.' She stood up and closed the car hood. Doubt still lingered in her mind, a doubt she needed to eradicate before she revealed David's secret to him. After all, she was told to get absolute proof before handing over the packet. One of the names Gil wrote was Dolie. Perhaps she was his mistress. She decided to ask his mother's name next, but she didn't get the chance.

'Are you two quite finished there?' bellowed Harry. He had just refueled both cars from a small store of gasoline cans. 'We need to get moving.'

Roger held up the empty water *debes*. 'We should refill these.'

'Later, at camp. We're too far from water now, and we can't waste time heading off to the river. Besides,' he added, 'we have five more cans tied

276

in that net behind my vehicle.'

Roger fastened the empty cans onto the Ford, and everyone clambered into their cars. This time Avery insisted on sitting in front with Roger to ask various hunting-related questions. Jade retrieved her hat and slipped into the back. If she hoped to hold a similar conversation with her two friends, she was sadly disappointed. Madeline, starved for information about fashions, discovered a willing informant in Beverly, and the two women happily discussed the merits of high versus low waistlines and the rise of hemlines.

Jade preferred trousers, hated sewing, and resented altering anything for some French designer's whim. Consequently, she soon tired of the topic and rested her elbow on the wooden frame, her cheek on her hand. The hot afternoon sun beat down on her, so she plopped her hat on her head and tilted the brim to shade her face. The brim also prevented her from seeing much more than the blurred scrub directly beside them. Jade drowsed. Nearly an hour had passed when their car lurched to a stop and woke her.

'Are we at camp?' she asked with a yawn.

'No,' said Madeline. 'The Dodge is steaming now.'

'Cripes,' groaned Jade. A huge cloud of steam issued from under the hood of the Dodge. 'That's really gone. It'll take a good half an hour in this heat to cool enough to remove that cap. Don't let them open it yet, Mr Forster. The steam'll come up like a blasted geyser.'

'Bloody hell,' muttered Avery. 'Do you think I

might scout for a bit while we wait?'

Roger shook his head. 'With all due respect, I don't know how good a shot you are, Your Lordship,' he said. 'Either Mr Hascombe or myself would have to accompany you, and I don't think Harry would appreciate any more delays at present.'

'I assure you, I am an excellent shot.'

'That may well be, sir, but we're rather close to some patchy wooded areas. They hold lion and rhino, neither of which readily welcome intruders.' Roger nodded to a stand of thorny *Commiphora* shrubs six hundred yards to his left. They, and similar patches, brandished the only bit of green to be seen in the harsh, dry landscape with the exception of a nearby straggly mimosa tree. Golden grasses and dried thorn-bushes covered most of the remaining area.

'There may be lion in that grass, too,' added Roger. 'Hard to see the cats. They blend right in. You have to watch for their ears twitching.' Avery scowled in disappointment. 'Don't worry, Lord Dunbury,' added Roger. 'You'll see plenty of action tomorrow and after.'

'Well, I hate to be rude,' muttered Beverly to her female companions, 'but I need to relieve myself. Madeline, you're most familiar with safaris. Just where does one do that sort of thing privately out here?'

'With this many men around? You don't,' she said. Beverly moaned.

Jade looked at the canvas canopy overhead and thought aloud. 'American pioneer women generally held up a blanket to act as a screen for each other. We could haul that canvas top off and use it the same way.'

'I don't think Mr Hascombe would like that idea,' said Beverly.

'Harry's approval is not your primary concern right now,' said Jade, 'but I suppose we should leave the car alone. For all I know, that canvas top holds the framework together.' She jumped out of the car and started rummaging around the equipment tucked behind their wooden seat. 'Surely there are blankets in one of these vehicles. We had some at the rail station at any rate.' She lifted up a box marked cook pot and found a bundle of gray wool. 'Here we go.'

Harry spotted her from the front of the Dodge and yelled at her, 'What the blazes are you doing, woman? We're not unpacking here.'

Jade held up the blanket. 'We ladies have some private business to attend to. So just hold your horses.'

Avery stepped out of the Ford and retrieved his rifle, a double-barreled .500/.450 Holland. 'I'll stand guard.'

'Avery, my love,' protested his wife, 'we are not wandering off anywhere. If we did that, we wouldn't need the damned blanket.' She kissed him on the nose.

'Don't swear, my dear,' said her husband. 'It's not becoming. And don't argue. I don't care to have a lion take a bite out of you while you are in, shall we say, a compromising position.'

Beverly rolled her eyes, and both Jade and Madeline smiled. 'Sometimes,' whispered Madeline to Jade, 'we have to indulge their manhood

279

or they become particularly sullen and irascible. But really,' she added, 'their desire to protect us helpless females is one of their more endearing qualities.'

Jade expressed her disbelief with an arched brow and opened the blanket. She handed one end to Madeline and held the other. Beverly stepped out of view of the cars. Avery stood guard a discreet distance away and watched the grass for those telltale ears or a tail twitch that might indicate a lion while each of the women took her turn behind the blanket.

Jade was refolding the blanket when she heard a loud hiss like a train's piston. Someone had opened the radiator cap prematurely. A cloud of steam belched upward, and the men scrambled away from the scalding rain.

Avery shouted, 'There's something in the brush!'

A distant clump of thornbushes shuddered violently as though a fierce wind pummeled them, and a puff of red dust rose along with a loud snort. The brush parted with a snap, and a monstrous black rhino trotted out. His ears twitched to put a lock on the strange hissing noise that had threatened his nap. It didn't take long. His keen hearing quickly located the Dodge. The beast pivoted lightly and turned his bulk in its direction.

When it charged, its agility amazed Jade. She'd seen the large bulls in the Spanish bullfighting arena run with such grace, but they had longer legs. This animal looked more like it should waddle, not canter.

'Don't stand there!' yelled Roger. 'Climb up the mimosa!' Madeline and Beverly raced up the nearest spiny tree.

'He's after the bloody motorcar,' swore Harry. He raced around the opposite side and tried to reach his own rifle. 'He'll gore the damned thing and then us if we don't stop him.'

Avery sighted down his Holland and fired. The bullet penetrated the thick hide and entered both lungs. Most other animals would have done their duty and died on the spot, but the rhino apparently didn't care to take the time. He continued his charge, puffing like a locomotive. Blood spurted from his nostrils and sprayed the grass. The rhino slammed headfirst into the side of the Dodge. The vehicle shuddered and lurched under the impact but remained upright.

The large nasal horn forced its way through the netting on the side and pierced several of the water *debes* at one time. Avery tried to fire again, but the animal had entangled itself in the netting and literally dragged the car a quarter turn, putting it between himself and the gun.

Jade never doubted Avery's or Harry's ability to finish the beast, but it did occur to her that she was missing one hell of a picture. She reached over the Ford's wooden side wall for her camera bag. As she tried for a foothold on a board, her left boot kicked one of the empty *debes* tied onto the frame. Her foot slipped and her hat fell onto the floorboard as she pitched forward.

The *debe's* sudden clang alerted the enraged, wounded rhino. It stepped back from the Dodge

281

and tossed the net full of leaking, gored water cans to one side with a shake of its monstrous head. Blood fell like rain and splattered the sides of the car.

'Jade! Look out!' shouted Beverly from her perch.

Jade looked up to see a dusty, dark, living tank thunder towards her. A ton of hatred powered the bayonet charge, all of it ready to gore her. No chance for the tree now. The animal would outrun her. 'Get ready, Avery,' she yelled. She still held the partially folded blanket in her left hand. With a snap, she opened it beside her like a cape and shouted, 'Hey-ah, *toro.*'

The rhino's dim eyesight caught the waving blanket's movement and it neatly pivoted towards it. It accelerated its charge. '*Toro!*' she shouted again and held her ground. The beast was nearly on her. The smell of hot blood, mud, and hide filled Jade's nostrils. She flipped the makeshift cape again. As the horn pierced the cloth, she leaped aside and left the blanket over the rhino's head. The animal thundered past. Jade put two hands on the car's sideboards, and sprang over into the seat and out the other side with her Winchester.

She didn't need the rifle. The animal was finally tiring from blood loss. It spent most of its remaining energy trampling the hated blanket into the red earth, goring it repeatedly. Avery repositioned himself and let fire the second barrel. This time the metal-jacketed bullet entered between the neck and shoulder and slammed into the heart. The rhino pirouetted once more to face the new threat, but it staggered and pitched forward, plowing the ground with its bulk.

'Stay!' Harry shouted and motioned for Avery to remain where he was. He fired with his own rifle into the rhino's neck vertebrae. The animal dropped onto its side and lay still in its own blood and dust.

For nearly a minute, no one moved. In truth, after the great animal had displayed so much stamina, no one really believed it was truly dead. Finally, Beverly called out from the mimosa, 'Is it dead now? May we come down? There's a thorn poking me in a rather tender place.'

Harry cautiously approached the bull, rifle at the ready. After kicking its rear to make certain it was really dead, he nodded to Avery, who answered them, 'Yes, you may come down.'

Jade leaned back against the Ford and breathed deeply, her head reeling with the giddy excitement only a matador experienced. She laughed aloud, and her green eyes sparkled through the sweat and dirt.

Avery knelt by the rhino and examined the large nasal horn. 'Shall I take your picture, Avery?' Jade asked. To her right she saw Harry bearing down on her, a dark scowl on his rugged, rectangular features. She ignored him. 'We must document your first trophy.'

'Splendid idea, to be sure,' said Avery. 'It's at least twenty-four inches long,' he said, estimating the horn. 'Come, Beverly,' he called to his wife. 'Look what I've done.'

Jade turned to reach for her camera while

Avery crowed before the admiring eyes of his bride and Madeline, but the energy surge was rapidly being replaced by a rubbery feeling in her knees. She started to drop. A firm arm grabbed her around the waist and hoisted her to her feet.

'Bloody little fool,' Harry muttered. 'You could have gotten yourself killed.'

'And just what should I have done? The thing would have been on me in a moment if I'd tried to run for the tree. Damned beast should have had the decency to die when Avery first shot it.' She glared up at him defiantly. Her lips tilted in a slight smirk, and her black hair lay plastered in matted curls around her head.

'That's because a rhino is too busy trying to trample every blessed living thing into oblivion to take the time to die. He . . . you . . . Oh, the hell!' Harry pulled her towards him and kissed her firmly on the mouth.

Jade tasted the sweat and dust on his lips and discovered, to her amazement, that she felt the same thrill as when she was playing matador to the rhino. In Harry's kiss she felt strength, heat, and danger. Her head swam, her pulse quickened, and for a moment, she felt her legs begin to collapse under her again. Then the thrill of danger returned and she rallied herself to meet it. It intoxicated her, and she recognized the attraction. She was embracing Africa as much as Harry.

At that instant, she returned the kiss measure for measure and felt Harry's rapid heartbeat through her shirt. His grip tightened around her as he whispered her name to her lips. Jade recognized his desire in the huskiness of his voice, but knew hers to be less for the man than for what he represented. *Be blasted if I let him know it, though. Let him wonder.* When he finally released her, she just stared at him with an enigmatic smile and a sense of her own power. Harry turned and stormed back to the Dodge. Her smile widened.

Jade retrieved her camera and her hat before anyone else noticed what had just happened. When she looked back up and saw Madeline's knowing smile and elbow nudge to Beverly, she knew the women had witnessed at least part of it. She shrugged it off and inserted a sheet of film.

'Smile, Avery,' she said as she framed the shot.

'Wait, let me raise up the head,' replied Avery. He struggled with the massive square head and succeeded in lifting it up as he knelt next to the beast, his Holland rifle nestled in the crook of one arm. Jade took the picture.

'Splendid,' Avery said. 'But we should have one with you by it as well. That was magnificent the way you deflected his charge. Whatever possessed you to think of it?'

'A bullfight in Madrid. My parents took me to see one once.' She winked. 'You recall, I *am* part Spanish by descent.'

'More likely Spanish gypsy,' he retorted. 'But it was marvelous. And,' he added after a moment's thought, 'bloody dangerous. Beverly, if you ever try anything remotely like that,' he said to his wife, 'I shall be forced to turn you over my knee and spank you for it.'

Bev's teeth flashed in a wicked grin. She twirled one of her short blond curls around a finger. 'Almost worth the risk to try it then, wouldn't you agree, Madeline?'

Madeline chuckled and turned away.

A goodly assortment of ripe swear words concerning some rather improbable ancestry of the rhino assaulted everyone's ears as Harry picked up the torn netting and surveyed the ruined water cans. 'Punctured! Every blasted one of them!' He threw down the cans. 'Roger, how much water do you have left?'

Roger shook his head to indicate not enough. 'One *debe* and what little is in any of the canteens. How far are we from the river?'

'Too blasted far. The river bends away at this point. It won't come back to us until we're nearly at the base camp.' He threw his hat on the ground and stomped on it, reminding Jade of the angry rhino. 'Looks like you're going to have to drive to the river and refill your *debes*, Roger. Take one of the men. We'll wait for you here.'

'May I make another suggestion?' said Jade. She didn't pause for an answer. 'At the risk of sounding very unladylike, if you men haven't relieved yourselves yet, you're probably carrying enough, er, water to do the job. At least,' she added, 'once you throw in the canteens and Roger's last *debe*.' She grinned widely. 'We three females can, of course, avert our eyes, or you can always hold up a blanket like we did. Oops, I forgot; the rhino obliterated the blanket.'

Avery's eyes opened noticeably wider as the

286

significance of her statement sank in. Beverly put her hand over her mouth to hide her smile and turned away before it grew into audible snickers. Madeline joined her, but Roger's face kept his usual angry, bad-luck expression. Jade didn't notice any of them. She riveted her eyes on Harry Hascombe.

His lips tightened, his square-cut jaw twitched, his mouth opened once, then closed. Finally he put his hands on his narrow hips and looked at the Dodge. Gradually his shoulders began to quiver and then shook until his upper body rocked with silent laughter. Harry slapped his knee and called the native men over. When he translated her suggestion, the men roared with laughter. Avery blushed.

'Ladies, shall we retire to the shade behind the Ford while the men do their duty?' suggested Jade.

After the radiator was at least partially filled, and the rhino head dispatched from its body and strapped behind the Dodge, they drove west for another hour to the base camp. Their first clue to the river's presence was the tree belt that followed the Tsavo River's returning path and the distant herds found near water. Finally a ring of canvas tents appeared like quivering ghosts in the late afternoon's shimmering heat waves. One oxcart laden with three water barrels stood to the side, gasoline cans stacked under it in the shade. The two oxen grazed placidly nearby in a thorny *boma*.

Harry stopped the Dodge and greeted Ruta, the tall Maasai from Harry's ranch whom Jade

287

recognized as Biscuit's caretaker. She watched them talk for a while and from Harry's various gestures tried to deduce the subject of conversation. At one point it must have involved the cars since he pointed to the Dodge and then to the water barrel.

Jade got out of the car and stretched while keeping one eye on Ruta. Now, there was a curious man. She wondered about his seeming attachment to Harry. But as she didn't speak Maasai, it seemed unlikely that she'd ever pry any secrets out of him. At least, he understood some Swahili. That might come in handy. Beverly slapped her on the backside with a canvas duffel. 'I'm not getting your bags, dearie.'

'Some friend you are.' Jade watched the men struggle with the huge rhinoceros head. 'Aren't you glad he's not insisting on having the entire carcass stuffed and mounted?'

'Don't give him any ideas, my dear girl. It's enough that we have to haul the head of that wretched thing around with us. By the by, I noticed your ointment didn't keep the rhino away.'

'I told you it wore off the boots and belt. And if you'll remember, I wasn't wearing my hat at the time.'

Madeline came up in time to hear the last part and nudged Jade with her elbow. 'I noticed. And so did Harry, it seems. You really must try a better cologne. Harry doesn't seem to care for your essence of . . . what did you call it, Beverly? Incontinent ferret in heat?' She giggled, and Jade scowled.

'And you, poor thing, have to share a tent with that smell,' added Beverly.

'She doesn't need to if she doesn't wish to,' retorted Jade in a husky tone. 'We planned for enough tents. Madeline can occupy hers — *alone*.' She turned to get her gear from the Ford.

'I'm not at all certain that I'm brave enough to sleep out here by myself,' admitted Madeline. 'If that ointment of yours really does keep lions away, it might be worth putting up with.'

'Suit yourself,' said Jade. She smiled. 'Next thing you know, you'll be smearing it on the tent flaps yourself.'

Jade returned from the car with her camera bag, Winchester, and personal duffel and was headed for the tents when Roger spotted her. He broke off his relatively animated conversation with Harry and waved for her to wait. She did, and he ambled over to her, stopping far enough away to prevent another sneezing attack.

'I want to thank you for your assistance back there.' He nodded to the east. 'A bit unorthodox, but it did the trick.'

Jade wasn't sure if he meant her bullfighting with the rhino or the solution to the radiator shortage, so she only nodded and waited. She didn't want to stifle him once he'd finally started speaking.

'Anyway, I was giving some thought to your previous questions about my real father. I've always wanted to know more about him myself, you see. You being a journalist and all, I thought

289

you might tell me how to go about finding out, so I've been racking my mind for anything that might be useful. I can only think of one other thing.'

Jade felt inclined to encourage him now. 'Oh? What is it?'

'Well, I remember Mother telling me that he died before I was born. She held me very close and told me to remember that I was a very *worthy child*. I recall she strongly emphasized those last two words and I've always wondered if that was some sort of clue.' He frowned and shoved his hands in his trouser pockets. 'I don't suppose that makes much sense, though.'

'Actually,' said Jade very softly, 'it might.'

Roger pulled a small box from his right pocket. 'When Mother died, I found this among her things. I carry it with me whenever I leave the ranch in case anyone takes to robbing me while I'm gone.' He looked sideways at Jade and added, 'It's about all I have of hers, you understand.'

He opened the box and showed Jade a pair of cuff links. One was inscribed with a G and the other with a W. 'Do you think they mean anything?' he asked.

'Yes,' said Jade as she stared at the cuff links that she remembered seeing in Gil's portrait. 'What was your mother's name?'

'Dolly. Why do you ask?'

'We need to talk, Mr Forster.'

★ ★ ★

His suspicions were correct. The woman had tremendous courage. That was all well and good. Killing had almost become tedious, his victims presenting as much challenge as the goats he practiced on. In recent years, he'd come to appreciate the hunt almost as much as the final kill.

Almost.

20

'Most of the Big Four are only dangerous when aroused. Unfortunately, the rhinoceros and the Cape buffalo are aroused by your very existence. Indeed, both have made it their goal in life to trample anything in their path. But when ranking the Big Four, one must always keep in mind that the lions of Tsavo make their living eating buffalo. They'd eat rhino, too, if rhino were worth eating.'
— The Traveler

Jade leaned against the car and stared at Roger, searching for some fraternal likeness to David. 'Tell me everything you know,' she said.

'It's little more than what I already told you,' admitted Roger. 'I don't think my stepfather cared to hear about my father. The only thing else I recall my mother saying was how she got to Mombasa. Father, my real father, was very sick. They'd been prospecting somewhere when he took a bad turn. Some Afrikaaner named Kruger, I think, brought them to Mombasa. Mother went into labor and when she was released, she learned Father had died.'

Jade couldn't believe her ears. All the names fit, Kruger and Abel. Even his mother's name of Dolly was similar enough to Dolie to suspect that Gil spelled her nickname differently from most people. Then there were those cuff links.

She wondered if Harry had suspected all along. She decided to ask. 'Did Harry ever tell you why I'm out here?'

'Actually, I've heard talk that you're asking about Gil Worthy.' He looked at his boots. 'I admit it's why I even brought up the topic with you. I knew the initials on the cuff links might be a coincidence, but then I thought about what my mother said, and I wondered. Do you think Gil was my father?'

Jade nodded. 'Your mother's name matches, and I've seen those cuff links before.'

'No one else knows about them,' he said. 'They've always been part of my mother's secret. I'd prefer they remain a secret.' He looked at Jade with such intensity that she agreed even though she couldn't understand why.

'Of course, but you will probably have to produce them in London as evidence.'

Roger nodded. 'I understand. So what does this mean now? Am I rich?'

Jade recoiled a bit. She had been so intent on finding David's lost brother and fulfilling a vow that the mention of money seemed cold and heartless. 'I don't know,' she answered. 'I do have something to give you, and something else to tell you. Your father didn't die when you were born. He went back to England. Maybe he thought your mother died. Maybe he was delirious. But he did come back in 1915 to find you. It looks like he was murdered in Nairobi.'

Jade expected Roger to show shock or sorrow over his father's desertion or death. He didn't. But then, his father had been dead in his mind

293

for his entire life. Just then Harry bellowed for Roger.

'Whatever you have for me,' said Roger, 'give it to me tonight.' He left to find Harry.

★ ★ ★

'It's not good *enough*!' bellowed Harry. 'Make it thicker.'

Roger's scornful voice added, 'It's a wonder you lazy louts aren't dead and digested.'

The advance men had already built a *boma* for the oxen and nearly finished a similar thorny protective barrier around the tents, but both Roger and Harry saw too many thin spots for their liking. They insisted on strengthening it. Whereas Harry's order came off with the authority of a headman, Jade noticed that Roger's comments simply dripped with loathing.

'The Tsavo lions are a different breed,' Harry explained to the hunters. 'Larger, for one thing, and the males don't sport that big, thick mane. Their manes, what there is of them, look more like a juvenile's, sparse and short. The prides are smaller, too, so the males actually hunt.'

'How large is larger?' asked Jade.

'Males average four fifty to five hundred pounds.'

Jade whistled. 'That's grizzly size.'

'Colonel Patterson's people built *bomas*,' stated Avery. 'I can't say it did them any good. Those lions broke right through.'

Harry's laugh came out as more of a derisive snort. 'Patterson? I think the old boy was one to

294

embellish. But that was a particularly nasty lot of lions plaguing them; that's for certain.' He pointed to the *boma*. 'That's why we want this twice as thick.'

'I thought only wounded or sick lions resorted to man-eating,' said Jade.

'Not here in Tsavo,' said Harry. 'Here, the beasts make a habit of it. But then, look at their alternative and decide what you'd rather take down: a buffalo capable of stamping you into a bloody pancake or a very *tender* human.' He eyed Jade as he emphasized the word 'tender.'

Roger interjected. 'It's their heritage, too. This area used to be a part of the old ivory route, only ivory wasn't the only commodity taken through here. Slave trading was part of the bargain. Weak slaves were left to drop. That's an easy mark for any lion.'

'Yes,' added Harry in a sinister undertone. 'And the young ones learn from watching Momma and Daddy.'

'I have gleaned two facts from this discussion,' summarized Avery. 'Vigilance is critical, and I'll end up with a lion skin sans decent mane.'

'You'll be lucky if that's all you end up with, Dunbury,' said Harry. 'Don't go looking for trouble out here. It *will* find you first. Roger, check on the rest of the gear. I'm going to talk to the tracker.'

'*I'll* talk to Memba Sasa,' said Roger. 'He's temperamental and more used to me.'

Harry shrugged. 'Suit yourself, Rog. I'll see to the camp, then.' He turned to the others. 'You can choose your tents from the three central ones. Roger and I flank you on either side.' He tugged his hat brim in a parting salute. Jade grabbed Harry's sleeve to stop him as he turned away. Harry turned with a wide grin. 'Why, Jade. Hate to see me go?'

Jade released his shirt and laughed. 'Not at all. I just want to know where I should tell my gun bearer, Pili, to sleep.'

'Oh,' he said with obvious disappointment. 'We have tents set up behind this inner circle for the men, although most of the Wakamba porters prefer to sleep outside. Still, if we are bothered by lions, most don't recognize a closed tent as anything and pass it by. The men know that. Your man will take one of those tents.'

'Fine,' said Jade. 'And just so you know, I believe Mrs Thompson is bunking with me.'

'Right.' Harry turned on his heel and strode off to the other side of the camp.

Jade threw her duffel into her tent and set the Winchester on the cot. She fished her camera out of its bag, and her hand brushed the second ring box. 'I found your brother, David,' she whispered. 'And when we get back to Nairobi, I'll find your father's killer.' She tucked the ring box back into a corner of the bag next to the sealed packet, took up the camera, loaded it, and headed out to photograph the camp.

With all the delays, the day was well advanced by the time they arrived. The temperature had cooled into the low nineties, and long shadows stretched like a yawning cat along the ground. Somewhere to the west, Mount Kilimanjaro rose up, but Jade saw only clouds when she squinted in that direction. The mystical mountain, considered by some to be the soul of Africa, stayed hidden behind its veil, too proud to be ogled by mere mortals like her.

The great volcanic mountain left its calling card, however, in the black rock around it. The camp sat at the base of several smaller hills to the north and across the river to the south. The tree belt showed where the Tsavo River came into its own just west of them as the many tributaries flowed together under the watchful but hidden eye of Kilimanjaro. She felt a thrill run through her just knowing the mountain was there behind its veil.

Avery joined her. 'Not exactly the land of milk and honey, is it?' he said. 'Rather lean-looking territory. But I came to fetch you. Bev is insisting on a bath now,' he explained. 'Mr Hascombe is going to hunt for the pot, as they say, and I thought perhaps I would lend a rifle. Care to join us?'

'Does Harry approve of my tagging along on this hunt?'

Avery grinned as if to suggest it shouldn't matter whether he did or not. 'Your people are paying his fee,' he said.

Jade laughed. 'Let me get my Winchester and canteen.' She stopped and turned to Avery. 'I never thanked you and Bev for your letters of introduction and you for just bringing Bev out here. I missed her and,' she added quickly before she hurt his feelings, 'you, too.'

Avery smiled and bowed in a courtly manner. ' 'Twas no trouble at all, fair damsel. Bev and *I* missed you, too. But I'm offended that you're not taking your new Mannlicher.'

'I haven't even practiced with it yet,' she replied. 'You wouldn't want me to miss an antelope because the sights were off, would you? I'll target shoot later. Pili has charge of it now.'

Pili saw her emerge from her tent with her Winchester and insisted on accompanying her. He had exchanged his white robe for a shorter tunic that revealed khaki shorts, long green socks, and a pair of scuffed, clunky, thick-soled shoes. Jade wondered if the attire had been provided by Lord Colridge since neither Harry nor Roger had known he was coming. Besides, her safari outfitter, Newland, Tarlton, and Company, usually supplied their porters with long blue jerseys similar to those worn by police *askaris*, only sporting the letters N and T sewn in red.

That was when it hit her. None of the porters wore anything remotely resembling that uniform. She examined them more closely. They all dressed in a ragtag manner with assorted cast-off great coats, torn vests, frayed shorts, red blankets, holey cricket stockings, or no stockings. 'Well, I'll be horn-swoggled,' she muttered. 'He not only took over heading the safari, he took over the entire job.'

'Beg pardon?' asked Avery.

'Harry took over the entire safari. Look.' She pointed to a cluster of Wakamba porters. 'Newland, Tarlton, and Company make their people wear blue jerseys.'

They walked on towards the *boma* gate. 'Is

298

this a problem?' Avery asked.

Jade shook her head. 'I hope not. I mean, Hascombe and Forster know what they're doing. Maybe even more so than some people sitting in an office in Nairobi. But it is my safari, and I feel I should have been consulted first.' She expressed as much to Harry Hascombe at the *boma* gate, where he waited with Ruta.

'Harry, I'm sure you're a first-rate rancher and hunter, but you'd make a lousy business partner. I'd appreciate it in future if you'd clear any new plans with me before taking over anything else. You fired my safari company and took over on your own.'

He stepped back and grimaced. 'You prefer to see the men all dandied up like a field of blue flowers?'

'You can all go about in pink tutus if you like. What I *prefer* is to be consulted first. I have to explain all the expenses to my publisher, and if he expected to see pictures of neat, tidy porters, he's going to wonder why he has pictures of refugees instead.' She stepped forward. 'It will look as if *I'm* skimming money off the top. You could cost me any future work.'

Harry retreated back another step and coughed once. 'I'm sorry, Jade. I'll admit that possibility never occurred to me. Look, Roger needs money. The bugger is more desperate than he lets on, and I knew I could pay him more by handling the safari myself.' He started to approach her, thought better of it, and remained where he stood, next to the silent Ruta. 'Forgive me, but those asses in Nairobi waste too much money on French wines and crystal goblets.' He looked her over and smiled. 'You didn't strike me as the frivolous type, Jade. I assumed you'd rather the money be spent on the best game hunter in the protectorate.'

'And that would be yourself, of course.'

He touched his hat brim and bowed slightly. 'Always at your service, miss. In *any* way I can be of service.' At the sight of her continued scowl, he added, 'I'll chop *my* fee in half.'

'Keep your fee, Harry,' Jade said. 'Just don't try to pull anything else behind my back.'

Avery shifted his smaller-caliber Jeffery rifle in his hand. 'If we are all through here,' he said, 'might we go hunt? My wife fancies an antelope for supper.'

Jade laughed. 'Beverly and I ate enough horse meat with the French army that we should probably pick out a nice, fat zebra instead. Sauté it in a little Bordeaux, and we'll feel right at home after traveling all day in the flivver.'

'Your wife and Jade appear to be remarkable women,' Harry said.

Avery shook his head slowly and rolled his eyes. 'You do not know the half of it.'

Jade glanced around for the tracker. 'Where's Memba Sasa?'

Now Harry rolled *his* eyes heavenward. 'It seems *he* feels he is only here for the *important* hunts, whatever that means. Won't do anything as mundane as look for food. But don't fret your pretty head. Ruta and I can find game.'

The six of them set out on a southeasterly angle towards the river, Hascombe in the lead followed closely by his gun bearer, Ruta. Jade came next with Pili, and Avery brought up the rear with his bearer. They pushed on steadily in the open grass and avoided the stands of thorny shrubs. In the distance, a small herd of giraffes browsed on the taller acacia trees, and a few white egrets pecked around in the dust by their hooves. A large stork flew out of an acacia and turned towards the river, his long wings flapping languidly.

Ruta pointed into the grassland, and Harry nodded. Jade and Avery both knew enough about hunting to keep quiet and concentrated on detecting whatever the tall Maasai indicated. Jade spotted a small cluster of white birds that shimmered up out of late-afternoon shadows and resettled into the grass. Egrets. They followed herds and fed on the insects stirred up by the hooves. As yet, she didn't see the herd, but Harry and Ruta turned to a more easterly direction towards the spot where the birds had landed. That was where the herd would be.

Jade followed silently and kept scanning the grass to their sides for the telltale, softly rounded triangular ears that signaled a lion. Almost in answer to her unspoken thoughts, Harry stopped and pointed left. At first, she didn't see anything. Then the grass twitched. Jade froze.

A lioness raised her head about fifty yards away and yawned. The cat rose with a dancer's grace, stretched, and trotted off into the distant scrub. Jade heard a faint pounding and realized it was her heartbeat. And that, she thought, was just over seeing a lone female. She grinned at

Avery. He silently mouthed back, 'Simba Jike,' and pointed at her. Impulsively, Jade touched her wrist tattoo.

The cooler air from Kilimanjaro sank beneath the hot air of the plains and put a slight breeze against their backs. Not good. More of a chance of alarming the herd. They advanced more cautiously and skirted to the south to avoid directly carrying their scent to the prey.

Before long, a small herd of two dozen or so Grant's gazelles came into view. About the size of a white-tailed deer, the dun-colored antelope blended into the golden grasses. Only the occasional flash of their white rumps gave them away. She noticed their horns, which stretched over two feet with a graceful lyre shape on the males and only half as long on the females.

Ruta and Harry stopped about two hundred yards from the herd and crouched in the grass. Avery and Jade did the same. Ruta handed Harry his smaller-gauge rifle and pointed to a particularly large male at the far eastern edge of the herd. Harry shook his head, chose a smaller one, then pointed out two other males to Jade and Avery. Then he mouthed, 'On three.'

He waited until each of them had settled into their kneeling stance, shouldered their rifles, and nodded their readiness before whispering his count. On three, each of the rifles boomed, and the herd scattered. All, that was, except for the three targets. They leaped into the air, only to collapse immediately onto the rusty earth.

'Good shooting,' said Harry as they rose. 'There's meat enough for the porters as well as ourselves for a couple of days.' He fired twice in the air, waited a count of three, and fired again. 'I've signaled the camp. The Wakamba will come with poles to haul the game back. No need to stay unless you want to.'

'Shouldn't one of us remain here?' suggested Avery. 'Or there likely won't be anything left to carry back.' He nodded in the direction of the lioness.

'Ruta will stay. He's killed one lion with only his spear. I daresay he'd enjoy killing another even if it's only with my other rifle.'

Ruta grinned.

Back at camp, Jade went into the center tent with one four-gallon *debe* of water and a bar of soap and washed. When she set the near-empty can on the oxcart, two porters laughed.

'You do not drink away all the water like msabu with yellow hair,' said one man. 'She used three full *debes*.'

Uh-oh, thought Jade. Beverly was in danger of acquiring an unattractive Swahili name such as Big Bath or worse if she didn't intervene. 'Msabu Yellow Hair needs more water to clean her yellow hair than my darker hair,' she explained. The men nodded and laughed again. She decided to visit with these men. Maybe they knew something about *laibons* that could be useful when she returned to Nairobi.

They spoke willingly about the area wildlife, especially the predators, but when she asked them whether or not witches used these animals, they became mute. 'One does not talk of witches, Msabu Simba Jike,' the spokesman

303

declared with a nervous glance. She tried to coax more from them and asked if *laibons* ever attacked white men, but they remained silent. She thanked them for their information and left in search of her friends.

The other porters and Ruta returned with the gazelles. Soon a delicious aroma wafted over the camp as the cook prepared thick steaks and a fragrant-smelling rice dish for them and distributed cornmeal, called posho, and chunks of antelope to each of the men so they could cook their own meals. Beverly and Madeline sat in wooden camp chairs on the shady side of the Dunburys' tent, and Jade joined them.

'There you are,' said Beverly. She sipped from a glass of lemonade. 'We'd begun to think you'd run off.'

'It might interest you to know, Bev, that you are Msabu Yellow Hair,' said Jade as she settled into a third chair and examined her fingernails. She felt a mild sense of relief, knowing half of her quest was over, and she longed to relax with her friends for a while.

'Really?' Beverly patted her blond curls. 'I should have guessed.'

Jade flicked a piece of red dirt from under one nail and watched it fly. 'Don't be too proud. I gave it to you. It was that or become known as Mrs Hippo Wallowing in the Water.'

Madeline's laugh escaped as a sort of yip. Beverly shot her a nasty look.

'First impressions, dearie,' finished Jade.

'Ooooooh!' muttered Beverly. 'Well, I don't apologize for my bath. I had enough of filth in

304

the unit, carbolic acid flea belts and all.'

Jade nodded. 'Didn't we all. But remember, the men have to refill those water barrels from the river, and that's dangerous work.'

Beverly looked down at her booted feet and pouted. 'You're right, of course. I won't do it again. I can be just as frugal as you two. More so.'

'Well, I think I'm going to shock Neville and cut my hair,' said Madeline. 'It takes too much time to put it up and detangle it. Besides,' she added with a giggle, 'I want to be a bit of a trendsetter myself. Will you help me?'

Jade pulled her pocketknife from her trousers. She stood behind Madeline, removed the hairpins, and held a hefty strand of wavy brown hair in her hand. 'Are you absolutely certain you want to go through with this?' she asked. 'Neville won't divorce you or anything?' On Madeline's repeated assurance, and with Beverly's advice as to styling, Jade sliced away the hair and tossed it into a heap at Maddy's feet.

'I believe this calls for one of your famous piss-sonnets, Jade,' suggested Beverly.

Jade studied the situation for a moment. 'All right. Try this. There once was a lady named Madeline, whose head with tangles was rattlin'. She said, 'I don't care,' and sliced off her hair, but her husband still gave her a paddlin'.'

Madeline reached back to pinch Jade. 'Whoa, partner,' Jade cautioned. 'Never attack the woman with a knife in her hands.' Another block of hair fell away. 'Done!'

Madeline shook her head. 'I swear, my head

305

feels pounds lighter. How do I look?' she demanded. Avery appeared at that point, puffing away on his pipe.

'I beg your pardon,' he said. 'I seem to have intruded on a feminine sacrificial rite.' He stopped and stared. 'But I demand to be introduced to this charming young girl with you.'

Madeline blushed and protested, but the brightness of her eyes spoke of how genuinely pleased she was with the compliment. Beverly beamed appreciation of her husband's gallantry, and Avery informed them that dinner was being served alfresco, if they cared to join him.

Their cook had worked a miracle and produced a culinary feast out of his cooking *debes* guaranteed to please the palate of the most jaded city dweller. The meat was tender, flavorful, and cooked to a turn. Rice seasoned with cumin, cardamom, garlic, onions, and fresh ginger complemented the meat without over-powering it. A side dish of grated green mangos and cucumbers seasoned with salt, pepper, and lemon rounded out the meal. Only one other delight was needed to complete Jade's gastro-nomic pleasure, and Harry supplied it with a large mug full of steaming black coffee.

A blanket of star-studded blackness soon covered the camp. Roger put more wood on the fire, and everyone adjourned 'to the drawing room,' as Avery put it. Conversation around the fire turned to the hunt that had produced the night's main course.

'Your bearer pointed out a magnificent buck, Hascombe,' said Avery. 'But you chose another instead. May I inquire why?'

Harry drained his mug, refilled it, and passed the pot around the ring. 'That older buck would have been a lot tougher and not big enough for a trophy, and he was too much in his prime to take him out of the herd.' He stretched his long legs in front of him. 'If you want a good set of horns, I'm sure Memba Sasa will find one for you. He ought to consider *that* an important hunt.'

'Is he your usual tracker?' asked Jade.

'Not mine, Roger's.'

Roger Forster bolted up in his chair. 'Yes, right. He's one of the few Maasai living on my ranch. Quite good. It's as if he thinks like the animals. About the only native,' he added with a scowl, 'that was ever worth knowing.'

No one said a word, and Jade remembered Roger's rude comment on the day she'd arrived at the hotel. Whether he'd been hard put-upon or not, she found it difficult to be sympathetic to or even tolerate this man. The thought that he was David's half brother disgusted her, but while she was sorry that David's brother hadn't turned out to be a man worthy of her deceased beau, she could no longer deny Roger's legitimate — or illegitimate, as the case may have been — claim to Gil's inheritance. The cuff links proved that. *Well*, she thought with a sigh, *no time like the present*.

'Mr Forster, about that subject we discussed earlier.'

Roger's eyes glowed in the firelight. 'You mean my inheritance?' He glanced at the others and smiled. 'It seems I'm Gil Worthy's son.' Roger

307

waited while the others gasped and expressed their delight. 'Might as well have witnesses,' he added to Jade.

'As you wish.' Jade rose from her chair, and the gentlemen politely stood with her. 'If you'll excuse me, I need to fetch something from my bag.'

Beverly started to follow, but Avery held her wrist gently and shook his head. When Jade returned, she carried the small box and the packet. As concisely as possible, she explained David's last request, the ring, and her trip to the London solicitor. She omitted only her visit with David's mother.

Roger sat silently, hands folded in front of him, and stared at the dirt so no one could see his face. 'My father abandoned Mother and me,' he said finally.

'No! He was extremely ill with malaria when he went home. He returned near the start of the war to find you, but he died before he could.' Jade leaned forward and spoke in a big sister's firm but gentle tone. 'He *never* forgot you. He even left instructions for his son, his *other* son, to find you. David would have, too, but for the war. Finding you was his final request.'

'I'm a bastard after all,' Roger said as though the thought amused him.

'But a lucky bastard,' said Harry. 'Most bastards never know their fathers or are better off not knowing them. Yours apparently was decent enough to leave you a legacy of some sort.' He shook the younger man by the

308

shoulder. Harry's beaming face showed his genuine happiness at his companion's good fortune.

'Ah yes, my legacy,' said Roger, the gleam back in his eyes.

Jade passed the box to Roger and waited breathlessly while he opened it. For a moment, he simply sat and stared at the ring as though mesmerized by the fire's reflection as it danced in and out of the stone. His eyes seemed to flicker themselves and harden. Then he pulled the ring from the box and slid it onto a slender finger of his right hand. It slipped, and he refit it to the slightly thicker middle finger. 'A ring?' he exclaimed.

'It looks like the one you have, Jade,' said Harry. Roger looked sharply up at her.

'A matched set,' she replied and handed over the packet. She wondered if Harry would notice that Roger's was missing that additional line, Bev's tear, as she termed it.

Roger took the packet and tore it open along one end. He extracted two sheets of paper covered in a close, masculine hand, and read silently. Jade shifted in her chair with restless curiosity. She hoped her closeness with David and her job as bearer of the news would endow her with the privilege of hearing its secrets. Once Roger looked up and into the fire with something akin to hate and loathing on his face, but he never spoke. Finally, he folded the papers carefully, replaced them in the envelope, and silently set it beside him.

Harry possessed less tact than the others and

finally inquired with a blunt, 'Well, man? What the hell did it say?'

'What? Oh, it's rather personal. My mother and all . . . You understand.' He slapped his palms on his legs and sat up straighter. 'But he does speak of a box in London for me.'

'Yes, the solicitor has it,' said Jade. 'You'll have to go to London to claim it.'

'Does your father say what's in the box?' urged Harry.

'Nothing specific. He only speaks cryptically of *vast wealth*.'

'Well, there you are, man. Your troubles are over.' Harry slapped him forcefully across the back. 'That calls for a drink.' He rose to fetch a bottle from a supply box.

Roger had nearly fallen out of his chair from Harry's hearty congratulation. When he regained his seat, Jade noticed his smirk. Well, he'd at least be a match for Gil's widow, she thought. Like it or not, she'd done half her job and planned to finish the rest when she returned to Nairobi. The wonder was that she didn't feel better for it. If anything, she felt hollow now, as if David had been taken from her and given to another, one who didn't appreciate him.

'Did I understand Harry correctly, Miss del Cameron?' asked Roger. 'You have a ring as well?' Again, Jade noted that his voice sounded cold and formal.

She nodded. 'David gave it to me when he died.' She fought the urge to grip the ring under her shirt. What if Roger demanded it as his own? How could she lose the one part of David left to

310

her? After all, she rationalized, he didn't tell her to give that ring to his brother. She found herself growing more impatient with Roger.

No one else spoke as they stared into the fire. Harry returned with a bottle of scotch and some tin mugs. Only Avery took him up on a drink. Jade leaned back and scanned the sky. A shooting star streaked from Leo's tail and burned itself out before it struck Cygnus, the constellation she'd assigned to David after the *ngoma*. A sign of success? She shook her head. Her imagination was getting way out of hand here. Besides, if it meant success, wouldn't the meteor have touched the swan?

Harry's deep baritone finally broke the silence. 'We're a jolly group, now, aren't we? Please, try to restrain yourselves and show a little dignity.' Everyone roused themselves, and Avery inquired after tomorrow's agenda.

'I understand you want a lion, Dunbury. There's lion to be found all around here, but I thought to head east to Poacher's Lookout.' Harry pointed in the general direction of the hill, invisible in the blackness beyond the *boma*. 'It will give you a good look at Kilima Njaro as well, which should please Jade's editor.'

'What about the Chyulu Hills?' asked Jade.

Harry picked up a stick and poked the fire. 'That, too. I thought of the spot back when you first expressed an interest in my old partner Gil.' He glanced sideways at Roger and added, 'Your father, Rog. Gil and I tromped around this area hunting elephant for a while, before I decided enough was enough and parted company with him.'

Roger stared at the ring on his finger, his eyes looking beyond it. With mounting impatience, Harry kicked Roger's chair and nearly toppled it. Roger recovered in time to keep from tipping and apologized for his apparent lack of attention. 'Thinking about the hunt,' he explained. Jade didn't believe him. She presumed his thoughts were in Nairobi and with the newly widowed Leticia.

'Will your tracker be able to find lion for us there?' asked Beverly.

'Rest assured,' whispered Roger. 'Whatever you want, Memba Sasa will provide it.'

Madeline stifled a yawn and announced her urge to retire for the night. Everyone agreed to the wisdom of that plan and ambled off to their respective tents after congratulating Roger again. Roger went in search of Memba Sasa, and Harry saw to stoking up the fires for the night.

Jade lay on her cot after removing only her boots. 'Do you always sleep with all your clothes on?' Madeline asked.

'Saves time and embarrassment. I despise running in terror in just my undergarments.'

Her tent mate rebuttoned her blouse. 'Do you really think we're in danger?'

Jade regretted her attempt at humor and turned her head to better see her friend. 'Not with that *boma* and the fires. Don't mind me, Maddy,' she added. 'It's a habit I picked up in the corps. If I'm not in a proper house, I can't sleep without all my clothes on.'

'Well, that may be, but I believe I'll just adopt your strategy while I'm on safari.' She glanced at Jade's duffel. 'Do you have any more of that ointment?'

'You mean the eau de incontinent ferret in heat? Trying to court a ferret, Madeline? What would Neville say?'

Madeline frowned. 'I thought perhaps we might just go ahead and anoint the tent. I mean, as long as we're out here in man-eater country and . . . '

'And Bev's been telling tales about how I always seem to get into some scrape.' Jade sat up on her cot.

'It did protect you when you had the flat.'

Jade pulled the packet of ointment from her bag. She ran a swipe down the buttoned tent flaps and added a few spots along the tent walls and on her belt for good measure. 'I don't know what you're worried about, Madeline. Tsavo lions are *man*-eaters. We're women.'

Madeline didn't find the joke particularly amusing, and didn't reply. Jade hung up the lantern, turned down the wick, and made certain her Winchester was handy. Part of her was ready to head back to Nairobi and concentrate on Gil's killer, but she did have an obligation to her editor for a safari article. Besides, she reasoned, this would give the commissioner more time to track down those other guests. Maybe she'd visit the *mundu-mugo* again and see if anyone else knew how a white man could have annoyed a *laibon* at the time of the war. Finally she plopped on the cot and dropped off to sleep. Once again she dreamed of silence and menace in the tall grass.

Hours later, a high-pitched shriek of terror roused the camp. Jade jumped up with the instantaneous readiness that came from long experience, heightened by her dream. She snatched up her rifle and undid the tent fly, leaving Madeline to turn up the lantern. Then she raced towards the screams, oblivious to the ache in her left knee. Avery emerged bare-chested, pulling the suspenders of his trousers over his shoulders as Jade ran past his tent. Excited voices, some nearly hysterical, guided her to the porters' quarters, where men waved blazing firebrands in the pitch blackness. Harry arrived at the same time.

'Can you see anything?' he shouted to her above the din.

'No. Between the light and the dark, it's too hard.' She squinted, her pupils struggling to adjust. 'There!' she yelled and pointed to one of the tents. One side was slashed into shreds of canvas ribbons. Then Jade caught the unmistakable musky aroma of a large animal mixed in with the scent of human bodies and burning wood. 'Lion!'

Cries of 'Simba' rang in the air, and quivering fingers pointed to the boma wall beyond the tents. Two golden-green orbs flashed in the gloom. Behind those glowing eyes crouched the tawny body of a male lion. Most of him remained hidden in the shadows. He snarled, and his muzzle wrinkled back to reveal flashing white daggers in the firelight.

Harry raised his rifle and had drawn a bead on the beast when Roger raced up. He tripped and stumbled into Harry. The shot went wild. The great cat turned to leap the *boma* wall, and Jade saw its lush gold-and-black mane as it crossed part of the firelight. She fired one round, but it only nicked the animal's hind leg as it scrambled to safety in the blackness beyond.

'Bloody hell,' swore Harry.

'Sorry,' said Roger. 'Something was on the ground, and I tripped.'

Jade didn't see anything on the ground, but then it was too dark to see anything clearly. She looked back to the dark *boma* wall. 'I'm afraid all I did was nick it.'

'Bring that torch over to the wall,' Harry ordered one of the men. He examined the spot where the cat had jumped the wall and saw a streak of blood. 'It'll bleed for a while,' he said. 'That should give us a decent trail to follow tomorrow when it's light.' He looked around at the men. 'Is anyone hurt?' he asked first in English and then again in Wakamba.

Pili stepped forward, holding his right arm. He was bare-chested, his gold cross and his sweat glinting in the firelight. A gash ran from shoulder to elbow, but not deep enough to cause excessive blood loss or permanent muscle damage. 'The lion ripped through the tent. Before I could escape, it clawed me.' An expression of shame crossed his face. 'I am sorry, memsahib. In my fear I grabbed what was at hand and struck the lion on his nose.' He held up the Mannlicher so she could see the bent sights and broken stock. 'I

315

have ruined your new rifle.'

Jade peered down the barrel. Gradually her shoulders started shaking, lightly at first, then harder until she broke out in audible laughter. 'Ah, Pili,' she exclaimed, 'what's an untried rifle compared to a tried-and-true gun bearer? I'm happy you weren't hurt worse than that.' She examined the gash. The blood had clotted in spots, but she wanted to wash and bandage it before any infection set in. 'Come with me. We'll fix that right up.'

She turned and paused when she noticed that her knee ached in a dull throb. *Must be getting ready to rain.* After all, the danger was past and nothing had tried to kill *her.* As she limped to the front tents and the medical kit, she commented to Harry, 'Next time you promise us lion, could you keep it outside? It's a bit more sporting that way.'

21

'A seven-foot-long, five-hundred-pound killing machine looks fierce enough in the light of day, but it becomes more terrifying by the flickering glow of firelight. You no longer see an animal that can be wounded. You only view a powerful set of jaws, a lightning-fast, rapier-sharp set of claws, or a hypnotic pair of golden eyes that are fixed on you.'
— The Traveler

Harry roused the camp before dawn, and a groggy assortment of would-be hunters spilled out of their tents in search of breakfast. Jade found Pili and examined his arm before joining the others. A healthy-looking scab covered the deeper rakes, and the almond-colored skin showed no signs of inflammation around the wound.

'You were fortunate, Pili,' she commented as she rewrapped the bandage around his biceps. 'If you hadn't acted so quickly, he would have killed you.' She pulled the loose sleeve of his tunic down over the arm. 'But why would the lion choose your tent? Did you have food?'

Pili shook his head. 'The men slept outside the tents. They would be easier to take.'

'Perhaps the fires kept the lion away from them?'

'Perhaps,' Pili answered in a voice that

317

expressed his doubts.

'Well, tonight you must take the tent with the bathtub. We'll move the tub somewhere else. I have a special guard against lions. I'll rub some on your tent.'

'I hear the men say that it is a charm against witches, not lions, mistress.'

'Perhaps, Pili, but at any rate, lions don't seem to like it, either.' She patted him on the shoulder. 'Come, let's find some breakfast.'

The cook served up a delicious-smelling hash concocted of chunks of leftover gazelle and various diced tubers enveloped in thick brown gravy and dolloped on slabs of bread baked in round patties over hot stones.

'Are we hiking to Poacher's Lookout today?' asked Madeline.

Roger shook his head. 'Tracking that lion. Probably won't leave enough time today.'

'We can't allow any men to stay behind at this camp knowing that cheeky bast — er, cat is out there ready to come back,' added Harry with a sheepish sidelong glance at Roger. 'Besides, Dunbury wants a lion, and this one has a good story to go with it.'

Avery pushed his plate aside and took out his pipe. 'That alone increases the value of any trophy. It makes my rhino head worth many nights of brandy and cigars with my comrades. They only have worn-out tales of German fighter planes to rehash.'

'You'll have to tell me, Beverly, how long it takes before I'm no longer in the rhino story,' added Jade. 'I'm guessing by the second telling.'

Jade looked around as the tracker appeared at the *boma* gate and Roger conferred with him. Memba Sasa didn't have Ruta's height or easy grace, yet the man radiated arrogance. She tried to analyze what it was about him that did it. Posture? Mouth? His eyes! They bore through everything as though they saw inside people. Roger rejoined the others.

'Memba Sasa has spotted some spoor left by our nocturnal visitor. Shall we?'

Jade took up her Winchester, and Pili went to bring what ammunition she might need. At least her knee didn't ache. She retrieved her hat and camera bag from the tent and followed Harry and Ruta outside the *boma*. They looked west, and Jade stopped dead in her tracks, dumbstruck.

Kilima Njaro, the White or Shining Mountain, hovered in the dawn sky over a cushion of thick, snowy cumulus clouds. The ethereal peaks of Kilimanjaro, as it was known to the mapmakers, glistened as the sun's light danced off its crystalline glaciers. Born during the time when larger glaciers scoured Europe and North America, the giant volcano had bathed the region in lava and ash belched up from its depths. Now it shone white and benign, the antithesis of its fiery youth. The Africans said it descended from the sky, and indeed it appeared to float atop the clouds.

'Quite a sight, eh, Jade?' whispered Harry.

She nodded dumbly and fumbled in her bag for the Graflex. Then, with a sudden sense of urgency, she attempted to capture the hypnotic illusion on film. After her shot, the mountain tired of posing and disappeared behind the rising clouds.

'Does it do that every morning?'

'Only if you're lucky. You, miss, appear to be quite lucky. So is your gun bearer.'

Roger trailed the crew and secured the *boma* entrance. Since Jade's Mannlicher was useless, she handed Pili her camera bag, which he treated as seriously as he did the rifle.

'Over here,' said Roger. He led the way around the *boma*. 'Here's where the brute took the fence.' He pointed to a rivulet of brown dried blood nearly camouflaged on the thorny wood. 'Memba Sasa found more on the grass and followed it. These beasts are territorial. He won't have gone far.'

'Just how big a territory is being discussed here?' asked Avery.

'A few square miles, if the game is plentiful. This close to the river, it should be.'

Memba Sasa led them west towards a confluence of two tributaries, which carried melted snow and rain from Kilimanjaro and other uplifted areas into a union that gave birth to the Tsavo. Smaller gullies, called *dongas*, cut gashes through the thin topsoil and the hardened volcanic rock beneath. They were dry now in the winter season between rains, but the party still skirted them. More than once they heard the heavy snort of a rhino or buffalo rise out of the brushy depths.

For two hours they followed Memba Sasa at a swift pace through the thorny scrub. The man

320

walked like one certain of the path rather than one looking for a sign. Only twice did he stop to get his bearings and never did he actually bother to show them any spoor. Jade looked to see what the man followed and saw nothing. The scrub punished the hunters for their intrusion. Wait-a-bit thorns tugged at their clothes and scratched their arms, legs, and faces.

Finally they stopped while Memba Sasa crouched in the grass and examined the ground. Roger squatted next to him and Jade heard them exchange a few, brief comments in another language. Harry stayed with Ruta to the back of the group as a rear guard. Jade pulled a few ticks from her clothes and another from her arm while the tracker studied a wider circle around the area. She saw several bad rakes from the thorns across his bare legs. The left one in particular bore a fresh, nasty-looking gash along with older scars.

Suddenly Memba Sasa grunted softly as if to say 'aha' and pointed to a bare spot on the ground. Everyone crowded around and stared at the pug mark in the dust. The paw print was the size of a saucer and showed little sign of disturbance, which Roger pointed out as an indication of freshness. Everyone went instantly on alert as they peered intently into the grass for the telltale triangular ears. By gestures, they established that Avery should have first crack at the cat with the understanding that Roger and Harry were there for immediate backup. Another dry *donga* cut a winding swath ahead of them, and the tracker pointed to it and nodded.

'We don't go in there, do we?' asked Beverly.

'How's your throwing arm?' answered Harry as he hefted a volcanic stone in his right hand. He hurled the rock into the thorny brush and waited. Something rustled within. Harry nodded to Ruta, Pili, and the Wakamba man chosen to carry Lord Dunbury's second rifle. They sent a barrage of black basalt into the brush as the hunters slowly paralleled the ravine towards its upper end. Memba Sasa stood silently to one side, refusing to demean himself with such low labor.

An enraged snarl issued from the ravine. The brush shuddered from the force of a large body plowing through it, and the *donga* coughed out an immense male lion. It stood but thirty yards away and glared at them for a second before hunkering down in the grass. Only its golden eyes gleamed through the dry plants as it appraised its own situation. Ruta ran in closer and pelted it with another rock on its left flank. The cat snarled in rage and scrambled sideways farther away from the rock. It also moved farther from the ravine. Pili saw the plan and joined in, driving the lion more to their right and into the open.

As the assault continued, the snarls rose in pitch and volume. A rock struck the enraged animal on the snout; then one massive paw swiped a second rock aside. The lion tensed, gathering its muscular hindquarters beneath it to charge the throwers. Avery took careful aim with a Jeffery rifle and fired a soft-nosed bullet into the cat's side as it leaped. The shot diverted the

322

furious animal's attention from the gun bearers to the hunters but failed to pierce the heart. Now over five hundred pounds of dun-colored muscle hurled itself in Avery and Jade's direction.

The lion launched itself into the air.

'Shoot it!' screamed Beverly.

Two rifles cracked simultaneously as both Jade and Avery fired into the massive chest. The lion twisted in mid-air in pain and rage and fell in a heap four feet in front of them. Razor-sharp claws scrabbled in the dirt as it writhed. Its jaws convulsed once in a stifled roar, and the great cat lay still.

Harry ran up to make certain the animal was truly dead before allowing anyone else to come closer. 'Excellent shooting,' he said as he examined the lion's chest. 'Both of your bullets penetrated within an inch of each other and entered the heart.' He looked at Dunbury with a sly grin. 'You'll have to share this one with Jade.'

Jade shook her head. 'Avery shot first. It's his. I'm just glad it can't come back after the men tonight.' She stood apart and watched as the others swarmed over the carcass like hungry scavengers. Even Memba Sasa took part in the poking, measuring, and general conquest of the beast's remains. He drew a knife and, after using it to measure the hind limbs, cut a small bit of hair from the lion's very sparse mane.

'Hey!' said Jade suddenly. 'That's the wrong lion.' The others looked up in astonishment and stared at her as though she had spoken some foreign gibberish.

'Impossible,' declared Roger with more venom

323

than Jade had heard in his voice before. 'We tracked the blood trail from the compound wall itself.'

'No. This lion has no mane to speak of.'

'Of course not, Miss del Cameron.' Roger sounded like a weary adult instructing an annoying, ignorant child. 'The Tsavo males aren't the same as the Serengeti lions. We explained that to you yesterday.'

Jade clenched and released her fist with mounting impatience. 'That's the point,' she persisted. 'The lion in the compound last night *did* have a big mane. I saw it when he moved into the firelight just before he jumped the fence.' She looked to the others for confirmation without results. Madeline and Beverly had stayed behind in their tents, Avery had arrived after the lion cleared the *boma* wall, and Roger had fallen into Harry before the cat moved into the light.

Harry moved to the cat's rear quarters and examined the hind legs. 'If you need more proof, it's right here,' he said. 'There's a fairly fresh scrape on the hind leg where your bullet grazed it last night.'

Jade stepped forward and examined the leg. The wound looked fresh, and a spot of red came away on her fingertips. 'It's bleeding,' she said. 'It should have scabbed over by now.'

Harry shook his head. 'Not necessarily. Walking out here in all this thorn would either keep it open or reopen it easily enough. You probably saw shadows and thought it was the mane. It's what everyone expects to see.'

Jade scowled again but didn't answer his

patronizing suggestion. True, a running animal might bleed longer, but the wound itself looked wrong. A grazing bullet should have scraped off some hide on either side and made a trough-shaped wound. This looked too sharp and fresh.

'Photograph it, Jade, before the men skin it out,' said Avery.

Jade handed her Winchester to Pili and started to take the camera bag instead. She stopped in midreach. 'Is that the lion that clawed your tent, Pili?' she asked.

The young Somali shrugged. 'It was dark, mistress. I mostly saw his claws.'

Jade turned her outward attention to gratifying Avery's good-natured vanity. Inwardly, something didn't feel right about the entire episode, but she couldn't pinpoint what was awry.

The Wakamba skinned out the cat with swift, expert strokes before they hauled it back to the base camp. The rhino head had been attended to on its arrival to camp, and they stretched out the great lion skin near it. Avery examined his two trophies like a child with new toys, and Beverly smiled as she watched him. Her 'Isn't he wonderful' came out more as a statement of fact than as a question. Jade didn't bother to reply, but Madeline, more sympathetic to the emotions of a new bride, agreed. The two women discussed the relative merits of their spouses while Jade cleaned her Winchester. Eventually, Beverly noticed Jade's pensive silence and nudged Madeline.

'I'm dreadfully sorry, love,' said Beverly. 'Here

we are carrying on like two love-struck schoolgirls without a thought to you.'

'I assure you, I don't mind in the least,' replied Jade while peering down the barrel. 'I actually found it rather amusing.'

Beverly frowned. 'You really must stop dwelling on David,' she said finally. 'I know you miss him terribly, but you cannot' — she searched for the word she wanted — 'focus on him any longer.' She put a gentle hand on her friend's shoulder. 'There will be someone else for you someday; I know it.'

Jade looked at the hand and then locked her green eyes on Beverly's. 'You know nothing of the sort, Bev,' she said softly. 'But,' she added, 'I wasn't thinking about David just now.'

'Oh?'

'No. I'm still bothered by that lion Avery shot.'

'Roger's convinced it's the same one,' said Madeline. 'And Harry — '

Jade held up her hand to interrupt. 'I know you put prodigious faith in Harry, Madeline, including his ability to make me forget David.' She frowned at Madeline, and the latter ducked her head from Jade's penetrating eyes. 'Nevertheless, they're both wrong.' She finished with her rifle and set it on her lap. 'There's something wrong about a lot of things,' she muttered.

'Such as?' asked Madeline.

'Such as why the lion last night went for Pili in his tent rather than one of the exposed men sleeping outside. Such as the way Memba Sasa tracked today. Did you notice? He barely looked at the ground or the vegetation. I did. I didn't see any blood spoor.' She took a deep breath and exhaled in a loud huff. 'I don't like that man.'

'Who?' asked Bev. 'Memba Sasa? What's wrong with him?'

'I don't know for certain. Nothing and everything.'

'Oh, well, that's specific,' said Beverly in a sarcastic tone. 'Really, Jade, you are just overwrought. I worried that this entire assignment would be too much for you. We all know you're tremendously brave and positively splendid, but there is a limit to what anyone can endure. I'm just glad that your crusade to find David's brother is over.' She smiled and nodded in the direction of the men. 'You were right, darling. You did find him out here.'

'And how wonderful for Roger,' added Madeline. 'The poor boy's had such a run of bad luck. Maybe now he'll move on with his life and marry that silly Leticia.'

'Who's Leticia?' asked Beverly.

'A local girl,' answered Madeline. 'Very pretty, but a little fool, if you ask me. Her father fell into debt and was bought out by Godfrey Kenton with Leticia thrown into the bargain even though Roger loved her. Godfrey was a bit of a dolt and a rounder. Pity how he died though.' She shuddered. 'It was horrid finding him.'

'We don't know how he died,' said Jade. 'I still think he was murdered and his body tossed onto Colridge's land to confuse the issue. That car proved he was at the flumes.'

'But not that he was killed there,' added Beverly. 'I'm inclined to agree with the

327

commissioner. He may have been drunk, passed out, and died of exposure.'

'And his body just happened to get hauled for miles?' Jade asked.

'Maybe Leticia shot him,' suggested Madeline. 'But I can't see that little thing moving his body. She'd need an accomplice. Just about everyone hated him. I know Harry did.'

'So did Donaldson, and Roger's still in love with her,' said Jade. 'At least if the way he behaved at the Muthaiga Club is any indication.'

'Well, then, perhaps Roger will get Leticia after all, if that Mrs Estes person takes her claws out of him,' added Beverly. 'I got the impression he was one of her toys, her *many* toys.'

Jade rose from her seat. 'How can anyone keep up with these webs that people weave down here? I just want to find a killer. But with Kenton buried, we're not likely to find the real cause of death, and everyone has a motive. With Gil, I know *how* he died; I just have no idea why.' She headed for her tent.

As she turned away, Bev called after her, 'How is your knee handling the walking?'

Jade stopped and shook her leg. 'It's fine. In fact it only seems to hurt on two different occasions. One, when it's going to rain.'

'And what's the other occasion?' prompted Bev.

'When something's about to kill one of us.'

★ ★ ★

Later in the afternoon, Roger led the crew out to hunt for the pot. Harry had scheduled a day trip to the Chyulu Hills and they needed enough food to last the meat-eating Wakamba until they returned. This time Memba Sasa came along, but Jade noticed he acted more like Roger's bodyguard and less like a tracker. Pili insisted on accompanying Jade. The Mannlicher required considerable repair to be usable; consequently, there was little need of a gun bearer. Jade reasoned that he wanted to make amends by being responsible for her camera if not for her extra gun.

He was certainly an interesting young man, she thought. Handsome, too, with his finely chiseled features, glowing bronze complexion, black hair, and clear hazel eyes. Before this hunt, she'd examined his wound for any sign of pustulance and discovered he spoke French. At least he swore in that language when she peeled off the stuck bandage and took a few arm hairs with it. Well, he was French Somali, and Jade recalled that Lord Colridge said he went to school at the mission. That certainly reckoned with the gold cross and chain around his neck. Perhaps she could write an article about him. She made a mental note to ask him about his life working for the flamboyant old horse breeder.

Two rifle reports disrupted her thoughts. Madeline brought down a Thomson's gazelle with her shot, but Beverly, who had never hunted before, attempted to use her husband's larger-caliber rifle. The sharp recoil brought her onto her backside as neatly as Madeline's shot

329

brought down the Tommy. Jade stifled her laughter by looking away. Beverly kicked her friend in the ankle anyway.

'That's for thinking about laughing,' she said and then broke out in a melodious chuckle. Her husband pulled her up and kissed her while the others pretended not to see.

Harry and Ruta followed the herd in hopes of bagging a second animal and left Roger, Memba Sasa, and several Wakamba to deal with Madeline's Tommy. Soon after, they heard the report of Harry's rifle. Roger dispatched a couple more Wakamba to assist with whatever his partner had bagged.

'You chose a good man for a partner,' said Avery.

'Who, Harry? Yes, he's quite a good chap,' replied Roger with little feeling. He peered at Jade. 'You're a cool one, too, Miss del Cameron,' he added. 'After watching you toy with that rhino and fire into the lion this morning, I doubt anything rattles you.'

Jade was too taken aback by the personal comment to reply. Beverly jumped in.

'She is positively amazing, Mr Forster. It's no wonder your brother took such a fancy to her. The only time I ever saw our Jade rattled, as you put it, is when she had to transport a load of shell-shocked soldiers and they started laughing in the most insane — ' Beverly saw Jade's lips tighten and stopped. 'I'm sorry, love. I shouldn't have brought it up. I'm a bloody fool.'

'Quite all right, Bev,' Jade whispered. But it wasn't. The reminder of that terrible experience

330

sickened her. Jade declined Harry's offer of an evening stroll just outside the *boma* and retired early that night, grateful that no unwanted visitors entered the compound.

★　★　★

His body swayed rhythmically to the barely mumbled chants as he sat naked on the ground. No chance for a fire here. Too many nosy humans about. He put a piece of dried weed under his tongue and let its magic work through him, feeling it dribble first down into his stomach, hot and potent. The heat entered his blood and coursed through his arteries, feeding his muscles. Though his eyes were shut, he could see. He saw the wild predators of the night and mentally sorted through them all. The jackal was too small. The leopard turned and ran when he bent his thoughts to it. None would face the ointment smeared on the heathen's tent. No worry, the heathen would fall. And the woman? She was too clever, and consequently, too dangerous. He would take care of her himself. There would be an opportunity soon enough.

22

*'The Shaitani lava flows at the western edge
of Tsavo are less than two hundred years old.
Local legends say that many villagers were
trapped and buried by this cataclysm, and
some claim that their plaintive cries can yet be
heard issuing from the many lava caves
nearby. It's not good to investigate those cries.
The caves can be treacherous, as the bones of
many hapless animals attest.'*
— The Traveler

A half dozen Wakamba men toted various parcels
to the cars the next morning, and Jade found
Harry supervising. She handed him a mug of
steaming coffee and a slab of grilled meat rolled
in stone-baked flat bread and bit into her own
portable breakfast.

'I presume we're taking the cars today?' she
said between mouthfuls.

Harry gulped some coffee and nodded. 'The
cars were Roger's idea. I wasn't too sure about
them myself, but I'm beginning to appreciate
them. Tsavo's a hell of a place to walk in.'

'Assuming they don't run dry.'

'Assuming. But we're close to the headwaters
of the river.' He nodded in the general direction
of Mount Kilimanjaro. 'Between snowmelt,
runoff, and springs, most of the headwaters flow
year-round. Should see some good game there.

332

Elephants. Interesting scenery, too.'

'The Chyulu Hills?'

Harry nodded. 'You'll get a good view from Poacher's Lookout.' He turned abruptly to one of the porters. 'Not the Ford, the other one. Careful with those petrol cans.'

'I should leave you to your work,' she offered and turned to go.

Harry dropped his tin coffee mug and grabbed her arm. 'Don't go.'

Jade pretended not to understand. 'I shouldn't go to Poacher's Lookout?'

Harry frowned and pulled her closer. 'You know damn good and well what I meant, Jade. You're too clever, and I'm being too obvious to let you misunderstand.' He sniffed at her loose black hair. 'Ah, for once you aren't wearing that awful hat.'

'Yes, I know. Beverly insists it smells like something rude.'

Harry laughed a deep bass rumble. 'I just bet she does. Dunbury's a lucky man. I should be so lucky.' His voice sounded seductively husky.

'Harry,' Jade began. He shushed her with a scarred finger to her lips.

'I know all the objections already. I'm forty-two years old, and you're still in love with a dead man. Probably more in love with him because he's dead.' He held her to him and bent down to her face. 'But I promise you I can help you get over him if you let me.'

Jade put her own hand over his mouth before he could kiss her. 'I'd be lying if I said I didn't find you very attractive, Harry, but I need time.

333

Lots of time.' She felt his sigh shudder from his chest and down his arms like the early rumbling warnings of a volcano.

'You'll think about it then?'

'I have been already,' she replied.

He kissed the fingers that rested on his chin. 'Guess I can't ask for more than that.'

He released her, and Jade walked back to the tents, conscious of his gaze on her the entire way. Madeline and Beverly met her by the *boma* gate and pretended to only then discover her.

'Oh, there you are,' exclaimed Beverly. 'We were looking for you.'

'Liar,' said Jade. 'I'm sure you knew the cook gave me Harry's breakfast to take to him. How long have you been spying on me?'

'Spying?' protested Madeline. 'It's too dark yet to be spying.' She didn't continue after Jade glared at her.

'Oh, give it up, Madeline dear,' said Beverly. 'Our Jade knows us too well.' She fixed her own soft blue eyes on Jade and smiled an enigmatic Mona Lisa smirk. 'In answer to your question, long enough. Do we congratulate him? He's a lucky man, or at least a very brave one.' Bev ducked, and Jade's empty coffee mug flew harmlessly overhead and clattered on the ground.

'There's nothing to congratulate him about,' Jade said through gritted teeth. 'Unless you count my turning him down as grounds for congratulations.'

Madeline pouted, and Beverly scowled. 'He's worth a fling at least,' offered Beverly.

'I don't fling.'

Beverly glanced back at the coffee cup on the ground. 'I don't know about that.'

Jade casually picked up the dirty coffee cup and walked to her tent. 'Better pack it up,' she called over her shoulder. 'We're heading out soon.'

Jade rode next to Roger in the Dodge with Pili, Ruta, and Memba Sasa. The route was too bumpy to allow much conversation. Once she tried to discern his future plans, but Roger said little and only smiled when Leticia's name came up. 'You could rebuild your ranch,' Jade suggested, 'and stop running safaris.' A particularly nasty bump that Roger could have avoided put an end to all conversation.

Harry and Roger stopped the cars near an ancient baobab tree next to the northernmost tributary of the Tsavo. Long shadows sprawled westward, fleeing the rising sun.

'We'll head on later to the Shaitani lava flow, but for now, I want to take you to the top of Poacher's Lookout,' said Harry. 'You'll get a grand view of the Chyulu Hills from there.' He pointed across the tributary to a tall mound. 'No sense chancing the cars across the riverbed. We'll walk.'

'Is it safe to cross on foot?' asked Avery.

'Up here it is. Crocs don't seem to like the shallow, fast-moving water. But anytime you have to cross water, you cross as a large body, not as individual tidbits.'

'Lovely,' exclaimed Beverly. 'I don't fancy becoming an hors d'oeuvre to a handbag.'

'I assure you,' said Harry, 'the view will be *well* worth the hike.'

They crossed the tributary and trudged up the rocky slope of Poacher's Lookout. Black basaltic boulders, nearly bare of lichens, stuck out at sharp angles and provided steps to the top. Jade reached the summit first, climbing from rock to rock like an agile mountain goat. Pili followed at a slightly slower rate, trailed by the Dunburys and Madeline. Harry and Roger along with Ruta brought up the rear for protection. Memba Sasa stayed at the cars, aloof as usual.

Jade's eyes had no room for anything besides the magnificent, snowcapped volcanic mountain of Kilimanjaro to the southwest. 'My stars,' she exclaimed. 'And I thought the Rocky Mountains were beautiful.'

She took one exposure and cursed herself for not bringing twice as much film. Now that half her task was over and the rest waiting until she returned, Jade again felt she could take a moment and enjoy the view. She drank in the mountain's softly rounded shape, the low white skirting clouds, and the hazy landscape in the crystalline-clear blue morning sky. Miles of open land and ages of time stood between her and the mountain. It was unapproachable.

She had felt this way when she first saw the Grand Canyon. The other side seemed so remote, so aloof, and no matter how far down she went, the rims and walls kept their distance. They surrounded her yet would always evade her. Kilima Njaro, the Shining Mountain, had that same cool pride mingled with its condescension to humans. Mortals might look at it when it allowed, but they must respect its superiority. As if in response to her rude stare, the mountain raised its cloudy veil higher. *Very well. I'll look the other way.*

The view to the north was less soul-stirring but still intriguing. Harry was right. She could spot the game from up here. Clusters of black-and-white zebras mingled with a variety of antelope and long-legged storks at the edge of a spring-fed watering hole. Farther away at the foot of some hills, a mass of large gray shapes paraded.

'Who has a pair of field glasses?' Jade asked. Roger pulled a pair from a pack and handed them over.

'What do you see, Jade?' asked Madeline.

Jade focused the lenses, and the gray blurs formed into a majestic matriarch and her cohort. A baby ambled among the elder's legs and explored the possibility of being fed by its mother. 'Elephants,' she answered without withdrawing the glasses.

Harry produced another pair of glasses and handed them to Madeline. 'I used to come up here with Gil when he first arrived. I hadn't been long in the country myself, and looking for ivory seemed like a fast way to get rich.'

'Was it?' asked Beverly.

'Do I look rich?' he answered. 'Elephants are smart and dangerous. Even the Tsavo lions leave them alone.'

'What are those beautiful little blue mountains

337

over there?' Jade pointed north-northeast.

'Those, Jade, are your Chyulu Hills. Volcanic. Everything around here is volcanic.' Harry pointed to the spread of black, tarry terrain at the edge of the hills. 'That's the Shaitani lava flow, about as barren a place as you'd ever care to wander in. No water there.'

So this is one of the places Gil came to, she thought. 'There's water someplace,' Jade said. She nodded back at the elephants.

'The Chyulu rock is porous. Water runs into the craters and comes out as springs. Lots of cavernous holes in the hills.'

'Just think, Roger. Your father hunted here. Isn't that exciting?' asked Madeline.

Roger stared silently at the gently rounded, blue-green hills, which contrasted sharply with the black lava fields and rocks. 'Yes, very,' he answered after a moment.

Jade followed his line of sight across the river and saw a smaller black outcrop just under a softly folded ridge. She raised the binoculars for a closer look. Perhaps, she thought, he saw an animal in the rocks. For a moment, she didn't see anything but blackness in the grassy mound, a cave maybe. Before she could explore the area more, Beverly interrupted her.

'Now what are you looking at?' she asked. 'You are being a terrible bore keeping those field glasses to yourself, you know.'

Jade handed the glasses to Beverly. 'There's something across the way; a cave, I think.'

'Where?' asked Beverly as she tried to find it.

'You're looking too far to the right. There.' She

put her arm in front of Bev's face and pointed straight out from her nose. 'See where the river bends sharply? Now look across it at the dark spot. It's peeking over the grassy hill just like a little — ' She gasped.

'Like a little what?' Bev asked.

'Ghost,' said Jade in a hushed voice. She pulled the ring from inside her shirt and studied the etching. 'Mr Forster, you recognized it, too, didn't you? The ring etchings are a map.' She felt a surge of excitement course through her. Perhaps she could learn something else about Gil there that would help her understand why he was killed.

She held out the ring and pointed to one side. 'Look!' she commanded. 'This crossed line here represents the railroad and its terminus.' Sharp intakes of breath punctuated her words as her excitement grew. 'Remember, the line wasn't finished then. This trough is the Tsavo River.'

She turned the ring over. 'This side holds a more closeup view. That bigger mound is Kilimanjaro. This smaller one is Poacher's Lookout. We look across the river to the hills and see the little cave peering over the other side.' She looked at Beverly. 'Remember? You said it looked like a little ghost peeking over a hill.'

'Yes, I do remember. This is marvelous! Mr Forster, don't you agree?'

Jade looked at Roger to gauge his response. He kept his excitement highly controlled, but a sudden tightening of his lips and a slight flare of his nostrils flashed across his face. His eyes held more fire than she'd seen before, too. What surprised her more was Harry's *lack* of reaction. His face didn't register any change, almost as if he had expected this discovery. Then she remembered. He had seen the ring before. She glared at him as if to convey the fact that she had found him out.

'It was fortunate you insisted we come up here, Harry,' she said. He smiled and touched his hat brim.

'Where's the tear in the ghost's eye?' asked Beverly as she peered through the glasses.

'What do you mean?' demanded Roger with renewed interest.

'I mean the etchings show a tear trickling down from the little ghost figure, that is, from the cave symbol. Where is it?'

Roger examined his ring more carefully. 'I don't understand what you mean.' He glared at Jade. 'What does she mean?' he demanded.

Beverly took his hand and turned it so she could see the etchings. 'There,' she began and stopped. 'Oh, it's not on this one.'

'The rings are different?' Roger's anger intensified. 'You said they were the same.'

Jade's ring dangled from its cord around her neck. Roger grabbed for it, and Jade stepped back out of reach. The rashness of the move made her wary, and Harry's apparent knowledge made her suspicious. 'I said they were a set. I must not have noticed that the tear, as Beverly calls it, was absent from yours.' It was a lie, but she felt no need to explain herself.

Roger stepped back and took a deep breath. When he regained his self-control he spoke. 'I apologize, Miss del Cameron, for being so rude just now. You must understand my excitement. *Please*, may I see the ring?' He held out his palm expectantly.

Jade reluctantly slipped the cord from her neck and handed it to him. 'There *is* another line on this one,' he said after comparing both rings. 'Perhaps it's a path, a trail.'

Jade held out her hand and waited for Roger to hand back her own ring. 'I suggest we go across and find out, Mr Forster.' She slid the cord back over her head on her way down the hill.

The short distance to the Chyulu Hills was deceptive, especially when the cars needed to wend around ravines and lumber over the bumpy, dried wallows. Jade felt a rising tension in her gut and tried to amuse herself with the gambols of frightened ostrich that raced beside them or the sudden run of a startled warthog, but her thoughts kept returning to David. She longed to take his hand again and tell him she was still on the quest. She and his brother were about to discover his father's secret legacy.

Gil had mapped this general area on paper, and more specifically on the rings, for a reason. He'd been planning to return here before his murder. Surely she'd learn something in the cave that would help find his killer. For too long she had felt responsible for David's death, believing his recklessness was an attempt to ultimately gain her acceptance of his proposal. Now, perhaps, the burden of guilt would be lifted from her heart.

The cars finally sputtered into the desolate, rolling black pillows of the Shaitani flow, waves of lava frozen in mid-ooze and baked into a miserable mockery of land. Once, they stopped to add water to both cars before they overheated, and Jade noticed the Ford purred less and chugged more asthmatically as they continued. This time, she rode with Harry and spoke her observation aloud to him.

'It's running rough,' she said as she leaned over so he could hear her better.

'Well, what do you want me to do about it?' he asked. 'And get that stinking hat away!'

She took off her hat and held it in her lap. 'It's the carburetor. It's all fouled with dust.'

'Is this a desperate situation?'

'No, but it needs to be cleaned soon or it could become desperate later.'

He pointed to the bleak landscape around him. 'I should prefer not to stop here. These rocks get blistering hot in the afternoon sun.'

Jade nodded. 'Later, at the hills. I can take care of it then.'

Harry turned his head and opened his eyes wider as he caught her meaning. '*You'll* take care of it? I forbid it.'

'Forbid it? Who's paying for this safari? You?' Jade sat back in her seat. 'I'll do it.'

Harry muttered something disparaging about independent women under his breath, and Jade smiled. She put her hat on and winked at the two women behind her before she turned back to the lava fields.

The inhospitable Shaitani flows lacked nothing in drama. If the stories about the doomed African villages held any truth, then the flow must have been fast and probably occurred at night when everyone slept. *Dangerous business, sleeping.* Heat waves rippled off the black rock and gave the illusion that the lava was still in the act of cooling.

'Almost out of it,' said Harry. 'We'll leave the cars below on the grass and take the rest on the shank's mare.' He slapped his leg to explain his meaning.

'Is it always this hot out here?' asked Beverly as they filed out of the cars.

'No. Sometimes it's hotter,' replied Harry.

When Jade picked up her camera bag, she saw a small, greasy-looking spot at its bottom. *Blast it*, she thought. She'd thrown the rest of the Kikuyu sorcerer's ointment in the bag after swiping down the tent flaps, and it had leaked. Jade handed the camera to Pili, added the Swahili book, a metal tin of exposed film and another of unexposed, then fished out the greasy amulet bag. 'Ick,' she muttered and tossed it onto the back floor of the Ford. Ointment covered her hands. She had wiped half of it off on the car's side when she stopped and looked at Pili.

'After that lion attack, you could stand a little more protection yourself. Hold still,' she added when he wrinkled his nose and stepped back. 'Remember, it keeps lions and witches away.' She swiped her hands on his dusty tunic, repacked her camera equipment, and gave Pili the bag.

Several more rounds of ammunition went in her pockets before she started up the hills with her Winchester. Once again, Memba Sasa stayed behind at the cars while the rest began the climb.

Roger was well in the lead already, but Jade soon reduced the distance between them. Pili followed closely on her heels.

The hills formed a long, humped chain resembling the vertebral column of a gigantic prehistoric beast that had long since been covered with plant life so that only the form remained. The sides weren't steep, but many of the exposed rocks were loose, so Jade took care before setting her weight on them. Fat, furry rock hyraxes scampered off through the oat grass into small crevices. She and Roger soon outstripped the others. Jade felt a sudden elation rise up inside her.

'Mr Forster,' she shouted, then decided to break down his barrier of formality and called him by his given name. 'Roger.' His head peeked around a grassy knoll at her. 'Exciting, isn't it?' she said as she trotted the rest of the way to him. 'Could there be diamonds here?'

'I am trying not to be too hopeful, *Miss* del Cameron. Perhaps Gil left a cache of ivory behind.'

'You may be right. It's probably wise not to risk disappointment.' Jade nodded at his ring. 'But no matter what, you also found that your father cared enough to try to find you,' she said. 'Add to that a very special brother who was also determined to find you.'

'I suppose that *should* be worth something,'

said Roger. 'But I can't pay my creditors with sentimental thought.' He lifted his head a little higher. 'If there *is* nothing here, I am still the sole surviving son and heir to at least part of his London estate.'

'Of course,' said Jade. In her mind she wondered again how much of a fight Mrs Worthy would give him. *That's Roger's battle. I'm staying out of it.* She started to reach out to pat his shoulder, but he backed away in his usual scornful manner. Jade didn't repeat the attempt at familiarity. 'Shall we find that cave then, *Mr* Forster?'

'It should be just over this small ridge,' he replied. 'You wait here.'

Jade shook her head no. She had no intention of staying back.

Pili arrived at that instant, and Roger immediately turned to climb the last ridge. Jade caught the scowl on Roger's face. She knew he held Kikuyu and Wakamba natives in scorn, but why Pili? Was Roger also prejudiced against Somali or did he carry the general distrust of mission boys that many settlers evidenced? Jade shrugged. Whatever it was, it was Roger's problem.

The cave entrance turned out to be a large lava tube tall enough for them to enter with only a slight stoop. If there had been a trail leading off from it once, there was none to speak of now. Jade looked at Roger to see how he took this new disappointment, but his moody face betrayed none of his usual frowns or scowls. If anything, he looked more alive.

'Can we go in?' she asked.

'Too dark,' said Roger. 'The sun isn't penetrating inside and what indirect light we have is sucked up by the black lava. These tubes are treacherous. There can be sudden drops, or perhaps the crust is thin and cracks open beneath you.' He took a deep breath and put his hands on his hips. 'I'll need good torches and lots of stout rope to explore these.'

The rest of the crew arrived just in time to hear these last words and expressed their disappointment in an assortment of moans, groans, and muttered mild expletives. Jade noted the 'I' portion of Roger's declaration.

'Cripes,' fumed Beverly. 'This entire side trip is literally 'on the rocks' then. I wanted to explore inside a volcano. I'm no fraidy-cat.'

'Of course not, Lady Dunbury,' said Harry. 'You've been splendid. But Roger's right. At least in part. I think we can do without the rope if we don't venture too far. There's plenty of firewood here to make torches.' Roger protested that they must consider the ladies' safety, but the company overruled him. Beverly called him a fussbudget, but Jade assumed he didn't want to share any discoveries.

'At least let's go back down to the cars for lunch first,' Roger suggested in exasperation.

'If he's hoping that we won't want to hike up this hill again, he's mistaken,' confided Beverly to Madeline and Jade. 'I intend to look in that tube, or cave, or whatever it's called.'

Since Roger led the way back down the hill to the cars, they had little choice but to follow him.

As Jade watched, the young man trotted ahead and made straight for Memba Sasa. After a short discussion in which Roger appeared to issue orders, the grizzled tracker nodded and headed off into the brush. No one else seemed to notice.

'While you eat, I'm going to get under that car and clean out the carburetor jet,' declared Jade. 'I don't fancy having a breakdown and sitting out in the plains past dusk.'

'Aren't you going to eat first?' asked Madeline.

'I will if you make me a sandwich while I find the tools.'

The ladies sat on various rocks, putting chunks of smoked gazelle meat on slabs of flat, round bread. Jade bolted her meal down and rummaged in a side box for tools while Harry and Ruta gathered wood for torches. Roger sat alone, and Avery stretched out in the Dodge for a nap.

Beverly watched her American friend from a shady rock. 'Jade,' she called. 'Do you still have that Swahili grammar? I want to look something up.'

'In the camera bag.' Jade proceeded to slide on her back underneath the Ford.

Beverly found the book and sat back down to flip through various pages.

'What are you looking up?' asked Madeline.

'Shaitani,' replied Beverly. 'I wonder what it means.'

'Satan,' said Madeline. 'Swahili has some Arabic roots.'

Beverly beamed. 'How smashing of you to

347

know that straight off. But then, you must be quite fluent.'

Maddy shook her head. 'You would think so, but I have to speak Kikuyu more than Swahili. I really am not as fluent as I should be.' She looked up as Roger Forster walked towards them. 'Hullo, Mr Forster.'

'What the hell does she think she's doing?' he demanded, pointing at Jade.

'Fixing the carburetor,' replied Beverly nonchalantly. 'The only way to get to it in a flivver is from underneath. That is,' she added with an impish grin, 'unless you want to roll it over on its back. Isn't that right, Jade?'

'Most definitely,' Jade shouted back from under the car over the sounds of metal pieces dropping to the ground.

'Well, stop it at once!' yelled Roger. His voice rose to a near hysterical pitch.

'Don't be silly,' said Beverly. 'We told you she's a top-notch mechanic. Your car couldn't be in better hands.' She held up a slab of bread. 'You're just overexcited about the cave. Have some lunch.'

'Beverly,' yelled Jade, 'while you're studying that book, look up 'Pili' for me. I thought I saw it the other day and wondered what it meant.'

Beverly looked first at Madeline, who shrugged, then flipped through the pages. Roger shouted, 'It's not Swahili, and it means warrior. Now get out from under that car!'

Jade didn't obey, and Roger stormed off. The ladies presumed he went in search of Harry.

'My stars,' Beverly exclaimed. 'Is that man

348

always so high-strung?' Just then Jade gasped.

'Are you all right?' the women asked simultaneously.

'Hell's bells and sweet mother of pearl!' Jade whispered. Then she added, 'Is he gone?'

'Is who gone?' asked a rich baritone voice.

'Harry? Where's Roger?' asked Jade from under the car. She slid parts of the dismantled carburetor out from underneath. 'Bev, blow out the intake jet, will you?'

Bev took the part as well as the hint to move out of earshot and motioned for Madeline to help her. Harry knelt down next to the car and peered underneath.

'What's going on here?' he demanded. 'I heard Roger yelling a moment ago.'

'He wasn't happy to see me under the car, and I think I know why.' She removed a carefully bundled brown sack and pushed it over to Harry. 'He didn't want me to find this.'

Harry took the sack gently in his large hands. 'What is it?' he asked.

'I'm assuming your partner is smuggling something, and considering the state of Mrs Estes in Nairobi, I'm betting it's heroin.'

'I'll be damned,' swore Harry.

'We can hope not, but he might well be,' replied Jade. 'He probably figured it would be safe from detection tucked up above the works under the chassis.'

'It's a fair bet he didn't expect to have one of his customers be so eager to spend time underneath it, either. Damn!' he swore and pounded the dirt near Jade's head. She coughed as the dust settled in her throat. 'Sorry,' he added.

'What should we do?' she asked when she stopped coughing. 'Pretend we didn't find it, or try to talk some sense into his head?'

'No use pretending ignorance. I'll talk to him,' said Harry after a brief pause. 'Maybe with this inheritance, he'll be willing to give up selling drugs.' He hefted the bag. 'To own the truth, I hoped he might rethink coming in as a partner with me and join up our land as one ranch. He's been struggling unsuccessfully to stay afloat, and I need more acreage for my cattle.'

'You knew about this place, didn't you, Harry. You recognized the marks on the ring.'

Before Harry could admit or deny the accusation, Beverly returned with the newly cleaned intake jet. Jade quickly put the carburetor back together. She had skootched out from under the car with the aid of Harry's strong right hand when a high-pitched scream ripped through the air from beyond the first low ridge.

23

Shaitani means devil.
— The Traveler

The scream held as one long shrill shriek before it ripened into a low, quavering moan. By that time, Jade had snatched up her Winchester from the car and covered half the distance up to the ridge. Energy born of fear coursed through her body, and her long legs ate up the ground. Like the wounded rhino, nothing short of a fatal shot could have held her back. Not even the stabbing ache in her knee. If anything, it spurred her on. The sound of many booted feet, including Harry's larger, heavy ones, pounded the dirt behind her. Who had screamed? Avery? Roger?

'Go!' She recognized Pili's voice. Jade shouldered her Winchester and slowed to a trot. She trained her line of sight down the barrel and rotated from side to side, wary of the sudden rush of a cornered predator. The shout came again directly ahead, punctuated by the clatter of rocks. A low, menacing growl followed, guaranteed to turn solid leg muscles to a quivering gelatinous mass. Jade hastened forward before her head had time to advise her legs differently.

A flash of dusty white tunic peeped out of a rocky crevice. Pili struggled to press himself farther into the crack and out of the reach of the razor-sharp talons that searched for him.

Another rock flew out of the meager sanctuary and hit the lion on the nose. The cat retreated several yards, screwed his face into a snarl, and roared. The noise echoed off the rocky hillside until it sounded like an entire pride of demons. Jade blinked in disbelief. The cat appeared to have something stuck in its thick black mane. A bone bead!

'Don't move!' cautioned Jade as she edged in closer. 'I have him.'

She slid around and aimed for a spot behind the shoulders to penetrate the heart. She squeezed the trigger. A split second before her cartridge exploded from the barrel, someone else fired from above. The second person fired short, and the lion jerked up and back just in time for her bullet to only graze his underbelly. Jade absorbed the recoil and chambered another round to fire again, but the beast had pivoted and retreated rapidly into the thick brush. She fired repeatedly into the dense vegetation, and an enraged scream of pain rewarded the effort.

Harry pulled Pili from his protective crevice and examined him for injuries as Roger scrambled down from the rocks above. Avery, who had held Madeline and Beverly back, released them, and the two ran to Pili. Ruta, who had also followed, stepped back.

'Blast the bad luck. We missed him,' Roger exclaimed.

'I had him, dammit,' Jade snapped, 'if you hadn't spooked him.'

Roger's face colored under her attack. 'Easy to lay blame on another, Miss del Cameron. But so

352

far, I haven't seen anything to make me trust your aim. You grazed the first lion back at the compound as well. Seems we're always out tracking a dangerous animal that you wounded and made even more dangerous!'

Jade's eyes flashed. No one accused her of incompetent shooting and got away with it. 'See here, Forster. In both cases, your meddling cost the killing shot. The first time, you tripped and fell into Harry. This time, you undershot and hit the dirt.' She stuck out her chin and started to edge closer to his face. Harry grabbed her around the waist and dragged her back while Avery planted himself in front of Roger. She felt the throbbing ache in her knee and wondered if Harry's proximity constituted serious danger. After all, the lion was gone.

'Easy there, Simba Jike,' Harry said. 'Put your temper on safety and cool down.'

Jade wriggled free of his grip and stepped aside. 'Sorry, Mr Forster,' she said. 'I was worried about Pili, and I suppose I took it out on you.'

'Apology accepted, Miss del Cameron.'

Jade noticed he didn't offer one of his own. She turned to her gun bearer, but Madeline and Beverly were tending to Pili's scratches, most of which came from the sharp volcanic rocks.

'What happened, Pili?' she asked.

He looked up and shook his head. 'I heard someone call to me, mistress. I thought it was you so I came to this spot. I didn't see you, but I heard something breathing.' He passed one slender hand over his face and shuddered. The other hand gripped the gold cross around his neck. Beverly sat down beside him and spoke soothingly till he regained his composure. 'I felt something . . . evil. Then that terrible lion sprang out from the brush. I could not run from it.'

'You did very well, Pili,' said Jade. 'It was clever of you to seek shelter in that crevice. I'm only sorry I didn't kill it.' She shot another angry glance at Roger.

'What I find most curious is why two lions have both taken it into their heads to go after your gun bearer,' said Avery. His eyes looked beseechingly at Jade, begging her to explain this to him.

Jade stabbed the air with her forefinger. 'No! Not *two* lions!' She looked around at their confused faces and open mouths and explained. 'Don't you see? It was the *same* lion each time. Remember? I said the one in the compound had a thick mane. You didn't believe me.' She pointed with her rifle in the general direction in which the lion had escaped. 'Now I *know* you saw the mane on that one, or at least Pili and Roger did. You also said the Tsavo lions rarely sport those big manes. So just how many big, hairy beasts can there be out here?'

'You've got to admit, she makes a good argument,' said Avery. 'We may well have killed the wrong lion the first time.'

'But I thought Memba Sasa tracked it from the blood,' said Madeline. 'Didn't he?'

'He did,' said Roger, his voice defensive.

'By the way, Rog, where is your tracker?' asked

Harry. 'I haven't seen him since we first climbed up to the cave.'

'I sent him off to scout for game while we ate lunch. He should have been back by now.'

'You don't suppose the lion got to him first?' suggested Beverly. Her voice cracked as she tried to control her fear.

'Not a chance,' said Roger. 'Memba Sasa out-thinks lions.'

Ruta snorted, and Roger glared at him. Jade again observed that Ruta could follow their conversations. He not only understood Swahili but English as well. He just refused to admit it.

'Well, we can't wait for him,' said Harry. 'We need to bag this bloke before he turns back on us.' He shouldered his rifle and saw Jade's distant stare. 'What is it?'

'There's something very wrong about this lion,' she said softly. 'I saw a big bone bead in its mane.' A chorus of exclamations ranging from a questioning 'What?' to a despairing 'Oh no' went up from the group. Harry spat out a ripe 'Damnation.' Roger's eyes narrowed.

'Now see here,' Roger said. 'I believe your imagination is running away with you, Miss del Cameron. A combination of the heat, the stress of these attacks, and your yet recent personal trials have taken their toll on you.'

Jade faced him coolly. 'You don't know a blessed thing about my recent personal trials, Forster. But whatever they may have been, I am *not* a hysterical female, as you imply.' She started to edge closer again and winced. *Blasted knee.* 'I do not imagine things, and if you — '

Pili sprang up from his seat by Beverly and Madeline. 'I saw it, too.'

Roger coughed in deprecation, but Avery interrupted before another accusatory outburst followed. 'The debate is moot at best and can only be settled by bagging the blasted lion. If it is following us, then I say we finish it first.' He nodded in the direction of Ruta, who leaned against the rocks, arms folded on his powerful chest. 'I daresay your man is more than capable of tracking that lion.' He looked at the Maasai for confirmation. Ruta nodded once slowly.

'Well then, it's settled as far as I'm concerned,' Avery said. 'Perhaps we four chaps can have a go at the brute.' He nodded at Harry, Roger, and Ruta. Before Jade could reply he added quickly, 'Mr Pili is injured, and while I can't speak for Mrs Thompson, I'd rather Beverly stay behind to look after him. I'd feel much better, Jade, if *you* remained to protect *them*. You're a better shot than my wife, I know.' When he saw Jade hesitate, he leaned in closer and met her eyes with a pleading look. 'Please!' he begged. Jade nodded.

'Please be careful, love,' said Beverly. Her voice quavered again as she made an outward pretense of calm. 'If you get hurt, I shall express my unhappiness by burning that dreadful rhinoceros head in front of you.' Avery blew her a kiss in reply.

Harry leaned towards Jade. 'Any such tender words of caution for me, Jade?' he asked.

'Yes. If you get killed, you don't get paid.'

356

Harry chuckled. 'Careful now. Such sentimental talk might inflame my heart.' He pointed to the brush with his rifle. 'Come along, gentlemen. *Simba* awaits.'

Roger held back. 'No offense to Ruta,' he protested, 'but I'd really rather wait for Memba Sasa. He's more experienced at tracking.'

'Nonsense, man,' snorted Harry. 'Ruta comes with us because he's Maasai and an experienced lion killer, not to help us find the beast.' He pointed to the fresh blood on the rocks. 'A child could read that trail.'

Ruta stood a little taller and straighter, if that were possible, before he led the way down the rocks and into the thorny grassland beyond. Avery and Harry fell in behind him immediately. After a moment's hesitation, Roger joined them. Jade reloaded her rifle.

The men had trekked only a few hundred yards when a shrill trumpeting blasted the afternoon stillness. A throaty roar vied for supremacy with the elephant's angry call. Suddenly, a hideous, snarling, agonized scream, such as the ones demons must have howled when the angel Michael cast them into the pits of hell, ripped the air and resonated in their ears.

'Merciful heavens!' shouted Beverly. Her hands trembled. 'What is that?' She ran to the edge of the ridge and stared out into the grasslands. A bulky form thrashed about in the distance and raised clouds of reddish dust.

'Elephant,' answered Madeline. 'And something else.'

The throaty screams died to a quavering

357

whimper, but the angry trumpeting continued.

'Whatever it is, the elephant is getting the better of the fight,' said Jade.

'It is the lion,' announced Pili. 'The elephant hates the lion and has killed it.'

'How convenient for us,' suggested Jade.

'Avery won't be happy,' commented Beverly, relief that the killer lion was dead evident in her voice. 'He had his heart set on a full-maned lion. I shall have to have a wig made for that one we shot by mistake.'

True to Beverly's word, Avery appeared shortly after with a very dour-looking face. Harry and Ruta followed, laughing and joking together in Maasai. Roger tailed them, ashen-faced.

'We followed the trail, and I think you might guess where it leads,' said Harry. 'Straight to that matriarch out there. The old girl must have been charged by a lion as a calf, because she certainly took it into her head to eliminate this one.'

'Did you see the lion itself?' asked Beverly. 'Did it have a bone bead?'

Harry seated himself on a rock and wiped his brow with his sleeve. 'I don't know that we'll ever resolve that issue, Lady Dunbury. I wasn't about to get any closer to an angry elephant, and the remains are probably, let us say, indistinguishable from mud at this point.'

Roger's face went a bit whiter, and his hand went over his mouth.

'Are you all right, Mr Forster?' asked Beverly. Roger ran behind a rock and threw up.

Harry watched him run off and frowned. Ruta said something in Maasai and laughed, but

Harry shushed him with a stern look.

'Did you speak to him yet about the car?' asked Jade.

Harry shook his head and checked the sun's position. 'We should leave soon if we're going to get back to base camp before dark. This place is too dangerous to dawdle in, and I'll feel safer once I have you all out of here.'

In the distance, a pack of hyenas began calling to each other in their high-pitched, rolling laugh. 'Sounds like they've discovered the remains of the lion,' Harry added as Roger reappeared looking shaken and worn.

Jade listened to the babbling calls and shuddered visibly. The sounds of that shrill, disembodied laughter rippled up and down. It transported her back to the war and that terrible day when her shell-shocked, wounded patients woke and turned the rear of the ambulance into bedlam. The shudder turned into a cold shiver. Jade hugged herself and closed her eyes to fight the memory. It didn't help. All she saw in her head was the endless, shell-blasted road before her and all she heard was the incessant, raving laughter chasing her.

'Jade, *Jade*!' Beverly's voice broke into the waking nightmare. She gripped Jade by her shoulders and shook her gently. 'Don't make me slap you.'

'What?' Jade muttered as reality slowly dawned on her. She pushed her friend away from her. 'Try it and see what happens.'

'That's my girl,' replied Beverly with a strained smile. Then she led Jade to a rock and seated her. 'It was that laughing, wasn't it?'

Jade nodded and looked around at the concerned faces with growing embarrassment. 'Stop staring, please. I'm fine.' She took a drink of water from a nearby canteen and wiped her mouth with the back of her hand. 'Just a bad memory, that's all.'

Harry continued to stare at her, his lips tightly pressed together through the growing stubble of facial hair. Finally, he looked away and repeated his suggestion that they leave.

'We can't leave yet,' protested Roger. 'We still haven't discovered what the etchings on this ring mean.'

'To hell with the ring, Roger,' answered Harry. 'You've lived this long without knowing anything about it. You can wait and come back later. Besides, the answer's probably tucked in a box in London.' He turned to go down the ridge.

Roger reddened. 'Easy for you to say wait, Harry. You haven't lost everything you ever wanted.' His voice rose in pitch and volume. Harry stopped but kept his back to Roger while the tirade continued. 'Are you trying to make me leave because *you* want to come back first? You aren't begging for more time from the bankers all because of some sniveling maggot till you have to resort to — ' He broke off his angry flow and looked up the path to the caves.

'We saw the underside of the car, Roger,' called Harry as he turned slowly. 'We know what you've resorted to.'

Roger spun about. A flash of loathing crossed his young face. Then he squelched it and adopted a look of bewilderment. 'I . . . I don't understand,' he stammered.

'Mr Forster, give it up,' said Jade. 'I don't know what the penalty is for running drugs here, but we'll bury the damn stuff and never say a word if you'll quit. We need to stick together here.'

'We can't leave anyway,' advised Avery. 'Not without Memba Sasa.'

'He still hasn't shown up yet?' asked Harry. Jade shook her head, and Ruta shrugged. 'Roger?' he asked.

Roger blinked several times as though confused, glanced once at the ascending trail, then surveyed the surrounding grasslands. 'I'll go look for him,' he said softly.

'Take Ruta with you,' said Harry.

'I don't need you or your damned gun bearer to help me,' yelled Roger over his shoulder. 'I can find my own tracker.'

They watched him stomp off down the ridge and into the grassy plains. 'Mr Hascombe, aren't you going to stop him?' begged Madeline. 'He could get killed. Please, let's just go home.'

'We can't leave a man, Mrs Thompson. Besides, Roger's perfectly capable of handling himself alone,' added Harry by way of reassurance. 'I think the better plan is for Ruta and me to do a search of our own.' He looked around him. 'We can eliminate the lava flows or this ridge of hills. Roger's got the right idea. If Memba Sasa went to scout game, he went into the grasslands. But it's a big area to search.'

He loaded his rifle and handed a second one

361

to Ruta. After a brief conversation in Maasai with the tall, laconic gun bearer, Harry turned to Jade and Avery. 'You two are the best shots. But you might want to go up into the cave anyway to be safer.'

'We'll build a fire near the mouth,' suggested Jade.

'Good idea. There's canned meat in the Dodge, and plenty of water in the springs around here. But be careful. Other animals like the springs, too.'

The two men walked down into the grasslands, while Jade and Avery retrieved bedrolls for all, some food, the remaining weapons and ammunition, and toted it in several trips up the rocky path to the cave. Beverly, Madeline, and Pili worked to gather a store of firewood.

'What I don't understand,' said Beverly as she dropped a load of sticks by the cave's entrance, 'is why Memba Sasa had to wander off to look for game. I'm no tracker, but even I can stand up here and see every herd for the next fifty miles.'

'What was all that business about drugs, Jade?' asked Madeline.

Jade shook her head. 'You might as well know. There was a packet of heroin hidden under the car. I found it when I dismantled the carburetor.'

'Heroin!' gasped Madeline.

'That explains Cissy Estes, doesn't it?' said Beverly. 'Roger must be her supply line.'

'Maybe, maybe not,' said Jade. 'It's certainly incriminating enough, but maybe Roger's just the dupe in all this. Someone brought those cars up from Mombasa and sold them to him. Perhaps they intended to get the heroin after the cars made it to Nairobi. I assume Roger planned to put them on the train and take them back there.'

'Here's a nasty thought,' added Avery. 'What if *Harry* is the drug runner? After all,' he explained, 'he hired Roger for this job. He might have suggested that Roger bring up these cars.'

'Oh no,' protested Madeline. 'Not Harry.'

Jade smiled. *Poor thing, she's so desperate for Harry and me to get together, she'd hate anyone to think ill of him.* 'Harry said the cars were Roger's idea,' she offered, 'and Roger's claims of innocence were pretty weak.'

'Could Harry be taking advantage of it?' asked Bev. 'Maybe Roger's angry because Harry's accusing him.'

'I don't know who's to blame for the heroin,' said Jade. 'Maybe both of them. But you may be right. Harry may try to blackmail Roger into selling his land to him.' Jade looked across the river to Poacher's Lookout. 'Harry knew about this place. I think he recognized the etchings the first time he saw the ring.'

'Do you think he suspected or knew that Roger was Gil's son?' asked Madeline. 'Is Roger in danger now like Gil was?'

Jade shook her head. 'I have no idea.' Then she remembered the snippets of conversation between Harry and Roger that she had heard when the first car overheated. 'So far no one's tried to kill Roger.' She squatted down beside the cave's mouth and arranged the wood for a fire by putting smaller kindling under a tepee of twigs and thin sticks. 'We need to get a fire going here and stay behind it.'

Pili reached into a metal box and handed a match to Jade. She swiped it across a rock and set it against the grass kindling. As the fire grew, she added a few larger sticks to feed it.

'Thank you, Pili,' she said. She eyed his scratches. 'You were lucky that lion didn't drag you out of that crevice.'

'He tried, Mistress Jade, but remember? You protected me with the old sorcerer's paste. The witch lion could not stay close for very long.'

'So you believe this lion belonged to a witch, Pili?' asked Avery. He leaned forward, eyes alert.

Pili nodded. 'Yes. It carried the mark of a witch, too. The bone bead.'

'Most interesting,' murmured Avery. 'But supposing there are such things, why would the witch send an animal all the way out here?'

'And why would it attack Pili? Twice,' added Beverly. 'Wasn't the *laibon* supposed to be angry with *you*, Jade, for killing its familiar the first time?'

Jade nodded. 'You're both right. It makes no sense.' She sat down beside Lord Colridge's personal servant, horse handler, and gun bearer. 'Pili, what are your thoughts on this? Why would a witch send an animal all the way out here to come after you?'

Pili stared at the flames for a while as he pondered the question. Finally he spoke. 'You ask two questions. One I do not know the answer to. I do not know why a witch would come after

364

me. But you also ask why a witch would *send* an animal all this way out to the edges of Tsavo. I do not think that is the case.'

'What?' asked Jade. 'But you said the lion belonged to a witch.'

'Mistress, the lion *is* the witch. The witch did not *send* the animal out to us. The witch himself is here among us.' He paused while the others exclaimed incredulously among themselves. Beverly huddled closer to Avery and clung to his arm.

Only Jade sat silently, her green eyes fixed on the handsome young Somali and his clear hazel eyes. The eyes, she noted, showed no trace of hysteria. Instead, they reflected a quick wit and a clear-thinking, intelligent mind. 'Go on, Pili,' she said. 'Who is it?'

Beverly gasped audibly. 'What? It's someone we know?'

Jade and Pili both nodded. 'Who was not here when the lion attacked me either the first time or the second time?' asked Pili.

'And who,' added Jade, 'led us to kill the wrong lion?'

'And who,' finished Madeline, 'has not shown up since . . . Oh my lord,' she gasped.

'Memba Sasa?' breathed Beverly.

'The swine!' cursed Avery.

'What's more,' added Jade, 'I think our safari leaders know or at least suspect. Think about it,' she added when they looked at her with open mouths. 'Was either of them thinking of Memba Sasa when it was time to leave? No. Harry just wanted to go, and Roger only had thoughts for

365

the secret of those ring etchings. It was Avery who remembered him.'

'But they're out there looking for him now,' protested Madeline.

'Naturally,' explained Jade. 'Once we observed that he was missing, they could hardly just say the hell with him and go off. They at least need to make a show of it. And,' she added quickly to alleviate some of Madeline's distress, 'I may be wrong about one or both of them. Maybe they didn't know.'

'So we should be safe now, shouldn't we?' asked Beverly. 'If that elephant really trampled the witch, then the danger is gone, isn't it?' Her voice, Jade noted, betrayed more fear than Jade had ever heard from her friend during their entire time in the ambulance corps. But then, they never dealt with witches in the corps, just howitzers.

'I suppose so,' agreed her husband. He, too, didn't sound certain.

Jade didn't answer. She was busy trying to figure out why the witch would attack Pili. That it didn't go after her again was no surprise. After all, she wore the protective paste and the witch knew it. The paste had succeeded before in keeping the big cat at bay when it came into her hut and again when she changed the tire. According to the Kikuyu, no witch could get too close to her when she wore . . . Her thoughts trailed off abruptly as a new and more awful one took its place. The lion was not the only creature that wouldn't approach her when she wore her protective hat. Harry stayed away from her at those times, too. It was at Harry's hut that the first lion stalked her, and Harry knew the Maasai and had a menagerie of animals. She and the Thompsons never saw what lived in the distant pens. They only had Harry's word about the ill-tempered baboons.

She shook her head. No, it was too preposterous an idea. She tossed it, but another took its place in her mind. The hyena had borne a bead and carvings to mark the *laibon*'s control over it. This lion had a bead, too. Even if Memba Sasa could transform himself, did that bead mean he was under the control of a stronger *laibon*? The old Kikuyu said he saw two witches in his dream. His words came back to her. *The new witch is younger and very powerful*. Was it Ruta?

Pili's voice brought her out of her macabre musings.

'I was very young when my mother died, and the fathers at the mission taught me many things about God.' He fingered his gold cross. 'They also taught me to be wary of Satan. They said to be alert. Be on watch! Your enemy, the devil, roams around like a roaring lion, looking for someone to devour.'

'Yes,' said Jade, 'that's from First Peter.' Somewhere in the back of her mind she realized that Pili had done more than just attend school at the mission.

Pili turned his face to her and met her gaze with one equally serious. 'Well, Mistress Jade, I believe that Satan is stalking us. And I do not think he is finished.'

24

'The animals in native legends are often capable of speech. Whether they've lost the ability to speak or we've lost the ability to understand is not known. But if the thoughtful person would listen to their cries and calls, they would still catch a glimpse of the animals' story. It is very like our own, filled with desire.'
— The Traveler

The sun had dipped more than halfway below the horizon when Harry and Ruta returned to the cave and the welcoming fire. Beverly offered them each a cold sandwich of hard bread and tinned meat before anyone asked them about their search. After all, they had returned alone.

'We didn't find him. Not so much as a trace.' Harry chewed a hunk of the stale bread and swallowed. He scanned the campsite. 'Roger's not back?' They shook their heads no, their mouths set in worried lines.

'Damn!' Harry looked up at the sky. Already, the first stars glowed weakly through a thin haze after the last gasps of sunlight played out. 'It's getting dark, and that veil overhead means rain later. Blasted fool,' he muttered. Jade didn't know if he meant Roger, Memba Sasa, or perhaps himself for suggesting they come here. She didn't ask.

'He should be able to spot the fire,' Madeline

368

suggested as more of a question of hope than a statement of fact.

Harry agreed and plopped down near the cave's wide entrance on top of a bedroll. 'Everyone needs to get some sleep. Ruta will stand first watch. When the moon's up, I'll take second watch.' He passed on the instructions to the Maasai warrior.

Ruta took his place at the cave mouth by the fire, and Jade retrieved a burning *Commiphora* branch to use as a torch. She led the others a few yards inside and made certain that the area was still safe. Jade saw no fresh animal sign and stuck the thorny branch in a wall crevice for light. Everyone rolled out the thin bedrolls and made themselves as comfortable as possible on the hard volcanic rock.

'I say, Jade,' remarked Avery, 'you wouldn't happen to have more of that stinky ointment around, would you?'

'Sorry. I left it in the Ford. It was leaking into the camera bag.'

'Well, maybe you should sleep to the outside of us all. You know, be a sort of protective barrier,' Avery suggested in a weak attempt at levity. Jade snorted in derision.

'Obstinate gypsy,' he muttered.

'Be quiet,' snapped Harry. 'Get some sleep.'

A heady, spicy perfume drifted across them, and Jade vaguely recalled that frankincense and myrrh were both extracted from some species of *Commiphora*. The fragrant scent lulled her into a drugged sleep where red eyes stalked her in the darkness.

★ ★ ★

The witch man watched with his predator's eyes. He saw the tall Maasai, Ruta, standing on one leg, storklike, with his left foot resting lightly on his right knee. The guard gripped a spear in his right hand. The others slept soundly thanks to the scented wood. The others, he didn't need them now. He could finish them at his leisure, revenge and sport all in one. The witch padded softly around the guard's right side and saw the Maasai pivot as his ears caught the stealthy sound. Then the witch whispered the guard's name.

'Ruta.' The voice came out rasping, almost growling, as though a man were injured. 'Ruta, help me,' the voice hissed in Maasai. The witch hoped to overcome the Maasai's wariness and make him think that one of the two missing men had returned.

As he watched from behind his rocks, Ruta trotted lightly towards him, his gaze piercing the black night for a wounded man. The witch knew exactly when the Maasai first saw his eyes, which glowed with a predator's night shine.

'Ruta,' he rasped once more. He saw the Maasai's face writhe and contort in horror when the warrior realized that the sound came from the throat of a massive hyena. The witch didn't allow his prey any more time and tore into Ruta's throat before he cried out.

★ ★ ★

370

Jade woke an hour before sunrise to Harry's deep, bellowing swear.

'What in blasted Hades? Ruta should have woken me hours ago. Where the devil is he?'

The torch had sputtered out long ago, and embers had replaced the bright fire at the entrance. Ruta certainly was derelict in his duties, and Harry got up to inform him of that fact. Jade went to the dying fire and stirred it back to life with some fresh twigs. Her head ached, and she felt drugged. An explosive gasp replaced Harry's Maasai curses. Jade took up a fresh torch and ran to follow him. She caught up with him at a cluster of rocks thirty yards away.

'Stay back!' he ordered.

The others stood clumped back at the cave mouth. Jade hesitated for a second, then ignored his decree and stepped to his side. The torchlight provided a dim illumination, enough for Harry to identify the heap in front of him. As its flame danced, the flickering torchlight caught the trail of sticky red blood and gave the illusion that it still bubbled and flowed from the large gash in the warrior's neck.

'His throat's been ripped out,' she whispered in horror. 'Lion?'

Harry shook his head. 'Bite looks too small. Whatever it was had powerful jaws. Maybe hyena, but I've never heard of a hyena taking a full-grown man like this. Ruta was no fool.'

'Any sign of Roger yet?' she asked.

'Did you see him inside?' Harry snapped as an answer.

'What's happened?' asked Avery as he came up behind them.

Jade and Harry turned to meet him. 'Ruta's dead,' Harry answered.

'Dead?' Avery looked over Jade's shoulder and his face betrayed his battle with disbelief, or rather, with not wanting to believe the truth in front of his eyes. His square-cut jaw worked as though words tried to form until finally one word managed to squeak out. 'How?'

'Some animal tore out his throat,' replied Harry loud enough for the others to hear.

Beverly shrieked, and Avery ran back to hold her. Madeline wept silently, and Pili stood next to her. Tentatively, his hand touched her shoulder. Madeline grabbed it and held it tightly.

'Roger's not back yet either,' said Jade. Her stomach churned as several possibilities popped into her mind, and she fought down a rising taste of stomach acids. It wasn't the sight of a man with half his neck missing, or even the staring eyes that disturbed her. She'd seen as much if not worse while moving wounded men in France. It was the thought of losing David's brother so soon after finding him. *Where can Roger be?* That thought was replaced by another. *Is Memba Sasa still alive after all?*

'Back to the cave with you and stay there,' ordered Harry. 'It'll be light in an hour. I'll look for Roger, but I want the rest of you to be ready to leave. If necessary, I'll stay behind with one of the cars and follow after I've found him.'

Jade refreshed the fire and took up a fresh brand. Then she went into the cave to retrieve her Winchester from where she'd slept. Only a dark blank wall met her. 'Who moved my rifle?' she asked. 'Pili, where did you put my rifle?'

'We did not bring the broken one, mistress. You kept the other beside you.'

'Well, it's not here.' She held her torch out at arm's length and made several sweeps of the floor with it. On her third pass, a horrid sound welled up from the ground below. The high-pitched, giddy laughter of a hyena echoed from beneath her feet and the surrounding walls. It rose and fell in its senseless babbling. The undulating laugh bounced off the hollow rock and added more voices till it grew to a lunatic chorus.

Jade dropped the torch and put her hands over her ears to shut out the hellish sounds. It didn't stop. She ran past the others from the cave and down the trail to the motorcars. There she nearly collided with Harry as he stood staring at the Dodge. She followed his gaze and sank to her knees in shock. Something had ripped two of its tires to shreds.

25

'It is very easy to become caught up and lost in the life of Africa; in its tales, mysticism, beauty, and blood. Perhaps that is why so many of the colonists still insist on maintaining their own traditions of dressing for dinner and using fine crystal even on safari. Many of them claim that to do anything less would be uncivilized.'
— The Traveler

Disbelief replaced the shock, which in turn gave way to anger. Jade scrambled to her feet and kicked the slashed tire savagely. 'Blast it all to hell!' she shouted. Harry reached for her and dragged her back from the car. 'Let go of me,' she yelled and dug her heels into the dirt.

'Easy there, Jade,' he said. She swung her right fist around in an attempt to hit him in the side. Harry stopped pulling, and she wrenched herself free and spun around to face him. Jade stood a yard away, feet apart, fists clenched at her side and black curls tousled, just as she had the night he pulled her from the scalding coffee. Her green eyes blazed. Harry couldn't resist the smile of admiration. 'Easy, Simba Jike,' he added. 'I'm on your side, remember?'

'Are you?' she demanded.

Harry jerked his head back as if slapped. 'What do you mean?'

'I mean that, right now, I don't know who to

trust. As far as I know, you're the one hauling heroin from Mombasa.'

Harry opened his mouth to speak, then clamped his jaw shut. His face darkened with a flush of anger, and his broad chest rose and fell with the intake of a deep breath. 'I'm not, and you'll just have to trust me on that.' Seeing no change in her face, he added, 'What else am I accused of?'

Jade debated whether or not to reveal her darkest thoughts, including her fear that Roger and Ruta had both been murdered. After all, Harry had brought them here to this site. And he wanted them to leave, which would make it much easier to explore the caves himself. 'You saw the ring in Nairobi. I think you knew about the cave, or suspected its existence.'

'And if I did?' His voice growled, low and rumbling.

'All that time you spent out here with Gil for nothing, or so you thought. And now your partner is missing. Maybe you knew more about Gil than you've admitted.'

Harry took a menacing step towards her, but Jade held her ground. 'You think I killed them? You think I hauled a hyena into the Norfolk and killed Gil? Just *what* the devil are you suggesting, Jade?'

'The devil is right, Mr Hascombe. And I think there will be hell to pay before long.' She turned on her heel and strode towards the others, who waited halfway down the slope. Harry ran and caught up with her in two long strides. He grabbed her arm and spun her around to face him. Jade remembered she wasn't wearing her hat.

'I'm not sure what rot is forming in that pretty little head of yours, Jade, but I had nothing to do with Gil's death or Roger's disappearance or even Ruta's death, for that matter, and I can't imagine why you'd think that.'

'Oh, can't you?' Her face was only inches from his. She stared coolly up into his eyes. 'You told me you were forming a partnership with Roger. If you're his business partner, then maybe you can lay claim to part of his inheritance as a business debt owed to you.'

Harry released her suddenly. 'We discussed it and yes, I pushed for it, but for Roger's sake, not mine. And no, Roger hadn't agreed to sign anything yet. He's still his own man. There's no way I could legally lay claim to whatever is waiting for him in London.'

'London, no,' Jade replied. 'But what about whatever's in that cave? Not to mention the fact that you'd have an open opportunity now to buy up Roger's land. Maybe *you* started that anthrax rumor that nearly ruined him. Did you kill Kenton, too, before he could ruin you with a similar false anthrax scare?'

'You are insane! You know that? Insane!' Harry stormed off up the trail to the others.

She watched him go and suddenly felt tired, confused, and a little silly. Maybe he was right. Maybe she was crazy. Still, she couldn't help feel that Harry was keeping secrets. He hadn't denied her challenge that he suspected the cave's existence from the beginning. She turned to rejoin the rest of the safari, what there was left of it, and arrived in time to hear Harry describe the slashed tires.

'But only the Dodge was slashed?' asked Avery. 'Why would some beast do that, and why the devil would it do that to one car and not the other?'

'I can answer that,' said Jade. All eyes turned to her in expectation. Maddy especially gazed at her with the pleading look of someone begging to be rescued. Pili still stood next to her as though to protect her. 'I left the rest of the anti-witch ointment in the Ford.'

'You don't think this is a witch again?' asked Madeline. Her voice rose higher with a hint of hysteria. 'I thought Memba Sasa was the witch and the elephant killed him.'

'He may not be dead after all,' said Jade.

'Memba Sasa a witch?' asked Harry. 'When did you arrive at that wild conclusion?'

'Last evening, while you and Ruta were off searching for him.' Something in Jade's tone suggested she questioned how well he had searched. Harry caught it, glared at her, and then looked away.

'Witch or no, we're down to one vehicle with one man dead and two missing. Even supposing the tracker is dead,' Harry added hastily before anyone could voice their opinion, 'Roger is still out there. *I'm* going to find him, and *you're* going to wait *in* the cave behind the fire. If I'm not back by early afternoon, you *will* pack yourselves and your ammunition into the Ford and drive back to base camp. Follow the damned

377

river, and you'll get there.'

Various protests about them leaving without Harry came from Madeline and Beverly. Avery, whose main concern was seeing his wife and the other women back safely, nodded his agreement to the plan. Only Jade kept her opinion to herself. That fact didn't escape Harry's notice, and he turned towards her as though daring her to oppose him. Jade merely smiled sweetly.

'I'm going with you.' If he thought he could get them to leave so he could take whatever Gil had left in the cave for his sons, he had another thought coming to him.

Harry took a menacing step towards her. 'No!' His voice was soft but firm. It expressed an absolute unwillingness to relent. Jade steeled herself to do verbal battle, but Avery intervened.

'I'll go with him.'

'Avery, no,' pleaded Beverly. 'Don't leave me.'

Avery put his hand to her cheek and stroked it. 'Now listen here, dearest. Mr Forster wandered off alone and look where it got him. We can't risk that happening to Harry as well. Two people are far safer than one, and,' he added with a nod to the cave, 'four people in the cave with a good fire at the entrance should be very safe. Ruta died away from the fire.'

Beverly had far too much faith in her husband's ability to doubt him, and too much classic British reserve to make a scene even if she did. She swiped her damp eyes with the back of her hand. 'Of course, darling. You are absolutely in the right of it.'

Jade was less doubtful of Harry's ability to

face any dangers on his own. But she would question the veracity of any report on his solo search, so she also agreed. Avery would make a truthful witness and, at present, Harry could have no personal vendetta against him. Harry also couldn't expect them to leave as long as Avery was with him or missing. 'Don't fret. We're all armed.' Then she remembered her missing Winchester. She'd use Beverly's Enfield if need be.

'Watch your back, Avery,' Jade whispered before the two men left. 'I don't trust Harry.'

Back at the cave she asked Beverly for her rifle. Pili raised his white tunic and exposed a large, mean-looking knife. 'I am armed, Mistress Jade. I took this from Ruta's body.'

'Good. You shall be a warrior as your name implies, then.' Pili opened his mouth to speak, but Jade had already taken a fresh torch and started to explore the interior of the lava cave.

'Where are you going?' whimpered Beverly. 'We're supposed to stay together and you have my rifle.'

'We're supposed to stay in the cave behind the fire, and I am.' She continued to inch her way back into the dark recesses. 'If this ring's etchings really do mean something, I want to find out what it is.'

'Well, wait for us,' ordered Bev. 'We're not letting you out of our sight.'

Jade smiled reassuringly at her friend. She had no illusions that Beverly was being overprotective. The woman was plainly fighting back terror, but Jade had never seen Bev so afraid before.

'Bev, remember what the commandant would tell us?'

Beverly thought a moment. 'No heroics. We don't need anyone awarded the order of the wooden cross.'

'That's right, and I don't plan on doing anything foolish now.' Jade waited a moment for them to each fetch a burning branch and then moved with cautious steps to the rear, easing into each step in case a thin shell of lava broke through beneath her. About seventy yards later she found her answer. A narrow side trail sloped down to her right.

'I think I found where your little ghost's tears run, Bev.'

Beverly and Madeline clustered close by and peered into the gloom. 'My word,' whispered Beverly. 'Another tunnel. Do you think it's safe?'

'I intend to find out. But stay back, all of you. Please,' she added as an afterthought. 'I know you think you're giving me more light, but you also risk pushing me down a hole.' Her friends drew back. 'Pili, guard the rear.' She handed him Bev's Enfield.

'No one will harm your friends from behind,' said the young man.

They inched onward and slid their feet to ensure a solid footing. Jade tested each step to see if the ground would hold her weight before putting full pressure on it. Lava tubes often had thin floors if another tube ran beneath. So far, this one seemed solid enough. She called back to the others, 'I've been told to go to Hades often enough. Looks like I found the way.'

The tube descended gradually until it seemed that they'd been going down for a very long time. The air was moist, but not musty, and much cooler. That meant they'd moved far enough underground that the surrounding rock quit absorbing the daytime heat. Jade's torch flared in spurts as the fire ignited pockets of resin. The heady aroma of spices flooded the cave.

'Jade,' called Madeline. Her voice quavered. 'Perhaps we shouldn't go much farther?'

Jade was about to agree when something off the far wall sparkled back at her. She crept forward to investigate. Rows of twinkling star shines winked at her. Whatever it was, it ran in a vein along the wall. She brought the torch closer for a better look. The reflection came back in brilliant greens, just like . . . 'My ring! These are the stones in my ring.' Her voice reverberated in the tunnel. Jade quickly spun around as she recalled the hollow echoes of maniacal laughter from the night before. Had someone been in this tunnel? If so, was there another way in? She didn't get an opportunity to investigate as the others crowded closer for a better look.

'You're right,' exclaimed Beverly. 'This is what Gil Worthy intended his sons to find. Roger will be so excited.' She gasped and put her hand to her mouth as she suddenly remembered Roger was missing.

Jade grimaced. Was David's brother dead by now? Had she brought destruction on Roger as she had on David? She suppressed a rising sense of anguish. 'We'd better head up. Harry and

Avery could be back soon, and hopefully, they'll have Roger with them.' Besides, her knee had started its dull, aching throb and the last thing she wanted was to be stuck down here. She had turned to go when her torchlight reflected off a duller metal surface. 'My Winchester!' she exclaimed. 'But how the blazes did it get down here?'

They returned to the surface more quickly than they had descended and found a thick layer of towering white clouds overhead. The wind moaned mournfully past the cave entrance, bringing the scent of rain. Echoes of the sorrowful wail rippled up through the walls as the wind found its way into the lava tubes. Gray sheets already hung over a distant part of the grasslands as the sky drenched the ground. *That explains my knee. This time it really is rain and not some threat making it hurt.*

'Rain,' Madeline said in echo of Jade's thoughts. 'The long rains are over, but a few storms still creep into June.'

They hurried to move the dry wood into the cave and started a new but smaller fire just inside the mouth. They finished just as the sky deepened to a dark, leaden gray.

'Hulloo,' called Avery from below. Water streamed from his clothes, and his voice betrayed his fatigue. Apparently, the rain had already found them.

'Avery,' answered Beverly from the entrance. 'Any luck?'

He shook his head, and drops of water flew from his soggy hat brim. 'None that's good. We found his hat and shirt, or rather, what was left of them.'

Madeline moaned and sank to her knees on the floor. 'Poor Roger.' A large tear rolled down her cheek.

'Where's Harry?' asked Jade.

Avery jerked his head to the side to indicate that Harry was coming. Just then, the sky flashed brilliantly, backlighting the scattered trees. Then as the lightning faded, the clouds ripped open and disgorged their rains on the two soggy men. Jade heard Harry mutter a curse and watched him climb up the wet rocks to the cave. He held a sopping hat in his left hand. *Roger's hat. David's brother's hat. David's dead brother's hat.*

'Forgive me, David,' she murmured. 'I failed you.' Now she had not only Gil's death to avenge, but also Roger's. When would this penance for David's death end?

Avery had entered the protective shelter of the lava tube and the warmth of both the fire and his wife's smile when Harry shouted. They turned in time to see him jump backwards, slip on a loose, wet rock, and tumble down the hill.

'Harry!' they all called in unison; all except Pili. He leaped from the cave, his knife in hand, and raced towards the rocks. For a moment, Jade thought the young man had lost his mind and intended to kill Harry. Bolts of lightning shot up from the ground and split the sky. In their brilliant but unstable flashes, Pili appeared to move with the discontinuous motion of a hand-cranked nickelodeon film. First he was on

383

one rock; then he was on the next. One of the rocks appeared to crawl on its own, shape-shifting in the storm. Then Jade saw the flash of Pili's knife as it drove home and severed the head of a hideous snake, a cobra. She dropped her rifle, snatched up her hat from beside her bedroll, and raced out to help the fallen man.

'It's broken,' groaned Harry between gritted teeth. 'My leg is broken.'

'Don't move,' Jade commanded and held up three fingers. 'How many fingers?'

'Three. I didn't hit my head,' he said.

Jade ran her hands along his body, probing for injuries. The rain pummeled her mercilessly with thousands of tiny fists. She felt each painful drop stab her back with icy ferocity. Water streamed off her hat brim and down her already soaked back. Harry shivered from the cold deluge, and Jade yelled to the others to help her get him inside.

'Get a bedroll to carry him on,' she shouted. Avery had anticipated the need and was already on his way down with one. 'We're going to roll you over on your side, Harry. You ready?'

He nodded, and Jade rolled him onto his good leg. Harry screamed in pain as the other leg tried to follow. Avery and Beverly shoved the bedroll under his back and then rolled him back onto it.

'Madeline, support his head,' Jade ordered. 'The rest of you, get a corner and part of the middle. Ready? On three. One, two, three.'

They hoisted the tall, heavily muscled man in the air and proceeded cautiously along the slick and dangerous path to the cave. Madeline

384

walked backwards so they could advance with Harry's head first and keep it elevated. Jade's muscles burned under the strain, and she shivered as the heavy, cold raindrops slammed into her skin. Water ran down her pant legs in a steady stream and dribbled into her boots. Her soaked knee throbbed in pain, but thankfully it never weakened. After a few minutes, which felt like hours, they had Harry inside the cave and near the fire, just in time for the deluge to end. Beverly and Madeline worked to remove his wet shirt and cover him with the remaining dry bedrolls, while Jade sliced open his pant leg with Pili's knife.

'Bev,' Jade said, 'do you still recall how to set a fracture?'

'Of course.' Bev's voice had lost all its timidity of the tunnel exploration and resumed its old, self-assured quality now that she had a job to do.

'I know, as well,' echoed Madeline with less assurance in her voice. 'We need something straight for a splint, don't we?'

'One of the planks from the Dodge,' suggested Avery. He left to remove one from the useless car below.

'Good,' said Jade. 'We need to get him back and to a doctor. You two take care of the leg when Avery gets back. He can help hold Harry down while you reset it. Pili, you come with me and help strip down the Ford. We'll have to leave things behind to make room.'

'You saved his life, Pili,' said Beverly. 'You were splendid killing that wretched snake. You really lived up to your warrior name.'

Pili shook his head. 'Mistress Dunbury, I tried to tell Mistress Jade before she went back in the cave. My name does not mean warrior.'

Jade looked up in surprise. 'No? But Mr Forster said — '

'My mother was French Somali. She spoke French, but she kept house for a Boer and lived away from Somaliland for so long, she also spoke Swahili and gave me a Swahili name. It means second son.'

Second son. Abel, my second son. 'Son of a biscuit,' muttered Jade. 'Son of a biscuit! Now I understand. Where's Roger's gear?' She ran to his bag, which she'd hauled up with the other supplies, and rifled through it. Her searching hands found the packet.

'What's going on, Jade?' Beverly asked.

Jade ignored her question and read Gil Worthy's letter. 'Pili,' she called, 'where did you get your cross? Let me see it.'

'It was my mother's. The fathers gave it to me when I came of age.' He handed it to her.

'The fathers at the French mission? They raised you?' Jade asked. Pili nodded. 'The woman's grave at the French mission,' she murmured to herself as she turned the cross over. On the back was an engraving: 'To be truly worthy.' That was the motto above Gil's portrait.

Jade glared down at Harry. 'You knew it, too, didn't you, you dirty, double-crossing son of a hyena. You knew Roger wasn't Gil's son at all.' She raised her hand to slap him, and Beverly rushed to restrain her. She shook her off. 'He's not worth the effort.'

386

Harry didn't deny her accusation. 'I swear I never meant to hurt you, Jade. But I didn't know about Pili. That's the truth. I just wanted to help Rog. I figured you'd never find the actual son, so why not let the inheritance help someone else?'

'How did he get Gil's cuff links? Did you kill Gil, too?' demanded Jade. 'That's why Pili needed to die. The cuff links weren't the proof. The gold cross was the proof — it's in the letter.'

'What cuff links?' protested Harry. 'I only told Rog the names on that envelope and map of yours. I found them in your suitcase.'

'I don't understand,' said Beverly. Avery had returned with the board and looked from one to another for some explanation.

Jade handed Gil's letter to Beverly. 'Read this. It will explain it. You stay here and guard them, Avery. Pili, you come with me.' Jade grabbed her Winchester. She checked the magazine, worked the lever to insert a round into the chamber, and slung the gun around her shoulders before heading back down the long slope to the cars.

Pili and Jade retrieved the necessary cans of petrol from the Dodge and began removing the extra boxes of foodstuffs and blankets from the Ford. Jade threw herself into the task with a vengeance, letting the work release some of her rage. If they hacked out the wooden bench, there should be room for Harry and the others to crowd onto the wooden floorboard in back. She would drive and let Avery ride shotgun.

She found a crowbar and handed a hammer to Pili, and together they began to rip up the bench from the wooden floorboard. They worked silently. All the while her stomach and mind alike churned over the latest revelation and the resulting questions. Had Harry actually killed Roger? Finding a hat and torn shirt was certainly a convenient explanation for his disappearance, especially when the cloudburst washed away any trace of blood. If Harry had killed him, then it would explain why he had had to kill Ruta, too. He was a witness. And Ruta had never called out, which suggested he was surprised by someone he knew, someone he trusted. Yet how, she wondered, could a man, no matter how strong, tear out another man's throat? Were the witch stories really true? Could a man actually do more than train and control wild animals? Could he become one himself? Memba Sasa, the old witch, was dead. She was pretty sure of that now. But Harry knew the Maasai and their ways. Just how *well* did he know them?

Then Jade heard a sound that made her blood run cold and her legs turn to jelly, the unmistakable cackle of demented laughter. With it came the dawning realization that the rainstorm had washed away the last of the protective ointment from her hat. Her hands trembled violently and the crowbar clattered to the ground.

Louder and louder rang the undulating call. She clasped her hands over her ears and shut her eyes. In her mind she couldn't drive fast enough. The laughter still followed her. She couldn't escape the psychotic cries. Now they hit the back wall of the ambulance with their heads. She could feel the reverberation echo down the

388

driver's seat, down her back. *They're on my back. My God in heaven, where's the damned hospital? Did I lose it in the moonless night? This is hell, and I'll drive the damned forever.*

All sense, all reason, all sanity fled from the incessant giggles and guffaws. The world was mad. She was mad to be here. What the hell was she doing here? Protecting David? Doing her bit? Vomiting she could handle. Gaping wounds and moaning men she could handle. But not this. She wanted to stop the ambulance and jump out. She wanted to escape the laughter. They weren't men. They were demons from the seventh pit of hell. Someone screamed. It wasn't her.

'Mistress Jade. Help me.'

Jade opened her eyes and the horrors of the front vanished. Pili stood backed against the Dodge, holding a hammer upraised to strike. An enormous spotted hyena menaced him, jaws open. Dripping saliva slathered its teeth as it tensed its stiff, sloping hindquarters to spring for the young man's throat.

Find my brother. Jade heard the words in her head as clearly as if David stood beside her. She woke from the nightmare as if someone had slapped her.

In a flash she slid the rifle off her back, slammed it against her shoulder, and aimed. 'No, damn you to hell. You can't have him, too!' Then she fired.

The hyena leaped into the air and spun around to face her. It coughed, and blood dribbled from its gaping maw and a thin hole in

389

its side. She sighted more carefully down the barrel and proceeded to work another round into the chamber. But her recent horror left her trembling, and her wet finger slipped from the trigger. Her next shot went wild. In that time the hyena turned and staggered into the brush.

Avery and the others were too far away to help, so Jade ran off on her own after the injured animal. From the blood trail she could clearly see it was seriously, if not mortally, wounded. *Probably dead already.* Pili followed hot on her heels. In front of them loomed a brushy thicket of thorny *Commiphora.* The trail ended here, and they approached cautiously. From within the brush they could hear the animal's labored, rattling wheeze as it choked on its own blood. Jade sidestepped, her rifle up and ready. She rounded the shrub and stopped dead in her tracks. Her olive face turned ghostly pale at the sight before her.

26

'Africa. We speak the word as if it were one place with one people rather like we say England or America. But this incredible continent holds more than a diversity of wildlife and people; it also holds a diversity of time. Mysteries and cultures from the dawn of antiquity rub against modern culture and sometimes, just sometimes, there are sparks.'
— The Traveler

There was no wounded hyena in front of her. Lying in the thorns, blood running from his mouth and side, lay Roger Forster. His eyes jerked frantically from Pili to Jade. His hands clutched at his chest. Jade's hands trembled, but she didn't lower her rifle.

'Pili, hold something to his chest to stanch the bleeding. I'm taking this son of a bitch back for trial.' Roger gasped, terror flooding his eyes, but whether it was fear of a trial or of death, Jade couldn't tell. She didn't care.

'You killed Ruta, didn't you? Godfrey Kenton, too?' Roger nodded weakly. Jade kept her eye on him along the Winchester's barrel. 'Then you read the letter in the packet. You found out that Gil's mistress was a Somali woman named Dolie, and you suspected that Pili was the real son. You had to kill him.'

'Needed . . . that . . . cross. Proof,' his voice

391

croaked out as a ragged whisper.

'You had Gil Worthy's cuff links. You killed him. Why?'

Roger's weak voice rasped back at her. 'Hired to . . . Needed money. First time to . . . kill a white man.'

'Were the cuff links proof of that job?'

Roger shook his head once, which set off a racking cough. Blood erupted from his mouth. 'Souvenir. Wallet was . . . proof.' Despite his weakened state, he managed a thin smile as he met her eyes. Jade could read the hate within. 'Stickpin was . . . souvenir . . . too.'

Jade felt her stomach twist in revulsion. Even now the man felt no shame for his deeds, only a gloating joy in his kills. He'd been a witch too long to remember civilized emotions. 'You registered as John Smith, didn't you? Then you waited in Gil's room for him to come back. You . . . ' She searched for the word, still disbelieving the reality. 'You had transformed yourself and killed him.'

By now Avery, Beverly, and Madeline had run down to see what had happened. Madeline screamed when she saw Roger's bloody form lying in the bushes. Pili still knelt beside him, pushing a new blood-sodden rag against his wound.

'Jade, what have you done?' wailed Beverly.

'He tried to kill Pili just now.' She turned back to Roger, whose blood flow, though held back by the canvas rags, still drained his life away.

'Did Memba Sasa teach you?' Jade demanded.

Roger nodded faintly. 'Power,' he gasped.

392

'Jade, stop it,' urged Avery. 'Can't you see he's too weak to talk?' He stepped towards her and put a restraining hand on her shoulder. She shrugged it off.

'He's a witch and a murderer, and I'll know *everything* before he dies,' she answered with so much force that no one contested her. They backed away, and she turned to Roger.

'Who hired you?' Jade demanded. 'Tell me!'

Roger's glazed eyes told her she'd never know, but she had her suspicions.

27

'Visit Africa. Live there. Make her your home and court her like a lover, but she will never divulge all her secrets.'
— The Traveler, France — *August 1919*

Sunlight filtered through the window into the private railcar. Avery had spared no expense on this train trip through the French countryside. Only the best would do and that included the education he had promised Pili. 'It's the least I can do for you, Jade, and for David.'

For David. Jade stared out the window, looking for familiar landmarks. 'That's the spot over there,' she said. 'That's where the last evac hospital stood.' The fact that David's plane had crashed a few hundred yards away was left understood. 'Of course,' she added in an attempt to lighten her own mood, 'the 'smells' are all gone.'

Pili, in particular, looked on with keen interest. Poor Lord Colridge, Jade thought. He never could quite understand why Pili left his service. She had explained it to him several times, but the old aristocrat had still resisted understanding. For that matter, so had she. She closed her eyes and took her mind back to Colridge's farm and their last meeting, which had also included the Thompsons and the Dunburys.

'He needs to come to London with us to claim his inheritance,' she said.

Colridge pointed to Pili. 'So *his* father was Gil Worthy?'

'Yes,' Jade replied. 'And I should have thought of that myself after I visited the French fathers at the mission. They told me about the abandoned young Somali woman and her child. Her people disowned her because the child was not one of theirs. But, like everyone else, I made assumptions. The gold cross proved Pili's parentage. Gil's letter in the packet said that he had left the gold cross with the mother as a sign of promise. He described the beautiful Somali woman, Dolie, whom he met near Kilimanjaro, where she kept house for Mr Kruger.'

'But I thought you said Roger Forster was Gil's bast — er, illegitimate son.'

'No. He only claimed to be after Mr Hascombe put the idea into his head to pose as Gil's son. But Roger himself knew it wasn't true. Roger's mother had married Roger's real father a year before he was born.'

'Well, why the blazes would Forster or Hascombe do such a fool thing anyway?'

'Harry knew Roger needed money. I think he honestly thought he was doing the man a good turn. And once Roger had money of his own, he might finally abandon his pride and consent to a ranching partnership with Harry rather than continue the risky business of running safaris. He never expected me to find the real son, anyway.'

Jade took another swallow of coffee before she

continued. 'What Harry didn't know was that Roger was trying even riskier methods. Apparently being dirt poor and losing his Leticia were more than he could handle. He desperately needed money and ran heroin from Mombasa to people like Cissy Estes. He also committed murder for hire and killed Gil. That's how he got Gil's cuff links. He said they were a souvenir.' She shuddered at the memory. 'He needed land, so he used Memba Sasa, a Maasai witch, to frighten the neighboring Kikuyu into leaving. Memba Sasa taught him the art himself, but Roger became more powerful than his mentor. Roger had a dilemma, though,' she continued. 'Once he read the letter in the packet, he suspected Pili was the real son. He had to kill him and get the gold cross to claim any inheritance. And he still wanted vengeance on me for killing his hyena earlier. So he turned hyena to do the job himself. He knew the sound of that crazed laughter would terrify me.'

Colridge snorted and waved his hand. 'Pish toffle,' he said. 'People don't turn into lions and hyenas. I can believe Forster went after you and Pili, but you just imagined the rest. Female hysteria and all that. You shot Forster in self-defense and that's the end of that.'

Jade didn't press the issue. She knew what she'd seen, and she had one witness as well, Pili. But a Somali would not count in Nairobi courts as a credible witness. Everyone else had been with Harry up in the cave. And if Colridge didn't believe it, he'd never believe Roger had controlled the jackal that startled his horse, the lions that stalked her at Harry's and by the road, and whatever animal had killed Godfrey Kenton. Memba Sasa himself was the lion that had attacked Pili both times at Tsavo, under orders by Roger.

Jade recalled the fresh scrape on Memba Sasa's leg and knew it was where she had grazed him with her bullet. It explained why Roger had interfered each time when they tried to shoot the lion and also why Memba Sasa had deliberately led them to a wild lion. But the last time he didn't escape so easily. A furious elephant meted out justice. That left Roger no other choice but to do the job of killing Pili and Jade himself, a choice that cost him his life and probably his soul. She was unsure about the snake that struck at Harry. It may have been a coincidence, but the jury was out on that one in her mind.

'Sorry business, all of it,' Colridge said. 'Forster was a good chap. Sorry to lose him.' The old man gazed at his feet for a moment. 'At least Harry is all right. His leg is mending.'

Madeline took the opportunity to ask Jade a question. 'But Roger even told you his middle name was Abel. How did he know that was supposed to be the name of Gil's son?'

'Harry knew,' said Jade. 'Remember when he went to my hotel room to help bring down my luggage? He rummaged through the bag and saw the envelope plus the names on Gil's map.'

'The irony is,' added Beverly, 'that wasn't the name of the son after all.'

'No,' agreed Jade. 'Gil may have told his

mistress to use that name and assumed she did, or it may have just been a metaphor for a second son, since Abel was Adam and Eve's second son. He even hinted as much on the map. When I heard that Pili meant 'second son,' it clicked. Pili's mother simply chose a Swahili version of the same thing. Perhaps she thought it was more appropriate for her child. I've defied the lawyers and read everything in the packet. Gil explained his love affair with the Somali lady and the guilt he later felt at leaving her an unwed mother. He also enclosed a map to the gem vein and an explanation of the ring markings.'

Avery roused himself. 'So Gil found a vein of those green stones, whatever they are, did he? But that land won't belong to Pili. What good will it do him?'

'Probably none, unless he wants to risk everything trying to mine them. But I suspect there's a strongbox full of them in London. That and a share of Gil Worthy's estate.'

'There's just one more question,' said Beverly. 'Who hired Roger to kill Gil?'

Jade studied her friend for a moment. 'Who gained the most by his death?'

Beverly gasped as comprehension sank in.

'But,' continued Jade, 'even if David's mother hired Roger, I'm not sure I can get proof. Still, we need to keep Pili's whereabouts in England secret.'

And, she thought, *I'll need to watch my back.*

★ ★ ★

'We're here.' Beverly's melodious voice brought Jade back from Africa to the French countryside and to the present. Both of the Dunburys knew how important this trip was to Jade, and she felt a surge of gratitude towards them for making it possible. The steam engine chugged to a stop.

The walk from the station to the cemetery took them through the French village to a quaint stone churchyard. Jade marveled at how quickly the townspeople had repaired many of the buildings. Even the earth had healed itself and spread a lush carpet over the hillside as green as the rare green garnets that Pili now owned. Together, the four of them found the grave site and the simple marker.

Lt. David R. Worthy, RFC
May 1918

Beverly and Avery placed a wreath of roses over the stone. Jade let a silent tear fall onto the grave. It was her gift, one from the heart.

I found out what happened to your father, David. I found your brother, too, and brought him to you. She paused and conquered the tightness in her chest. *He's a fine man and truly worthy.* She bowed her head. *Thank you for entrusting me with the task. I think I know who hired Forster to kill your father, and someday, I'll get the proof.*

Jade looked up at David's brother and smiled. Her own green eyes sparkled like the mysterious stones. She remembered the ring she still wore under her blouse. Technically it, too, belonged to

Pili. She took it from around her neck and held it out to him. 'This is yours as well.'

Pili gently closed her fingers over the ring with his slender hand. 'My brother loved you. He wanted you to have it. Perhaps if you had married, you would be my sister, and I want my sister to have this ring.'

Beverly came forward and hugged them both. 'David can be very proud of his brother. You'll have a good life ahead of you.' She turned to her husband. 'Avery, tell them our news.'

'We've decided to settle in British East Africa,' he said. 'We bought Leticia Kenton's farm from her. We're going to raise horses, and once Pili has finished his veterinary courses, he's going to be our partner. Neville and I are making plans to get an aeroplane and start that safari guide business we talked of.'

'And, Jade, we want you to come stay with us,' added Beverly. 'There's plenty of room for you. Maddy can't wait for you to be one of her neighbors. You know she's started her first book, don't you? It's all about you. I think she needs you around for more material.' She took Jade's hand in hers and pleaded. 'Oh, please say you'll stay with us.'

'I'm very happy for all of you,' Jade said, 'but, Bev, I can't — ' Her throat caught and the remaining words died before they came out. 'I have no idea what I'm going to do right now, Bev,' she said finally. 'The magazine wants me to write more articles on Africa, so I promised I would. After all, Africa's gotten under my skin.' She fingered her lion-tooth tattoo. 'But I don't think I can stay in Nairobi.'

As she said it, she wondered what sort of life lay ahead for her. She'd paid her debt to David, but she felt no release. Maybe it was the war. Maybe it would always haunt her. She did know this: she'd never feel settled anywhere. If anything, she'd use her new job as an excuse to travel, to wander, to search over that vast continent. It would be easier if she knew what she was searching for.

Author's Notes

The premise for this story comes from an interesting tale. Bror von Blixen (husband of *Out of Africa* author Isak Dinesen, and a famous hunter/author in his own right) was once asked to shoot a particularly troublesome hyena. The tribespeople claimed it belonged to a witch and feared revenge if they tackled it themselves. Blixen shot the animal but only wounded it at first. He followed the trail, flushed it from some brush, and shot it again. Baron Blixen claims that when he finally came near the carcass, there was no hyena, but a man with two bullet holes. This tale and similar stories of vengeance animals can be found in *The Tree Where Man Was Born*, by Peter Matthiessen, and in *Death in the Long Grass*, by Peter Hathaway Capstick.

Any of the books that Jade found or looked to find in Gil Worthy's library will also give the reader insight into colonial Africa. All of these can be borrowed through interlibrary loans. Other excellent and more accessible resources include any of Elspeth Huxley's books, such as *The Flame Trees of Thika* and *The Mottled Lizard*, as well as books by Isak Dinesen and Beryl Markham. Osa and Martin Johnson wrote several books on life in 1920s Africa, including the famous *Four Years in Paradise* and *I Married Adventure*. Information on the Johnsons is also available at the Martin and Osa

Johnson Safari Museum, which has an excellent Web site (www.safarimuseum.com) and an even more magnificent research library in the museum in Chanute, Kansas.

★　★　★

For more information on women ambulance drivers, the reader can start with *Gentlemen Volunteers*, by Arlen J. Hansen. There is a chapter devoted to women drivers and tremendous resources listed in the back of the book. An excellent fictionalized version is *Not So Quiet . . .* , a novel by Helen Zenna Smith. This novel, printed shortly after World War I, was banned in some places for being too controversial.

Other titles published by
The House of Ulverscroft:

MORTAL REMAINS

Kathy Reichs

John Lowery was declared dead in 1968, the victim of a Huey crash in Vietnam, and buried in North Carolina. Four decades later, Temperance Brennan attends the scene of a drowning in Hemmingford, Quebec. The corpse is identified as John Lowery. But how could Lowery die twice, and how did an American soldier end up in Canada? Tempe exhumes Lowery's grave in North Carolina and takes the remains to the U.S. military in Hawaii for reanalysis. Soon another set of remains is located — complete with Lowery's dog tags. Three bodies — all identified as Lowery ... Then Tempe is contacted by Honolulu's medical examiner, needing help identifying the remains of an adolescent boy found offshore. Is he the victim of a shark attack? Or something more sinister?

THE ATTENBURY EMERALDS

Jill Paton Walsh

It was 1921 when Lord Peter Wimsey first encountered the Attenbury emeralds. The recovery of the magnificent gem in Lord Attenbury's most dazzling heirloom made headlines — and launched a shell-shocked young aristocrat on his career as a detective. Now it is 1951: a happily married Lord Peter has just shared the secrets of that mystery with his wife, the detective novelist Harriet Vane. Then the new young Lord Attenbury — grandson of Lord Peter's first client — seeks his help again, this time to prove who owns the gigantic emerald that Wimsey last saw in 1921. It will be the most intricate and challenging mystery he has ever faced . . .